'Funny and heartfelt'
Spectator

'Joyous and full of light. I only meant to read a
chapter and I greedily gobbled down the whole lot
in one go. He is a beautiful and empathetic writer'
Cathy Rentzenbrink

'A fascinating story, gripping, moving and
exquisitely written, this is a wonderful gift of a
book from one of the best writers working today'
SJ Watson

'Brilliantly sustained'
Rachel Johnson

'A beautiful novel about longing,
growth, music and family'
Queen & Country Magazine

By Patrick Gale

PATRICK GALE

TAKE

NOTHING

WITH YOU

TINDER
PRESS

First published in Great Britain in 2018 by Tinder Press
An imprint of HEADLINE PUBLISHING GROUP

First published in paperback in 2019 by Tinder Press
An imprint of HEADLINE PUBLISHING GROUP

5

Cataloguing in Publication Data is available from the British Library

ISBN 978 1 4722 0535 3

Typeset in Sabon 10.75/14.75 by Jouve (UK), Milton Keynes

Printed and bound in Great Britain by Clays Ltd, Elcograf S.p.A.

Headline's policy is to use papers that are natural, renewable and recyclable
products and made from wood grown in well-managed forests and other
controlled sources. The logging and manufacturing processes are expected
to conform to the environmental regulations of the country of origin

HEADLINE PUBLISHING GROUP
An Hachette UK Company
Carmelite House
50 Victoria Embankment
London EC4Y 0DZ

www.tinderpress.co.uk
www.headline.co.uk
www.hachette.co.uk

For Aidan Hicks

CHAPTER ONE

At an age when he was reassured that life was unlikely to surprise him further, Eustace found, in rapid succession, that he was quite possibly dying and that he was falling in love for the third time. Up to this point he had been a not-able survivor geographically as well as medically, a relic almost, having lived his three decades as a Londoner in a white-painted terrace house off Kensington High Street, while all around him sold up, subdivided, reunited and remodelled. The street, prettily lined with flowering cherry trees, went from being artistic, even Bohemian, to being colonized by expatriate bankers. Now, with a smattering of oligarchs and CEOs, it housed more homesick nannies and maids than its Victorian developers could ever have imagined there.

Since turning fifty, he took a circuit-training class twice a week so as not to have to give up cake or wine. Friends said it sounded hot because the instructor was an ex-marine who called it Boot Camp but the reality was cosier than their fantasies: a mixture of men and women, from rounded young mothers to retired plumbers, from buns of steel to daily bun-habit. He was fitter than most, which was entirely down to dog-walking since not even at school had he taken much exercise. But he was not so fit that he could lie on a sweaty mat for a round of reverse crunches or Complete

Bastards and not wonder if his heart might be about to burst. Classes took place in a church hall, one of those pockets of self-sustaining parochial life that came to seem increasingly miraculous in affluent central London.

Occasionally he overdid it, especially if he found himself sharing circuit stations with one of the fitter, sexier men and was driven unconsciously to compete. He was used to waking with a stiff calf muscle or a wrenched shoulder, and assumed that the mild discomfort in his neck was just another such sprain. The ex-marine was ingenious in regularly throwing new exercises into the mix, so it was nothing strange for a new muscle to complain at being rudely rediscovered. The discomfort persisted, however. It was not quite a sore throat, more like the sensation of strain after mistakenly swallowing too large a bite of hard apple. He fancied there was a persistent dryness in his mouth as well but, having irritatingly developed an allergy to tree pollen in his forties, he wondered if this were simply a bad reaction to early summer or the polluted London air.

Eustace was not one of nature's doctor-botherers, a reaction to having grown up in a household in which to be written a prescription was more validation than misfortune. It was a deep-seated reaction, too, to his having survived the eighties and nineties almost unscathed; like many in his position, he made no attempt to hide his scars, but preferred not to dwell on the claws that had left them.

He bore with the throat discomfort, sucking painkilling lozenges when he remembered, until he was due for a routine check-up. He then brought it to the nurse's attention in case it turned out to be some form of thrush. She took a good

2

look, said there were none of the infection's usual signs but took the customary throat swab for analysis and made a note of his symptoms. He often joked that he had never been so healthy as since Gwyn made him HIV positive; he received far more medical supervision than most men his age and the analyses of twice-yearly blood tests meant he was highly unlikely ever to have one of the late diagnoses that were so often the lot of doctor-shunning men.

The falling in love was Naomi's fault. To say she was one of his oldest friends was misleading, as it implied friendship of a long duration. In fact they had briefly been friends in circumstances of some intensity, as cello students in their distant childhoods, then rediscovered one another when he contacted the Royal Academy in search of a cellist to play at his lover's funeral. In the interim she had enjoyed a strato-spheric career as a performer, playing the Elgar concerto at the Proms in her late teens and releasing a string of prize-winning recordings before overwhelming performance anxiety abruptly caused her to retire.

'Naively I thought I could just kick the concert habit and do a Glenn Gould, record in studios, but nobody wants the girl they can't see,' she explained the first time they went for a catch-up-on-our-lives drink together. 'And, hell, I needed to break down a bit, become a proper woman, grow hips, all that stuff, and the record company wanted this nervy little pipe-cleaner girl who couldn't stop throwing up.'

Instead she followed the example of the great teacher they had briefly shared and reinvented herself as someone who trained musicians but no longer performed herself.

She taught at the Academy but also took on a series of much younger, less ambitious pupils, many of whose parents had no idea she had briefly been something of a star. He loved how the adult Naomi looked. She had retained much of her beauty but nerviness had been replaced with generosity, edginess with naughty wit and he was touched that he seemed to fill a sibling-shaped hole in her life as she did in his.

Her friendship, based on their almost identical ages, overlapping childhood experiences and the fact that they had, in different ways, gone through emotional battlefields and rebuilt themselves was of such help to Eustace, as he worked his way through the hard labour of mourning, that he soon found the perfect way of stitching her into the fabric of his life.

He lent Naomi his beautiful sitting-room for her private teaching two days a week in exchange for her minding and walking Joyce while he caught a train to visit the woman she called 'your depressingly indestructible mother'. Quite often Naomi stayed over because there was room, they enjoyed cooking together and they always had too much to talk about. It had been during a long evening of do-you-remember that she first made him play her cello to her and the almost animal joy of it came back to him. She lent him a spare instrument so they could have fun playing De Fesch and Bartók duets together. Then she found him one to buy and coached him for his audition with a local orchestra.

They didn't often play duets after that unless they were drunk. Eustace found the memories stirred up by playing alongside her almost too much and they were not all of things he found he could share, even with her. As for the orchestra, they agreed that she might occasionally help him with fingering a passage but that he would never subject her to one of its performances. Amateur music making was all about enjoying the pleasure of rehearsals and minimizing the pain of concerts. It wasn't a bad orchestra – this was central London, after all, and many of the players were highly trained teachers of their instruments and they had an excellent conductor and hired the best soloists they could afford. Each season began for him with high hopes, however, and ended in the cruel reminder that, for all their professionalism, they sounded like an orchestra that rehearsed for two hours a week, not thirty.

For reasons she couldn't be drawn to explain, Naomi lived in an ex-council tower block in an ungentrifiable pocket of North London she called 'a bit stabby'. She claimed she was visually illiterate but knew his house would reassure the parents of children who came to learn with her there.

'Don't you remember?' she said, when he teased her about this. 'It wasn't just the lessons that were special but the place where they happened.'

'Yeah,' he said, thinking back to a beautiful, shabby house in Clifton where nothing mattered so much as art. 'You're so right.'

To his horror, it was only after Gwyn had dumped him that she admitted how ghastly she had found him.

'If you'd succeeded in moving him in,' she said, 'I'd have

stopped coming round. He clearly answered some masochistic need in you, but it wasn't a side to you I liked to see encouraged.'

'Why didn't you say?' he asked, horrified at how close he might have come to losing her.

'That's not what proper friends do: they love whoever their friends love. If they can. And keep supportively schtum if they can't.'

And yet, the falling in love was Naomi's fault. She had little patience with any signs Eustace gave of pining since becoming single again. She cajoled him into downloading a dating app to his phone by way of healthy distraction having had, she claimed, startling successes with its heteronormative equivalent. It was a brutally frank business. Vital statistics were loaded, from height, weight, age and furriness to itemizing the depressingly reductive *types* the user favoured. Rebelling by instinct, Eustace began by ticking every box only to get soundly told off when hairless ladyboys or latex-wrapped control freaks came on to him and, through increasingly aggressive questioning, obliged him to admit that they would never have been a match.

He limited his range a little but he soon found, as countless other men must have done, that being set free simply to chat, flirt and lead one another on opened up a world of possibility from which inhibition would have cut him off entirely in a dinner party or bar. He chatted with men who wanted him to dominate them then, through some accidental reference, would find himself discussing Pablo Casals recordings with them or how best to nurture a *tibouchina urvilleana* through the winter, sex sidelined by far more nourishing interests.

Nothing about his meeting of Theo was promising: Theo was twenty years younger, he was in the army and he was pretty. Pretty would normally have put Eustace off – he tended to be drawn to men with rough edges, evidence of wear and tear, a bit of heft or receding or departed hair. He had always found prettiness poignant, doomed as it was to pass, and outright beauty utterly daunting. His possibly unfair assumption was that beauty went with a need for reassurance whereas imperfect men would be grateful for the attention and accordingly generous. However, the desert camouflage and boots, the occasional sweat patch or glimpse of an enormous and unambiguous gun about his person seemed to balance out Theo's puppyish looks. As did his fearless persistence.

'You forget there are two of us making choices here,' Theo texted when Eustace had felt obliged to post a suggestion that he would usually have gone for grizzled sergeant major over smooth-skinned captain. 'But our names are impossible together. We sound like cat breeders.'

'I was nicknamed Stash at school,' Eustace admitted. 'And Sluice.'

'I think I can cope with Eustace.'

Theo spent several days after that pretending he wasn't really a rufty-tufty soldier at all but the company's cook, whose pride and joy was his cake decorating and pastry-making. He sent photographs of a succession of birthday cakes for the officers and men, each camper than the last, each bravely greeted by Eustace with another compliment. Finally he confessed that the pictures had been random finds off Google to test and alarm. He was actually a fairly senior officer doing something clandestine. There was sand, though, and date palms, and once a glimpse of spectacular ruins that looked like, but couldn't have been, Palmyra. He also admitted he had landed his job because of his two degrees in Arabic.

At this point they stepped away from the app and on to Skype, because Eustace pretended not to believe him about the Arabic. Goaded to prove it, Theo chatted away in a surprisingly deep voice, while shaving topless, and driving Eustace wild by refusing to speak a word of English before grinning, reaching out to the shelf above his sink with a soapy finger and hanging up.

It was a short step to texting one another images or bulletins from their wildly contrasting days. Eustace introduced Theo to his whippet, Joyce, to his cello, to Kensington Gardens and to the assembling ladies of the orchestra's cello section in exchange for meeting a tank full of sweaty squaddies, a scorpion and a full moon reflected in an oasis. Then Theo happened to Skype while Eustace was having supper and, amused, went to fetch his own tray of food and can of Coke. And so they slipped into the comforting habit of weekly supper dates. They made a point not only of regularly eating together but downloading the same books to read or, when army broadband permitted, watching the same television programmes simultaneously, Eustace on the sofa with Joyce, Theo sprawled on his bunk.

The move from text to video allowed Eustace to latch on to, and collect, the little imperfections which only made Theo more endearing: the small chip off one of his incisors, the way his thick eyebrows didn't quite match, a slight tendency to stutter when he was excited as though his thoughts outran his tongue. And the intimacy of their conversations threw up intriguing parallels between them – less than perfect childhoods, an unfashionable tendency towards monogamy, a belief that dogs were sent to teach us how to love.

Eustace dreaded ringing him at a bad moment.

'You mean with bullets flying? I hate to tell you, but I probably wouldn't answer.'

'That's even worse. Now if I ring and you don't answer, I'll be thinking IED.'

So they agreed Eustace could text whenever he liked but that Theo would initiate all calls, as his life was more complicated.

Because they had deleted what Theo called the App of Doom, and become roundedly human to one another by talking rather than texting, they resisted doing the usual sordid, appy things, like beating off in unison although – thanks to a waterproof cover on Theo's tablet and a cunning suction pad Eustace found for his – they did take a couple of showers together. For the most part they talked, as any new lovers must. They told their stories. Eustace learnt that Theo was teetotal because his parents were drunks and confided in turn that his relationship with Gwyn had verged on the abusive and that his one with his mother wasn't straightforward either. They laid tentative then increasingly definite plans for Theo's next home leave, which was in four months.

Naomi demanded details, of course, encouraging him at

every turn and brushing aside any doubts he expressed with characteristic pronouncements.

'Prudery at our age is as unconvincing as home dye jobs,' was one. 'You're scared he might rearrange your tidy life,' was another. Her final pronouncement, after she had been briefly introduced to Theo at the start of a Skype call before coming over all girlish and making a hasty exit was that this latest twist in his life story was almost unbearably sweet. 'If I'm honest, I only got you on the app to get you some healthy rumpy-pumpy to help you forget Gwyn. Only you could dive into a lake of pure sex and come up like some Labrador with something so bloody wholesome.'

The results of his blood tests led to Eustace being called in for another consultation and an X-ray. He had come clean to Theo weeks back about his HIV status, popping his daily dose of medication on camera and showing the labels on the pill pots in close-up. Theo just grinned, nodded, apparently quite unbothered, although the connection sometimes wavered, which could make expressions hard to read if they weren't backed up by words, and held up a bottle of his own.

'Prep,' he said with another grin. 'I used to be in the Scouts.'

At which Eustace had nodded, smiled back uncomprehendingly then raced to Google to find out just what Prep was. He didn't like to tell him about this latest hospital visit though. As Theo had already joked, their age difference was completely immaterial, as they were never going to meet 'in the real world'. Eustace wasn't sure if this was a joke or not and hoped his face hadn't fallen too obviously at it.

And he certainly didn't tell him that the X-ray results came through, and he had a papillary thyroid carcinoma and would need an operation at the first opportunity. He wanted to tell him but found he couldn't. He told himself it was because a man in a war zone had no need of bad news from home; he was almost convincing.

They had one of their weekly Skype dates the night after, however: pizza at either end and *Vertigo*, because Eustace had horrified Theo by admitting he had never seen it. Joyce had learned to recognize Theo's voice and responded when he called her name, even though they were fairly sure she couldn't see things on screens as she barked or whined in response to noises on a show's soundtrack but sat calmly through any silent imagery of cats or rabbits, both certain to send her into a frenzy in the flesh.

To Eustace's dismay the Skype call had barely begun with his lover greeting Joyce and her frantically sniffing the screen and whining to get at the nice man who knew her name when Theo started weeping, lent courage by the fact that there was nobody in the other bunks.

'What?' Eustace asked. 'For God's sake, what? Theo?'

Theo mastered himself then cracked again.

'Take your time,' Eustace told him gently. 'I'm here. I can wait.'

Theo had not long before adopted a local dog, a mixed breed who looked as though she or a parent had once herded animals. Perhaps rashly, he had christened her

Audrey and taken to feeding her leftovers from the mess. She had taken to sleeping beneath his window and joining him enthusiastically when he went jogging. But that day he had found her shot dead in a ditch. He was desperately upset. There had been no enemy action for days, or nothing near the camp, and he had a horrible feeling she had been killed by one of his fellow soldiers who could occasionally become trigger happy, shooting birds or rats when nervous or bored.

'I've been out here too fucking long,' he whimpered, after blowing his nose, his face blotchy with tears.

'When's your next leave due? I mean proper leave, back here?'

'Five weeks now,' Theo said.

'Hey! So we can go to Battersea Dogs' Home together. Maybe find a friend for Joyce to tear around with.' *What am I saying?* he thought, but he said it anyway. 'She's an egomaniac; it would do her good not to be an only child at last.'

And Theo mumbled, 'Really?'

'Sure. Why ever not?'

'I love you.'

Theo meant it. He wiped his nose again and turned the full wattage of his big eyes on to the screen, where he had somehow achieved the perfect, most flattering lighting.

A few days before, regaining ground after letting herself be flustered by their Skype introduction, slightly peeved, perhaps, despite her denials, that the app she had recommended for mere curative diversion had so rapidly thrown up what was looking like another relationship, Naomi had snatched his mobile to examine several photographs of Theo with a connoisseur's frown before reluctantly declaring him *Pornstar Bambi*.

'I love you,' Theo said again. He didn't smile.

'Fuck. I think I love you back,' Eustace told him, unmanned.

So there it was. He was in love again, this time with a man he'd not even kissed yet, after not so much as a whiff of pheromones and after the most chaste courtship of his life to date, far purer than anything he'd experienced in his teens.

And he had cancer.

He told Naomi of course, about the cancer, because he needed her to come and stay while he went to hospital to have the thyroidectomy. One of the by-products of his period in his early twenties employed as a quant in a merchant bank was private health insurance he had never got around to cancelling. He could have the operation swiftly and in a private hospital he could see from his guest bathroom at the back of the house. They wouldn't be sure until they opened him up but the cancer might not have metastasized yet. They would have to remove some lymph nodes as well to check.

Eustace told Naomi to her face and she gave him a warm hug but was bracingly calm afterwards. And then, because she knew him so well he could never keep anything hidden from her for long, he told her about the love.

Theirs wasn't one of those friendships in which the single straight woman looked to the gay man for a relationship surrogate. She had always been clear that what she liked about being around him was precisely that they weren't lovers, that they were 'grown-ups' who could be as refreshingly honest with one another as siblings and as supportive as true friends. Over the years since they had rediscovered each other, she had pursued a discreet love life, giving him so few details that he had always assumed she preferred her men married and only sporadically available. Men had let her down, however, as Eustace's friendship had not, and he knew she would miss him if he disappeared into another exclusive or possessive relationship.

'He's on active deployment,' he felt he needed to point out. 'You'll hardly notice the change . . .'

She chose not to rise to this but parried his comment with a joke. The scarring would be minimal, she said, and with the calibre of surgeon he'd be getting up the road, they could give him a facelift in time for Theo's leave.

'You can be surprised when you open the door and carry on looking surprised throughout the honeymoon. You've got to tell him, though,' she added.

'He's in a war zone. Someone just shot his dog,' he said, petting Joyce for reassurance. But the dog chose to pull back and look at him with a whippetty directness that somehow only echoed Naomi's. 'It's the last thing he needs.'

'But you might be really ill. Would you want to start a relationship with someone who was dying before you met them?'

'Jesus, Naomi!'

'Sorry, but would you?'

'Well let's see. Let's let the oncologist read my entrails for signs before we start seeing vultures wheeling over W8.'

The operation was remarkably simple. His thyroid was removed, leaving a small horizontal scar in the front of his neck that soon began to heal once the skin clips were removed and which he rubbed religiously with calendula cream to make it disappear more quickly.

Still he said nothing to Theo. Although, as Naomi loved pointing out, in a literal sense they had *been seeing each other* for some time, although he had seen Theo cry, although he now knew him well enough to recognize the way he invariably glanced to his left when saying something painful or unconsciously rubbed an earlobe when something turned him on, Eustace still felt Theo was too much a stranger to be so confided in. Until the scar had blended in with the other all too numerous lines on his neck, he avoided sitting too close to a light source on their date nights and only sent selfies after judicious cropping.

The date for Theo's leave was now only a fortnight away. Theo had a father still living, but they were not close because of the drinking, in which he persisted. There was an aunt he loved, however, who was on the Isle of Wight. So, assuming their first meeting in the flesh would not be a disaster, they'd laid a plan to go there for a few days, staying on a houseboat in Bembridge harbour because the aunt was beyond hosting visitors. Then they would travel on to Dorset to walk some of the coast path. Joyce would come too. To Eustace's slight relief, there had been no follow-through on the rash but impractical suggestion that they adopt a rescue dog together. Theo's leave was for two whole weeks.

Then the oncologist announced that the thyroid had indeed been cancerous and that Eustace would be needing radioactive iodine treatment to make sure that any thyroid cells left behind by surgery would be destroyed. 'You'll take a single capsule of I-131. That's the radiation bit,' she explained. 'It will make you entirely radioactive for a day or two, depending on the size of dose and your metabolism, which is why we'll have to perform the treatment in our dedicated suite – what I like to call the Lead-Lined Room. Once your readings are below a safe level we'll let you out but it's simplest to bring only clothes and possessions like paperbacks you don't mind leaving in the bin at the end.'

Still he didn't tell Theo. The treatment date fell after their last date night and his next duty visit to his difficult mother and two days before the date of Theo's arrival.

'You don't have to stay,' he told Naomi. 'Honestly. You have a life. I can easily put Joyce in kennels for once.' Joyce looked at him as though outraged but then, a little like a Sealyham terrier's, her facial markings meant that outrage or disgust seemed her permanent expression.

Naomi stroked her. She was always far softer on the whippet than she was on him. He liked to tease her she'd have made a natural mother had she not been born aromantic.

'Don't be ridiculous,' she said. 'You've seen where I live. Coming here will be a holiday.'

She was just the same with him when she arrived for her

day of lessons and he set off to visit his mother, but there were small marks of tenderness when he returned. She booked a table at their favourite restaurant for supper (he paid, but it was the thought that counted). And she had bought him a very soft bamboo T-shirt, boxers and socks, 'to pad around your cell in. It's always hot as hell in those places; you won't need layers'.

She insisted on walking him the short distance to the hospital and checked him in, mischievously playing the role of his significant other in front of the nurses. And then, as a surprise, just as she was leaving him, she pressed a tiny MP3 player and earphones into his hands, betraying a small tremor of emotion in the gesture.

'It's only a cheap one they were giving away on a flight once,' she said. 'You can throw it in the bin when you go without a backward glance.'

He smiled, making her push her hair off her face in the impatient way she had when feelings were required of her.

'Is it all cello music?' he asked.

'Of course,' she snorted. 'What other kind is there? What was it Jean used to tell us all the time?'

He pictured Jean, their formidable shared teacher, her leonine face, her daunting, oracular air.

'When everything has been said,' he began and they finished in unison, 'the cello sums up!' And they both laughed.

'I put all your favourites on there,' she added. 'And maybe a few surprises.'

'Is it all you?'

'Not entirely,' she said. 'But other people's recordings can be so bloody irritating. Is that self-centred of me?'

He kissed her as response, which raised a smile from the nurse who was waiting to usher her from the lead-lined room.

'You're allowed to visit him tomorrow,' the nurse said. 'Just not for very long and you'll have to keep your distance by sitting right over there.' She pointed to an unappealing chair in the corner.

Naomi glanced back at the chair. 'No thanks,' she said. 'I don't want to glow in the dark.'

Bring nothing with you that you don't mind leaving behind. Like that daunting instruction he was sure nobody in a plane ever obeyed that, after an emergency landing, you should take absolutely nothing with you, it was an injunction that might have been designed to arouse Dante-esque thoughts of transience.

The corner room was featureless but Eustace had lived long enough under the influence of an art-dealer lover, then that of his collection, to prefer a blank wall to bad art. There was a plane tree outside. A yard of dirty sky. Pigeons. A police helicopter. He could even see across the lower block of flats between to the roof and upper floor of his house, whose chimney pots were distinctively modelled like chess pieces.

He poured himself a glass of water. The introductory booklet said that the more he drank, the swifter his radioactivity would be safely flushed away underneath unsuspecting Kensington and Chelsea.

He changed into the bamboo T-shirt, socks and boxers, left his other clothes, shoes and wallet in a bag by the door as instructed, climbed into bed, because he thought he might as well, plugged in the little ear buds and picked up the MP3 player. It was so small, with a cord so it hung around the listener's neck like a pendant, that it took him a while to work out how to set it playing. Then his head filled with a watery piano introduction so instantly evocative of boyhood it made him smile in recognition: Saint-Saëns' *The Swan*.

CHAPTER TWO

Eustace lived in Hell, or at least its antechamber. Or perhaps Purgatory was a fairer comparison, since he was not unusually abused, and he was clothed and fed, and with both parents still living. On the rare occasions when people asked where he lived, they tended to exclaim,

'Oh Weston-super-Mare! How lovely! Lucky boy! It must be like being on holiday every day.'

And he knew they were thinking seaside, sunshine, donkey rides on the beach. But Weston had estuary mud, not proper sand, and was no sunnier than anywhere else in England.

His surviving granny said the rain came across the Bristol Channel directly from Wales, which made it more penetrating and with a tendency to leave coal streaks on drying laundry. And if you lived in a place where people came on holiday, it made things like going to school harder and when you tried to do holidayish things on your doorstep, like going to the beach, you felt people stare. And if the sun did come out, it was crowded down by the water, and he had taken on his mother's horror of crowds. Only she didn't call them crowds but trippers. Weston, his mother said, attracted something called the Rougher Element, and a few ugly incidents where the sons of visitors had thrown sand in his eyes or kicked over his carefully constructed sandcastles apparently confirmed this. And donkey hair made him wheeze. So, although their house in Royal Crescent was close to the water, Eustace rarely went there for pleasure, preferring to ride his bicycle aimlessly around the streets or to find a shady corner of a public park.

Even without the Rougher Element, people in unwise shorts, people exposing too much sweating flesh, people who ate and drank in the streets when it wasn't even a mealtime, Weston was full of people who were a source of unease. Many of them were very old, as a lot of them chose to come there to die, apparently, but there were also others adjusting to life outside mental hospitals and more of whom his parents darkly muttered 'rehabilitation'. These were often painfully thin but otherwise could only be distinguished from the ex-psychiatric patients by the bad teeth and skin they often had or by their way of looking for things in litter bins or abruptly asking if he could spare any money. All three groups had a tendency to talk to people who weren't there and to be alarmingly unpredictable. However compelling they were to watch from a safe distance, they were best avoided. Unfortunately, while the really old residents liked to bask in the sun like lizards, the people adjusting and the people in rehab seemed as drawn as Eustace was to the few shady corners of the town's parks and gardens.

There was little respite at home since that was also a home with a big H. He had overheard visitors describe Royal Crescent as *distinguished* and knew from Granny that it was a reminder of how refined a resort the little town had been before the arrival of the railway and the Rougher Element. Their house should have been lovely. It had spacious rooms, high ceilings, a pretty conservatory and a calm, ferny garden. Several of the bedrooms, including his, had glimpses of the water. However his father had turned it into one of the town's many old people's homes so there was always a pervasive smell of cabbage water or worse and, except in the deepest reaches of the night, rarely a half-hour went by without the ringing of a bell or the sounds of the demented elderly. Depending on the resident, these ranged from cackling merriment to naked anguish. Eustace was used to both smells and sounds, of course, since he had grown up there and they were his normality, but they made him reluctant ever to bring boys from school home with him. Also there was something about being a child in such a place, that encouraged the old to be forever reaching out with hands or voices, so that to enter any of the public rooms was to feel prodded and challenged in ways he did not welcome.

Apparently the change to home with a big H had come about by degrees. 'Stealthy degrees,' his mother said, implying she had been hoodwinked into allowing it.

His father had grown up there, in what had still been a pleasant, spacious family house. He was the youngest of four brothers, a crowded luxury Eustace found unimaginable, but three of the brothers had died in the war and then his grandfather had died of grief and Granny had taken to her room and lost the use of her legs. So she had needed someone to cook and clean and care for her. His parents had met somehow – at a dance, Dad claimed, though that was as unimaginable as having brothers – and married and her father, Grandpa, needed help as well, as he was confused and used to having things done for him because of the army. So, with two parents living with them and needing help, which was expensive, it made sense to take in a few other similarly needy residents, carefully vetted because Granny had ferocious standards, even when confined to her room. And of course this meant his mother did no cooking or cleaning like other mothers, which was nice, but also meant they never knew what was for supper and had to live with the smells and noises.

He had yet to master the art of making or, more complicatedly, keeping friends. Occasionally, though, a boy from St Chad's had casually taken him back home and Eustace had been struck each time by the relative silence and cosiness of normal houses, their lack of bells, their compact sense of family. His lack of siblings left him feeling exposed and outnumbered. He felt oppressed by the need to behave well and unobtrusively at all times and thought that, in principle, it would be good to have a brother or sister so that he could be childish sometimes. In fact, the lack of one meant he had never really learnt how to play. At school he would naturally gravitate to the nearest available adult, who would be unnerved or irritated by his interest, which did not win him the trust of other boys.

He assumed a brother or a sister was a possibility – he wasn't a fool – but something forbidding in his mother's manner warned him off asking her about the matter. When he tried asking his father, he characteristically joked his way out of having to answer the question.

'Much better being an only. Your mother was an only and look how well she turned out! This way you get more cake! And all our attention!'

(They were taught at St Chad's only to use exclamation marks sparingly but Father spoke with them all the time.)

It was Granny who told him, when she grew bored of playing bezique with him.

'You had two older sisters,' she said.

He hadn't even asked her a question. They hadn't been talking about families. She just fixed him with her gloomy gaze, her blue eyes made even bigger by her thick glasses.

'You had two sisters, twins, four years older than you. But they died. One died being born, strangled by the other's cord and the survivor lived an hour then sort of gave up. The other was bigger and stronger but the little one's cord got her. So. You were very welcome but you'll be the last and you can never talk about it. Your mother nearly lost her mind with it. Now, fetch me a barley sugar from my dressing table and take one for yourself.'

The taste of barley sugars, not a sweet he or any boy he knew would ever actively choose for themselves, was always associated for him with the peculiarly burdensome sensation of secrets, of knowing a thing yet being unable to share it.

To have shared it with any confidence, he'd have needed to understand what he was sharing and there were elements of the revelation that baffled him. He had watched pregnant women out of the corner of his eye when out shopping, knew the way their extra bulk changed their gait, and failed to imagine either his mother or Granny in such a condition. And he knew husbands were involved in the process but Granny's gladiatorial talk of cords and strength alarmed him.

It offered an explanation, at least, for why his parents were so unlike the ones on television or in children's stories. Their connection to one another seemed arbitrary; their characters lacked common ground.

It seemed to Eustace that his father could quite happily have remained a bachelor. He was a happy man – *flippant*, his mother called it – entirely lacking in the energy to go out and make money, build tree houses, play football with other fathers on Saturdays or assist in the making of further babies. He had never settled in any job, *drifting* (his mother's word again) from National Service to helping run a factory that made wooden toys, to working at Wilton Carpets before marriage and fate handed him the endless job of running his mother's house as a Home. Now he did things like change lightbulbs or re-stock bathrooms with lavatory paper and did them with a cheerful slowness that could have been designed to make Eustace's mother cross but was probably no more than what it seemed: light-hearted, oblivious self-absorption. Eustace had always taken his jokey manner at face value; his father was a happy sun to his mother's clouded moon.

After Granny's shocking revelation, however, Eustace reassessed him. As the father of two dead daughters, and a man with three dead brothers, he should have been crying all the time. His father's cheeriness now seemed brittle and unconvincing, a clay mask which the wrong response might cause to crack, revealing something frightening, something not quite a face.

Eustace was essentially a kind boy; he knew that when people were sad, you were supposed to reach out to them to make them feel better, but he began, if not actively to avoid engaging with his father's constant jokes and irony, then to treat them with wariness. Those exclamation marks were like little prods now, keeping one at a distance.

Mother was not like the other women in Weston. She had a lot of headaches, which involved her retreating to a darkened bedroom where she was not to be disturbed and which seemed to be directly related to sunny weather or being cross. And she was cross a lot.

When she was in a good mood, though, which she often was in the mornings before she was dressed, she liked to talk about her own mother. She had several photographs of her mounted in silver frames. Maman had been a prima ballerina, and was pictured impossibly balanced on one foot, arms and other leg raised in a graceful arabesque, or lifted high by a man in make-up, both of them looking as though there could be nothing sadder than to weigh no more than a pretty cloud. In some pictures, newspaper cuttings mainly, she was pictured after a performance, her eyes still painted like a pharaoh's daughter, her taut body wrapped in a fur coat, clutching a huge bunch of flowers, surrounded by older men who all looked at her as though she was the best possible food.

Mother said Grandpa was one of those men at the stage door night after night, an army officer who couldn't believe his luck at being singled out but who thought it entirely unremarkable that his wife should turn her back on dancing and adulation to live on an army camp where the only theatre was a Nissen hut and where the only music was the blare of a regimental band or the wheeze of the chapel harmonium. Dancers ceased to dance in their thirties or once they became mothers, apparently, so it was not really fair to blame Grandpa. If they hadn't married, Mother would not have existed. She blamed him, still, not just for snuffing out Maman's glamorous career but for passing on his genes so that his daughter had his big, practical ankles and not Maman's slim, artistic ones.

There was just one significant photograph of Eustace's mother as a young woman. Around the time when her engagement to his father was announced, she was chosen for the Girl in Pearls feature at the front of *Country Life*. The picture showed her smiling (though showing no teeth), looking very clean and hopeful in a white lacy dress and pearls, with her glossy hair held back by a pale velvet Alice band. She did not look like a young woman about to spend her life in an old people's home in Weston-super-Mare. The page from the magazine was in a silver frame in his grandfather's bedroom, and looked like an image from an earlier, more confident era and so utterly unlike the mother he knew that it was some time before Eustace had made the connection between her and the stylized image.

It was undoubtedly his mother's fault – because she made all the decisions requiring artistry or taste – that he had been given such an impossible name. He had no idea it was impossible at first, thought it no stranger than living in a houseful of old people who weren't relations.

Inspired, perhaps, by the keen interest he'd been showing in the photographs and clippings of Maman, Mother took him to see *Swan Lake* when a touring company brought it to the Bristol Hippodrome.

Eustace was transfixed by the music, the drama, the athleticism, the men wearing tights. Having seen nothing like it in his short life, he bombarded his mother with questions about it for days afterwards. If the same ballerina danced both the white and black swan, by what magic did she briefly appear both in the ballroom and outside the ballroom window? Why didn't the men dance on their toes like the women and how on earth was choreography written down? It amused and gratified her and she followed up by buying him both *Stories From the Ballet* and the Ladybird Ballet book, which demonstrated the five foot positions and some of the basic French terminology. If he was really keen, she said, they could find a ballet class for him. Classes were always short of boys.

So one day he was playing the Tchaikovsky dances and, remembering the ballet, began to mimic what he remembered of it in a loose, even wild sort of way, dancing around the place, gaining courage as he went and snatching up a crocheted shawl as a prop to whirl about himself. Two of the elderly lady residents parked in the conservatory to enjoy spring warmth encouraged him, laughing and clapping. It was so unusual a sensation that he danced on, even pretending he knew how to dance *en pointe*. His father laughed at everything, so naturally Eustace continued to dance when he appeared in the doorway. But far from laughing, his father scowled and shouted, 'Stop it. Stop it at once!' He dragged the arm off the record so roughly there was an awful noise and the record was scratched deeply. 'Now apologize to the ladies for that disgusting display.'

Eustace apologized to the old ladies, who continued to giggle, excited by his father's shouting. There was no further discussion. The Tchaikovsky record disappeared and was replaced by *Going Places* by Herb Alpert and his Tijuana Brass, which wasn't the same at all.

Instead of the promised ballet classes, Eustace was signed up for clarinet lessons. No one asked him which instrument he'd have liked to learn. Apparently his father had found an old clarinet in a second-hand shop and that dictated the matter. Left to his own devices, Eustace would have opted for something showier, like the harp. Mr Buck, his teacher, was a strange, humourless man with smelly hair but extremely clean hands, who lived in one of the down-at-heel art deco houses near the station. Eustace saw no more of the house than the hall and front room, where lessons happened, and felt no wish to explore further; it was so gloomy and colourless. The only decoration was a bust of Beethoven, perched on the upright piano, and a spider plant so dusty it was hard to see how it remained alive. Lessons took place after school on a Monday and, after an initial, rather stiff introduction by his mother, it was decided he was old enough to walk to them and home again unaccompanied.

Mr Buck taught him to read the treble clef. Every Good Boy Deserves Favour At Christmas was how to remember the notes on lines and, for the notes in the spaces, the illogical Boys Dance For All Cows Eat Grass, Boy. As for

29

the clarinet, all Eustace knew was that it smelled of ear wax and he couldn't put it in his mouth without wondering who else had put it in theirs before him.

Mr Buck produced a fine, full tone without hesitation but Eustace either blew too hard or not quite hard enough, so that he elicited either alarming squawks or whispery stutters: nothing that sounded like music. Obediently he learnt fingerings and battled his way through the short pieces in the book Mr Buck sold him. These weren't really pieces, he soon realized, but themes lifted from proper works, curtailed and simplified. Their familiarity was designed as an incentive to the early learner but the gap between the stump of melody and its more glorious source material was simply humiliating. What was worse, the book included pop songs alongside the classical morsels, so Eustace would have to go from picking out *New World Symphony* to squawking *Yellow Submarine*. He knew he had to practise. Mr Buck filled out a little notebook each week with what he had to have done before the next lesson – *B flat major scale, Da Doo Ron Ron* or whatever – and he knew the lessons cost money so were not to be squandered but, even shut in his bedroom, he was self-conscious about the noise and felt it must be as unwelcome and raucous as a trumpet's parping. And then people would comment on it in ways that made him sure the sound was awful.

He knew how clarinets could sound – on a trip to Bristol he had bought an 'Exploring the World of Music' recording of the Mozart Clarinet Quintet and Concerto with his pocket money – but there was an agility and humanity to the tone when proper players performed that he felt he could never achieve. In his hands the instrument remained a crude machine, smelling of someone else's decay, which would never sing.

But then, all at once, Mr Buck was removed from his life.

'You can't have any more clarinet lessons,' his mother flatly announced. 'Mr Buck has had to go away. Awkward really, as we hadn't had his bill for the last three—'

'Yes, well,' his father cut in, in the way he did when he wanted a subject dropped.

'Do you mind very much?' she asked.

'No,' Eustace told her, heart soaring. 'I mean, I love music but . . . I don't think the clarinet is for me.'

His parents managed a smile at that, so he knew he must have unwittingly used an adult turn of phrase.

'Perhaps the violin,' his mother suggested.

'Perhaps,' he agreed. 'Or . . . the harp!'

'No. Not the harp,' she said. 'I think that's for women, really. We can sell your clarinet in the local paper and I'll ask around.'

It was only through boys at school he heard that Mr Buck had been sent to prison for being a *kiddy fiddler*. This was surely an unjust mistake, he thought, since Mr Buck was a clarinetist. Then an older boy explained and Eustace was obliged to deny that Mr Buck had ever touched him or taken naked pictures of him for his collection, which he kept upstairs, apparently, and which was extensive.

In the weeks that followed, during which he ceased learning scales and fingerings on the clarinet, since there seemed no point, he experienced moments of odd excitement at having spent time alone with a known criminal and moments of equally odd disappointment that, given ample opportunity, Mr Buck had never touched or asked to photograph him. Had Eustace been off-putting? Rude? Insufficiently alluring? He found himself obsessively reliving the dreary hours of their lessons, the lugubrious house, Mr Buck's unsmiling demeanour and very neat fingernails, the way the place felt quite unlike a home. But perhaps upstairs was different. Perhaps upstairs Mr Buck expressed himself in lavish, even exotic ways, and a world of unspeakable wonder had lain waiting to be discovered, beguiling yet frightening, had Eustace only thought to ask to visit the lavatory or requested to go upstairs to admire the view of the station.

He noted, in the light of the kiddy-fiddler revelation, that no adult asked him if Mr Buck had done anything to him.

It wasn't that he revised his opinions – Mr Buck had been joyless and uninspiring – more that it was a revelation that a person could have so much more to them than they showed. It made him aware that he might have secrets in turn and grow to be someone other than the ordinary boy for whom people took him.

CHAPTER THREE

'It's a recital and we're going,' his mother announced by way of explaining why they couldn't watch *World About Us*, which was a Sunday evening custom for him and his father, like winding the clocks and taking out the dustbins. 'God knows, we get little enough high culture in this town. When we do, it needs supporting.'

She had even dressed up in a long black dress and silver sandals, which meant he had to wear his school uniform and his father, a suit and tie.

The recital happened in St Joseph's, the Catholic church, which was an adventure in itself, and was given by a cellist called Carla Gold, who had inexplicably moved to the area from London, and a pianist from Bristol.

Eustace was resentful at missing *World About Us*, since he disliked changes in routine, but forgot everything, television, homework, the hardness of his chair, the moment Miss Gold strode on to the stage. She was young, younger than his mother and tall and very striking, with a great mass of tawny, curling hair like a mane, a dramatic nose she regularly turned aside on her longer bow strokes and hands and arms as gracefully controlled as a ballerina's.

Her pianist was as glamorous as she was and wore white tie and tails, which set off his olive skin and neatly trimmed black beard. He had an exotic surname.

'Persian, apparently,' his father informed them, rather too loudly, 'or must we say Iranian now?'

They played two sonatas. The third Beethoven one and the one by Rachmaninov and, for an encore, Carla Gold returned to the stage alone and finally spoke. Her voice was warm and lightly accented.

'Told you,' his father told his mother, again too loudly. 'She was born Goldberg or Goldstein. They often do that.' His mother shushed him and he laughed, nudging Eustace so they could be boys together, united against the impossible woman with whom they lived.

'Thank you so much,' Carla Gold said. 'I'd like to play you the Prelude from the third Bach Suite. It begins with the C major scale and arpeggio, which my incredible teacher, Jean Curwen always said was all anyone starting the cello needed to play for their first year. And I like to think it shows Bach taking an instrument, which until then had been largely for accompaniment, and demonstrating just what it was capable of. It begins with the downward scale and arpeggio and then he opens the range out and out until it soars like a great C major eagle. So . . .'

There was a titter then an awed hush as she sat back on her piano stool, thrust out a shapely sandalled foot to her left, gazed up at the top left-hand reaches of the church, took an audible breath as though about to sing, and began to play.

She didn't simply play the notes; she played as though urgently communicating. *Listen!* her playing said. *This really matters!*

Eustace was enthralled and clapped so enthusiastically

when she was done that his father laughed and his mother murmured, 'Not the harp, then?'

Had Carla Gold silenced the applause and said, 'Now you must leave everything behind and follow me wherever we must go,' Eustace would have obeyed her without a backwards glance. As it was, he was struck quite dumb as they all stood to file out, the adults chattering noisily as they went, many, astonishingly, about things other than the music.

Unusually the two musicians were standing by the doors as people left, quite as though they had just thrown a rather large dinner party and were politely seeing their guests off the premises. This slowed everyone's exit because, naturally, so many people wished to thank them or say 'lovely' or whatever. When they drew near, Eustace was fascinated to see Carla Gold's eyes light up at the sight of his mother, quite as though she'd recognized a kindred spirit.

'Snap!' she said and pointed her foot to show that she and his mother were wearing identical silver sandals.

'Isn't this where you ladies have a cat fight?' his father asked.

Miss Gold said, 'Not at all. We both have marvellous taste. And I love your dress. Is it Indian?'

His mother said yes but that she had cut the little bells off, as they were a bit much.

'I say,' she added. 'I don't suppose you give lessons?'

'Of course. For you?'

'Oh. No!' His mother laughed. 'Far too late for me. For our son, Eustace,' and she laid a hand on Eustace's shoulder and Carla Gold turned the full force of her glamorous attention on him.

'How do you do, Eustace?' she said and he could tell she thought his name was a bit funny.

'I'm afraid he doesn't have a cello yet.'

'Good. Much better. I'll lend him one of mine then we can find one of his own if he gets serious, find one that really fits. Cellos are like friends, Eustace. We choose them with care.'

Eustace was too awestruck for speech.

'I'm in the book,' Miss Gold added to his mother as she turned to the next well-wishers. For a moment Eustace found himself looking at the exotic pianist with the tidy beard who was smiling secretively and looked at him with an odd kind of recognition, and then they were out in the night which no longer felt like an ordinary Weston-super-Mare Sunday night but was transfigured by the spell of music and the lingering trace of Carla Gold's spicy scent.

Most of the boys at St Chad's read comics – either *Beano* or the crudely drawn and, to Eustace, quite inexplicable ones devoted to football or the Second World War. Eustace had learnt to feign interest, just as he was learning to pass comment only on the women pictured in the greasy old copies of *Health and Efficiency* kept hidden in the school locker room and occasionally taken out by the older boys and passed around in a tense atmosphere of pious awe. The men in the magazines, fat, thin, old and young, all quite ordinary-looking, all indiscriminately naked, he saved up in his head to pore over later.

What truly captivated him, however, were his mother's copies of *House and Garden* and *Good Housekeeping*. She flicked through them when they were fresh, occasionally attacking them with scissors to remove a fashionable look she wished to emulate or a recipe to pass on to Mrs Fowler, who did all the cooking (and disliked novelty). She then left the magazines in the conservatory for the residents, from where Eustace would bear them briefly off to his bedroom before they became crumpled and soiled. He loved the smell that came off them, which was probably no more than glue and ink but which was encountered nowhere else in his life so became the odour of luxury itself, the essence of stylishness and escape.

He would shut the door so as to be undisturbed (having only one child, his parents were respecters of privacy) then study the magazines with something of the reverence the older boys brought to the pages of nudist campers playing netball or grilling sausages. He didn't read every word, but he looked at every page to examine the men and women within for keys to unlocking the life of glamour, happiness and style. He had no desire to be the women, although it would be good to have them as friends one day, have them pour out their troubles or share their secret joys. He also sensed he could never be the men, manly but oddly innocent as they enjoyed the latest home saunas, open-topped roadsters or invigorating showers. The hairy, gold-watched wrist of an airline captain changing gear in a sports car while enjoying a Rothmans cigarette stood for all he could never be, even as it opened out a little hollow of confused desire within him.

Entering Miss Gold's home was like entering the world of those magazines so that at first it made him so shy he could hardly speak. Luckily his mother had come with him, as it was his first lesson, and was talking for two, introducing herself, admiring everything. Eustace had never seen her like this before; she was cooing like a dove and smiling. She was not a great smiler, as Maman had told her it was the swiftest route to dewlaps and crow's feet, but it made her look much more attractive, like a room when someone turned off the overhead light and lit a table lamp instead. *House and Garden* had taught him the importance of table lights. Accent lighting, it was called.

Miss Gold didn't live in a house, but a rented flat in one of the older houses, converted into flats in the late Victorian era and carved out of the first floor. It was brilliantly sunny and furnished with bright, happy colours, everything very modern and possibly brand-new. It was like a flat in a film, somewhere Julie Christie might live but rarely be home. There was a shaggy white rug that made Eustace think of her bare feet, and a big, white leather sofa he longed to flop on full length. A big steel bowl piled high with shiny mandarins and lemons echoed a set of bright orange saucepans. The only touches of the antique were a railway clock ticking above the cooker and a funny old railway poster for Weston framed over the fireplace. He felt immediately at home there. So, evidently, did his mother, who so enjoyed being shown around that she feigned surprise when Miss Gold said it was time to start the lesson.

'But perhaps we should meet for coffee,' she added and, to his surprise, his mother smiled with none of her usual stiffness and said that would be delightful. 'I'm always free on Mondays,' Miss Gold said and touched his mother's elbow as she showed her to the door.

The music room was what would have been the second bedroom. There was a sofa and upright piano and a bookcase full of neat stacks of cello music and a sort of family of cellos hanging on pegs on the wall or nestling in velvet-lined cases.

'Are these all yours?' he asked.

'Cello is all I've ever done,' she said. 'So, yes. I started when I was very little, five or six, on this eighth, so I grew up through the quarter and the other sizes. You're going to be tall like your parents, I expect, so you'll start on the three-quarter. Then these full sizes are for teaching on, performing on or lending to students.'

'Do they all sound the same?'

'No. All different. That one I always use in chamber music as it's such a good blender, whereas that one is super loud but *fantastically* resonant high up, so good for orchestral work where the big cello tunes are often in the upper register of the instrument so they cut through the texture. And this yellowish one – it's a quite early English one – is sweet but so quiet, so very good for practising at night or for playing Bach or Telemann on. So. First things first. Sit. That's it. No, that chair's too low for you. Your thighs must be parallel to the floor or pointing slightly downhill towards your knees. Try that blue one. Perfect! Now. Make yourself comfortable. Sit well back. Have a little stretch and a yawn. Loll a bit.'

She laughed at him.

'Right. So this is how you will never EVER sit when

you play the cello. Nothing wrong with being relaxed but I want your spine rocked forwards on your pelvis so that the two of you can dance more easily. You and your cello. So always choose a chair with a flat seat and always sit on the front of it. And sit up. That's it!'

She clapped.

'Remember how that feels. You're relaxed but alert and you're ready to dance. Now . . . Ivan? Meet Eustace! Spread your knees and extend your left foot a little further out than your right one. Eustace? Meet Ivan!'

She brought him her three-quarter size, showed him how to extend and adjust its spike and let him just get used to the feel of it against his upper chest, explaining that she wouldn't give him a bow for a week or two, while he trained his left hand to find the notes. She guided his left hand to a strip of blue Dymo tape she had stuck across the finger-board so that his first finger could find first position.

'Ivan is your friend,' she joked, 'and first position is your home. When you're not dancing with Ivan, you'll feel bereft and when you're not in first position, you'll be on an adventure.'

She taught him a string of useful words when getting to know Ivan: pizzicato, fingerboard, bridge, pegs, neck, tail-piece. Then she had him pluck the four strings with and without his first finger pressing on them and then, while he did that again, she sat opposite him with her cello and plucked a melody so that the sounds he was producing went from being merely plonky notes to becoming music. She laughed as they played. It felt more game than lesson. It was very different to learning the clarinet with Mr Buck.

She wrote in a little marbled notebook for him then, having established he could read a stave, gave him a book of extremely simple music and taught him how to read the bass clef (Good Boys Deserve Favour Always!) before letting him introduce his second finger to the string so as to pluck out the first tune in the book while she played a sort of descant on her cello. The hour went by too fast.

'So Eustace,' she asked him. 'Are you going to enjoy playing the cello?'

'Oh yes,' he told her. 'Very much.' And she laughed and pointed out how he had instinctively dropped an arm around Ivan as though to stop him being taken from him. 'I can see Ivan has made a friend. I don't teach just anyone who asks, you see,' she explained. 'I can't bear teaching children who are only doing it to please their parents and be good. There'd be no point in that and music is too precious. Do you know what I mean by passion?'

'I think so,' he said, though he wasn't sure.

'Passion is a special word,' she said, 'because it means love, the sort of love that burns you up from inside, but it also means suffering. This isn't a hobby. If you want a hobby, take up birdwatching or collecting stamps. This, my boy, is a passion. Are you with me?'

He nodded, too excited to risk speaking, and she smiled again.

'Good for you. So. This time next week you'll play me those first two pages of tunes. Oh. Tuning! I nearly forgot.' She swiftly established that he didn't have perfect pitch but was reassured that he could hear a perfect fifth when she played one.

41

'*Twinkle Twinkle*,' he said.

'Yes,' she told him, 'or *Georgy Girl*. You know that song?' And she sang it while accompanying herself by strumming her cello like a guitar.

Then she showed him how to use a tuning fork. (She suggested that his lovely mother buy him one at the music shop towards the Odeon.) He was to strike it on his knee or any hard surface then sound it by holding it near his ear, and then twist the tuning knob on his A string to have it match, then tune the next three strings to perfect fifths below it. Finally she showed him how to tuck and strap Ivan securely into his soft canvas case so he could take him safely home.

'Thank you, Miss Gold,' he said as he stood in the doorway.

'My pleasure,' she laughed. 'Be good to Ivan. Play with him every day.' He was half-way across the hall when she called out to him, 'Eustace?'

'Yes?'

'Would you mind if I met your mother for coffee?'

'Of course not,' he said, although he did feel a small stirring of jealousy and he added, a little disloyally, 'She doesn't really have friends, so it would be nice for her.'

She smiled at that. 'Good,' she said. 'But I promise not to teach her the cello.'

'Good,' he said and they laughed because she had sensed his jealousy.

He bought the tuning fork on the way home; spending his pocket money rather than asking his parents for it made the purchase feel somehow weightier. He took Ivan and the tuning fork straight to his room in the attic when he got home and immediately set out a corner as a dedicated practice area, as he never had for the clarinet, with a music stand and a chair he had to borrow from the dining room, as he immediately worked out that the chair at his bedroom desk was both too soft and a little too low. It was still his bedroom, still the room of an odd, rather shy boy in a house that periodically smelled of old people or kippers where normal houses smelled of frying bacon or wet dog, but he liked that the first thing he now saw on waking was the chair and music stand and waiting cello. He liked to think he had re-created a small part of Carla Gold's flat in his room, a space where he could dedicate himself and, if necessary, suffer.

St Chad's had always been a trial for Eustace. He found gangs and crowds oppressive and tended to respond to dread by tuning out at just those moments when some key feature of Latin or football was being explained. He wasn't stupid but he was fatally inattentive, preferring to daydream than to memorize chunks of seemingly pointless fact. He liked the idea of Latin in principle – there was a romance to a dead language that had once been the tool of a superpower led by men in leather skirts – but for a small word like *cum* to have so many meanings, or for quite so many declensions to be necessary seemed to him arbitrarily cruel. When not being asked without warning to parse a word or writing Latin proses along the lines of *O slave, thou hast betrayed the camp. At length many men must die on account of your perfidy* they were translating their way doggedly through Caesar's *Gallic Wars* around the class.

Eustace would feel the blood drain from his face when it was suddenly his turn and always seemed to miscalculate when trying to work out in advance which clause or sentence would fall to him. Science was little better. As in football, the other boys all seemed to have absorbed the basics at home, along with speech and how to hold a knife and fork. They could dribble a ball, understand the offside rule and knew the difference between density and mass.

He longed to be one of them, part of the pack, able to catch a cricket ball without for one second worrying it would snap his fingers back, able to feel keen interest in this striker or that goalkeeper. He didn't want to be special or superior, he didn't wish to shine, but merely to pass muster. Being a bit dozy or even downright ignorant in class was no problem; it was usually preferable to being thought a swot, unless one was also good at games. Sport was Eustace's downfall. He was malco-ordinated – *malco* was the insult most often shouted at him by others – never reliably able to catch a ball, never reliably able to throw or kick one in the direction required. He was all too able to lash out with his boot and miss a ball entirely and, were a racket or bat introduced to the challenge, the result was no better.

Sport shouldn't have mattered. It wasn't a subject in which you sat exams and it surely wasn't the reason some parents paid fees to have their children learn more or less the same things they could learn up the road for nothing, but with added Latin. And yet it seemed to matter more than anything else. The height of social ambition at St Chad's was to pass on to Millfield, one of the nearest public schools, which was renowned for its sporting prowess and sounded, to Eustace, horrific.

Sport took up half the boys' conversation; the other two quarters were devoted to last night's television and the spreading of jokes and gossip. Sport also accounted for more than half the cups given out on prize day. Clearly it must have a deeper significance that had eluded Eustace. He asked his mother, who never showed the slightest interest in any sport except tennis during the Wimbledon season, and she said she supposed it was a good way to avoid becoming fat. He asked his father, who laughed of course and said sport was metaphorical: battles without bloodshed.

Happily there was a handful of boys similarly useless at games. Rossiter was immensely fat and so unfit he turned an alarming colour at the slightest exertion and Sprague was so unco-ordinated and feeble it was almost a disability – his arms and legs flew out at unexpected angles when he ran and he had a delightful way of losing his temper really badly at the least provocation. Clearly it would not have done to befriend either of these boys but their presence was a daily comfort as it showed Eustace he was not quite at the bottom of the sporting heap.

Then there was Vernon. Vernon was not especially fat, although he did have asthma and hay fever so wheezed rather when pushed. Vernon's failure at sport was a matter of magnificent choice. He *chose* not to be interested. Vernon amused Eustace's father, who said he was like 'a late-middle-aged man unexpectedly landed in a small boy's body and making no allowances for the change of habitat'.

Vernon read nothing but novels by Trollope, whom he declared no genius but simply amusing, and, although he rarely smiled, Vernon liked to be amused.

Vernon was almost entirely unsociable away from school and it was hard to imagine him doing anything so ordinarily youthful as mooching around the town on a bicycle or sitting on someone's bedroom floor to play with a *Scalextric* set, although he once laconically admitted to enjoying a week-long game of *Diplomacy* against himself. After a cricket game in which they were both batsmen who, inevitably, were never called, Vernon appeared to recognize Eustace as a kindred spirit.

It started with Trollope. Inspired by Eustace's unusual first name, Vernon told him the plot of *The Eustace Diamonds*. All the plot. Eustace must have been a good listener because Vernon followed this up with the plots of *Can You Forgive Her?* and *Barchester Towers*. They became experiment partners in science and Vernon, who was effortlessly good at Latin, helped Eustace remember third declension endings. A few times he came home with Eustace for tea, which is when he so amused Eustace's father. He said he liked old people, which was no surprise, because rumour had it his own parents were ancient, and he spoke to the residents with great formality and close attention.

Vernon was quite unmusical. He claimed he quite enjoyed Gilbert and Sullivan and the *Pomp and Circumstance Marches* and some rock albums but said that the rest of music, from Couperin to The Carpenters, struck him as no more than noise and he preferred silence or birdsong. He respected Eustace's cello lessons and the new devotion they involved, however, which Eustace was touched by. He liked hearing about Carla Gold, whom he likened to a character in his beloved Trollope, and he seemed to enjoy dramatizing his situation.

'You'll need to see less of me to concentrate on your music,' he said. 'But that's perfectly all right. It might become your calling and one should respect callings. There again it might be a hobby like plastic models or stamps, but I hope for your sake that it isn't: hobbies are so predictable and demeaning.'

He pronounced *hobby* with an exaggerated H that amused them so much it became code between them. If either of them came across a boy involved in some traditionally male pursuit that struck them as especially pointless, oiling a cricket bat, say, or collecting Dinky toys, Vernon would draw them out into expressing enthusiasm and then say, 'It must be good to have a . . . hhhobby,' and Eustace would have to walk smartly away lest his giggling give offence.

Miss Gold had cast a powerful spell and Eustace proved an apt pupil. He continued to practise religiously every day, sometimes more than once and he soon found that he was thinking far more about it than any classroom subject. This might not have been the case had any of his schoolteachers been glamorous or even attractive. They were all male, which made the spell of Carla Gold's floaty clothes, tumbling hair and delicious scent all the more potent. Her focus was total. Music mattered to her, whether she was instructing him in the mysteries of bow hold, harmonics or tuning. She also had few of the usual personal boundaries of a teacher and freely revealed herself in chance comments, frank opinions and little rags of colourful gossip.

He progressed rapidly through the positions, at least from half to fourth position. Fifth position and the daunting sounding thumb position had to wait, she said, until his tone was fuller and more confident. She was very keen on confidence. Also on posture. Soon after his first few lessons she had produced a framed reproduction of a very dramatic-looking cellist called Madame Suggia, painted by Augustus John.

'I want you to look like her when you play,' she said. 'Not the mad expression or the dress, of course,' she laughed, 'but her bow hold and posture. See how her left foot being stuck out like that balances her right arm as she extends it? But look at her wrist! So flexible and such good pronation in her upper bow arm. Yes, you produce the sound with the bow on the string but you draw out that sound with that left foot, with your right elbow, even with your neck and the small of your back.'

This sounded completely mad – *barking*, as Vernon said when Eustace told him – but when she encouraged him to adopt Madame Suggia's posture and to perform what she called swan bowing, he could hear the difference. Suddenly he was playing loudly, really loudly, without pressing especially hard. And she laughed at his surprise at the sound he was making.

'That's it!' she shouted. 'Now you're playing! Reach for that sound when you play scales, when you play anything. Anything else and Ivan is speaking, not singing. Can you feel the difference?'

He nodded.

'Where do you feel it?'

'Well . . .' Eustace thought. 'In my ears, obviously, but also in my chest and knees.'

He came to love that sensation of each note vibrating through the body of the instrument and into whatever part of him held it, his knees, his chest, his left hand. She encouraged him to play each scale slowly at first, not letting go of any note until he had found its core. *Mining the note*, she called it, finding the gold in each one, even on parts of Ivan where the tone could be a little woolly, like fourth position on the C string. She made it sound like a moral imperative. However apparently banal the exercise or tune he was playing, she expected his tone to be evenly rich, his tuning perfect.

'Otherwise there's no point. Otherwise you're not bothering and you might as well play football.' Miss Gold despised football. It was a point of agreement between them that sport was largely without purpose, benefit or beauty, though she admitted to a guilty crush on George Best and watched Wimbledon for Nastase and Borg.

Towards the middle of his second term with her, she invited him to join Cello Club. This was when she brought all her students together in a nearby church hall. Most of them were far more advanced than Eustace but Carla Gold was kind and made sure his music was never more than he could manage. The benefit was the thrill of hearing a group of cellos playing together. She sat them in a circle which she joined, sitting between Eustace and a very solemn young girl playing a tiny quarter size. First they played scales and arpeggios to get used to one another's sound, then they played games, launching the scales and arpeggios in succession to produce shifting chords. Then they played some rounds and canons. Finally Carla Gold produced pieces she had adapted, or that her own teacher had once arranged. These were cleverly scaled so that the most advanced players were up in thumb position or carrying melodies while players like Eustace and the solemn girl had their moments of glory, too, playing pizzicato accompaniments or holding crucial bass lines which felt like weighty foundations to the harmonies soaring above them.

Walking home, he felt everything in his life shift a little as the idea of becoming a cellist for a living took root.

He told nobody, certainly not his parents or Miss Gold, but became even more assiduous, routinely practising before and after school and paying special attention to his scales and arpeggios now that Carla Gold had shown him these were music and not simply chores. The only person he eventually told was Vernon. Vernon was a superb keeper of secrets. He harboured his own ambition to write a magnificent and devastating novel about the state of the nation. He then planned to die at thirty-two, so as to die younger than either Mozart or Jesus.

'Good for you,' he said solemnly when Eustace told him. And his quiet respect for the ambition was all the more valuable for music and the pursuit of music being mysteries to him.

The realization that he wanted to be a cellist when he grew up improved Eustace's focus on his school lessons. What had previously seemed largely unbearable suddenly fell into perspective as a mere stage to be worked through. It was like thumb position. He had shyly asked one of the most advanced pupils about this at Cello Club, an impossibly sophisticated teenager called Gabriel, who had hair just like Leo Sayer's and called Miss Gold by her first name.

'It hurts at first,' he said, 'especially if you've got steel strings, because they can dig into your thumb like cheese wire, but then you develop a pad next to your thumbnail and before you know it, no more pain and it feels totally natural.'

To his amazement, Carla Gold shared his dislike of school. 'Maths was the worst for me,' she confessed, impressed that this was his one really strong subject. 'I was sick one term and never caught up. I used to pretend I needed the loo and then hide there for as long as I dared, so of course my maths got worse and worse. But Jean sorted me out. Jean Curwen.'

'Your cello teacher. She sorted out your maths?'

'Jean's amazing. She's no ordinary cello teacher. She saw I was suffering, saw it was getting in the way of me progressing, so she sat me down one afternoon and instead of teaching me the Mendelssohn sonata we were working on, she helped me understand algebra. In forty minutes. She's an incredible communicator. You'll meet her one day. When you've cracked thumb position. She was one of those players who could have been a household name – she had the gifts, the passion, the support of Casals for heaven's sake – but she'd decided you couldn't be a good soloist and a good wife and that her calling was to teach instead.' And she went on to mention two famous players Jean Curwen had taught. 'She runs a cello school. They teach just enough subjects there for it to pass as a school – only subjects she approves of, mind you, like French, Italian, German, music, art history and she drags in some poor mouse of a woman once a week to teach maths if need be – but really it's all about the cello. Hours of practice a day. One-on-one lessons from Jean at least twice a week. Terrifying and utterly transformative.'

'And you went there?' Eustace asked.

She nodded. 'She gave me one lesson then offered my parents a full scholarship. Actually it was no such thing. She simply took me on as a charity case at her own expense but I imagine there were enough fee-paying students there to subsidize me. I stayed for two and a half years.'

After his first evening at Cello Club, everything that had bothered Eustace at school, teachers who sneered, boys who teased, *fero-ferre-tuli-latum*, the causes of the Hundred Years War and his inability to kick a ball with any accuracy fell into perspective. He now had a clear ambition in life that lay beyond them, and he saw they would last only so many terms. He realized he had been too passive, letting awful things happen to him. He determined to meet them half-way. He might not be able to kick a ball with any vigour or do anything about boys who knocked his books on the ground and laughed but he could make a point of asking teachers to explain things he didn't understand and tick off mysteries in Latin or physics the way he now ticked off scales and exercises. Countless boys had tackled them before him; how hard could they be?

Added to this was something he couldn't even share with laconic Vernon: a sense that he had become one of a lucky few admitted, by the almost accidental process of coming to have cello lessons with an inspirational teacher, into the blessed circle of the musical, for whom nothing, neither maths, nor food, nor Latin, nor friends, was as important as music.

CHAPTER FOUR

'It's time you had your own cello,' Carla Gold told him. 'You're growing out of Ivan already and I think all this is taking hold, isn't it?'

'Yes.' Eustace nodded, thinking suddenly how awful it would have been if she had said, *Actually I think this is a complete waste of both our time and I think you should stop.*

'Good,' she said. 'I'll have a word with your mother and tell her the time has come to spend some money. There's a good dealer we can visit in Bristol.'

It might have seemed odd, her saying she'd talk to his mother, since he never saw them together, always arriving at and leaving lessons and Cello Club on his own, but he knew they saw one another. They met for coffee and cake sometimes and occasionally his mother would let slip that they had gone to a concert together, usually a lunchtime one, in St George's Brandon Hill. This last detail gave him a little flash of jealousy because Radio 3 sometimes broadcast concerts from there, so it carried the same distinction in his head as the equally mysterious Royal Albert Hall or St John's Smith Square.

Before Carla Gold, his mother had not really had friends. His father had no friends either but then he was laughing and friendly with everybody so went through his days with people being nice to him. His mother was aloof, however, and full of judgement, so he had sometimes worried that she might be essentially unlovable and friendless.

His mother had always been overtly dismissive of friendship between women. It was childish, she said once, to pursue such a thing after one was married, and she often repeated an anecdote in which a new woman acquaintance had alarmed her by taking her on one side at a party to ask, *Would you be my friend?*

'So pathetic,' his mother said, having imitated the woman's wheedling tone, 'and a bit creepy, really, like some overgrown schoolgirl.'

This new friendship made no difference to her at home. She continued to complain bitterly about the same things she always had, but her discreet, offstage outings with Miss Gold were clearly having an effect. She began to dress a little more like her, acquiring the sort of floaty dresses and ethnic shoes Miss Gold favoured, and she started to wear her hair in a looser, more natural style, which his father said he preferred. There were changes around the house as well, notably big, framed posters – one of a voluptuous Klimt woman lapped in gold leaf, and one of a mournful Burne-Jones redhead, who Eustace privately thought looked as though she was on the point of being sick.

'Your father and I have agreed it's time you had your own cello,' his mother announced. 'I've some money set aside for it and Carla says we can go to Bristol to choose one. Good ones are usually a shrewd investment apparently, so if you ever give it up, we can always sell it again.

We can stay overnight, to make a thing of it. I know it's not far, but it's never a quick decision,' she added, as though she had been buying cellos for years.

It was the Easter holidays, after he'd been learning the cello for over a year. During the spring term he had been allowed to join St Chad's little orchestra. This was a rag-bag of players brought together at random, far too many trumpeters, lots of timid violinists and one, hunted-looking viola player, but he looked forward to their Friday after-noon rehearsals, and not just because they took the place of games. He liked Mr Ferguson and appreciated that he was doing his best to have them play proper music, even in easy arrangements. The March from *Aida. Chanson de Matin*. The *Lieutenant Kijé Suite*. It was a revelation to find that boys Eustace had always thought of as the Enemy played instruments and had this softer side. Jarvis, his ter-rifying football-mad house captain turned out to be a violinist and seemed to think Eustace slightly less useless now that their eyes were meeting across a music stand. There was only one other cellist, who sat in the senior position because he was older, and he seemed incapable of playing in tune or producing even a trace of vibrato. It made Eustace realize what a good teacher Miss Gold must be.

So, strangely, he found he was missing school. Not only was there no orchestra in the holidays but no Cello Club and no cello lessons. Carla Gold had said there was no rea-son why lessons shouldn't continue if he wanted them to but he had heard his father sigh heavily over the bills so lied and said perhaps it was best not, in case they went away. But they never went anywhere ever; the implication being that there was no need since they were lucky enough to live in a town with a beach.

Guessing all this, it seemed, Miss Gold said he could always call round during the holidays to talk things over or to *have a little play* if he felt his practice was losing direction. He was very tempted but didn't like to as, in his father's eyes, taking advantage was nearly as bad as showing off.

Going away to Bristol for the night with his mother and Miss Gold felt a bit like a holiday, to them as much as to him. Both women had chosen rather carefree floral dresses, as if by prior agreement.

'Snap!' Miss Gold laughed when they collected her.

Everyone was in high spirits and Eustace had to make an effort not to talk too much with the excitement of having his two worlds align so pleasingly. Taking him aside after breakfast, to slip him some spending money – something he did only very rarely – his father specifically warned against this.

'Remember not to do all the talking,' he said in a funny man-to-man way. 'They may have, you know, grown-up lady things they want to discuss without you butting in.' And he laughed, to show it was not serious, although it clearly was a bit.

So after initially showing off a little, and leaning between the front seats to make comments, he was good and sat back in his corner of the rear seat while his mother drove them, and he enjoyed doing the reverse of showing off, which was to sit so quietly and unobtrusively that people quite forgot you were there. His mother liked driving and drove rather fast once they were out of town. She laughed a lot and said naughty things about people like the headmaster's awful wife at St Chad's and a new resident they had, who was a brigadier's widow and so bossy his father had taken to calling her the Brigadonna behind her back.

'Though Brigantine would suit her better as she has a bosom like the prow of a ship,' she told Miss Gold and it struck him that perhaps his mother was showing off as well, just a little.

They had stayed in Bristol overnight before, in a small hotel, which, for all the novelty, had been depressingly like an old people's home and therefore just like where they lived. But Miss Gold, who insisted Eustace must call her Carla in the holidays, said that they were staying with her accompanist and his artist friend in Clifton, as they had lots of room.

'Two chaps,' she added, with a sort of backwards nod to indicate Eustace in the back seat. 'Is that OK?'

'Of course,' his mother said. 'But better not tell your father, Eustace, all right?'

'All right.'

'His father can be a little old-fashioned,' she explained. 'But what fun. And the money we save can go on a really nice lunch. Escape!'

They all laughed and Eustace accepted one of the blackcurrant éclair toffees Carla passed around and sat on quietly in the back seat feeling an unusual twinge of disloyalty towards his father.

They went directly to the string dealer's, a rambling

shop on Park Street. Carla knew the owner of old and said he was one of the best luthiers in the region – he made and repaired string instruments as well as selling them. There were racks of violins, violas and cellos, each with a little paper label tied to one of the pegs, not giving the price but a number by which it could be looked up in a ledger that showed who was selling it, what was known about it and how much the seller was asking.

'You'll need a bow as well,' Carla said.

'Really?' his mother asked, sounding briefly like his father.

'Afraid so. Well the bow he's been using really goes with that cello and it's a bit short and light for his arm length now. You're going to be tall, like your father,' she added to Eustace. 'And I think we need to allow some room for growth.'

It was bewildering to face so much choice but Carla said they could discount a lot of them as being *professional* and therefore out of his price range.

'But he needs a good instrument with a full tone and some welly to bring on his technique,' she told his mother. 'Some so-called student instruments are a bit blah. So . . . I think we need a couple of brand-new ones for comparison and a few older ones with a bit of soul and character to them.'

She found him a quiet corner in one of the small rooms at the back of the building, where she brought him a chair. Then she conferred with the owner and found him six cellos to try out and some bows she thought would suit. Curiously she made him choose a bow first. He had no idea how much bows varied.

'If you end up taking this seriously,' she said, 'you'll want two or three for the different weights. One for orchestra work, say, and one for chamber music and one for disasters. But don't worry,' she added with a grin at his mother, 'just the one for now.'

His mother had found a chair as well and sat in the corner, beneath a shelf of violas, much as she had sat in a department store chair while he was fitted for his St Chad's uniform. He hoped she was enjoying as much as he was this visit to a world where art, headily, was everything.

Carla made him play a slurred C minor scale on one of the modern cellos with each bow. He disliked the cello, whose sound was bright to the point of metallic, but there were two clear candidates among the bows, whose balance and length felt just right.

'I'd better take whichever's less expensive,' he said and was pleased that this turned out to be his favourite of the two.

Knowing he would feel self-conscious about playing in a shop, Carla had thought to bring along a music stand and a piece he'd been learning, the Fauré *Sicilienne*, and she set these up before him much as though he was having a lesson. She tuned each instrument with expert rapidity and passed them to him to try, suggesting he play both the opening phrase and a passage from the piece's curious middle section, which would test an instrument's higher range.

The variety astonished him. The first instrument was heavy. The second was lighter and had a sweeter tone but sounded harsh in fifth position. He decided at once that he wanted an old instrument, one with a few dents and scratches – what Carla called *dings* – so that he wouldn't worry about its being perfect. And he knew from his mother that old was often better than new and liked the idea of being able to say that his cello was an antique. But deciding between the older instruments was hard. There was a very red French one, which Carla said had been restored by Guivier's in London, which was good, and had a bright tone. He preferred the look of an almost honey-coloured English instrument she said was from about 1820 but then she passed him a German one, very battered because it had spent time in a boys' boarding school, but which was structurally sound and had such a strong tone that his mother stopped searching in her handbag for something and said,

'That's nice. I like that.'

And finally there was what Carla said was a clever fake Stradivarius, provenance unknown but probably French again. That was undoubtedly the prettiest, with a hand-some scroll and elegant back. But when he played a C minor scale on it, he found a bad wolf-note on the C string's A flat, which no variation in bowing pressure seemed to relieve. So the choice was between the red French and the boy-battered German.

'Would you like me to try?' Carla offered.

He nodded and they swapped places. She played the French one first, thrilling him by playing the first solo passage of the C major Haydn concerto on it so loudly that people started to gather in the doorway behind her to listen. Then she took the German instrument and played exactly the same bars.

'No question,' she told them. 'This is your baby,' adding, to his mother, 'if you don't buy it, I will. It's a steal. The only reason it's been in stock so long is the state of the varnish but that's purely cosmetic. How on earth did a boarding school end up with such a good instrument? Maybe they had no idea what they had.'

'What's wrong with the French one?' he asked, for hearing her play it, he had decided it was rather glamorous and heard himself telling people, 'Oh, do you like it? It's French, early nineteenth century and restored by Guivier's.'

She glanced dismissively back at the French one, which he was still holding. 'Bit woolly in fourth position,' she said, wrinkling her nose prettily. 'I think that gloopy varnish may be hiding a repair that didn't quite work. We can always get this chap tidied up for you but looks really aren't everything. And the back is perfect, look!' And she swung the instrument back to front between her long legs to that he could admire the unscratched butterfly symmetry of the wood on its back. He liked that it was obviously old and that it was unshowy. He also liked the rich clear tone emerging from such an unpromising-looking front.

He had no idea what it would cost, he realized, or how much of her savings his father was allowing his mother to spend. He looked to her for guidance.

'What do you think?' he asked and she shrugged.

'It has to be your decision,' she said.

'But you liked this one's sound?' he asked.

'Yes,' she admitted. 'I had no idea until Carla played them both how much a difference the choice of instrument made.'

'I'd like that one,' he said. 'Yes please.'

'Good choice,' Carla said. 'And there's an approval period, so if for some reason it doesn't work out, we can bring it back and change it within the month for a small fee. Now . . .' She stood again, the heels on her boots making her seem suddenly extra tall in the confined space. 'Brace yourself.'

She glanced at his mother, who said sharply, 'I thought you said this was a steal.'

'It is but . . . Don't look like that. Well within budget. But it'll need a good hard case. We can't trust this to a child's fabric one, not if he's carrying it through the streets.'

He had quite forgotten about the need for a case. Happily the dealer also sold second-hand ones, no doubt those in which the second-hand instruments arrived. They found a sober black case with crimson velvet cushioning inside. There was a leather strap to hold the cello in place by its neck, cushioned pockets for rosin and spare strings and a holder for a second bow, should he ever reach that stage. Nestling the new cello into it felt extremely grown-up after the childish soft case in which he had been carrying Ivan around until now.

'Isn't it awfully heavy?' his mother asked.

'No,' he lied. It was quite heavy but the weightiness was part of the adult burden he was to take on, like responsibility, like scales every day and not just pieces, like passion. 'I can cope.'

'He'll soon get used to it,' Miss Gold said.

And so a cheque was written, with one of his mother's customary girlish muddles: did she have her cheque card, should she write her address on the back too and had she remembered to fill out the stub so she didn't get told off later? And minutes later they were back out on Park Street and he was carrying a new cello.

Although it was well into the afternoon, it was decided they needed lunch. After persuading a taxi driver he could take the cello as well as three passengers, they rode to a proper Italian restaurant with real Italian waiters who knew Miss Gold. Eustace was bought a pizza that completely hid the plate beneath it and his mother and Miss Gold had spaghetti with clams and a big carafe of white wine. He had special water with minerals and bubbles which he thought tasted a bit salty but made him feel as grown-up as the new cello, and the olives and anchovies on his pizza.

After a curt reprimand from his mother, while Miss Gold was in the lavatory, he made a special effort not to show off. In practice this meant being largely silent and listening to the grown-ups, which was no great hardship.

His mother encouraged Miss Gold to talk about herself. Inspired by his mother's story of growing up in the shadow of a prima ballerina, she described how her talent and interest in music had startled her parents; she thrilled Eustace by describing them as *utterly unambitious, three-piece-suite suburbanites*, a phrase he stored up to tell Vernon later.

'They were people with no books or piano. They had me signed up for lessons as my mother had decided it was a pretty, ladylike thing to learn, like flower arranging, and it caught fire in me.' She laughed, shaking out her hair with a flick of her hand as she gazed at her wine glass, remembering. 'I took it so seriously, played so loudly, that I think it unsettled them. My teacher put me in for a competition. What they used to call festivals. Lots of children playing endless pieces for a long-suffering, stony-faced judge. Only in this case the judge was Jean Curwen, and she changed my life.'

'And now just look at you,' his mother said and both women laughed. They had drunk all the wine and had little glasses of something with a burning coffee bean in it, so were possibly rather drunk.

'You know, she runs holiday courses for younger players. It's recruitment really as it gives a taste of the real thing but it's inspiring. Jean is incredible. I think she'd like you!' She turned her attention to Eustace in a way that made him see how much she had been looking at his mother up to that moment. 'I was going to suggest we send you once you've mastered thumb position.'

'When am I learning thumb position?'

'It sounds excruciating,' his mother said.

'It is when your skin's young,' Carla told her, wincing. 'But you adjust. This term,' she added to Eustace. And with a smile she handed him a paper bag from the shop, something she must have bought while his mother and her chequebook preoccupied him. It was music: a series of exercises and melodies called *Introducing Thumb Position*. The notes looked extremely simple until you saw the treble clef and realized how high they were played on a cello's fingerboard.

'Thank you,' he said. 'Thank you very much.'

'You shouldn't have,' his mother began but Miss Gold silenced her with a little gesture of her wine glass.

'It's a treat to have an apt pupil,' she said. 'Maybe later we can christen the new cello with a little lesson on this stuff? Would you like that?'

He nodded, conscious that he was showing off slightly again and wondering if he might be a bit tipsy from the diluted splash of wine his mother had poured for him. 'Where are we staying?' he asked.

'Not far,' his mother said. 'We can walk from here.'

'Ebrahim – that's my pianist friend – lives near here with a painter called Louis. It's a wonderful old house overlooking the gorge. You'll love it. But first, she's bought you a cello, so I think we should get your mum to buy herself something.'

'No, I shouldn't,' his mother said.

'There's a lovely boutique in a mews near here. At least come and see. I want something, too. I think we should all have treats today.'

Insisting again that he call her by her first name, Carla prevailed. His mother had drunk at least one glass more of the wine than she had; he had been keeping count. They strolled up the road to an enticingly gaudy shop presided over by a woman with waist-length platinum hair, a flowing black robe and an array of silver jewellery so that she looked like a kindly sort of priestess. Her shop sold women's clothes but also pottery and glass, candles and joss sticks. Eustace sat quietly in a chair while his mother and Carla became like girls, swooping and exclaiming, holding things up to the light and each other. They both fell in love with the same dress, a long peacock-blue thing with trailing sleeves and silver embroidery around the neck and cuffs. The woman in black came to the rescue by selling his mother the dress and Carla a matching jacket with a pair of black silk trousers they all agreed would look very dashing when she played the cello. And as she was wrapping the clothes in tissue for them and putting them into pretty bags, the proprietor winked at Eustace and threw in a packet of joss sticks for him as a reward for his patience.

'Not many boys will sit quietly like that while their mother shops for clothes,' she said.

Carla smiled back at him and said, 'Eustace is no ordinary boy.'

And he felt a shiver of excitement as they returned to the pavement, for he realized the shopkeeper didn't know which woman was his mother.

He trailed along behind them, distracted by shop windows and people. He tried to imagine a different history in which Carla, not his mother, had married his father and realized that he couldn't get beyond the slightly awkward handshake they had exchanged after her concert. They belonged, as Granny said of people sometimes, *in quite different parts of the zoo.*

Ebrahim's house was just as Carla had described it: a battered Regency showpiece near the end of a row overlooking the gorge and the suspension bridge. It had delicate wrought-iron, covered balconies wrapped around the first floor and the rooms, hall and staircase had the same pleasing proportions as their house in Weston, but without all the old people and with rugs and sanded floorboards instead of fitted carpet. The biggest difference, though, was the art. Their pictures at home were all fairly small, antique prints and engravings, apart from the two posters his mother had put up under Carla's influence. Here the art was all very new; modern paintings, some recognizably of objects or people but most of them just big shapes and blocks of colour. Very little of it was framed and some of the biggest were simply leaning against walls.

Carla had him leave his new cello in the hall then gave them a little tour, because his mother said she was dying to look round before the *boys* came home.

'Where do they go to work?' Eustace asked. 'If they're an artist and pianist?'

'Oh, artists and musicians have to work to pay for all this,' Carla laughed as she led them upstairs. 'Ebrahim is rehearsing with his piano trio in some Baptist church they always use and Louis is at work in his studio, which is basically a disused car showroom he rents with a couple of other painters in a really rough part of the city. He used to work at home but Ebrahim said the paint fumes were making them both sick. Ebrahim is sensitive. Like you!'

There was a big sitting room that took up all the first floor then two bedrooms and a bathroom on the floor above that and a little flight of steps to the sunny roof garden where chimney stacks on two sides and bamboo screens to the front and back gave total privacy.

'Great for parties,' Carla said. 'And you can sunbathe up here without a stitch on and no one would know.' His mother cleared her throat and Carla winked at Eustace. 'I never said that,' she murmured.

On the way back down they glanced into the *boys'* room, which was very masculine, with dark brown walls and old mahogany furniture. Eustace was fascinated at the idea that two grown men shared a bed but sensed from the way the women also glanced at the bed, the big, unignorable fact of it, that sleeping arrangements were not a topic for discussion.

Across the landing lay the spare room, which was a bit smaller but had the same spectacular view as the boys' room. It seemed to double as the house library. Every wall was filled with bookshelves, even over the window and the door. They were rammed so full that books were now being slotted in on their sides here and there. There were photographs propped up randomly as well, pictures from holidays, from parties. Eustace itched to be nosy and examine them.

Every inch of the little bathroom tucked in under the eaves had been wittily papered over with a varnished collage of people and images clipped from magazines, quite a few showing men wearing very little. They were sportsmen and workmen, Olympic swimmers or divers or men in advertisements for pants or bathrooms, but the hand at work had enjoyed pasting them into surprising contexts: a gathering of debutantes, a stiff eighteenth-century group portrait, a flock of sheep, a procession of laughing nuns. Again Eustace wanted to linger, preferably unobserved, but they were being moved on.

'You two can sleep up here,' Carla said, 'and I can take the little bed in the basement.'

'I wouldn't hear of it,' his mother replied. 'Eustace is

getting a bit grown-up to want to share with his mother any more. Besides, he's a fidget in his sleep and he'd keep me awake. You could cope with me, couldn't you?'

'Well. Yes. If you're sure . . .'

'Actually wine at lunch has wiped me out rather,' his mother added. 'As we're going to be sociable tonight, I might take a nap here while you two play with the new cello.'

So they all returned to the hall, where his mother gave Eustace his pyjamas and washbag from her overnight case before disappearing for her nap while Carla led Eustace and his cello down to the basement. The bedroom down there was tiny, below street level with no window. But the music room beside it had a grand piano and gave directly on to the ferny area from where steps led up to the pavement.

'You're well insulated down here, so you can play your heart out without bothering anyone. Ebrahim often plays at night, when he has insomnia or he's getting over jet lag. So. Come on. Let's hear this beauty again!'

She set up the thumb position book on a stand and found him a suitable chair while he rubbed rosin on his new bow and took the cello from its velvety case. Carla sat on the piano stool nearby, played him a D minor triad to tune to then, smiling, said,

'Give me a C minor scale, melodic, three octaves, as slow as you please.'

The acoustic was wonderful, a little like a bathroom's. He enjoyed the scale.

'Now major,' she shouted as he neared the bottom again

and this time she threw off some jazzy chords to accompany him. 'G major next, then D minor harmonic,' she called and he played out, excited by the rich tone the battered old instrument produced for him. 'Are you happy?' she asked when he'd finished.

'Very.'

'Good. I think it's pretty special. It'll certainly see you through to the next level. Your mum loves you very much.'

He wasn't sure what to say to this. 'I know,' he muttered gruffly. 'So . . . how does this work?'

She laughed at his embarrassment but took pity on him by delivering some swift instruction. She showed him how thumb position used the principle that a thumb pressed down hard an octave above the open A on the A string could form an anchor position in which notes could be sounded with the four fingers just as in first position but an octave higher. The difficulty, apart from any initial pain, was that the higher up the string a player travelled, the closer together the notes became and therefore the harder they were to play in tune. In addition, effectively shortening a string this way drastically reduced the instrument's resonance.

His new cello no longer sounded rich. It sounded like an owl, an out-of-tune owl at that.

Carla smiled, wrinkling her nose in sympathy.

'So what's the point?' he asked her.

'Apart from the enormous range it gives us, thumb position's what separates the sheep from the goats. Most cellists learn it – you can't really get to Grade 8 without it, not that I want to put you through all those boring exams. They learn it, they know the principle, but they're never confident, they're never really in tune and they'd avoid it if they possibly could. For me, that's the definition of an amateur cellist.'

Hearing this naturally made Eustace determined to master the new skill. She left him to explore the book while she, too, took herself off for a nap. It alternated increasingly difficult exercises with melodies arranged to use the hand stretches or string crossings. How challenging could it be? He resolved to work his way through the book within the year and to begin every practice session with a page of it, however tedious or screechy, even if his thumb bled.

He lost track of time. After a while the pain in his thumb wasn't so bad, unless he attempted vibrato. The sound became a little less like an owl, he discovered, if he adjusted the distance of his bow from the bridge and didn't press as hard into the string with it as he usually would. Since his father's ban, he had often read his mother's old copy of *Ballet Shoes*, no longer enviously dreaming of ballet classes but simply reading ballet as a tidy metaphor for any life of art and discipline. He watched old films like *Intermezzo* and *Red Shoes* in the same spirit, with a kind of thrilled recognition. He decided this pain in his thumb was like the necessary agony of young ballerinas learning to dance on points, aspiring to grace even as their shoe tips filled with blood.

He completed the first and second sections, resisting the lazy impulse to play on because sight-reading was easier than true practice, worked through them again, trying to show no mercy to poor tuning but wishing, too, that he had more slender fingertips to make accurate tuning easier. *Amazing Grace* proved especially challenging, because of the string crossing and the sudden large interval at the end of the second line. He played it again. And again. He tried playing it much lower, in first position, perfecting the tuning at that pitch, then in fourth and then again with his thumb pressed over the fingerboard. He was concentrating so hard that he didn't know he had an audience until a man's voice said, 'Hello,' between attempts.

Startled, he turned and recognized the pianist friend he had not seen since Carla's long-ago Weston recital. He seemed quite unchanged, still neatly bearded, tanned and slight, leaning in the doorway as a satyr might have leaned against a tree. He looked different now, of course, in jeans and a cheesecloth shirt rather than white tie and tails.

'Er, hello,' Eustace told him. 'I'm trying to learn thumb position. Sorry.'

'No pain, no gain. You must be the famous Eustace. I'm Ebrahim.'

'I remember. I came to your concert in Weston.'

Eustace made to stand but Ebrahim waved him back to his seat and came to sit at the piano. 'Try that again.'

'*Amazing Grace*?'

'Yes. Let's see if I can put you off.'

So Eustace played *Amazing Grace* in thumb position while Ebrahim improvised an accompaniment of chords and ripples that started traditionally enough but soon introduced blue notes and remote, jazz harmonies.

'Another verse!' he called out as Eustace reached the last

line. 'Let's try it quietly.' So Eustace played it again quietly, using the side few hairs of his bow as Carla had taught him, to produce a glassy, ghostly tone while Ebrahim played chords on just the second and third beats of the bar, turning the song into a sad waltz. 'And one more time,' he said, '*Appassionato*.'

Eustace dug in his bow and attempted some vibrato, though it was hard to do so and stay in tune so high, but somehow Ebrahim, playing a sort of Liszt parody, made his efforts sound convincing and he laughed when he reached the end.

'You're getting there,' Ebrahim said.

'I hope to.'

'That's the new cello?'

'Yes.'

'Let's put her through her paces.'

'You think it's a girl?'

'Don't you? She has hips. And she's been around a bit. Do you know any Fauré? The first sonata, maybe?'

Eustace admitted he had recently learnt the *Elégie*.

'Of course you have,' Ebrahim said, letting Eustace see he was a bit of a tease. 'It's every cellist's first grown-up showpiece, isn't it?'

He played the solemn introduction but Eustace could manage no more than the first phrase before confessing he hadn't memorized it yet. Suddenly businesslike, as though this was a lesson, Ebrahim riffled swiftly through a shelf of music beside the piano, found him the cello part and began again, still playing from memory himself. It was daunting, because Eustace had learnt the piece but never performed it and, of course, the copy had none of his own fingerings written in. But he found he was remembering most of them and the new cello's sound made it ring out. Ebrahim made no allowances, playing out so that Eustace had to play out as well to match him.

'Good,' he said at the end. 'Where'd all that passion come from? You're what, eleven?'

'Twelve. But you don't have to try so hard, I think, because it's such a sad piece.'

'Do you know *Après un Rêve*? It's only an arrangement of one of his songs but it works so well. Here. You're not scared of sight-reading?'

'I love it. Carla says I should sight-read less and practise more.'

'And Carla is always right. But good for you.' Ebrahim dug out a single sheet of music and put it on the stand. 'We'll take it pretty slow,' he said. 'Just remember it's a song. Yearning and regret. That sort of thing.'

And he launched into the introductory bars, barely giving Eustace time to note key signature and tenor clef. It was beautiful, with the sad restlessness that seemed to be Fauré's hallmark. He fluffed a couple of notes, stammering apology as he did so, but Ebrahim seemed quite unbothered.

'You've a good legato,' he said.

'Thank you.'

'But you need to be less rigid about tempo. Enjoy the turning points of the melody, like here.' He played a section. 'And here. Any accompanist worth their salt will be flexible and follow and anticipate you. You never want to overdo rubato, or it gets mannered and irritating, but in a piece like this, a song basically, where you have a singing line throughout, you need to flex to bring it alive. Want to try again? I love this piece.'

'Yes please.' Eustace couldn't believe he was playing with a professional. Ebrahim made it seem entirely normal, but then music was his life. And the second time through, Eustace allowed himself more time to indulge the melody.

'That's more like it,' Ebrahim said when they'd finished. 'Do you sing?'

'Not really,' Eustace admitted. 'In fact, no. I don't, except when we have to in school assembly.'

'Pity. Listen to singing, then. There are song recitals on Radio 3 almost every day of the week. Learn to play like a singer. Because they're having to use their breath, singers really think about the shape of a phrase, its high points and how to support them, and you can recreate that with your bow. Listen to me. I'm going on and I'm meant to be cooking. Cup of tea?'

'Oh, I'll practise a bit longer, thank you. But thanks for playing with me.'

Ebrahim grinned. 'My pleasure.' He stood from the piano and stretched so that his shirt rode up out of his jeans. 'Are your mum and Carla out, then?'

'Oh. No. They went upstairs for a nap,' Eustace said. He caught a flicker of amusement in Ebrahim's response.

'Ah. Best not disturb them, then. Just come and find me in the kitchen when your poor thumb gets too sore.' And he shut the door behind him so Eustace wouldn't feel self-conscious about continuing.

Finally Eustace stopped because someone came down the outside steps with a bicycle and then in through the basement door and there was soon the sound of conversation added to the cooking smells coming down from the kitchen and he sensed he should be sociable rather than self-indulgent. He packed the new cello away, carefully wiping off rosin powder and finger marks with a handkerchief first and telling himself that now he had a cello all his own, he would do so every time he played it.

Ebrahim had thrown on a striped navy-blue apron and was frying spices and onion and chopping something. Another man, who seemed frighteningly large, with muscles that actually bulged and hair cut so short that it was a blond fuzz across his tanned scalp, was straddling a stool to watch him work, nursing a mug of tea in enormous, paint-splashed hands. He swung around and held out a paw to shake Eustace's.

'Eustace,' he said. 'I'm Louis. Have a stool. Tea? *Stroopwafel*?' He had an interesting guttural accent that wasn't French or German. 'I'm Dutch,' he said, with a wolfish grin. 'I'm also profoundly psychic.'

He tugged out a stool so that Eustace, too, could perch like him to watch Ebrahim cook. He poured him a mug of tea from the pot and passed him a deliciously chewy biscuit. It had a buttery layer in its middle.

'This is very good,' Eustace told him. 'Thank you. Is that toffee inside?'

'Treacle. *Stroop*. My mother thinks I'll starve so she posts them to me from Gouda, where they make the best ones.'

'Because of course nobody here knows how to bake,' Ebrahim said, adding something liquid to the pan and shaking it so it sizzled. Their pans were quite unlike Mrs Fowler's pans at home, being cast iron with wooden handles.

'You like her *spekulaas*,' Louis said.

'And her chocolate *lebkuchen*. I like her everything. It just amazes me she thinks Victoria sponge and scones and gingerbread and Christmas cake don't count as baking.'

'She knows they count. She's reminding me where I come from.'

There was an attractively grainy quality to Louis' voice enhanced by all this talk of cakes and biscuits.

'Is my mother still napping?' Eustace asked. 'She never normally goes to bed in the afternoon.'

This wasn't strictly true – his mother often used her recurrent headaches as a pretext for a siesta – but the kitchen clock said it was nearly six fifteen and he didn't want Ebrahim and Louis to think her slovenly.

The others seemed to exchange a smile, although their eyes barely met to do so. They were quite unlike his parents, he realized, in that so much of their communication was unspoken, just somehow implied.

'I'll take them both a cuppa,' Ebrahim said, pouring very brown tea from the pot.

'I can do it,' Eustace offered.

'No, you stay here and eat another waffle and talk to the Dutchman. How does she have it?'

'Oh. Well. She really likes weak Earl Grey, so it's hardly coloured. And no milk.'

'Ah.' Ebrahim passed a mug of Indian tea to Louis. 'You can have that,' he said and started afresh with a daintier bone-china cup and an Earl Grey teabag. He caught Louis' eye as he headed out to the stairs. 'Could you, er?'

'Sure,' Louis said and stood to stir the contents of the saucepan. 'Your eyes are on stalks, Man-Cub,' he added softly.

'Oh. Sorry,' Eustace said. 'I didn't mean—'

Louis' tone was kind and amused. 'Anything you want to know, you have only to ask.'

'Oh. Thank you. Yes.' Only he wasn't quite sure what Louis meant.

'Are we your first gay couple?'

'Yes.'

'Well, apart from the obvious, we're no different to other couples. Sooner or later it's just domesticity, you know? Did we remember to buy firelighters and why is your sister coming to stay yet again?'

'My father's mother lives with us. And my mother's father.'

'That must be terrible. Or is it OK for you? I mean, grandparents are different, right?'

'It's OK,' Eustace said, enjoying his second waffle and knowing Weston could offer nothing closer to such exotic pleasure than a Wagon Wheel. 'They're very old now. But they've been there all my life, so I suppose that makes it normal. Have you always known you were . . . ?'

'An artist? Always. I was never like the other boys.'

Eustace was confused and felt himself blush stupidly. Louis smiled and looked down to pick at some dried paint on his wrist. 'Don't worry. I know what you meant but the answer's sort of the same. Either way there's that period of worrying you're the only one, of worrying you're wired differently from everyone in your class. Two things you'll learn as you get older: no, you're not the only one and yes, you're wired differently and that the difference is fantastic!'

Eustace felt they were talking in a code which only one of them fully understood but it left him feeling privileged, as though he had suddenly been admitted to one of the exclusive little gangs at school.

That dizzying sense of having gained access to another realm stayed with him all evening, as Louis taught him to make vinaigrette and let him lay the table, and as Ebrahim came back downstairs shortly followed by his mother and Carla, all of them rather giggly, all of them, he noticed, even his mother, shoeless. It was as though they had been drinking wine; only they had no bottle or glasses with them. They ate delicious food, all of it quite unlike the plainer things they tended to eat at home, because of the elderly residents' delicate digestions. Louis set out little bowls of smoked almonds, olives and stuffed vine leaves and fingers of raw vegetables to dip into a mixture of Greek yoghurt and some sort of Indian pickle whose spiciness made Eustace's nose tickle but left him craving more. Then they had a chicken curry bright with fresh coriander, which Eustace had never tasted before, and garlicky naan bread – another first – to mop up the sauce. And pudding was figs baked with chocolate inside them served with vanilla ice cream Ebrahim had actually made himself.

'Do you always eat like this?' Eustace asked them and they laughed.

'I love cooking,' Ebrahim said.

'People who work from home,' Louis added, 'tend to crave distraction.'

'Time you went to bed, young man,' his mother told him. There had been something different about her all evening and now he realized it was because she had been laughing. It made her seem younger than she did at home, where the tone of her better moods rarely rose above a dry and weary wit.

'Are you going to tuck me in?' he asked and was pleased that they all laughed.

'Don't push it,' she said and the others laughed some more. 'Sleep tight and if you wake very early, practise your thumb position very, very quietly.'

He impulsively kissed her cheek as he left the table and she surprised him by giving him a little hug as he did so. 'Thank you for my cello,' he said. 'And for my thumb position book,' he told Carla. 'And for supper,' he told the others. 'It was delicious.'

'Bed,' his mother told him. 'And don't read too late.'

They were all quiet until he had left the room and closed the door behind him. He resisted the temptation to loiter outside and listen as their chatter resumed. He brushed his teeth swiftly then went to bed without showering, as strange bathrooms were unnerving. But with the bedside light on the little bedroom was cosy, despite the oddness of having no window, and having his new cello standing in its smart case at the foot of the bed gave him a feeling like Christmas and birthdays were supposed to feel and so rarely did.

CHAPTER FIVE

He decided to try sitting in the armchair for a change. He was not ill, after all, not in a way that gave him symptoms at least, so lying in a hospital bed made him feel fraudulent. He also worried it might stop him sleeping later. He experimented with watching television, flicking impatiently until he found a news channel, but realized he was taking nothing in beyond it seeming a report of wall to wall pain and bad tidings, so he switched it off and plugged in his little headphones instead and returned to listening to Naomi play the first Brahms sonata.

It was impossible to remain disengaged from music. The sonata was so familiar to him – his left hand could even summon its fingering with a little concentration – that it had the quality of an old friend, demanding attention as a right. He had bought a newspaper on the way in but had set it aside as an indulgence for later on. He had only briefly regretted forgetting to pack the eminently disposable novel he had set out by his case. To listen to music for a change, without either being in a concert hall or performing some domestic task at the same time, was a meditative treat.

Exciting though live performances often were, he knew too much of the strains involved ever to watch entirely without anxiety. Before Naomi re-entered his life as a friend, he had visited hers purely as a punter, watching her perform twice, with a pianist at the Wigmore Hall and in front of an orchestra at the Proms. He did not yet know what torment she had been going through but he sensed it, as everybody did. One of the things that people loved about her performances was her evident vulnerability. The sound that emerged was superb, the technique flawless, but the human cost was writ large in the way she paused to wipe her hands and brow between movements, and in her naked, laughing relief when each performance was over.

Her brother, Ralph, now played with a Canadian string quartet and she envied him his career. His quartet wasn't world-famous but it was constantly in work. He was on the less showy second violin line and quartet players perhaps felt less exposed than soloists did, but she was the first to admit that Ralph had the cool head she had always lacked.

'I became too hysterical,' she sighed. 'Jean would have been disgusted,' she added, referring to the teacher they had briefly shared.

Naomi now looked sufficiently different to Naomi then, to Naomi the star, that she was never stopped in the street unless she was carrying her cello as an aide-memoire and, even then, walking beside her, Eustace had watched people think they recognized her then dismiss the notion. She had cut the hair that once had lashed dramatically across her shoulders into an elegant, lower maintenance bob, and was judiciously admitting silver to it. And she was now a healthy weight. As a student and performer, she had been twig-thin, with fatless arms in which every tendon could be seen.

She spoke only rarely of her time as a performer, preferring to talk of the years before or since. Sometimes she referred to herself as *a recovering performer* and the details that she let slip since re-befriending him were akin to those of ruinous addiction. She had trouble with crowds and stress, occasionally melting away from a gathering without explanation or apology. She had trouble with her teeth, which had had their enamel fatally weakened in her performing days from the impossibility of not throwing up backstage before every concert.

'It was that, or beta blocker dependency, in common with half the soloists out there. But I hated the blankness they brought on. I hated being sick but I was an adrenalin junkie and performing without it felt like performing on tranquillizers – the lack of nerves was nerve-wracking in itself!'

Naomi worked hard with her academy students at impressing on them the need to stay grounded, to avoid becoming hooked on the performance high, to curb the impulse to lacerating self-criticism, just as they needed to remember to eat normally. But she knew it was a doomed challenge, that they thought she was teaching because she had been too weak to cope.

'And I was, for Christ's sake. I watch them sometimes,' she had told him the other day, picking grapes off his bunch rather than pinching off a handful, precisely because she knew how much this irritated him. 'I watch them when they're lost in playing me some sonata finale or some cadenza or other, and all I see are those terrifying Olympic gymnasts, all spangles and killer attitude. And that's just the boys.'

It had been a while before Eustace realized that his friendship with Naomi had given him the sibling he had dreamed of in boyhood. Already long used to a brother, she unconsciously adopted the same manner with him that she did with Ralph: frank, dismissive, fiercely loyal. He worried that he would lose her, that she'd suddenly meet someone and move on, heedlessly in love. He had already decided that anyone new in his life would have to accept her as an intrinsic part of it, like a sister in fact. And he hoped she knew that her approval or disapproval would dictate any future he might have with Theo.

When Eustace prodded her on the subject, she said that she felt it was time she put aside love, erotic love, as a recovering alcoholic progressively puts aside mouthwash, painkillers and even coffee.

'I'm done with extremity,' she claimed. But he wasn't sure he entirely believed her. She still noticed men, builders, waiters, passers by; he saw her appreciate them. And she had a way of opening out to their attention, laying herself wide open sometimes, that worried him.

He nearly missed the phone call to alert him to the imminent delivery of the radioactive iodine because his head was full of Naomi's Brahms. Luckily the bedside telephone also had a flashing light, which he saw from the corner of his eye. An extremely polite nurse was calling to say his dose was ready and that they were on their way to deliver it. Eustace recognized the voice. It was the same

Ghanaian man who had run through other formalities on his admission, weighing him to calculate his dosage precisely, taking his orders for lunch and supper.

He knocked and entered shortly, his crisp uniform adding to the conscientious air he had of a priest-in-training. He bore before him a metal canister, like a modernist version of one of the three magi bearing precious gifts. A suited woman was with him.

'Myrrh for time of burying,' Eustace told them.

'I'm sorry?' the woman asked.

'Nothing. Nervous joke.'

'There is nothing to be nervous about, I assure you.' The formality of the nurse's manner was deeply soothing; he'd have done well in a euthanasia clinic. 'This is Dr Searle, the hospital physicist.'

'How do you do?' she said, shaking Eustace's hand. 'You'll see me and my Geiger counter later,' she added. 'For now I'm just here to oversee safe practice. This canister contains your dose of I-131.The layers of metal prevent the radioactivity contaminating anyone or anything in transit. The dose is in pill form.'

'Are you good at pill swallowing?' the nurse asked.

'Expert,' Eustace assured him. 'If I have water.'

'It is not so very large. I shall unscrew the canister in a moment then use this special wand to pick out the pill safely and pass it to you to swallow immediately. Do you understand me?'

'Perfectly.'

Dr Searle coughed, impatient perhaps, but the nurse smiled seraphically, giving Eustace the impression that he enjoyed both the ceremony and the playfulness. The nurse fetched a glass of water from the bathroom. It was unexpectedly hot.

'Warm water helps with the uptake of the iodine,' he explained. 'After we give you the dose, you may experience some nausea. Constipation, diarrhoea or a dry mouth have also been reported. Most patients only experience a dry mouth. I'm afraid you can have nothing to eat or drink now for two hours, to ensure you absorb all the iodine. After that, it is business as usual and we'll want you to drink lots of water to speed the radiation out of your system.'

'How does it actually work?' Eustace asked.

Dr Searle answered. Eustace tried and failed to imagine the journey whereby a woman became a physicist in a hospital lab. It was hard to imagine her walking a dog or tending a flower garden. 'Your thyroid absorbs any iodine in the blood. It continues to do that even when affected by a carcinoma. Although you had a thyroidectomy, the scan we performed afterwards showed you still have small pieces of thyroid left. These will now draw in the iodine and its radioactivity will destroy their cells. It's a little like that poison you put down which ants carry back into their nests to feed their young.'

Perhaps she was a gardener after all?

Eustace indicated that he was ready and the nurse set the canister on a table, unscrewed its heavy lid then used his ingenious transparent wand to draw up the pill and pass it, at arm's length, into Eustace's cupped hands. Now it felt less like a magi's gift than an administered sacrament. He rinsed it down with a good gulp of the warm water. The nurse took the glass from him and immediately ushered Dr Searle from the room. Soon after, Eustace heard the second door closing on him.

He sat on the bed for a while, waiting to see if he'd feel sick but he didn't. What he did feel, now that he was nil by mouth for two hours, was a hankering for a large glass of something crisp, some dolcelatte and oatcakes to go with it. Perhaps with some green olives. He returned to the chair, angling it directly to the window, thinking its view would distract him.

He put the earphones back in and pressed play on the little MP3 player, but his thumb was too big for the delicate controls and it lurched over several tracks and was no longer playing Brahms. It was something contemporary for solo cello. It took him a second or two to place it. Then a melody emerged from the flashy accompanying figures and he recognized a sly encore written for Naomi by Thomas Adès or Mark-Anthony Turnage or some other playful genius. Over a crazily difficult introduction and background of pizzicato strumming, spread chords in the style of Bach, knocks on wood and punchily rhythmic riffs worthy of Led Zeppelin, a tune emerged which any cellist could play after only a few lessons: the childishly simple and monotonous melody of *I Will Survive*.

Although it invariably brought the house down, Naomi had never recorded it because of a difficulty with the holders of the rights to the original song. She had recorded this, he understood, just for him. When she reached the end, he could hear birdsong recorded through his garden windows as she murmured, 'Get well soon, babe.' He swiftly fiddled with the buttons to make the track play one more time.

From where he sat, he could see the house where he lived so clearly he half-wondered if he'd suddenly spot Naomi at an upstairs window. But she would be downstairs, of course, teaching for most of the day. Years after moving in there, he still didn't think of it in any way other than as Gilbert's house or *Maison Gilbert*, as his lover had liked to call it.

Although one was a lover and the other a pseudo-sister, Eustace could never remember Gilbert now without thinking of Naomi or think of Naomi for long without remembering Gilbert. Their presences and influences in his life were so enmeshed, he was always pulled up short by any reminder that they had never met.

In his early twenties, when he had found himself earning far beyond what he felt was his worth as a mathematician in a banking firm, Eustace was scooped up at the end of a sweaty night in a club under Charing Cross by an older man who described himself as second generation South Ken French.

'My name is Gilbert,' he said, touching his chest and inclining his head with disarming formality.

They danced to three songs, each pretending to enjoy the music, kissed extensively against an alley wall, made love on Gilbert's sofa then showered before sitting up in bed half the night to talk. It was like finding the big brother he had never had. Worldly-wise, funny, Hollywood handsome, Gilbert was flattering, kept saying things like, 'Why has no one else snapped you up yet? What's wrong with you? There must be something wrong. Stay for lunch while I work out what it is!'

The rest of the weekend vanished in a heady continuum of talk, sex, more talk, and so much kissing their faces became raw. In one of the intervals – 'intermission', Gilbert announced it, as though the bedroom were an old-fashioned cinema – he led Eustace around the house, showing him the paintings he was waiting to sell and see-ing if he could guess the ones he half-hoped wouldn't leave the house just yet.

As Gilbert fed him little plates of luxury from the fridge – manchego, jamon serrano, white peaches ripe to juiciness – he asked, clearly fascinated, just what a quanti-tative analyst did and how it was that a bank made use of a mathematician if not simply to add and multiply num-bers. He made Eustace draw explanatory equations on a notepad to demonstrate risk and the potentially enormous gains to be made from shouldering then subdividing other people's debts. Gilbert was clever, but it was plain he did not really understand or take Eustace's work especially seriously, as though banking were a game. And Eustace realized, with an unfamiliar pang, that this lightness in him recalled being a chubby little boy riding a Sunbeam Winkie with a flag on the handlebars back when his father was alive and still made light of everything.

Emboldened by a large glass of icy Manzanilla, he made Gilbert explain his work in turn. Gilbert had two jobs: one as an expert on late nineteenth- and early twentieth-century British art at Christie's and one as a private dealer. Most of the paintings in the house belonged temporarily to

Gilbert but once in a while he would sell several simultaneously to the same collector.

'A lot of my clients are completists. I introduce them to an artist whose work they like and then they want them all. And of course I work with several interior decorators. They love a set of paintings – it makes a bold statement and the repetitive colour palette is easier for them to work with than the visual *macédoine* of things people inherit.' He pulled what Eustace would soon come to know as a very Gilbert face, expressing a blend of Gallic scorn and English amusement.

Eustace finally returned home late on the Sunday night to the flat in Finsbury Park he shared with near-strangers. He was wearing clothes Gilbert had insisted he borrow and went to work as usual on the Monday, feeling lightheaded from lack of sleep and self-conscious about a persistently pink mouth and cheeks he was sure everyone was staring at. He spent that night at the flat after a ninety-minute phone conversation with Gilbert about nothing and everything then never slept there again; he moved in with Gilbert the following night.

He earned well and could easily pay his way but Gilbert was casually generous. Perhaps precisely because he was a dealer, he had an almost negligent attitude to property.

'It's only stuff,' he would say. 'This is all that matters,' kissing one of Eustace's nipples, 'and this,' with a kiss to his forehead.

Gilbert had been taken under the wing of an older lover back in the sixties and regarded it as only right that he should be passing on the favour now. He marked the morning after Eustace's formally moving in with the opening of a joint bank account and, to Eustace's bewilderment, by the roping-in of his cleaning lady to witness a fresh will leaving him house, contents and business.

'We have to take steps to help ourselves,' he said with a shrug. 'No one else will,' adding, with a characteristically Gilbertian twinkle, 'these are all steps I can reverse if you fail to please . . .'

They enjoyed just four years of unalloyed happiness before Gilbert had to be hospitalized with a bout of pneumonia, the first of a succession of debilitating HIV-related infections.

Eustace had himself tested frequently, enduring the days' long wait for the results to come through. Against all the odds, Gilbert had not passed on the virus.

'Even my generosity has its limits,' he joked on hearing the news.

Eustace found himself rapidly becoming an expert in palliative care and took time off from work to nurse Gilbert, before impulsively throwing in his job. He sank his last bonus and savings into buying a bargain flat in Olympia that needed only better lighting and German taps. To improve it further, Gilbert added a few of his paintings and Eustace sold the place at an embarrassing profit, which he immediately rolled over into buying two more of what Gilbert called *fixer-uppers* in an up-and-coming area just south of the river. And so, with his heart and mind almost entirely focused on a shrinking man in a hospital bed, he ceased to be a quant and became a property developer.

By the time Gilbert finally gave up the struggle, he was

blind, prematurely demented and so light Eustace could easily hold him in his arms and carry him from bed to bath and back again while a nurse changed his sheets. Eustace's life had undergone a radical transformation. His work suits and dress shirts were sidelined in his wardrobe for weddings and funerals and his days became like one extended weekend. The period of nursing Gilbert and the evident inability of some people to cope with his lover's diagnosis swiftly cut their address book by a third. In the same period London property values continued to rise, unchecked by crises in the stock market or in banking. Eustace emerged into the nineties as a rich survivor from a war to which many of his neighbours remained oblivious. He became a keen gardener and theatregoer, an adeptly apolitical charity fundraiser. He changed his body shape by joining a gym, reclaimed control of his mind by learning and practising meditation and let Naomi bully him into taking up the cello again after a twenty-year gap. His hair turned prematurely silver and he took to having it cut short every week by a mournfully sexy Turkish barber who trimmed eyebrows and nose hair without being asked.

He had flirtations and adventures but only one significant relationship after Gilbert. To the dismay of friends, of Naomi in particular, he became involved with Gwyn, a febrile, bad-tempered pharmacist he had befriended when volunteering on the ward where Gilbert had been a frequent patient. Gwyn was seriously ill when they met, and neither man had any reason to believe he would live another two years. But then the new combination therapies arrived, the AIDS wards began to empty of gay men,

Gwyn's symptoms abated and his viral load shrank. They were forced to admit finally that their pairing had been based on the dubiously romantic assumption of it being cut short by Gwyn's death.

Gwyn's legacy was to have infected Eustace in the process. Eustace would be on pills for life and was obliged to call in on a clinic for a battery of blood tests twice a year but otherwise, in the new coinage that was meaningless to those outside the gay sexual playground, he was said to be *undetectable*.

CHAPTER SIX

Grandpa died.

It was entirely to be expected as he was nearly eighty-four and confused but it still came as a shock because he had given no warning signs and was in apparently robust health apart from the confusion. One of Eustace's regular chores was to escort Grandpa on his constitutionals in case he lost his way, although this had happened only once, when he made the mistake of helping an even older man home with some bulky shopping, which took him too far from his usual route for landmarks to lead him back. As a rule his walk was unvarying: along the front to the right, past Knightstone Island, along Manilla Crescent and Birkett Road, past the Old Pier and then back along the higher route via Prince Consort Gardens and Grove Park, where he paused to feed the birds two slices of yesterday's stale bread. Eustace had trouble keeping up with him. He tended to march wordlessly until they reached the ruined pier, where he invariably made some comment about *trippers from Cardiff* or said it reminded him of somewhere he had been during the War. When feeding the birds he would usually ask Eustace a question or two that seemed to reveal a residual sharpness beneath the mental fog. Did he only play French and German composers? Did he prefer playing on his own or with the school orchestra?

Whatever answer Eustace gave seemed to give him food for thought as he would then fall silent, but sometimes he followed up with an apparently unrelated statement. The most recent of these was the pithy, 'Awfully glad you never took to football; useless bloody waste of time.'

Nervous of his grandfather when he was small because he was tall and military and never cracked jokes like his father, Eustace had grown fonder of him recently. He liked the quiet elegance of Grandpa's barely varied jackets and ties and the way he kept his brogues so well polished and wore a Homburg in winter and a Panama when the sun shone. He rarely commented on how slovenly so many other men looked but Eustace could tell from the way he narrowed his eyes or emitted a kind of growl as they approached some man in T-shirt and shorts that he was appalled. On their last walk together he had paused at the end of the bird-feeding ritual, turned his watery blue eyes on Eustace with concern and, enunciating with care, asked, 'You don't ever intend to wear flip-flops, do you?' and when Eustace, who was never allowed summer footwear less formal than his Clark's Lysanders, said certainly not and that he always thought they looked most uncomfortable and likely to make one trip, Grandpa's relief brought real kindness to his expression. 'Good man,' he said quietly. 'That's the ticket.'

As it happened, he died while bending to lace the second of his brogues. He keeled over sideways off the end of his narrow single bed, making a thump loud enough to alarm people eating breakfast in the dining room below. It meant the undertaker needed only to tie the second shoelace before carrying him away already perfectly dressed for his coffin, although Eustace later discovered that his mother had substituted paperclips for his gold cufflinks, which Grandpa wanted Eustace to inherit, and removed his Jaeger-leCoultre wristwatch, which she took to wearing herself, saying it comforted her.

Death was a regular caller at an old people's home, of course, especially in the spring, when the turning-down of central heating and opening of windows seemed to make the residents' birdlike grip on their perches less tenacious. Eustace had observed that, far from upsetting the survivors, death was as much a provoker of excitement as a visit from a minor royal or the winning of a premium-bond prize. A funeral was an excursion of sorts, with all the fuss and novelty that entailed, and there was always a tea party afterwards, at which his father served sherry, which went down very swiftly and made everyone a bit noisy and even less steady on their feet.

But this was the first death of someone Eustace knew and loved and he cried a little, in his room, on his own. Not that he was sad at Grandpa going – he was glad for him. He wept, he realized, at the irrevocability of the change, the never-more it represented.

'Be careful around your mother,' his father told him, as they stood respectfully to attention in the hall while the undertaker and his apprentice carried Grandpa out in a temporary coffin. 'She'll take this to heart.'

Eustace would never have predicted this. His mother's talk had always been of Maman, of her beauty and artistry and how they'd been sacrificed to her father's selfishly male requirements. He had never heard her breathe a word of praise or affection for her father, for his achievements in the army, which, an obituary in the *Daily Telegraph* informed them, were considerable. If she spoke of him at all, it was with a sighing tone, as people spoke of an elderly dog, and she left the care of him, the washing and the dressing to the staff. She said she did so to maintain his dignity and privacy. But Eustace could not remember any signs of tenderness between them beyond her occasionally running the hall clothes brush over his coat shoulders for him, as his arthritis made it hard for him to reach. She did always call him Daddy, however, behind his back and to his face, as though a part of her had remained, or wished to remain, his little girl.

His death saw her take to her bed and stay there in the darkness for two whole days, leaving his father to liaise with doctor, undertaker and parson and to make short, awkward phone calls to the members of Grandpa's dwindled family and acquaintance.

'It's only to be expected,' Granny pronounced when Eustace visited her with the news. 'She feels guilty that she never did enough for him. Daughters always feel guilty. It's their lot.'

Granny's habitual gloom and tendency to harsh judgement came into full bloom with a death in the house. Unable or reluctant to leave her room now because her legs were ulcerated and she didn't want to reveal herself in public as *one of those ghastly old bats with bulgy bandages*, she relied on Eustace to bring her every detail, along with cups of tea. She declared herself fond of Grandpa, although they had persisted in addressing one another formally with surnames, but shed no tears because, as she said, he was *overdue*. 'No merciful release for me,' she added. 'The women on our side go on and on. It's a curse.'

When his mother emerged on the third day, just as Eustace was leaving for school, she was in a black polo neck, like Audrey Hepburn in *Funny Face*, and big dark glasses. 'You'll play at the funeral, won't you?' she said. 'That folk song you used to play. He liked that.'

'Did he? *The Green Bushes*?'

'That's the one. You can play that. Without a piano. It'll be haunting. And then, at the end, *The Swan*, to honour Maman, as he loved her so. And I'll get a bugler from his regiment to play the Last Post at the crematorium. And we'll sing *Crimond*. He liked that tune. And maybe the organist can play *Nimrod*, but only if she's up to it.'

Eustace was bewildered. To his knowledge his grandfather had barely acknowledged the presence of his cello in the house, apart from those few indirect comments on their walks, and he had thought their rooms far apart enough for him not to be disturbed by Eustace's practising. His mother's words made him realize the old man must not only have been listening in but talking about it.

'Of course,' he told her. 'I'll run through them with Miss Gold in my lesson tomorrow,' and he hurried off to school, guiltily aware of being excited that he was to perform. But then, as he thought about it, he became nervous. Music at a funeral had to be perfect without drawing attention to the performer.

Carla understood his nerves perfectly. 'They're ideal pieces,' she said, 'as they both have a good singing line but don't require agility of you. When you're tense, the last thing you need is to be playing something with lots of hopping about.'

The Green Bushes was a Howard Ferguson arrangement. Since it was to be unaccompanied, she suggested he play it as though singing the folk tune, taking the first statement of the sad little melody and repeating it twice, once more assertively, once with wistful softness. *The Swan* was more of a challenge. He had played it at a school concert a few months before with another boy – a show-off he didn't like much – playing the piano part a bit too fast, and had retained the little pencil mark he had made on his fingerboard to help his third finger find a flawless top D without hesitating. The difficulty was that this time he'd be accompanied by the church's lady organist.

'The organ isn't nearly as expressive as the piano,' Carla said. 'So you'll just have to use that and heighten the expressiveness of your line.' She made him think of Saint-Saëns' phrases as literally phrases: statements, questions, replies and a summary, this one assertive, that one retreating, less here, more there. 'See? Obviously it's reductive to think of music like that, it's music first and foremost, but it can really help with a piece like this that's basically a wordless song. Were you fond of your grandfather?'

He nodded.

'Well I'm very sorry he's gone but when you're playing, you mustn't think about him. Think only of the music. You'll find it's a relief, especially if it's your first funeral. You can think about him before and after, of course, but when the cello's in your hand, think only of the cello and your relation to it.'

He had just one rehearsal with Miss Duffy the organist, the evening before. She seemed very old, and wore disconcertingly thick glasses but she had a kind voice. She had an endearingly plain face, like a bulldog's, and was evidently rather shy so he wondered if she had taken up the organ as a way of hiding herself away. The organ was off to one side, he saw to his relief, so he could be playing unobserved. She had him tune to the organ, as it was a little flat, then suggested he play *The Green Bushes* first to get used to the acoustic. She walked off into the nave while he played, where she startled him by singing along with the third verse in a rich contralto. Stupidly he hadn't thought of it as having words.

'I'll buy you fine beavers an' a fine silken gown

I'll buy you fine petticoats with a flounce to the groun'

If you will prove loyal and constant to me

And forsake your own true love, I'll be married to thee . . .'

She walked back to the organ bench when he was done. 'Lovely,' she declared. 'There won't be a dry eye in the house. You can take more time, though. Enjoy yourself. Milk it a little. Now, let's try *The Swan*.'

She launched into *The Swan*'s accompaniment, which did indeed sound a little pootling and comical on an organ but, unlike the show-off at school, she played it quite slowly and he had no trouble keeping up with her or finding his creamiest top G at the end.

'Very nice,' she said when he'd finished. 'You'll do him proud.'

As he left the church so that she could practise other

things, she launched into a blazing, flashy piece so at odds with her quiet appearance that he wondered whether she was simply softly spoken and not shy at all.

On the day of the funeral, he wore his school uniform and polished his shoes extra well in Grandpa's honour but it was a great relief, given how many people seemed to be crammed into the church, that he was not to follow his parents and the coffin into the body of the church to sit at the very front but was to hide away with Miss Duffy and turn pages for her at the beginning and end.

It felt odd being off to one side, more spectator than participant. He couldn't see the coffin or the priest or his parents wheeling in Granny. Miss Duffy had placed a service sheet on his music stand so he could follow proceedings but he felt self-conscious joining in the hymns when she was playing the organ beside him and he did not like to stand for them as that would have meant laying his cello on the floor and it was a comfort to have it to lean against. Instead he merely read the hymn words in his head as everyone sang them. There was a rather long address about Grandpa and who he was and what he had done, during which his attention drifted, then there were some prayers, including the Lord's Prayer, which he dutifully spoke, though without kneeling, just as Miss Duffy spoke it under her breath at the keyboard. Then it was time. She had been solemnly decorous throughout the service and looked almost tearful as he played *The Green Bushes*, but as she began the accompaniment to the Saint-Saëns, she cast him a broad, toothy smile that stopped him feeling remotely nervous and let him pretend that the rest of the church was quite empty.

The priest said some words of dismissal then Miss Duffy launched into *Nimrod* and the bearers carried Grandpa out and everyone followed them. When Miss Duffy finished, she locked the organ up while he shut his cello back in its case, then she surprised him by shaking his hand.

'You're really rather good, you know,' she said. 'I hope you're taking this seriously.'

'Well,' he said. 'Thank you. I'd like to.'

'Good,' she said. 'Keep at it,' and she melted away through the crowd chatting outside. Quite suddenly there were lots of strangers congratulating him or thanking him, and then they parted and there was his mother.

She was in her best black suit and crisp white blouse and she had done something to her hair so that it was high and more regal than usual. She had on her sunglasses which had their usual effect of turning her face into a mask, but seeing him, she crumpled her lower lip and he worried she might be about to cry. But she only drew him to her and hugged him, which was not a thing she ever did, especially not in public.

'Thank you,' she murmured. 'I wish Carla could have heard you. That was . . . special. Thank you.'

His father was watching from nearby, tense, perhaps, because of all the old men in medals and because of the strain of not being able to crack his usual jokes. But even he shook Eustace's hand, which was very odd indeed, and said,

'I know we hear you practising at home all the time but, well, I had no idea.'

Eustace was not expected to go with them to the

crematorium but instead had to drop off his cello at home and make his way to school for the rest of the day. It was still quite early and he arrived in time for a maths lesson before lunch. They were doing calculations involving log tables, which he usually enjoyed, but he kept being distracted by the odd, not entirely pleasant fizzing sensation performing at the funeral had engendered.

CHAPTER SEVEN

Now that Eustace had turned twelve, St Chad's began to exert new pressures on him. Until then he had thought of the hours he spent there, the weeks in uniform, the months of submitting to arbitrary regulations and exercises of authority as necessary evils. His father had once said as much.

'The thing about school is that it seems to take for ever when you're in it but it passes, and quicker than you realize at the time.'

It had seemed to him that there was no choice involved; he had to go to school because it was the law, and he had to go to the school his parents had chosen for him. His mother regularly reminded him that it was a *good little school* and that he was lucky to be sent there and not to the less rarefied local equivalent, which was free but where he'd not learn Latin or Greek or play in a school orchestra. But now he began to be aware from things other boys were saying, that a great dividing of the ways would soon be upon them.

Like the vast majority of his contemporaries, he was to sit Common Entrance in order to secure a place at a public school – possibly the terrifying sounding Millfield, possibly his father's old one at Clifton – where he would have to board, a prospect that alternately thrilled and frightened him.

A handful of boys, identified afresh now that they were suddenly corralled into a class of their own, had taken the eleven-plus exam already, as their parents were sending them to the local grammar school where they could still study Latin and Greek, wouldn't have to board and would be spared the regular, embarrassing conversations between their parents about fees. Eustace envied these boys. It seemed to him they had the happiest year ahead of them and the easiest future. He had not been entered for the eleven-plus, however, as his mother said they wanted him to *broaden his social sphere* and that, in her experience, grammar-school boys were *neither one thing nor the other* and tended to be *chippy*.

Another handful of boys, who were the cleverest in all or certain subjects, was shifted up into a class called A1, a sort of intellectual peak, where they were taught by Dr Figgis the headmaster himself and only the most senior teachers, and prepared for valuable scholarships at various more or less famous public schools around the country which would give them a free education if they won them and, one assumed, profound humiliation if they failed. Eustace knew a few of these boys but, once they were elevated to A1, found they no longer seemed to know him very well, withdrawing into their cleverness as though further contact with the commonplace pained them.

Several boys had vanished from the school since the last holidays. None of them was a friend or an especial tormentor of Eustace's so he didn't notice their absence at first, merely assuming they had done better or less well than him and been moved to a different class. But gradually he came to understand that they had been removed to be enrolled in Broadelm Comprehensive, the mixed state school that had been a byword for terror ever since he began to attend St Chad's.

'But what will they *do*?' he asked his mother, after glimpsing a couple of these exiled boys at a bus stop with some older, noisy girls who were showing off their skills with bubble gum.

She sighed, in the way she did when a topic bored or repelled her. 'I suppose most will leave school at sixteen,' she said, 'and get jobs. You know. Apprenticeships and things. Some might join the army, of course, or the navy. And I believe there's a sixth-form college now for the ones who think they have a chance at university. Not that university's crucial; you can become an accountant or a solicitor, I think, without getting a degree first.'

And then there was Vernon. He had calmly revealed that he would be going to Broadelm next because, for all that they had enough money, his family had left-wing principles. 'Well, my father does. Before she died, my mother made him promise I'd come here first, so I'd pick up Latin and things and make what she thought of as *suitable friends.*'

'Like me.'

'Precisely.'

Eustace was upset. He had come to rely on Vernon as a regular, phlegmatically supportive presence in his life and had vaguely assumed they'd be going on to the same public school next. 'We can still see each other in the holidays, though?' he asked.

'Oh yes. But I doubt we will. You'll have a whole raft of new friends and I'll be too busy shagging *le tout* Weston.'

Vernon was an early developer and had already begun wearing Tabac aftershave and trying to interest Eustace, with little success, in much-thumbed pages from *Playboy* passed down to him by the school's under-groundsman. But he had yet to set aside his devotion to Trollope and his involvement with the opposite sex remained entirely imaginary. Eustace felt a pang at this casual dismissal of their friendship and hoped it was only bravado speaking. It was impossible to picture Vernon in the comprehensive; until now his interests had seemed far too rarefied, but perhaps well-thumbed naked ladies would provide a sort of entry visa.

He continued to like coming around to sit in Eustace's room to read while Eustace practised and, as the weather improved, they also took to spending time up in the Fort, a hilltop Iron Age encampment site beyond where the houses gave out. This had long since become so overgrown as to be more woodland than archeological site. People exercised their dogs, teenagers went there to smoke and drink cider but Eustace suspected it was the Fort's popularity as a lovers' meeting place that drew the increasingly hormonal Vernon to want to linger among the ivy, discarded crisp packets and used condoms.

But one day after school when they seemed once again to be drifting towards the steps that led up there, he dared to challenge his friend. 'Why do we never go to your house?' he asked.

Vernon shrugged. 'It's really not very interesting. And

with no mother it's not terribly homely. Are you so very keen?'

He said this in a way that usually would have obliged Eustace to deny any interest and to change the subject out of politeness. But it had been a bad day at school with both boys and teachers sneering and Eustace was feeling uncomfortable in his skin and bloody-minded.

'I am, really,' he admitted. 'But only because you're a friend so, naturally, I want to see where you come from. I'm curious.'

Vernon shrugged again, so that Eustace worried that, for the first time in a friendship without arguments, he might have offended him. Vernon led the way back down to the water and along the front, past Knightstone Island, Eustace's house and the pier and the worst gathering point of the Rougher Element and then turned sharp left, off the front. Naturally Eustace was agog, because in all their years of friendship he had only very roughly narrowed down Vernon's address to a handful of streets off the prom the other side of the Winter Gardens.

He turned out to live in one of the handsome houses on Ellenborough Crescent, whose once-private garden square had long since become a rather feral public park, but whose houses had never lost their air of remaining elegantly set apart from the hurly-burly and chip fat. They reminded Eustace of the houses near Louis and Ebrahim's place in Clifton and several were similarly now under hippyish multiple occupancy or even harbouring squatters. A big *Atomkraft Nein Danke* sun dangled across the upper window of one while another had a Union Jack in a window and stars and daisies painted across its crumbling stucco. Vernon's house, though, was in fairly good repair. His father was evidently a keen gardener as the neat gravel path led through a pretty succession of rose arches to a recently repainted front door with close-clipped bushes to either side.

'My father's an artist,' said Vernon as they walked up the path. 'He mainly paints naked women, so don't be shocked. And . . .' He broke off for a moment and looked at Eustace as though gauging his reaction. 'He's not at all well.'

'Well I can come back another time. When he's better,' Eustace offered, feeling bad now.

'No, I mean he's really ill. He won't get better. It's Parkinson's. He can still walk and talk but he's a bit wobbly. Just so you don't think he's drunk.'

'God. Of course not. But are you . . . ?'

Ignoring his little show of decent dithering, punishing his curiosity perhaps, Vernon strode ahead. He unlocked the front door then held it wide so that Eustace had to follow.

Houses like this, older houses, tended to look a certain way, Eustace thought. He had pored over plenty of magazines so had a good idea of what was tasteful or usual. This house broke all the rules. There was no wallpaper for a start, just really bold blocks of colour. At some point even the floors had been painted and then rugs thrown on top. There were books everywhere. Rooms full of books. And, indeed, many, many paintings of naked ladies, all in white or silver frames so that they stood out from whatever bright colour the wall was painted behind them. And

111

yet it also looked like a house in an advertisement, because it was very clean and neat, except it was far more interesting, full of antiques and strange or beautiful objects.

'Where's your room?' Eustace asked.

'Upstairs,' Vernon said. 'But it's just a room. Pretty boring really. Come and meet my father. I never bring anyone back so he'll be interested.'

He led the way along the hall and through a big kitchen where gleaming pans hung from a rail and knife handles protruded from a block. There was a huge, full wine rack. When Eustace's father produced a bottle of wine it was usually singly and to mark a special occasion, with much examination of the label and a big fuss made about decanting. Vernon's kitchen felt more like the Italian restaurant he had been taken to in Clifton that time.

There was rock music playing in the conservatory beyond. The intervening windows and the one in the door had been painted out with whitewash, like those of a closed-down shop. Vernon tapped smartly on the door but didn't wait for anyone to speak before opening it. A big woman with dyed blonde hair Eustace was fairly sure worked on the cold meats counter in the Wavy Line was sprawled on a rumpled daybed stark naked. Vernon didn't flinch, and neither did she but simply said, 'Hello boys,' maintaining her pose.

A man was perched on a stool, drawing rapidly with what looked like stubby crayons made of lipstick. An older, more handsome version of Vernon, he was in pyjamas and a dressing gown and smoked as he worked. His right hand and the cigarette were bright with pigment smears. He glanced their way.

'Oh good,' he said. 'Put the kettle on, Vernon. There's a love.'

'Of course,' Vernon said, and ducked back to fill the kettle.

'Lovely afternoon,' said the naked lady.

'Yes,' Eustace said, only glancing her way momentarily because of bosoms.

'Are you nearly done, Viv?' she asked. 'I've got to get the girls their tea.'

'Just finishing your foot,' Vernon's father mumbled. 'So you must be the famous Eustace,' he said.

'Yes,' Eustace said.

'So are you going to sort Vernon out for me?'

He glanced at Eustace over his sketch pad. His eyes were an icy blue where Vernon's were cattle brown. His speech was halting and slurred, as though he had been drinking but his keen gaze was intelligent and full of irony.

'I wasn't aware he needed it.'

'I'm done with you now, Jen. Thanks.'

'Thank Christ for that,' the model said. 'My neck was seizing up.' She sprang up with surprising agility, giving Eustace a flash of white thigh and dimpled bottom as she disappeared behind an old-fashioned screen to dress.

'She's modest once she's in motion,' Vernon's father said.

'Oi! I heard that.'

He tore out the sketch he had been working on and laid it alongside several others already ranged along a paint-spattered table, then he carefully draped a sheet of tissue paper over them all.

113

'My late wife,' he told Eustace, 'used to say that all boys needed sorting out. Some of us repeatedly.' His slow laugh gave way to a nasty smoker's cough. 'Filthy habit,' he added, emptying his ashtray into a dustbin under the table. 'I never bring it into the house because of the boy. Come on. Tea.' He drew a few pound notes from his wallet, called out to Jen that he'd left them on the table for her then led Eustace back to the kitchen.

Unexpectedly domestic, Vernon had not only boiled the kettle and made a pot of tea but laid the kitchen table with proper cups and saucers, a milk jug and a plate of neatly sliced Battenberg and chocolate finger biscuits. There was even a tea strainer. There was no place laid for Jen, who let herself out through the conservatory.

Vernon's father was extremely tired after his exertions and yawned repeatedly, apologizing every time he did so. It was fascinating catching traces of Vernon's wit and politeness in him, even with the slurring. Vernon unfussily served them all, and the way he put cake and biscuits on his father's plate for him made Eustace wonder what other assistance he gave him. His father's movement was clearly impaired as well as his speech. Eustace noted how Vernon was careful not to fill his cup too full so his wobbling hand didn't spill it. Did he help him dress and undress, he wondered. Did he help him in and out of the bath? He could not imagine helping his own father to undress but presumably situations like that arose slowly, eroding inhibition by degrees.

Vernon's father quizzed him much as his own father had Vernon, asking him about his parents and what he liked and disliked about school, but what really seemed to interest him was Eustace's cello-playing.

'It's good you take it seriously,' he said. 'This place is basically a dump, so it's important to have a window in your life. Like all those novels Vernon reads. You must play to me one day, like you play to this cloth-eared boy. Thanks, I will,' he said as Vernon offered him more tea. 'And someone pointed out that teacher of yours to me the other day. She's a serious babe, isn't she?'

Eustace wasn't sure how to answer but guessed the question was rhetorical. He hedged his bets by simply saying, 'She's pretty amazing.'

'She was walking along the high street and I swear that, just for that moment, she was head and shoulders taller than anyone else in view, like a Masai among the pygmies. Incredible. I'd love to paint her.'

'Like Madame Suggia?'

'Sorry?'

'The Augustus John portrait. Of the cellist in the red dress.'

'Oh. Yes. I didn't know what she was called. Yes. You know your art, then?'

'Not really,' Eustace admitted. 'Just that one. Perhaps she'd sit for you?' He had been going to add something about Carla keeping her clothes on but decided it would have been presumptuous.

'Dad doesn't really paint any more,' Vernon explained quietly. His manner since they arrived had been subdued, respectful even, and Eustace decided he wouldn't press to visit again but would wait for an invitation.

'No really about it,' his father added. 'Can't hold the brushes and I refuse to do fucking finger-painting. Pastels are a compromise.'

Soon after that he announced he was tired.

'I should go,' Eustace said. 'Thank you for having me. It was lovely to meet you, sir.'

Vernon's father's hand was rough and dry to the touch. He laughed at being called 'sir'. As Eustace left, he was already climbing the stairs, leaning as heavily on Vernon as on the banister.

Eustace became aware of what Granny called an atmosphere between his parents. Quite suddenly he found he was no longer being sent to bed at a certain time but left more to his own devices after supper, which meant he picked up on more snatches of conversation he was not meant to hear. There was a heated discussion about St Chad's latest bill – a document rather cruelly delivered in the same envelope as his end of term reports. He overheard discussions of scholarships and bursaries, and his mother referring to him as 'really a thoroughly ordinary child'. His father, who had never passed any comment on his school reports suddenly observed, 'Your maths is still excellent. That's good. But perhaps you could try a bit harder in the sciences? Is it so hard? Isn't maths the hard bit?'

Eustace said he would try. The trouble was that his relationship with maths was entirely instinctive and nothing much to do with teaching. He had always felt at ease with numbers and their patterns. Maths, like music, existed in a pure atmosphere whereas science seemed to consist of inelegant attempts to make sense of the world, attempts that formed no pattern but only clumsy lists peculiarly hard to memorize. History was no better. Having always been a muddling through in the lower middle sort of boy, he had drifted to the bottom of A2 class, suddenly sharply attuned to the future and the need for competitive achievement.

Miss Gold had held off from entering him for any Associated Board exams apart from Grade 5, which she said was useful for the scales and theory. But now she announced that she had been talking things through with his mother and he was to be entered for the music scholarships at Clifton. Most music scholars had two instruments or offered an extra skill like composition or harmony, none of which Eustace had, 'So we have to get your playing pretty spectacular,' she said. With this in mind she began to push him harder. He had to work at a different Duport study each week as well as his scales, and he was to learn and perfect a whole sonata of Grade 8 standard – she suggested Beethoven or Brahms and, to show off his tone and sense of line, the slow movement to the Rachmaninov sonata. 'Quite achievable,' she said. 'I was playing all those at your age and nobody has to lean on you to put in the hours, which is a good sign as it means you're self-sustaining.'

Suddenly the pressure was turned up in music room and classroom alike. And, of the two, music always won out over schoolwork. It wasn't that he was stupid but he needed to be set tasks. A list of quadrilateral equations or a story from the English Civil War would hold his attention but if Mr Payton rambled on about the ablative absolute or Mr Jordan banged on about Milton, Eustace soon found he was staring at the way a tree was moving outside the window or the curious pattern some boy's hair formed on his neck. But with his cello and bow in hand and faced with a high Brahms phrase not yet quite in tune, he could play the same fifteen or twenty notes over and over for an hour and be surprised by the passage of time. When he was practising he felt himself utterly present, not least because of Carla's insistence that he play with his whole body.

Vernon still enjoyed sitting in on the occasional practice session, saying he liked the constant repetition and the infinitesimal changes of detail. Interestingly the steady exposure to classical music he was gaining at one remove this way was making him appreciate his father's rock music more, even though he still couldn't have told Mendelssohn from Martinů. He said he found it 'very Zen' and inexpressibly soothing to sit reading in the presence of Eustace's intense concentration and that he was starting to appreciate his cello-playing the way he did the persistence of boys repeatedly tapping a ball in nets or heading a football in a corner of the playground.

Actually Eustace did make an effort in class now. He knew it mattered. It had often been impressed on him that all subjects mattered equally and would continue to do so until he was sixteen and could finally give up all but three of them. Now that his teachers were regularly springing sample Common Entrance papers on the class, it was having the intended effect of making him panic at intervals that he seemed as far behind the herd as if he had lost two terms to sickness or tragedy. Did he remember how to form the subjunctive in either Latin or Greek? Did he remember the difference between a sepal and a stamen or what were the primary causes, detriments and benefits of Henry VIII's break with Rome? He tried taking Kennedy's *Primer* to bed with him and relearning one lesson each bedtime, he took to revising French verbs at breakfast but found that, for all that the stabs of terror his apparent failure to absorb learning caused him, he still couldn't care about exams the way he cared about strengthening the fourth finger of his left hand so that his A flats and C sharps were not foggy. When he heard himself produce a sourly tuned note due to weak finger placing or over-hasty inaccuracy, he felt a kind of deep-seated shame he never felt on the sports field or standing to read aloud in a Greek class. But he breathed not a word of this to Vernon or his parents. He confided only, and only slightly, in Carla. When she once interrupted her flow of talk during a lesson on the Brahms sonata he was learning to ask offhandedly, 'But school's all right, isn't it? You're not harming your chances of anything, are you, with all this playing?' he admitted that, no, school wasn't brilliant, that he had fallen behind in every subject but maths because music was now all that really mattered to him. She broke off writing notes in his little notebook to look at him solemnly a moment and said, 'OK. So this scholarship really matters.'

Soon after that his mother made the surprise announcement that, at least until the day of his music scholarship exam, Miss Gold was to give him an extra lesson a week. 'Don't worry,' she said, parrying the objection she could tell his father was about to make in the name of economy. 'She's not charging. She insists. But the only time she can fit you in is early on Saturday mornings in Clifton before the first sensible train would get you there. So we've agreed that I'll start taking you there on Friday nights and staying over.' She glanced at his father in a way that betrayed a conversation to which Eustace had not been a party. 'So that, well, so that you have someone else in the house with you and those chaps . . .'

He had not stopped thinking about their night in Clifton since his mother had driven him home with the new cello. From the beauty of the house and contents, the sense it was a place in which the arts came before everything, including the obligation to be normal, the paintings everywhere, a tiny bedroom off what was in effect a temple to music, the homemade granola and yoghurt at breakfast, to the giddy good mood into which the visit had spun his mother, and the glorious weather they had for the drive home: the memory had become a glittering toy for him, a thing he took out in private to wonder at afresh. And a part of that had been the way his mother casually said, in the course of the drive home, that it was probably best if he tried not to go into too much detail about their overnight stay as his father could be old-fashioned and there were things about it he might not like or even understand. 'He's a dear, dear man,' she said, 'but he's often not as sophisticated as we are.'

Eustace had nodded uncertain agreement but sensed she was paying him a compliment. An intrinsic part of the thrill of the visit had been that their hosts were both men, who shared a bedroom as though that were perfectly unremarkable; it was an experience he assumed would never be repeated.

But it turned out Carla stayed there quite often because most of her pupils were in Bristol and she saw them on Fridays and Saturdays. Louis and Ebrahim were trying to persuade her to stop renting in Weston and become their full time lodger. She often called on Ebrahim's services as accompanist to her more advanced students and Eustace was now among their number as he was to accompany him for his scholarship exam.

His only confusion and slight disappointment was that his mother was to come along too. He assumed this meant she had told his father after all about Ebrahim and Louis sharing a bedroom, despite having hinted that she needed discretion in the matter. He would have enjoyed the adventure of going there by train without her.

'Couldn't I have gone on my own?' he asked experimentally as they set off on the first of their Friday nights away.

'Out of the question,' she said. 'Even though you're quite capable of catching the train and the bus, it still means hanging around in some pretty rough neighbourhoods and you can't run away from trouble with a cello on your back. Quite apart from your safety, I'm terrified of someone grabbing it off you.'

This sounded like a speech she had composed in anticipation and it was unanswerable. 'Not every mother would do this, you know,' she added. 'It's not exactly convenient and you know how your father frets when he's left to fend for himself.'

'I know,' he told her. 'I do appreciate it,' although he

suspected his father rather enjoyed the prospect of a night on his own when he could watch what he liked on the television and sleep like a starfish, rather than on one side of the bed. And there was no fending to be done since Mrs Fowler cooked his supper and would probably make him a special treat if she knew he was on his own. Neither did his mother seem especially burdened by the sacrifice, for she hummed along to Radio 3 as she drove and bought him a Crunchie when she stopped for petrol, which was quite unlike her as she had a tendency to mutter about cutting back his sugar intake.

A pattern to these nights away was tacitly established from that second visit. They arrived at about six o'clock and his mother went for a little lie-down as driving always threatened to give her a headache, while Eustace shut himself in the basement music room to practise for an hour or so. Invariably Ebrahim joined him after about half an hour to work on his pieces – he was full of useful ideas about phrasing and balance – while Louis and Carla made supper. Then they ate much later than he tended to at home and he was sent back down to bed once the grown-ups reached the coffee stage. After a delicious breakfast, Carla gave him the first lesson of the day while his mother enjoyed a lie-in and a late breakfast with *the boys* as she took to calling them, though Ebrahim came downstairs in the lesson's last third to work on the pieces with them. Carla seemed subtly different on these Saturday mornings, compared to during the lessons in Weston, a little dreamy, melancholy even, the music a constant, beautiful challenge for her. The room was much larger than her other teaching space, and she walked around him as he played, interrupting him to adjust his posture in small ways she said were crucial, left foot further out, right upper arm rolled inwards when the bow reached the tip so as to maintain strength and take the strain off the flexing wrist, back straighter. With the trace of percolator coffee and buttered toast still about them, and the occasional waft of shampoo from her still damp hair, she had never seemed more beautiful to him and his wish to please her had never been so strong. When Ebrahim joined them, she became at once more playful and more focused, teacherly, and their joint attention on his playing, two gifted professionals with a mere schoolboy, was almost overwhelming.

On the first Saturday, she began to express doubts about the Rachmaninov slow movement. Eustace thought it the saddest, loveliest thing he had ever heard, especially when Ebrahim added in the rocking then passionate piano part. But Carla sighed and frowned.

'I don't know,' she said. 'Perhaps you're just too young still. It's like Chopin. It can't be simply pretty.'

'She means you have to fall in love and suffer,' Ebrahim told him with a wink and she gently cuffed the back of his head in passing.

'We can fake it,' she said at last, 'and Ebrahim can help you. And no, it's not just love and sex, it's . . .'

'Regret?'

'Exactly.' She turned on Eustace. 'Regret. The whole movement expresses regret. One day you'll understand the kind of thing he means but for now just, well, think of how you feel when you remember a perfect day you can never, ever have again.'

Eustace must have looked blank because she shrugged and took up her cello too and played it with him. 'Just copy my phrasing,' she said. 'It's all in the rubato, those moments where he seems to be looking over his shoulder even as time and the piano are driving him on.'

Playing together was amazing. They seemed so loud, and the sound brought his mother in to stand in the doorway. Carla ignored her, watching Eustace closely as she played from memory. 'Here,' she said. 'He looks back. You see? And again here! And as we go up the final scale, you can *really* take your time before the last two notes. And . . . take your time. Yes!'

Eustace nodded, glancing at his mother. Carla swooped forward with her pencil and marked each of the points where she wanted rubato with a short wavy line above the stave. She wrote *Regret!* in her distinctive handwriting at the start of the movement. *You want it all again!*

All too soon the second pupil of the day appeared. When Carla taught him in Weston he felt no possessiveness towards her so he was surprised to feel an odd thrill of jealousy at the skinny girl in a tartan skirt coming down the area steps. He consoled himself with the knowledge that, unlike him, she had not spent the night there. And he fancied she was similarly taken aback, used to being the first pupil of Carla's Saturday.

Carla's goodbye was bright and professional – she had the other pupil waiting, after all, so didn't see them out – but Louis and Ebrahim gave his mother a hug and a cheek kiss on the doorstep. She softly whistled the minuet of the Brahms as she wiggled the car back and forth out of a tight parking space, so he could tell she was in a good mood. Normally parking manoeuvres made her cross.

'They're nice, aren't they?' he said.

'Louis and Ebrahim? Yes. Very. Louis is incredibly wise, like a very old man in a younger body.'

'What about? Painting?'

She laughed. 'Love. He's wise about love.'

This was a little unnerving; his mother never discussed emotions, especially not with his father, and Eustace wasn't sure what he thought of her discussing them with a near-stranger. She carried on whistling, tapping out a rhythm on the steering wheel so that her bracelets jangled. The bracelets were new.

'We should take a look at Clifton College on our way out,' she said.

'No,' he said, 'that might jinx it!'

'Course it won't. You'll sail in. Come on. Just the outside.'

She drove them as near to the school as the road would take them. He saw dignified Victorian buildings, a copper roof, a chapel, a sports field and a gang of tall boys in smart uniforms moving from building to building, some with briefcases like businessmen, others with their books under their arms. He spotted one boy with a cello case. It might have been him in the future, though the boy was tall and thin and had the chiselled features and tidy blond hair of Janno in *The Trigan Empire*.

'What do you think?' she asked.

He thought it looked amazing, after the streets of Weston, like a glimpse of a world purified, a world of rationality, where they'd let him concentrate on maths and his cello and never mind the other subjects. 'It's OK,' he said. 'Keep driving, though, or someone might see us.'

'Funny man,' she said, swiftly brushing his hair out of his eyes with cool fingers.

As well as working on his two pieces every day without fail, he recruited Vernon. Vernon invariably had his transistor radio about him because he liked irrelevant soundtracks to his reading, like ball-by-ball cricket commentaries and the shipping forecast. As well as testing Eustace on the long list of Italian terms, he began to carry around a copy of *Radio Times* so that he could test him on the composer of pieces thrown up when he switched on the radio at random intervals through the day.

Eustace couldn't get over his shock that Vernon was not sitting Common Entrance that summer. He realized he couldn't say he had assumed from Vernon's occasionally lordly manner and the rumours about his mother, that his family rejoiced in *Old Money*, that he'd had his name down for Eton or Winchester from birth. Vernon admitted his father had been to Westminster and his mother to Cheltenham Ladies' College but said his father was a bit of a Tony Benn. 'I'm rather looking forward to it actually. There'll be nothing like the homework we get now and no more being chased down the street because of the uniform.' Vernon had always been remarkably self-sufficient – it was one of the qualities that had first drawn them together – but it was hard to imagine Broadelm Comprehensive readily absorbing his quaintly Edwardian dress and manner even to the extent St Chad's had done. Vernon, he decided, was putting on a brave front and it would be a kindness not to discuss the matter.

Meanwhile, when a letter was sent requesting Eustace be granted a day off school for the music scholarship exam, the headmaster told him he was to be spared all games until the day so as to have yet more practice time. He was not let off gym, however, as that was somehow beneficial.

Because of the pattern set by the regular Friday nights in Clifton, Eustace had assumed that his mother would come with him for the scholarship exam and that they would spend the night before it there but Carla had a concert engagement in Edinburgh so couldn't be there. She hadn't liked to tell him earlier, she said, in case it made him nervous but he was well prepared now and would have Ebrahim to give him confidence from the piano, so he'd be fine. Besides, his father had had words with his mother on the subject apparently and suddenly announced that he was taking him, since it was his old school, and his father's before him, which was the sort of thing that might make a difference.

'So your mother's going to stay home and hold the fort for a change and it'll just be us chaps together. You do your playing in the morning then we get time out for some lunch then you have your theory and interview bit then they give us the results and then we come home. It'll be quite jolly.'

Eustace thought it sounded excruciating. As he got older and his body began to change in various unwelcome ways, it made him peculiarly sensitive to things about his father he found hard to bear: his nervous joking that never seemed to be funny any more and possibly never had been, the way his hair was thinning surreptitiously at the back, so that he wondered if his father had noticed, the hair on the back of his hands that was somehow different from the hair on Louis' wrists. Eustace caught himself watching him sometimes, when he was reading the newspaper or watching television, looking with a sort of horrified intensity for any similarities they might share. People often said they were alike – not least Granny, who so often gloomily remarked that he reminded her of his father at the same age that it must be true – but as yet he was glad to say he couldn't see the resemblance. He most wanted to resemble his mother, but she persisted in seeming quite apart from her menfolk, like a reluctant visitor from a distant, naturally elegant race.

She seemed quite oblivious to his concern about the big day. 'Being just you boys will be fun for a change,' was all she said. 'I'll organize something a bit special for supper and you can tell me all about it.'

Since his grandfather's death, Granny had gone into a decline, though no relation to him, and was refusing almost all food beyond Complan and digestive biscuits and the occasional mashed banana. She never left her room and now often elected to stay in bed all day despite cajoling to at least sit in her armchair. Eustace would visit her. There were times when her extreme gloom could feel bracing, even restorative, and the death of his grandfather had raised her value to him. He had overheard his father say he suspected she would slip away one night, which made Eustace conscious that every short visit to her might be his last.

After he had finished his third practice of the day on the evening before the scholarship exam, he went down to see her. Her eyes were closed when he came in but she opened them slowly as he sat in her bedside chair. There were seagulls making a racket on the flat roof below her window. She hated seagulls.

'Sorry,' he said. 'Did I wake you?'

'I never sleep now,' she told him. 'Not properly. There'd be no point, not unless it can be the rest from which we never wake.' She stared at him then realized she didn't have her spectacles on, so reached for them slowly from her bedside table before staring at him some more, eyes greatly magnified. Half a digestive and the last two spoonfuls of a mashed banana lay beneath her lamp on a tray. He was just thinking he'd make himself useful by carrying them down to the kitchen when she began to speak. She coughed first. She always coughed first these days because she spoke so little it was as though a sort of skin formed over her voice in the silent intervals.

'Big day tomorrow,' she said.

'I didn't know you knew,' he told her.

'If you keep as still and as quiet as I do, not much escapes you,' she said. 'Will you get it?'

'I don't know,' he said truthfully. 'But I've worked very hard. I don't think I could have worked much harder without stopping school to fit it in.'

'That's good,' she said. 'Regret's a terrible thing, and you'll know you gave it your best shot.' She stared at him in heavy-breathing silence for a minute, as though seeking out the hard work on his face. He thought of the Rachmaninov. She was the only person who could stare at him like that and not make him self-conscious. She had always done it, since he was little, and he had always broken the rules and stared right back. It was almost like a game between them and the chance really to examine the pouches, spots, hairs and discolorations of old age was compelling and instructive.

She broke off staring finally and raised a hand to the big chest of drawers behind him. He thought she was going to offer him a barley sugar but she directed him to the top drawer on the left; barley sugars, along with her antique passport, Kirby grips and corn plasters, were in the little drawer of her long-redundant dressing table, before the window. The top left drawer contained much complicated underwear and Eustace hesitated when he started to open it in case she was confused. She was, after all, confused most of the time.

'Go on,' she commanded impatiently. 'I left them on the top so I wouldn't lose them.'

He tugged the drawer a little farther open, releasing a strong smell of lavender bags and the Yardley's Sea Jade soap she favoured. There were two old photographs inside. One showed his father posing robustly with Clifton's Under 15 rugby team.

'He never made it to the seniors,' she said dismissively. 'Weak knees.'

The other showed the grandfather he had never known, looking rather surly in cricket whites. 'He was much better-looking than that,' she said. 'I married for love, which was possibly foolish. Go on,' she added. 'I don't need them. You take them, for luck. Neither of them amounted to much, really, but I think you might surprise us. Off you go, now.'

The audience was at an end. By the time he had closed the drawer again, gingerly tucking in a stray strap of some kind, then picked up her supper tray, she had removed her glasses and closed her eyes.

CHAPTER EIGHT

His mother had calculated correctly in sending him with his
father. She would have fretted about timing, parking, petrol,
what to wear, whom to speak to, which would have trans-
ferred to him as nervousness. His father, by contrast, was as
bluffly cheerful as though they were off to watch a new James
Bond film together. He knew exactly where to park near the
school and where Eustace could find him when he'd finished
the first of his two ordeals. Ebrahim met them outside the
music department, smartly but not too smartly dressed, so
that he looked just like all the masters and not a man who
lived with another male. He shook Eustace's father's hand
and said what a pleasure it was to meet him again.

Eustace's father then shook Eustace's hand and said,
'Good luck, old chap, but it's been sounding fantastic so I
don't think you'll need it.'

'No,' said Ebrahim. 'He's worked really hard. Carla
says the crucial thing today is to enjoy the music and convey your enjoyment to your audience. And to remember
they're an audience first, not examiners.'

And that was it. He led Eustace to register his arrival with
the school secretary then they joined a little clutch of boys
and their accompanists or on their own, in the case of the
two playing piano and organ, in a kind of waiting room. A
couple of the boys were in the uniform of the junior school,

132

the rest, like Eustace, were in uniforms from elsewhere. One boy, with too much unfortunately curly hair, who was nervously fiddling with his clarinet, had brought his mother as his accompanist, and she was tremulous with nerves and kept clearing her throat as though registering disapproval, which made Eustace appreciate Ebrahim's total calm.

'Should we give you his compositions now?' she asked abruptly, holding out a large portfolio to a passing teacher who assured her that later would be fine.

He didn't have to endure hearing too much of the brilliant competition before he was summoned. There was a burst of Chopin from one boy, and some extremely confident unaccompanied Bach violin from one of the junior school boys, all audible through the one intervening door.

After the Bach, the nervous mother cleared her throat and said, 'Well, the rest of us might as well all go home now,' at which everyone smiled a little tightly as it was just what they were thinking. Her poor son made an awful hash of a work Ebrahim murmured was by Schumann then played one of his own compositions, a piece of such chortling banality that smiles of relief were exchanged in the waiting room, although Eustace felt desperately sorry for him. At least candidates left by a different door, so were spared having to pass through their unofficial audience.

And then, all too soon, Eustace was called. Ebrahim stopped him with a gentle tap on the elbow as the school secretary disappeared back through the doorway. He smiled, said, 'Look at you,' and straightened Eustace's tie swiftly. 'Play for me,' he muttered. 'And remember you're not just playing, you're telling me a story.'

Quite unexpectedly the doorway gave on to a stage, with a grand piano on it, at one end of a large assembly hall. A plump man with a kind manner was there to greet them. He shook Eustace's hand and clearly knew Ebrahim already as he said, 'Ebrahim, what a treat. Now, Eustace, what are you going to play for us, once you've tuned up?'

Eustace told him.

'Excellent. We'll have the first movement of the Brahms, please, with no repeats. Then your Rachmaninov. Do you like Rachmaninov?'

'Very much, sir,' Eustace said, at which the man smiled.

Trained by Carla, Ebrahim didn't play an A for him to tune to but a D minor triad and, when Eustace was working on his C string, which had lost pitch in the warmth, discreetly explored an F minor one as well. When he was ready, Ebrahim looked across and smiled as though an audition were the most delightful thing and they launched into the Brahms. Eustace was nervous at first, and rushed the semiquavers a little, but Ebrahim held him back and his playing reminded Eustace of what Carla had said about how the Brahms sonatas, like their Beethoven models, were dialogues for two instruments, not showpieces for just one, so he remembered to play softly when the piano had the interest and felt again as he did so the keen pleasure of question and answer. Carla had written in her distinctive italic above some of the phrases. *Shall we do this? Or this?* then, a little later *No. Let's do this . . . and do it TOGETHER.* At the start of the coda she had written, *Life is so good and I LOVE my new cello!* She must have written it very discreetly after his last lesson with her.

When they finished, he found his heart was racing. She had warned him adrenalin did this sometimes, kicking in late so that it could destabilize a player or make them careless. He remembered her advice to take time to retune, even if the cello didn't need it, to reassert control. Then he glanced out at the head of music, who called, 'Whenever you're ready,' and then at Ebrahim who, only now, opened the Rachmaninov score, so that Eustace wouldn't feel he had been holding anything up. And before he began the bars of solo piano introduction he looked at Eustace without smiling this time and discreetly tapped a finger to his chest by way of saying, *Play for me, not them.*

With great cunning, he began at a fractionally slower tempo than Eustace was used to so that, from the first, Eustace's playing had an urgency to it, a sense of pressing forwards and, of course, it gave him space in which to let the passionate outbursts in the movement's middle section break into a tempo that seemed much faster while remaining at a perfectly comfortable speed. Again there was a pencilled message from Carla on the music: *You can never taste that happiness again. Never.* And then, when the theme was stated again towards the end: *But the pain of remembering is a kind of pleasure.*

He had absolutely no idea if his performance was good or indifferent; the piece seemed to be over almost as soon as they had begun. The head of music was busy writing notes when Eustace dared look his way. Ebrahim caught his eye and they stood, as though to take a bow, and the school secretary came forward to meet them.

'That was lovely,' she said. 'Always chokes me up, that

movement,' but Eustace felt she was speaking to Ebrahim, not to him, so hurried to put his cello, bow and music back in his case so they could follow her out by another door.

'Thank you, Ebrahim,' was all the head of music said as they left.

His father was waiting for them outside. 'Well?' he asked.

'If he doesn't get it,' Ebrahim told him, 'it won't be because of his playing. Well done,' he told Eustace. 'Good luck.'

'Thanks,' Eustace said, remembering his manners. 'And thank you for playing so beautifully. I'll do my best.'

An embarrassing little conversation followed in which, to his horror, Eustace realized his father was trying to work out if he owed Ebrahim money for having just accompanied the audition and from which Ebrahim backed off with a friendly wave of dismissal.

Insisting on shouldering his cello for him, his father steered them to a little café for lunch, the sort of place where people ate fried breakfasts all day. His father ordered a bowl of tomato soup and Eustace had cheese on toast, which was delicious but which he found he could barely swallow for tension. He wished his father would drive home with the cello and leave him to catch a train, but Dad chattered on obliviously, saying how silly it was still to be nervous of the masters on returning to his old school then reciting from memory what the unvarying lunch menus had been when he was a pupil there. Although their food was long finished, his father somehow still managed to make them nearly late so that they had to hurry back to the school, not quite running. Eustace was delivered back for the written section rather sweaty and red in the face and was the last to take his seat in the classroom but nobody seemed to mind and the boy with terrible hair seemed to have been crying, which stopped Eustace fretting about his own appearance.

It was a short test, delivered by a different music master. They each had a sheet of paper and a sheet of manuscript paper with some examples of chords and key signatures and so on written on it. There were no surprises. He knew all three of the composers and pieces they had to identify, was relieved they had to translate Italian instructions into English and not the other way around, and hoped he had got at least two thirds of the manuscript questions right. Finally, having handed in their papers for marking, they were each summoned in for a brief interview with the head of music.

Quizzed about his musical ambitions, Eustace said he enjoyed playing in an orchestra very much but hoped to play in a string quartet as that repertoire seemed so interesting, and it was not quite as daunting as playing alone. He said he was worried at the thought of learning a second instrument as he felt there was never enough practice time as it was but confessed he would like to be taught to sing better and wondered if his fondness for maths might suit him to learn harmony.

After the interview several of the boys left with their parents, either in despair or because they had long journeys and were content to receive any news by letter.

'I think we might as well wait, don't you?' his father said. 'Get it over with here and now?'

So they sat on with Eustace's cello beside them as the last few boys went in for their interviews. Eustace became

aware of his father's heavy breathing beside him and wondered if the others could hear it but reflected that at least
he wasn't cracking jokes. As with the auditions, they were
called in by one door and sent out through another, presumably to spare anyone witnessing sorrow or glee. They
were the very last to be called, by which point Eustace had
decided that a letter would have been easier to bear.

The school secretary ushered them into the head of
music's presence and he immediately came out from behind
his desk saying very well done and they were happy to offer
him the number two music scholarship, subject, of course,
to his passing Common Entrance in the summer.

Eustace was so happy and relieved that he found he
could show neither feeling on his face. He just glanced at
his father, who clapped him on the shoulder and quipped,
'Told you so,' and also shook the head of music by the
hand. They then had a quick manly chat about his father
being an old boy and the assumption that Eustace would
be applying to the same boarding house, interviews and so
on. And just when it all seemed to be over and Eustace was
starting to shiver with the relief of tension lifted, his father
said, 'And just to be clear, and I hope you don't mind discussing the matter so frankly, but needs must, I fear. The
scholarship doesn't just cover his cello lessons, does it? I'm
right in assuming it covers the fees?'

The teacher's genial manner cooled and he suggested it
might be appropriate if Eustace went out and waited for
his father in the quad.

The bench outside was a bit damp so Eustace stood on
the path with his cello. There were swifts swooping and

calling overhead and, from several open windows in the high Victorian walls, he could hear the murmur of lessons in progress. Someone was playing the organ in the chapel. There were pianos playing and a flute. None of the sounds went together and yet they seemed to make a perfect spring-time harmony. A soberly dressed older woman walked by on the path with a clutch of files under one arm and a very pretty dachshund clipping along beside her on a scarlet leather lead.

He must have been looking unhappy because she paused, with a look of unmixed kindness, and asked, 'Are you lost?'

He told her no, that he was waiting for his father and she smiled again and walked on. But he imagined telling her, 'No. I'm found!' That this was a place, like Ebrahim and Louis' house nearby, that he knew could pick him up and save him from everything in his life that was odd or wrong or eccentric or did not work.

His father's mood had altered entirely when he emerged. 'Come on, then,' he said and walked swiftly ahead of him back to their car, no longer offering to carry the cello. He drove in silence, then, as if the silence had become too much for him, with the radio intermittently tuned to some discussion programme of which Eustace's mind could make no sense. It was only when they were queuing in rush-hour traffic on the outskirts of Weston that his father abruptly turned the radio off and, still focusing on the traffic, said, 'I feel so stupid. I'd just assumed the scholarship covered everything, so had your mother, or we'd never have let you go through all that for nothing. I'm so sorry, old man.'

'Are the fees so high? Why am I doing Common Entrance if . . . ?' Eustace's response tailed off.

Traffic began to move again and his father, who was not good at talking and driving simultaneously, again fell silent and merely sighed once, heavily. When they parked and he cut the ignition he spoke again.

'You did so well today. It was a splendid performance.'

'Yes, but . . .'

'Times haven't been good. I've lost a lot of value from our savings. The cost of oil to heat this place is ruinous. And we've yet to find new guests since the last three departures.'

He always spoke of *guests* and *departures*, never residents or death.

'Will you rent out Grandpa's room as well now?'

'If we can. We need all the money we can get.'

'Should I stop my cello lessons, then?' Eustace could not believe he was making such an offer. It would be like stopping his own heart.

His mother had seen the car pull up and come out excitedly to hear the news. The car was becoming hot. Eustace felt he would soon be having trouble breathing. He could smell his father's Old Spice too strongly and tried not to picture the air in his father's lungs then going into his own. As in a silent film, he saw his mother's posture change and a furrow of concern replace the happy expectation on her face. She had been tidying the garden – actual gardening was left to Mr Willis, who came once a month – and had on her gloves and was clutching secateurs in one hand and a little fork in the other.

140

'Let me tell her, I should,' his father said, letting Eustace's question hang disturbingly.

'All right.'

His mother reached the car and opened Eustace's door. 'Well?' she asked. 'How'd you get on? What's wrong?'

'I got it,' Eustace told her, then worried he might be about to cry so got briskly out and pushed past her to open the rear door to slide the cello case out.

'But that's marvellous! Well done, darling! We must celeb— Eustace?'

He hurried into the house, careful not to hit Mr Palmer, an ancient, wordless resident, who was loitering on the porch on his Zimmer frame. He went directly up to his bedroom, stood the cello in its corner and lay on his bed. His window was slightly open, as the heat from downstairs made the attic stifling if not allowed to escape.

His parents had differences of opinion regularly, but it was an article of their marital faith always to present a united front to him at difficult moments, and to others always, and to air any differences out of his presence. She might say to him, 'Let me talk to your father about it,' and later claim to have changed her mind on a matter. Or he might say, 'Your mother and I came to a conclusion,' and in either case Eustace would know there had been a frank exchange of views and that one of them had won. His mother had once told him that Maman, being an artist, had a passionate nature and was known for her temper before she married but upon marriage had put her temper aside as one might fold up a pair of crimson evening gloves, because arguing with one's husband just wasn't done.

That evening, however, they argued loudly enough for even the deafest residents to hear. He couldn't make out their words and wasn't sure he wanted to – it was too mortifying – but he could tell they were moving from room to room. Just the occasional word or phrase reached him: his mother saying, 'Typical. Just typical!'

His father saying, 'So get a bloody job, woman.' Then, later, him shouting, 'I am not made of money,' and her lashing back with, 'That was pretty clear from the off, making us live in this godawful place with your mother.'

But then the volume of their disagreement dropped as abruptly as if an intervening door had closed and, instead of snatched phrases, he could make out only tones of voice: his mother's unhappy, quite possibly tearful, his father's low and emollient.

Relieved the crisis seemed to have passed, Eustace stared at a damp patch on his bedroom ceiling he had long thought of as a map to the island of Privacy. It was hard to believe that, after such a long preparation, the elation of his triumph had been so swiftly replaced by this odd mixture of disappointment and mortification. He had been encouraged to reach for something that was never his for the grasping. They had been reading *Coriolanus* in class recently and been taught the concept of hubris and how such fatal over-reaching could never go without punishment: it was the order of things.

How bad could Broadelm be? It had lain beyond his prospects for so long, been the place where only *other people* and the *less fortunate* went, that it was difficult suddenly to picture himself there. Although the revelation that Vernon was going had been a kind of rehearsal. And at least he would have a friend there, his only friend, if he was brutally frank about himself, and it was surely easier to start at a new school with one friend than with none? But then there was the humiliation of people in his class at St Chad's learning that he was no longer headed in the same direction as they were. Might he even be demoted from the Common Entrance class to A3, to be with other boys like Vernon, who were marking time until the end of the summer term?

He drifted from imagining the worst that could happen in his last few months at St Chad's to thinking guiltily about the cello. He knew how much lessons with Carla cost, knew from a glance at his mother's chequebook stubs that they cost more than Mr Buck's had. He hardly dared to add up what they had cost his parents to date and what it would save them for fuel bills and so on were lessons to stop and the cello be sold. He tried to be brave. He tried to imagine a future without his cello or Carla, glowing from the heart of it, and the prospect was unbearably bleak. But plenty of boys survived perfectly well without music in their lives. He could learn to draw. Pencils and paper were cheap, and he had seen books in the town library with names like *How to Draw Horses* and *How to Draw Ships*. Or he could read more, lose himself in long, inches-thick novels the way Vernon did. Or he could work much harder in school, not only at maths. At least for his last term and a half. He rather suspected there would be no Latin or Greek at the comprehensive.

'Eustace?' His mother's voice surprised him, coming suddenly from the landing outside his bedroom door. She sounded subdued, unlike her; possibly she was ashamed after all the shouting.

'Yes?' he said.

'It's time for supper.'

'Actually I'm not terribly hungry.'

'Nonsense. It's macaroni cheese. You know you like that.'

He did, and resented the way the savoury smell of it had started to reach in under his bedroom door, making his treacherous stomach gurgle when he had been prepared to be hungry and interesting.

His mother had laid a cheerful cloth on the kitchen table to make the meal more celebratory and his father poured a glass of red wine for him as well as for his mother. It was a deep red Hungarian variety he liked because it was cheap and which his mother liked because, she said, it was strong so went further. The meal was actually mercifully short – macaroni cheese followed by trifle made with Swiss roll and tinned mandarins – but seemed to last for ever because of the tension caused by both parents pretending nothing was wrong when they surely realized that he knew they had argued ferociously. The subject of the scholarship and unaffordable school fees went undiscussed apart from a fleeting acknowledgement when they first sat down to eat and his father raised his glass in a toast to Eustace, saying,

'Jolly well done today, old man.'

His mother, also raising her glass, said, 'Yes. We're so proud of you.'

But immediately she had tasted the wine she exclaimed how good it was and how cheap. And then they talked brightly on about nothing. It amazed him how good they were at talking endlessly about nothing at all. Vernon said his father had always maintained it was better to say nothing at all than to say nothing of interest but perhaps mealtimes at Vernon's were eaten in stony silence, broken only by the scraping of cutlery on plates, which would have been worse than empty chatter. Marginally.

At last, after obliging his mother by accepting a second bowl of the trifle, although Dream Topping always left him a little queasy, Eustace could stand the strain of good behaviour no longer so said, 'You know, I really don't mind. I'm fairly sure I won't have to do Latin or sport at Broadelm and, you know, Vernon is going there, which is nice.'

'Is he, now?' his father said and added something about unfortunate circumstances.

'Well your father's going to explain to Dr Figgis,' his mother said, 'so there'll be no misunderstandings or awkwardness.'

'And I won't have to sit Common Entrance!' Eustace told her.

'No,' his father said. 'There is that. Though you'll keep doing the classes right up until exam time. Might as well still get our money's worth.'

This earned him a quick glare from his mother, who then said, 'But because you did so well today, we've agreed to send you on the holiday course in Scotland, with Miss Gold's old teacher. You remember the one she mentioned? Because it does sound amazing. And there's absolutely no question of you stopping your lessons with her or selling your cello or any nonsense like that.'

'Unless you would prefer to stop,' his father said, earning himself a further glare.

'Maybe later on,' Eustace told him with a rare sense of wielding a little power.

And the odd, shattering evening ended on a giddy note because his parents no longer felt so bad. His father turned on the radiogram and played Charles Trenet to remind his mother of their honeymoon and Eustace enjoyed the unusual sight of them laughing together and looking younger than they had earlier, and the whole bottle of wine was drunk, with Eustace having a second glass without either parent noticing while they were having a little dance together to *La Mer*.

Alone in his room again soon afterwards he felt terribly giddy, saw black spots before his eyes and was sick into his bedroom sink. He saw macaroni in there and mandarin segments and red wine, which made him sick some more. The smell was awful and he had to use his toothbrush handle to mash the bits through the plughole. It was like flushing away the whole, ultimately toxic day and its fears and tensions and empty little triumph and catastrophic embarrassment.

He pulled on his pyjamas and brushed his teeth and climbed into bed to think about the mysterious Jean Curwen. She was a legend, Carla had said. He was going to learn from a legend.

CHAPTER NINE

The business of not being able to take up the scholarship, of hearing he was not going to have to sit Common Entrance after all but could drift through the rest of the school year, represented a dramatic slackening of pressure. Eustace still practised his cello but the edge of obsession had gone. It was a little like waking from a long sleep, and he found he emerged out of step with his contemporaries. He was not developing at the speed of Vernon and the others, which didn't bother him especially as, from what he could tell, puberty was a messy business and, in any case, inevitable as a speeding car. But he disliked feeling childish and he realized that all the shutting himself away for the hours of practice his cello demanded had left him outside the circles of the boyish norm and in danger of being left behind, the irritating child who couldn't keep up.

Without warning, Mr Payton, A2's form master, announced one morning that he was suspending their usual classes for the next two periods in order to give them a special course he called *How To Succeed as a Teenager*. During this he expected them all to take notes.

'I don't expect all of this to make sense entirely to you now,' he told them. 'But if you note it down, you'll find it better imprints on your memories and then, when occasion arises at your big school, as it surely will for you all in the next few years, you'll be more likely to remember what I'm telling you and benefit from it.'

The solemnity and anticipation were rather thrilling. Eustace exchanged a glance with his desk partner, Snell Major, a nice enough boy, though with no sense of humour. They each turned to a fresh page and gravely wrote *How to Succeed as a Teenager*. Eustace underlined the title in a different colour then paid close attention.

Mr Payton began with an excruciating talk on bodily change. It was hard to imagine he had ever been young. It was a talk that would have been more useful, arguably, a year before, which was when most of Eustace's contemporaries began to gain dramatically in height, to sprout hair in places formerly smooth and to smell strongly, often of the deodorant they were ostentatiously using to counteract their own odours.

'You won't all develop at the same rate,' he said. 'Some of you – Higgs for instance – have probably already finished growing. Others may have yet to start. Entirely to be expected. You'll all get there in the end. And you won't all develop in the same ways. Some men are hairy everywhere – arms, chest, even back – some hardly at all beyond their groins.'

There was a chortle at *groins*, of course.

'You're laughing because you're embarrassed,' he told them. 'All perfectly normal. So, while you're laughing, here are some pictures to give you an idea of the variety to expect.'

He opened his briefcase and took out a handful of colour photographs of completely naked men – blond, dark, hairy, smooth – which had been carefully cut from porn magazines and mounted, perhaps by Miss Packard, the broad-hipped school secretary, on to tidy pieces of white card and sealed under layers of sticky-backed plastic. He handed them to Higgs, the head of school, who sat in the desk nearest the door (six foot two, already quite hairy), and gestured for him to pass them around. Eustace's desk was in the farthest corner from Higgs, so he swiftly calculated that the pictures would reach him last and then stay on his desk.

'What about girls?' some idiot asked.

'Yes, sir?' Higgs asked, magnificently innocent. He had already passed the pictures on and the images travelled fairly swiftly, as though nobody liked to be seen to retain them for longer than anyone else. Eustace found their progress so distracting that he had difficulty taking in what Mr Payton was saying.

'How many of you have sisters?' Mr Payton asked and almost everyone but Eustace seemed to put up a hand. 'So you'll know that girls develop in much the same way, although your sisters may have been modest and done their best to hide it from you. At around the age of twelve they grow in height, they develop breasts and hips, with much the same variation in speed and size as the development among boys. And they grow pubic hair, of course. They also begin to have their *menses*, a Latin word meaning . . . ?'

'Months,' everyone called out with a kind of groan and one of the class swots added, 'From *mensis*, month, third declension, sir.'

'From which we derive which English verb?'

'Menstruate?' somebody suggested and there was a laugh.

Suddenly the photographs arrived, all together, on Eustace's desk. He had seen fully naked men before, sometimes caught windblown glimpses on the beach or dunes when they performed that comically modest dance to replace trunks with pants beneath a clutched towel, but his father had always been almost obsessively secretive about his body. Apart from the deep disappointment of the few men he'd glimpsed over other boys' shoulders in *Health and Efficiency*, he had never before been given them to gaze upon, under instruction even, except in art lessons and it was difficult to relate the saints and soldiers of Renaissance paintings to the hairy, sweating reality.

There were four photographs, and he took care to look at each in turn and not to linger unduly over any, although he was utterly fascinated. There was a Swedish-looking blond man, with very blue eyes and almost white eyebrows, posing with a striped beach ball under one arm. His body was almost hairless, like an overgrown boy's and had a pronounced scar where his appendix had been removed. There was a redhead with flaming tufts in armpits and groin and a rueful expression. There was a brown-haired model, locks to his shoulders, girlish as any Renaissance saint, whose genitals seemed curiously undeveloped beneath their tidy little thatch.

Lastly there was a black-haired man with a drooping cowboy moustache and an unbuttoned checked shirt. His big legs were as thickly haired as his chest. His cock stood to attention unlike the other men's and he gazed at the camera unsmilingly in a kind of challenge. Eustace stacked the pictures on the corner of his desk, with the black-haired man on top, then realized he was staring so flipped the stack over so the pictures were hidden and was startled in the process by his neighbour passing him the female equivalents he had not even noticed Mr Payton put into circulation, and had to fumble for all eight pictures on the floor. He looked dutifully at the naked ladies but as briefly as possible as he sensed he had an angry blush.

'Good,' said Mr Payton. 'Now that I've got all your attention, we need to talk about self-abuse.' Eustace had never heard this term before and had no idea what he was talking about. 'Contrary to what you may have read or heard, it will not make you blind or mad or give you hairy palms.'

A burst of nervous laughter here and Bailey, who was excitable, howled like a wolf.

'It's not a patch on the real thing but you're all several years off being legally old enough to enjoy that. And it's kinder on your sheets and pyjamas than wet dreams. But practice moderation. Don't get obsessed with it.'

Self-Abuse, Eustace wrote on his otherwise blank page. *Don't get obsessed with it.*

'You have already covered human reproduction in your biology classes. What you won't have covered is the law, and the law is very clear about this. Sex under the age of sixteen is illegal and you need to be eighteen before you can marry without your parents' consent. However, I'm not naïve. Your bodies are already awash with sex hormones and so are those of the girls you're likely to meet in the next few years. Just remember you only have to do it once to get a girl pregnant. So don't go all the way, however much she might lead you on.'

Eustace thought about obediently writing down this last command but nobody else was doing so and it frankly seemed a bit silly.

Then, to electric effect, Mr Payton added, 'There is a world of pleasure you can give one another with hands and mouths.' He said it quite drily, as they had heard him describe the formation and application of gerunds or summarize the different meanings of *ut* paired with subjunctive or indicative verbs. He was not a teacher even remotely associated with pleasure and Mrs Payton, a wintry fellow-classicist, appeared to have adopted disappointment long since as her default emotion, and yet something in his words had the salt savour of experience. *A world of pleasure. Hands and mouths.*

Mr Payton continued to lecture them, and Eustace continued to take notes, on contraception, on tobacco, on alcohol, on hormones and their effect on temper and energy levels, on the importance in one's teenage years of avoiding too much free time as apparently it was during idleness that one might fall prey to the many things that would make a teenager fail. It was a double period and a great deal of territory was covered but, like a wasp to spilled syrup, Eustace's mind kept returning to *mouths, hands, a world of pleasure.*

CHAPTER TEN

Eustace and Vernon had long established two places outside where they could go after school or meet at weekends. They had been going to them together for so long that it was rarely a matter for discussion. They would head to one or the other while deep in conversation. If it was wet, there was a dilapidated Victorian shelter in the network of paths on the edge of Prince Consort Gardens, which overlooked the remains of Birnbeck Pier. This had pretty stained glass, distant views across the water only visitors mistook for the sea and, because it had that telephone kiosk reek of piss and cigarettes, was rarely occupied by grown-ups. But their more usual haunt was the Fort, up its long flight of steps above the same headland grandly signposted *Ancient British Encampment.*

Vernon had grown so much recently that they no longer looked the same age and Eustace liked to think that old ladies they politely greeted in passing took them for older and younger brothers. Vernon's voice had broken during the holidays and he now had a thick layer of fluff growing along his jawline. He complained that all the growing he was doing made it very hard to wake up in the mornings and often gave him cramps. Two or three times he had very politely asked Eustace to massage away an ache in his shoulders or thigh, which naturally Eustace had done for him. He had been rather proud when Vernon said that cello-playing had given him a penetrating grip. He had never owned a dog or cat but now that Vernon was growing bigger than him, it was a little like having a large pet.

Naturally he told Vernon about Mr Payton's lecture on *How to Succeed as a Teenager*.

'I took notes,' he said.

'Let me see,' said Vernon and sprawled with a weary sigh across their usual heavily carved bench. Eustace sat across from him on a tree stump and dug out the relevant exercise book from his satchel.

As Vernon read, chuckled and murmured, 'Priceless,' his new favourite word, Eustace noted, where his outgrown trousers had ridden up above his socks, that he was sprouting black hairs on his legs as well now.

It turned out that all that year's school leavers had been given similar talks that morning but that the content and manner was left to the initiative of the speaker.

'Grenyer just showed us a film,' Vernon said. 'Actually not even that. It was one of those spacky wind-on reels, like the scripture lesson ones with the bible scenes, but with rubbish drawings instead of photographs. And there was a recording to go with it, so Grenyer could just press play then hide his blushes in the darkness and wind on to the next picture when a little ping on the tape told him to.'

'So what was in it? Drugs? Sex?'

'Neither really. Love and marriage. John and Mary fall in love over a game of tennis and get married. Then he lies on top of her to make a baby. Pretty off-putting really, though you got to see her breasts and everything as there was a pretty weird cross-section diagram after the romantic moon-light shot, showing how his cock fitted inside her lady parts.'

'Her vulva and vagina,' Eustace supplied, imitating the scrupulous W sounds of Mr Payton's Latin Vs, which made Vernon chuckle as he knew it would. 'Vernon?'

'Yes?'

'Don't laugh at me.'

'I wouldn't dream of it.'

'But what is self-abuse exactly? He went on and on about it and everyone else seemed to understand, so I felt a bit stupid.'

'Wanking,' Vernon said, stretching back in the sunshine with his hands behind his head. 'The solitary vice that never disappoints.'

'Ah.' *Now or never*, Eustace thought. 'So . . . do you do it, then?'

'Of course,' Vernon said. 'Don't you?'

Eustace was lost for words for a moment then had a brainwave. 'I'm not sure I'm doing it quite right.'

'It's not hard. Pardon the pun.'

'Yes but . . . nothing seems to happen.'

'You don't come?'

It seemed safest simply to shake his head and look blank. Vernon frowned thoughtfully. 'You're not circum-cised, are you?'

'You know I'm not.' They'd pissed side by side often enough, up there against the trees or in the sulphurous, oddly competitive urinals at St Chad's.

'Well look and learn.' Vernon glanced around then swiftly unzipped his trousers and tugged out his cock, which rapidly became hard so that veins stood out on it. Eustace stared. 'Impressive, huh?' Vernon drawled, in his Sean Connery voice. 'It's easy with a foreskin. We're lucky. You just take a firm hold and do this.'

He demonstrated the movement which Eustace realized he had seen countless times when older boys were mocking one another and which suddenly made insulting sense. Vernon seemed at once proud and touchingly bashful.

'You can have a go,' he said. 'If you like,' and he made a small gesture of invitation that had Eustace tumbling to his knees and taking hold. Vernon gave a little moan. 'You can hold harder,' he said. 'If you like.'

'Like this?'

'Oh. Oh God. Yes.'

Eustace moved his grasping fist as he had seen Vernon do, glancing around to check they were thoroughly hidden from the main path. If anyone came, he decided, he would pretend to have dropped something. He could feel a stirring in his pants. Luckily Vernon had his eyes closed.

'Faster,' Vernon muttered. 'Oh. Oh yes. Oh God.' And he lurched to one side of the bench so as not to make a mess on Eustace's school blazer.

Eustace sat back against his log and watched, intrigued, as Vernon spent himself prodigiously then tidied himself up with a neatly ironed blue tartan handkerchief.

'Thank you for that,' Vernon said at last, not meeting his eye.

'Here,' Eustace said and offered him a Cherry Drop from the packet in his pocket before helping himself. They sucked in companionable silence for a minute.

'I can't believe you've never done that,' Vernon said at last.

'Neither can I,' Eustace told him. 'It doesn't hurt, or anything? You looked as though you were in pain . . .'

'Far from it. The first time you think you're going to piss, a bit like when you have a wet dream, you know? Only it's so much better.'

Eustace nodded, although wet dreams were as yet still a mystery to him as well.

'But you don't pee,' Vernon explained, 'you just, well . . .'

'Yes. I saw.'

'Do you want me to . . . ?' Vernon gestured towards Eustace's trouser area.

'Er. Thanks, but better not.'

By unspoken agreement they stood and walked back through the Fort and down the steps to where they had padlocked their bicycles together. Unthinkingly Eustace scratched his nose and smelled the alien tang of Vernon on his fingers. It was foxy, like the strong smell of stinging nettles in flower, and not unpleasant.

'Well done on the scholarship, by the way,' Vernon said. 'Even if you can't take it up.'

'Thanks.'

'It won't be so bad at Broadelm. You'll see.'

'I know.'

'Just try and, you know, grow a bit taller before we start there.'

Eustace laughed and play-kicked him as they pedalled back downhill.

CHAPTER ELEVEN

The encounter with Vernon – Eustace called it that in his mind, he could think of no other way of describing it as it had been like meeting a new Vernon he hadn't seen before – changed the flavour of everything overnight. Not only did he find he couldn't stop revisiting its every detail in his head, the feel of Vernon in his hand, the gruff little gasps he had made, the colour and consistency of the stuff he produced, but he found it changed his view of everything.

He tried not to let it change the way he saw his parents however – it was far too weird to think of either of them, especially his father, in a sexual light – but at school, and in the streets to and from it, he began to find himself readily picturing certain people naked. The woman with red hair and huge breasts in the sweetshop. The man with tattoos down a hole in the pavement. Mr Jordan, his English teacher. It was incredibly distracting. He had never been the most focused student in the classroom but now his mind was an untrained puppy, chasing whatever it pleased. Suddenly the leering and jokes of the other boys began to make more sense rather than simply being alienating and frightening. He became aware that the handful of boys in his class who were boarders were having encounters almost every night, of an unromantic, competitive nature. There was much bragging about size, about quantity of *jizz* – a word he had often heard but never understood, and which he still wasn't entirely sure how to spell. To his relief he found few of the other boys piqued his interest. One or two of the teachers, however, the younger ones like Mr Jordan, marking time at the school after university while they decided on a career, were another matter. Mr White, who taught French and rugby, had hairy forearms. Mr Skipwith, who taught maths rather frighteningly and football even more so, had a fascinatingly large Adam's apple and a way of swinging his hips as he clacked aggressively with his chalk across the blackboard. Both wore daringly fashionable flared trousers rather than the drab suits worn by their older colleagues, and these were so mesmerizingly tight across the bottom and crotch that Eustace began to find himself reaching the midpoint of their lessons suddenly aware that he had been staring so intently he had taken in not a word they had been saying. And now that he had been shown, of course, he knew exactly what to do when he woke with an erection or when prolonged exposure to Mr Jordan's broad chest brought him to boiling point.

He tried to bear Mr Payton's proscriptions in mind and to confine his self-indulgence to once a day. He could not think of it as self-abuse, since it seemed to do no harm. If anything, it cleared his mind of clouds for a while, let him go back to thinking rationally about dates or numbers, declensions or the uses of the pluperfect. But he soon began to see the sense behind Mr Payton's warning. Once was rarely enough. This was an appetite in which, far from taking the edge off one's need, satisfaction seemed only to make it the keener. So he began to strike deals with himself in which two sessions a day were permissible if one only lay down for one of them and stood by the sink for the other. Self-indulgence in a school lavatory cubicle was more medicine than pleasure, he convinced himself, since the possibility of discovery made it so tense.

And with the convulsion this wrought in his life came the discovery that he had no control over his fantasies. The mind was unruly. He might lie down at night, chair silently wedged against doorknob in case, wad of loo paper carefully to hand and plan to think of some acceptable idol, like David Essex or Lee Majors, only to find quite the wrong person barging in on his decorously arranged scenario. Once or twice this was Louis but more often than not, and with volcanic results, it was Vernon.

He betrayed nothing, of course. When they met each day he was as studiedly offhand as usual, although privately he found he was now keenly aware of Vernon's physicality, of his appealing, nutty smell, of the growing heft of him, of the roughness in his deepening voice. And Vernon, in turn, seemed as studiously careful around him. Just once, as they were strolling along the front, sweltering in their uniforms between bare-legged, bare-armed holidaymakers, Vernon nudged him, prompted by the approach of a dazzlingly pretty girl eating a 99, and asked, 'So, are you succeeding as a teenager now on a regular basis?'

And Eustace had nudged him back and laughed and told him to shut up, but his scarlet face must have given Vernon all the answer he needed. Vernon had coughed and began to talk about Fanny Burney, whose immense novels

he had just discovered, and whose name he enjoyed pro-
nouncing with suggestive relish.

They still saw each other every school day, still tended to
walk to the Fort or the Prince Consort Park shelter for long
conversations about nothing much. And although Eustace
still practised his cello regularly even though there now
seemed nothing in particular to practise for, their encounter at the Fort must have made Vernon wary of stopping by
to listen and watch. But perhaps it wasn't that, Eustace considered. Perhaps it was just Vernon being sensitive to the
disappointment of not being able to take up the music
scholarship.

Vernon's birthday was approaching. It was a quietly
manly custom between them that they observed one
another's birthday but ignored the more vulgarized feasts
of Christmas and Easter. For the past two years they had
honoured one another's passions, Vernon giving Eustace
records of the Haydn and Boccherini cello concertos and
Eustace giving Vernon paperbacks of *Armadale* and *Felix
Holt*. But this year he decided to be bold.

He knew that boys his age often loitered in the magazine
section of Smith's – he had seen them – reading magazines
they would never be sold, tucked into a copy of something
innocuous about model trains or warfare, having stepped
a yard or two to the left or right of where they had dared
to tweak the magazine down. The Smith's staff didn't seem
to mind – at least they never intervened unless there was
an attempt to steal something – and there were always a
few grown men doing exactly the same so perhaps it was
an accepted pattern of male behaviour, something their

fathers did as well, but in other towns, perhaps. But to have grasped such a magazine himself and queued at the counter with it then handed it to the woman behind the till was quite unthinkable. In any case she would probably refuse to sell it to him, whatever story he told her. Most boys at St Chad's relied on the scraps of pornography hidden in time-honoured spots and mysteriously refreshed from time to time. But they were, quite literally, filthy, so long used and abused that merely to handle them was to feel a sense of pollution.

In the heart of the most touristy part of the town, where everything, even buildings, felt provisional, entirely geared towards rapid moneymaking not stability or elegance, was a corner shop so lurid he would never normally have entered even in an emergency. It sold tobacco, lettered rock, sweets, holiday postcards – including the ones with rude jokes illustrated by scarlet-cheeked, big-busted women and sweating, ferrety men. It also sold newspapers and magazines. It was known that the teenage girls employed there on a weekend heedlessly sold cigarettes to children.

Even so, Eustace prepared as for a commando raid. First he went to Smith's, where he bought a large brown envelope, a birthday card with Monet haystacks on it and a roll of wrapping paper. And, with beating heart, he swiftly lunged between the men crowding the shelves to check the price of the magazine he had settled on. Then he headed to the corner shop, checked that one of the girls, not the thick-armed owner, was on duty and walked in. As always the place was crowded but with trippers, not locals, nobody who would know him. As it happened, the girl was taking a telephone call as she served, so her mind was at the other end of the grubby, curly flex and barely on the job. She certainly wasn't engaging customers in conversation. Even so, he waited until there was no queue before seizing a copy of *Mayfair* and darting forward with exactly the right money – more than he would have thought it possible to spend on a magazine. She took his cash without meeting his eye, making encouraging, 'go-on' noises to whoever was on the other end of the phone call and, without asking, thrust his purchase into a striped plastic bag. He bundled it in turn into the new brown envelope inside his Smith's bag before heading home to privacy.

Had he needed confirmation that his circuitry was differently wired to that of other boys, the pictures provided it in abundance. Or rather, his lack of response to them did. He read the magazine with great care, as it was a present, and looked at every single page. The women in it were selected, he saw, to offer a range of appeals, from haughty to cheap, blonde to ginger, pert to ripe. He gazed, appalled and inquisitive, but felt not the slightest stirring and found his eye lingering not on parted skin or curling hair but extraneous details, lacy underwear, shiny high heels, a macramé potholder he would have liked in his own room.

He began to feel that telltale tightening in chest and y-fronts only when he passed beyond the pictures and reached a section never retained among the grubby fragments in the loo cubicles or changing room at school. It wasn't a letters page exactly, although it was entirely words and purported to be written by readers. It was a series of confessions – he suspected entirely fictional – sent in by

PATRICK GALE

women and men driven by guilt or an odd kind of generosity to unburden themselves. They told of passionate, shameless encounters in train compartments, hotel rooms, airplanes and a department store changing room – a lack of domesticity, a giddy sense of transience seemed integral to the narrative thrill – in which the narrators had sex with men or women or men *and* women whose need for immediate satisfaction overruled any sense of risk or decency or normality. They were utterly compelling, he found. And it was because, unlike the pictures, they involved the imagination. And men. He read every one and it was some time before he felt able carefully to fold the magazine away in wrapping paper and leave his room again.

Although the magazine was securely wrapped and even had the shop's plastic bag under the wrapping to be doubly secure, he did not like to risk taking it to school where a crowd might gather and boys insist Vernon open it there and then. He hid it carefully under his mattress – he had been changing his own sheets for some time now – and casually suggested Vernon come back with him for birthday tea.

One of the few good points about living in an old people's home was that there was always cake to be had at teatime. His mother was out, happily, so there was no call to socialize and they could raid Mrs Fowler's cake tin and take mugs of tea upstairs.

His mother had been out a great deal since the music scholarship exam. She seemed to have embarked on a period of self-improvement, taking herself off to Bristol to see exhibitions or matinées of the kind of subtitled films

164

that made his father fidget. And when not absent, she often seemed distracted by books borrowed from Carla. Her predominant mood had become scattily sweet and her punishing headaches, rare, so nobody minded the absences.

That afternoon his father was out as well, probably filling the car to its roof with loo paper and latex gloves at the Cash and Carry. Even so, discreetly pulling open his sock drawer to block the bedroom door from being opened would be less likely to unsettle Vernon, he decided, than resorting to his usual chair-beneath-doorknob solution.

They sat on the bed, sipped their tea, and Vernon dutifully laughed as he opened his card. But his *bloody hell* on opening his present was sincere and gratifying. His slightly adenoidal breathing thickened as he began to turn the pages. Eustace sat beside him, catching the Sunday roast scent of him. Since the photographs had aroused Eustace so little, he was interested to see their effect on his friend. Was it breasts that caught his eye? Faces?

'Bloody hell,' Vernon muttered again, flicking back for a second look at a giddy blonde in a rose-pink negligée and suspenders. Eustace nudged him playfully. Vernon glanced up. 'Thanks, Stash,' he said. 'This is . . . bloody hell.' He pushed a hand down the front of his trousers to rearrange himself.

'Show me,' Eustace said. 'What . . . Who do you like the best?'

'This one,' Vernon said. 'Her. Look. I mean Christ, Stash. Look at her!'

He had flicked back again to the rose-pink blonde. Eustace made a show of looking at her, too, but she seemed utterly ordinary to him. A little sharp-faced and cheap. He could imagine her as a Saturday girl in the very shop where he had bought her. Looking at her, he could think of nothing they would find to talk about. Except Vernon, of course.

He wants me so much and I just can't handle it, he imagined her telling him. *You know?*

Believe me, I know, he told her.

Help me, she told him. *Take him off my hands . . .*

Eustace took the magazine from Vernon and flicked to the back, to find the confessions again. 'OK,' he said. 'Just imagine this is about her. With you.'

And, keeping his voice as low and calm as he could, he slowly read the confession in which a shy but eager-to-learn nurse found herself trapped in a lift late at night with a handsome and powerfully equipped junior doctor wearing very little under his scrubs. As he'd hoped, Vernon couldn't help but unzip himself and he read on through a second story, about a bored housewife and a randy plumber until, with a hoarse curse, Vernon was done.

Then, rather than ask him if he wanted the favour returned, Vernon muttered, 'Your turn now,' and shifted so that he sat tightly behind Eustace, a thigh hot against each of his. 'Easier to do it right-handed this way,' he murmured as he unzipped Eustace and returned the favour. He restrained him tightly with his left arm when Eustace made a move to finish on his own, which made it all the more exciting, and continued to hold his chest until his panting had subsided.

Just as before, there was no acknowledgement from Vernon of what they had just done. Eustace felt slightly faint and must have closed his eyes because, when he became aware again, Vernon was over at the bedroom sink, washing and drying his hands.

'Thanks for this,' was all he said, picking up the magazine as Eustace tidied himself up, unpleasantly hot in the face. 'But could I keep it here, maybe? I'm not sure about carrying it home.'

Eustace was about to say there was an envelope and plastic bag then realized that the magazine gave a good pretext for a return visit. 'Of course,' he said, taking it from him and lifting the mattress to hide it. 'You can, er, come and look at it whenever you like.'

'Thanks. Well, I'd better be off.'

Eustace's father must have returned from the Cash and Carry. Eustace heard Vernon making conversation with him beyond the bend in the stairs, him sounding entirely innocent and calling his father 'sir'.

A discreet pattern emerged during the remaining weeks of term. He and Vernon would have their usual after-school stroll to the Fort or the shelter but once a week Vernon would say something like, 'I haven't heard your cello in a while,' and say so boldly, in front of other boys. And that meant that they walked back to Eustace's room instead. He always began by watching Vernon look at the magazine then he would read one of the stories and then Vernon would either play with himself or have Eustace do it. He was always polite about offering to *finish Eustace off* next but, mysteriously, because he wanted it more than ever, Eustace felt compelled occasionally to shrug and say,

'No thanks,' or 'next time, maybe.'

It was as though he needed to prove he had more self-control than his friend, although he felt he actually had less. And guilt at having used the cello as a pretext for the meetings would drive him to practise furiously in the hour or two that followed each encounter.

When his left hand was in second or third position, near his nose, he would catch musky reminders off it of what they had been about.

CHAPTER TWELVE

His last term at St Chad's drew to a close strangely. He was left to his own devices for hours on end while some of his classmates sat Common Entrance and others were whisked off to various single-minded public schools for scholarship exams or interviews. Rather than spend the time reading in the library, he asked for permission to bring his cello into school to practise, which was granted once it was ascertained that there was a practice room sufficiently isolated from the gym and school hall for the sounds he made not to disturb those working on exam papers. He set himself to learning as much as he could of the second Bach suite.

Vernon and the rest of A3, who were going on to Broadelm or comprehensives further afield, continued with ordinary lessons, though these were, Vernon said, largely pointless, but it did not seem to have occurred to Dr Figgis to have Eustace join them. He was, it seemed, a case apart, an anomaly, possibly even an embarrassment. It was good to work at something he loved in a school environment. He kept to school timetables, had breaks when the others broke for lunch or recreation. There was Sports Day, as usual, in which he and Vernon did their usual obligatory minimum, running a few races badly and tripping on some hurdles. There was the traditional Excursions Day, when they were all parcelled off into coaches, seemingly at random, to spend the day with harassed teachers at tourist attractions. Eustace got Windsor Safari Park, Vernon, a trip to a factory that made footballs. Then there was the usual interminable prizegiving ceremony, with prizes handed out by a television actor famous for a show children weren't allowed to watch.

Utterly unexpectedly, Eustace found himself awarded a record token for *Outstanding Effort put into Pursuing a Hobby*. There were cheers when he stumbled, blushing, up to the stage to receive it, a shout of *Hobby!* led by Vernon, and boys who never spoke to him actually clapped him on the back as he returned to his seat. It was as though, for ten minutes at the longed-for end of his time in the school, he became bewilderingly popular. His parents weren't there to see, not knowing he was to receive anything; it would never have occurred to him to ask them.

He walked home with Vernon via the town record shop, where he spent the token at once on the boxed set of Casals playing the Bach suites. There was a more recent recording by Paul Tortelier and Vernon lobbied for this, having recently watched Tortelier on television, but the Casals was better. Carla had told him.

'No, no,' he told Vernon, repeating her criticism because he liked the sound of it. 'His approach is too romantic. Casals' approach is cleaner, less obviously winning.'

It was his first boxed set. Having glimpsed what seemed like a whole wall of them at the house in Clifton, he fantasized that one day he, too, would have shelf after shelf of the things, along with an up-and-down light over his kitchen table and a walk-in wardrobe or dressing room with very calm, tidy shelves. His bedroom record player was a discard of his parents, very much mono, very much a Dansette but, as he had earnestly said to Vernon once, pre-empting a sneer, 'Carla Gold says serious musicians don't really bother with stereo systems; for them, records are just that, an *aide-mémoire* not a substitute . . .'

Vernon sat on the end of the bed while Eustace reverently opened the box. On the cover, Casals' egglike head had been given a blue filter. He didn't play the first suite or the third, although he knew Vernon would be more likely to enjoy them, but the challenging fifth. It was in C minor, a key whose darkness suddenly appealed to him. The magnificently sombre C octave with which it began seemed to fill the room, defying levity. The volume was a little high but he didn't care. He was thirteen. Such things would be expected of him.

They listened in silence for a while, awestruck. At least, Eustace was awestruck. Perhaps Vernon was too, because, when he began to speak, he had to clear his throat, as though tears had built up in there.

'What does it mean?' he asked.

'I don't think it means anything,' Eustace told him. 'There's no story, or message, or scene painting. It's just pure music.'

They listened on into the Allemande then Vernon glanced down at his lap pointedly and asked, 'Do you . . . ?'

The music had taken Eustace by surprise. It wasn't like the first and third suites, with their heart-on-sleeve joy, their unambiguous dance rhythms. Its high seriousness was a dare. He had left prep school. He was off on his course tomorrow and starting at a comprehensive in the autumn. Everything was about to change for ever.

'Only if we can kiss first,' he said.

It was a mad thing to suggest. He had no idea how to kiss other than what he had gathered from films and it was somehow a far more intimate idea, because of its involvement of mouths and faces, than the virile assistance Vernon had in mind. He was startled when Vernon simply said, 'Sure,' pulled his face to his and kissed him. They only kissed with lips at first, which was nice though a bit ticklish and Vernon tasted of that day's lunch, a rather sweaty steak and kidney pudding they were invariably served on Thursdays. But then Vernon pushed him back on to the bed and started kissing him deeply, thrusting his tongue into his mouth.

Eustace wasn't sure he could breathe then realized he could through his nose. He opened his eyes and saw Vernon's were tight shut. The weight on top of him felt good. Tentatively he pushed his own tongue into Vernon's mouth as well, feeling how their tongues slid over each other like fish. He parted his legs, to give Vernon more room and suddenly Vernon was thrusting into him.

The bed squeaked but Casals' cello was louder. Eustace reached an arm round to hold Vernon, which seemed only natural, but his hand landed on Vernon's bum, which was much harder than expected, as though Vernon went to PE classes in secret, and all at once Vernon was gasping and swearing and jumping off.

'Shit,' he said. 'Oh shit. I didn't mean . . .' They both

looked at where a very obvious wet patch was seeping through the front of his school trousers. Casals now seemed far too loud and inappropriate, like hymns at a party. Eustace rolled on to his feet to turn the record off. Vernon frantically sponged at himself with Eustace's face flannel from the sink, which didn't really help.

'I should probably go,' he said. 'Really. Er ... Enjoy your course.'

And before Eustace had finished putting the Casals record back in its sleeve and into the box, Vernon was thumping off downstairs. From the window Eustace saw his friend walk down the steps outside and not quite get astride his bicycle when Eustace's mother came back from wherever she had been and leaned against the car door to force him into clumsy conversation. Poor Vernon held the bike protectively between himself and her to hide the stain on his trousers with its saddle.

Eustace thought his mother looked almost flirtatious, as though sensing Vernon's eagerness to be off and enjoying the power his politeness gave her to force him to linger. But then she released him with a little wave, and lunged back into the car to retrieve a bag of shopping from Dingles in Bristol. And rather than walk smartly up into the house, as she usually did, she just leaned against the car again and stared up at the windows looking, for her, oddly defeated.

Eustace didn't want her to see him watching so stepped back, discomfited by the glimpse of her less than usual assertive self. He filled the sink with the hottest possible water and rinsed out the flannel Vernon had used, just as he always did now when he used it for the same purpose. The familiarly, oddly seasidey smell reached him in the steam, and made him think briefly of Mr Payton's startling exhortation during *How to Succeed as a Teenager*.

'You are now, most of you, of an age where you can start a life and take a life, become fathers or killers. Though it's a few years yet before the Law recognizes you as such, in the eyes of Nature, you are young men.'

He was not ready to be a man. All at once the prospect of going to Ancrum for the residential course, which had so excited him, filled him with fear.

Passing down to the bathroom on the floor below, he could hear his mother in the kitchen on the floor below that. He couldn't make out her words, just her distinctive voice, going on and on with the kind of animation that she reserved for half-truths and talking to Mrs Fowler. She would have one of her headaches, either later on, or the following morning, he could tell. That was probably preferable to her suddenly remembering he was off to Scotland on the train and making a great fuss about luggage and packed lunches and so on.

He locked the bathroom door and, as always, drew the curtains. He tugged down his trousers and pants and made himself look at his lower reflection in the mirror. Then he took down the nail scissors, which had gone slightly rusty in the damp of the bathroom cabinet and, pinching his pubic hair hard between finger and thumb, so that it raised the skin, cut as much of it off as he could. He rinsed it off the sink into the plughole so that it formed a clump he could easily lift up and flush down the lavatory. He looked again in the mirror and was even less satisfied. He wanted to turn back time or at least make it progress no further.

Putting the scissors back in the cabinet, he thought about using his father's still soapy razor, but decided he was too scared of cutting himself. Then he saw a tube of his mother's hair removing cream. He opened it and gingerly sniffed it. It smelled fine, if sugary sweet, like most women's products. He unrolled it enough to read the instructions. *Five minutes*, he read. He squeezed some out over the scrabble of hair the nail scissors had left behind, smeared it in then quickly rinsed it off his fingers in case it did something odd to his nails. They had recently learnt in biology that hair and nails were made of the same thing.

It began to tingle a little, then quite a lot, then to burn, but he imagined that was to be expected; hair couldn't simply melt away, after all, and it hurt if you pulled it. He shuffled over to sit on the lavatory, trousers and pants down around his ankles, looked at his watch and forced himself to be brave and cope with the pain for at least another three minutes.

Finally he could bear it no longer and lurched up to rinse the stuff off at the sink, using deliciously cold water. There was a violent stink of sulphur like the time he had cracked a bad egg into a pan. The skin revealed was an angry pink and continued to burn, but it was miraculously hairless. Looking at himself critically one more time in the mirror, trying to see his body as a stranger might, he was not sure it was an improvement, more a drastic alteration.

He dressed himself again after dabbing on some calamine lotion from an old bottle dating from a phase when his mother had briefly worried about sunburn, then retreated back to his room. His mother had stopped talking and was playing *Spanish Flea* loudly instead.

Supper would be fish pie and boiled carrots because it was Friday.

CHAPTER THIRTEEN

Eustace had never travelled so far from home in his life and certainly not on his own. His mother had lent him a folding, Black Watch tartan suitcase, which she said was lighter than the others. She had stored it with lavender bags in it to prevent it turning musty in the loft and he felt sure it would make his clothes smell like someone's grand-mother so packed it at the very last moment in case.

He had never paid much attention to his clothes before. He wore his school uniform most of the year but otherwise wore the clothes his mother bought him and which reap-peared in his wardrobe washed and ironed. He had black lace-ups for school and Lysander sandals for holi-days. His socks were all knee-length and either black or blue, his Y-fronts, all white. His long-sleeved shirts, like his father's, were all Tattersall checks; their summer equiva-lents were plain coloured T-shirts. His mother would countenance nothing with a picture or words on it. He had never considered any of this until required to pack the tar-tan suitcase with seven of everything, plus a jersey in case, because Scotland was colder than Weston.

Then it dawned on him he was not just going on a cello course, nor going for an extended music lesson, but spend-ing a week in a big house full of complete strangers who might judge him for what he wore. He was grateful that his mother had returned from one of her recent trips to Bristol with some new, flared jeans for him and a couple of cheesecloth shirts but decided to save these for later and travel in clothes he had already broken in.

As the journey was to take nearly seven hours, he packed two of his longest books – a collection of horror stories by H.P. Lovecraft, which Vernon had lent him, and E.M. Forster's *A Room with a View*. Louis had recommended he read the Forster.

'You're the perfect age for it,' he said in the tone he used in which Eustace could never distinguish kindness from teasing, 'as it's all about yearning and escape.'

Come the morning he had assumed he would catch a train from Weston but his mother, not smitten by the expected headache, insisted on driving him to Bristol to catch the train from there.

'It won't be complicated changing trains,' he told her.

'No,' she conceded, 'but you've your cello as well as the suitcase with you and it would be a disaster if you missed your connection.'

Although his father always had chores to keep him busy in the morning, he insisted on coming as well. 'Nonsense. It'll be fun,' he said. 'It's not every day you go on an adventure like this.'

But actually it wasn't much fun as his parents' forced air of holiday jollity and their slightly repetitive questions about the course kept breaking down into little irritated exchanges about his father's reluctance to overtake lorries.

'I'm sure they're going as fast as they can,' he'd say.

'If he misses his train, it'll be all your fault,' she'd snap back. 'So, is this woman giving you individual lessons, Eustace, or teaching you all as a group?'

'I think it's a bit of both,' Eustace started to tell her. 'Mainly it's ensemble work in little groups but she'll work with each of us in turn as well.'

Already her attention had drifted back to the road. 'Now,' she said. 'You can overtake him *now*! Oh really, what on earth is the point?'

As the car was not especially large, the cello case had to lie diagonally across the back seat, over Eustace's lap and obscuring his view. The boot was full of bags and boxes because his father had decided to combine the errand with a trip to the Cash and Carry afterwards. This meant that his suitcase, riding on top, kept bumping the back of Eustace's neck and giving off a powerful whiff of lavender bags. He concentrated on keeping his eyes to the front and breathing deeply and slowly in an effort not to become inconveniently carsick.

They arrived on the edge of Bristol for the start of the weekend crush – something catching the train from Weston would have spared him, though he didn't like to point that out. From cursing and bickering and presenting Eustace with questions, his parents fell into an increasingly tense silence. Then suddenly they were at Temple Meads Station and the squabbling began again as they searched for a parking space. They raced to the platform for the Cornish Scot, which arrived from Cornwall minutes later. The cello had to go in the guard's van but, as pleased as a child performing a conjuring trick, his father produced a plastic covered bicycle chain and stout padlock and locked the case securely to the guard's van cage around its neck and upper handle while his mother tied a large label to it which named him as the owner and said *Travelling to Berwick-upon-Tweed*. Then she insisted on finding him a forward-facing seat and stowing his case on the overhead rack, introducing him to a rather startled woman who looked like a retired schoolmistress, in the hope that she would watch over him. Finally she gave him a hug and a kiss, which was so unlike her it reminded him he had never gone on such a journey without her. His father handed him some spending money for emergencies and a packed lunch Mrs Fowler had made and told him to call them on arrival and reverse the charges. He also made a nervous joke about not talking to strange men. Finally the guard blew his whistle and they both jumped out and closed the door and waved like mad, so that he felt obliged to lift a hand to wave back.

It was a relief to pull away from the platform, which his father had jokily run along to keep him in sight, and to take the Lovecraft stories from his case and settle down in his seat. He caught the eye of the retired schoolmistress, who smiled kindly.

'Your mother didn't give me the opportunity to say,' she said, 'but I'm only travelling as far as Birmingham New Street. But you're a big, sensible boy. I'm sure you'll be just fine after that.'

'Yes,' he told her. 'Thank you.' And he began to read.

Apart from one boy who only had to come from Edinburgh, everybody else seemed to have come up on a train from

London. By prior arrangement they had also sat in the same carriage and talked and laughed and shared picnics and stories all the way up. Their train had arrived in Berwick ten minutes before Eustace's and they were waiting together in a happy, noisy cluster, marked out from everyone else on the platform by their instrument cases. None of them knew Eustace, of course, so there was no sign of recognition until, in a slight panic lest the train head on to Dundee with it on board, he hurried to the guard's van and unpadlocked his cello. Seeing him climb down with a cello case now, as well as his suitcase, the others cheered and waved.

Then a comfortable woman in a pink tweed coat and horn-rimmed spectacles hurried over saying, 'Eustace?' And shook his hand saying, 'I'm Peg, the Cello Centre administrator. We don't do surnames at Ancrum.'

She led him across the platform to the group. 'Everybody, this is Eustace, all the way from Somerset.'

'Hello!' everyone shouted. It felt as though he had arrived at a birthday party after the cake had been eaten and the jellies brought out.

'Do you all know each other already?' he asked the flame-haired boy beside him.

'No!' people shouted but the boy said, 'Yes. Some of us play together at school. I'm Ralph,' he added and shook hands with a solemnity that made Eustace suddenly homesick for Vernon.

'Now,' Peg said. 'Home to settle in quickly then out for supper. The minibus is this way.'

Following her, Eustace instinctively stuck beside Ralph,

as the only other one who had begun to speak to him. 'You're not a cellist, then,' he said, seeing Ralph had a violin case with him. 'Sorry. I'm stating the obvious.'

'Jean has to have a few of us, and a pianist or two, for the ensembles,' Ralph said gravely. 'But we still get a lot out of it. It's musicianship she teaches as much as specific cello technique.'

And, sure enough, Eustace spotted two or three violin or viola cases among the luggage being shouldered all about him. Two people had no instruments at all, only music cases, thus identifying themselves as pianists.

Their instruments and cases were piled into a van by a man Peg introduced as Young Dougie, who must have been at least sixty. Then three of the older boys climbed up front with him and the rest of them boarded the minibus driven by Peg. Eustace decided to sit and see what happened and was quietly pleased that flame-headed Ralph sat beside him. Ralph had kept his violin with him, Eustace noticed, and hugged it on his lap as a mother might a baby with wind.

'Do you ever let it out of your sight?' he asked him.

'Only when I'm asleep,' Ralph admitted. 'And, even then, I quite often reach out if I wake in the night, just to check it's still there. It was my grandfather's. It's the reason I began playing. I've just started at the Menuhin School. I'm mainly here because of my little sister, Naomi.'

'Oi!' A hand smacked Ralph on the back of the head. 'I'm only a year younger than you and much more mature.'

Ralph made a scoffing noise but was smiling and Eustace twisted in his seat. A very pretty girl with a savage haircut scowled at him.

'I cut it myself,' she told him, seeing him look. 'My friend has cancer and they can make a wig with it.'

'But not for *her*,' Ralph said. 'Our mother was so angry.'

'Was it very long before?' Eustace asked her.

'I could sit on it. I'm Naomi,' she added. 'And this is Freya, who is so scared she was sick on the train.'

'Eustace,' he said. 'I'm a bit nervous, too,' he told Freya, who had a woolly hat on, although it was quite warm, and looked as though she had been crying as well as sick. 'Are you a cellist as well?'

She shook her head then almost soundlessly said, 'Violin,' and gave him a heartbreakingly brief, crumpled-in smile.

Ralph and Naomi had been that Easter, they told him. Just like him, Naomi was taught by a former pupil of Jean's but they were both students at the Menuhin School. A couple of others, they'd discovered on the train up, were at somewhere called Chet's and another two were about to start at Wells. More than ever, listening to the casual way they described lives already dedicated to their chosen instruments, Eustace felt the want of his place at Clifton.

'So what's Mrs Curwen like?' he asked Ralph.

'We don't call her that. We all call her Jean,' Ralph said. 'Honestly.'

'Jean's amazing,' Naomi added. 'Nothing matters to her more than music. Not food, not housework, not gossip, not clothes.'

'Music is a religion,' Ralph cut in dramatically, 'and Jean's a priestess. She can be a bit terrifying.'

Freya looked tearful at that so Naomi added swiftly,

'But only if she thinks you're not taking music seriously. Or if you're rude about Haydn.'

Once they'd passed beyond the outskirts of Berwick, Peg followed Dougie's van through several miles of beautiful, rolling countryside dotted with mature oaks and handsome houses. It was not how Eustace had imagined Scotland. From films and shortbread tins, he had expected gloomy lochs, towering mountains and romantically ruined castles, but Ralph assured him that was the Highlands.

'This is the Borders,' he said, in a tone that summoned up Vernon. 'Walter Scott country. It's Scotland but completely different to the rest. You won't see much countryside beyond the park, in any case. Jean keeps us pretty busy.'

They drove in at the gates of a wooded estate. Angus cattle grazed alongside sheep. There was a little estate church then a bridge over a river and then, on a rise in the land, a handsome Georgian house with big white windows, and rambling extensions out to its rear. There was a pretty double-sided flight of steps up to a sort of terrace by glazed doors on the first floor but they drove around to a more serviceable entrance off the crowded courtyard at the rear. There was palpable excitement from Ralph and Naomi and the others who had been before. Eustace felt his own first-day-of-school apprehension was matched in Freya's expression as she pulled her hat even lower over her brow.

Jean came out to greet them, leading a small cluster of men and women. She gave an impression of height though that was probably an illusion created by good posture. She had thick, unruly dark hair tinged with grey and the lines of someone whose feelings were never hidden. As the other grown-ups ranged behind her, she laughed and began to hug anyone making a return visit.

'Welcome back,' she told them and Eustace decided she made him think of a lioness. She gave that impression of nobility and of coiled strength. 'And to the rest of you, welcome to Ancrum. I'm Jean and this is my husband, Fraser and two of our full time students Magda and Brigitte, all of whom you'll be meeting and working with. We need to settle you all in quickly before we take you to supper. Give your name to Magda here.' She indicated a grinning young woman with very straight blonde hair. 'She'll tell you which room you're in and which of us will be leading you there. All cellos into the ballroom please, where I promise they'll be perfectly, perfectly safe. There just isn't room for them and you and your suitcases in the bedrooms. But we make an exception for violins because we know how you worry!' This was said with an affectionate stroke to Ralph's cheek, which brought on a blush.

They queued to give their names to Magda to look up on her clipboard. Each adult was collecting a different cluster of them for a different part of the house. As he gave his name and Magda was examining her list, Jean called out, 'Eustace? You're with me!'

He turned and she shook his hand.

'I've heard all about you from dear Carla,' she said. 'How is she?'

'Oh,' Eustace said, uncertain. 'All right, I think.' And he was briefly unnerved by the directness of her stare. This

185

was not a woman from whom you could have secrets or for whom you would ever dare not to practise.

He was happy to find he was in the same room as Ralph and a tall boy called Fred who played the viola and seemed dauntingly grown-up. They were joined by one of the pianists, Pierre, and Jean marched them at speed through the house. They went via the huge ballroom, so Eustace could leave his cello there, then up an uncarpeted back staircase – what Jean called the *Maids' Staircase* in a tone that implied she might once have been used to maids – to a long room in the attic with five beds in it.

'Ralph can lead you both back to civilization in a moment,' she said. 'The boys' bathroom is just back along the corridor – girls are up a different staircase entirely – and we'll be off to supper in—' She glanced at her little gold wristwatch. 'Six o'clock. All right? Happy, Eustace?'

Eustace smiled and nodded and she briefly beamed back.

'Good boy.'

They deferred to the tall boy, Fred, who was clearly the oldest and let him take the bed slightly apart from the others and nearest the window. Eustace took a bed in the farthest corner, which, he was pleased to see, had its own reading light. Pierre, who had an accent, so was presumably French, immediately set about carefully unpacking his suitcase into a chest of drawers. Nobody else bothered.

Ralph led the way back down the Maids' Staircase. The family's rooms, he explained, were on the first floor, where a stuffed bear with raised paws warned against trespassing. They were staying where the rest of Jean's lucky handful of full time students lived during term times.

186

'Do they do nothing but cello?' Pierre asked. 'Surely there are laws about needing to learn other subjects?'

'Oh yes,' Ralph explained airily. 'They study maths and languages and they can do A levels in history of art and music, of course.'

'But Jean teaches them the cello,' said Fred a bit mournfully. 'And everyone knows that's what matters most.'

'Is there somewhere like this just for violas?' Eustace asked him and Fred seemed to notice him for the first time.

'I doubt it,' he said. 'Unlike cellists, we tend not to draw attention to ourselves.'

The others jeered kindly. Jokes at the expense of viola players were a musical tradition.

They came through a big panelled hall where a mounted stag's head looked down on a rocking horse and an array of wellingtons, walking boots, walking sticks and an old side table where a framed, signed photograph of Pablo Casals stood amidst a welter of unopened letters, including some bills marked URGENT in red letters.

At every turn there seemed to be rooms cluttered with music stands, standard lamps and antique dining chairs. There were oil paintings, many of them battered and even torn and patched, of horses, dogs, country houses and the men and women who lived in them. A deerhound the size of a pony emerged from her lair under a piano to nibble Ralph's ears and was introduced as Rowena.

Immediately breaking the group down into clusters of three or four to settle them in was good psychology. By the time Jean was striking a tam-tam to summon them down to the back door, tentative alliances had formed and there was chatter and laughter as they climbed into a succession of more or less filthy household cars. Jean and Fraser stayed behind but Peg and the younger tutors drove them to a large Victorian guesthouse a couple of miles away where, in the formal dining room, Magda led them in singing a grace in German. Then softly spoken local girls in uniform served them. There was a choice of three dishes for three courses but all of them, at Jean's insistence, were vegetarian. Pierre, who had sat with Eustace, Ralph and Freya (who was still in her woollen hat but seemed marginally less unhappy) was aghast.

'I have steak twice a week usually,' he said. 'Not this . . . rabbit food.'

But Eustace thought it sounded rather good. He had a glass of tomato juice to start then grated Double Gloucester with slices of Bramley apple on a bed of lettuce. Freya's nut cutlet and roast vegetables looked rather more sustaining. Ralph assured him the puddings were excellent and said the menu never varied so one could work one's way through all options. Fred was at a different table, Eustace saw, where his height and good looks had left him surrounded by girls, including Naomi, but she saw him watching and gave him a private smile that seemed to say, 'I know. We're ridiculous.'

In the course of the meal it emerged that Eustace was the only one at his table not attending or about to attend a school noted for its music department. Even Freya's eyes widened when, prompted by Pierre, he told the sad story of his music scholarship.

'A comprehensive?' she murmured, her voice much

188

richer and deeper than her wan expression led one to expect. 'You poor thing.'

'It's really not that bad,' he said, instantly warming to the kindness in her tone. 'I'll still have lessons with Carla Gold – she's a pupil of Jean's – and I can join the local youth orchestra once I'm fourteen.'

'But it's the practice. When will you practise?'

Eustace told them he would practise after school, the way he always had, but both Pierre and Ralph pointed out that their schools made both solitary and supervised practice a part of the daily timetable. Freya rather boldly added that practising outside school hours required more discipline.

'Half of us would probably grind to a halt,' she said, 'if we didn't have parents or teachers pushing us.'

'What would you do if you stopped?' Eustace asked her.

She looked at him owlishly, scratched an itch on her scalp through her hat. 'Climb trees?' she suggested. 'Read books? Get a boyfriend?'

The other two laughed at her.

'Don't be absurd,' Ralph said. 'She's easily the strongest player in our year,' he told Eustace. 'You know you are,' he added when she flicked a pea at him. 'You'll play the Britten concerto next term. You'll be in the Royal College at eighteen and you'll go and do postgrad abroad then become a soloist.'

She shrugged and returned to picking at her food. 'It doesn't mean I wouldn't rather climb trees and read books,' she muttered.

'Does your mother push you?' he asked Pierre.

Pierre pushed away his plate with a pout. 'She's a tyrant and a bitch,' he sighed. 'And completely unreasonable. But I happen to love what she makes me do. Yours?' he asked Ralph.

'Oh,' Ralph said. 'Ours is famously unhinged. She played Casals recordings to Naomi in the womb. Jean taught her, you see, and she never got over Jean's disappointment when she stopped playing to get married. Naomi didn't stand a chance. I'm just along for the ride.'

'So not true,' Freya said.

Once again Eustace felt himself singled out for not having a mother who pushed him relentlessly or even at all. He did not admit this however, covering up by making the others laugh with an entirely untrue story of how his mother used to go through his weekly practice book and quiz him to check he had done everything listed there.

'Have you done D minor? Well, have you?' rapidly became a catchphrase the others repeated to each other as supper progressed and he felt guilty for turning his mother into a joke.

After supper, because apparently it was some kind of tradition, those who had been before led all the others down to a recreation room in the basement where there was a ping-pong table. There were only two bats but they played an elimination game called Round the Table. This involved everyone squeezing into a circle revolving around the table, hitting the ball just once then slamming the bat back down for the next person behind them. It was easy enough to start with but, as people were eliminated for failing to snatch the bat in time or wildly mis-swiping the ball, the atmosphere became hysterical. Eustace surprised himself by staying in quite long. The last two, reduced to having to spin once on the spot between hits, were Naomi and Freya, both experts and briefly savage in their determination to win. When Freya caught Naomi out with an especially fast return, Naomi shouted, 'Did you do the D minor? Well, did you?' so that Eustace knew his joke about his mother had spread to other tables. They played twice more until Magda fetched them out via the door into the garden.

Girls his own age were a rarity, something Eustace had not known since the primary-coloured idyll of his Walliscote kindergarten class before starting at St Chad's. He realized half-way through the furious, clattering progress of the third game that girls on the course had been a source of dread to him. He had worried their presence would expose or test him, that, being male, he'd be expected to approach them in some peculiarly male manner. He had foolishly made no allowances for their being free agents and was surprised to find them approaching him, talking to him and, strangest of all, finding him funny. He had never thought of himself as funny before, apart from privately with Vernon, thinking himself strange and intense. Perhaps girls' humour was different to boys', relying more on words and less on physicality?

As they took their seats in the minibuses he found himself surrounded by girls as Fred had been on the way from the station and at supper. They were very inquisitive, he discovered. He had thought the conversation at Ancrum would be all of music, but they wanted to know where he lived, if he had siblings, what he did for pleasure. As he tried to answer them in ways he hoped would hold their interest or make them laugh or like him, he realized he was shaping a persona, a version that was and wasn't quite himself. It was at once protection and another source of worry. Could these girls, from unhappy Freya to the two contrasting sisters who lived in a very grand public school where their father was organist, tell he was not like other boys? Could they sense it off him, like a sweet, unmanly smell? Was that why they seemed so immediately confiding and comfortable with him as they weren't, say, with the older boys? Perhaps they were unconsciously treating him as another girl?

When they returned to the house they were directed to the ballroom where chairs and music stands had been set up, not in a conventional orchestral layout but in two generous semi-circles facing another chair, which, in its emptiness, radiated a kind of power. Like most of the furniture he had glimpsed in the house, the chairs were antiques, an array of dining chairs, many of which seemed still to have their original upholstery on them, the silk rotten from sunshine, with horsehair and wadding showing through in places. They all took their instruments and bows and clustered the cases together in a big bay window. Suddenly Jean was among them, also holding her cello and bow. She was smiling. It was as though the palpable excitement in the room and the simple presence of young players keen to play gave her joy.

'Sit wherever you like,' she called out. Her voice was quite high but commanding, her accent evocative of the past, like that of an old BBC announcer. She wore brown leather court shoes, a tweed skirt and a pink silk blouse. With her thick, unruly hair and lack of make-up or jewellery, and her craggy bird-of-prey profile, she could not have been less like Carla. She would have looked quite at home serving tea and slices of cake at the Women's Institute. And yet something in her voice, in her effortless authority, made him want to please her any way he could. Suddenly she pointed to the chair nearest her.

'Sit here, Eustace, so I can hear you.'

She sat in the central chair, facing them all, rapidly tuned her cello then played an A for them all to tune to. She smiled around the room as they tuned. Her posture was extraordinarily upright. He couldn't help but notice the way she stuck out her left foot just as Carla had taught him to do from the start.

'Chord of C major,' she called out. 'Any note in the triad you like.' Lots of people started on a bottom G or a C then changed their minds. Eustace picked the E above middle C as it was easy to tune.

She looked around her as the chord hummed and buzzed. He noticed she was playing a high C, in thumb position. She had found it without so much as a glance.

'And listen. And tune to each other. Good. Now C minor.'

Eustace obediently shifted down a semitone to E flat, again a note he felt confident finding and tuning.

'Everyone who's on the fifth, sharpen it. That's better. Now for something fairly unrelated. F major.'

There was a momentary hesitation then a blurring as people chose their notes, then a condensing of harmony so pleasing he couldn't help but smile. Jean looked around the room and smiled back at him.

'Now. Anyone born in January, add in an E flat.' She unerringly took in that Eustace and Freya had each added the dominant seventh. 'Only two of you! So. Quieter. If you can't hear Eustace and Freya, you're too loud. Balance to them. That's it. So. Good.' She held up an eloquently bony hand and they all fell silent. 'Hello Rowena,' she said to the deerhound, who had briefly come to look in from the doorway. 'Later.' Rowena walked away with a sigh. 'So. I am Jean Curwen, for those of you who don't know me, and this is my calling: the cello is my life. I happen to think music, not money or being clean and tidy, or doing brilliantly at exams or being pretty, is the single most important thing in life. Music knits. It heals. It is balm to the soul but it is also the refiner's fire. It requires rigour and application and although you're only with me for this one precious week I expect rigour and application from you all while you're here. But we will also have fun.' And her face was wreathed in a mischievous smile.

'Now, before we play anything, I notice that two of you have steel strings.' There was some glancing around to spot the guilty parties – one of the older boys on viola and a girl cellist who looked about ten but was possibly just very small. 'I'll find out your reasons for playing with these later, but let me just demonstrate something. Eustace?' She stood, gave Eustace her cello to hold then held out her hand for the girl's instrument. 'May I?'

Blushing, the girl passed it to her. Jean sat again and played a little half-scale on the A string.

'Thank you.' She handed the cello back.

'Now listen.' She took her cello from Eustace and played exactly the same figure with exactly the same bowing pressure and speed. 'Do you hear the difference? Yes, gut strings are harder work, because there's a natural friction there that forces you to seek out the tone with your bow. And you can always compromise and use silver on gut, which speaks more readily than gut alone. The steel string lets you sound those notes more easily but there's a natural pulse to the gut resonance, which the steel lacks. And steely players are obliged to confect a pulse through too fast a vibrato or by gushy bowing and the effect is falsely passionate. In the worst cases it becomes hysterical. You probably think I'm quite mad. Eustace certainly does.' This with a glance at Eustace. 'But I know what I'm saying as the cello is my life, and I have been crucified for my truth.'

This last declaration came out with a terrifying crackle in her voice so that nobody knew where to look. She broke the momentary harsh atmosphere with a handclap.

'So,' she said, 'let's celebrate new friendship by playing Fauré. There are several great composers who never understood the cello or any stringed instrument really, like Wagner.' Somebody hissed theatrically. 'Yes, quite. But Fauré understood strings intimately and wrote especially well for us cellists. This is an arrangement of the *Libera Me* from his Requiem. Violins and violas, there are parts for you. The rest of you, I'll give you parts at random. Just play whatever lands up on your stand. It's a very fair arrangement. You all get the big tune at some point!'

She handed her cello to Eustace again and swiftly distributed music across the room.

'It will feel glorious playing together at last and your instinct will be to show off and play out. Please don't, even when you have the tune. This week is all about chamber music and half the art of chamber music is listening to each other. If all you can hear is you, you can't very well listen to your neighbours. So . . .'

She took back her cello with a polite, 'Thank you, Eustace,' then counted them in. 'One, two, three, four.'

Once the pizzicato introduction had begun, she sat down to join in. She was playing from memory, he noticed. She had given him a part that began with the melody. Was this on purpose, so she could hear his playing? He played it confidently, knowing two or three others were on the same line, including Naomi. It lay exactly in his comfort zone, in third and fourth positions, where he could reach for the kind of resonance Carla called *searing and true*. At least it did at first. Glancing ahead down the handwritten page, he could see there was a middle section where it strayed into thumb position.

Jean seemed to be having fun, turning her smile this way and that across the room like a lighthouse, for all that she was paying close attention to everyone's playing. She sang as she played – sang the Latin words in a high, girlish voice at odds with her leonine looks. He found he was transfixed by her long right leg and caramel-coloured court shoe thrust out to balance her bowing arm, presumably as she had taught Carla and precisely as Carla had taught him. He was moved and reassured by the familiar gesture as he was by her elegantly extended bowing arm and supple strength in her wrist as it flexed to begin each up-bow. It so mirrored Carla's technique as to be like spotting a family resemblance in a relative never met until now.

Suddenly they were in the middle section, lots of them scaling in thumb position in thirds, and it wasn't so bad because there was safety in numbers and the music was still glorious, but different, glassy and nervous. '*Tremens, tremens factus sum ego,*' Jean sang. 'But hush! Yes it's high and hard but *piano, piano*. We're scared for our lives! That's it! And here it comes again. Dum-dum. Da dum-dum. Da dum-dum. Nice rounded pizzicato hands, please. No need to be timid. It's the relentless tread of the advancing angel. It's the End of the World and there's no escape. Yes. Yes! And here's the heavenly tune again. But this time it's bigger because you've prayed and there is no hope but GOD! And GO!'

And she stopped talking to play along with the melody only now she wasn't smiling; she was in character, utterly solemn, eyes briefly closed. When they finished, she roared approval and clapped.

'Sometimes,' she said, 'I think there is no better composer for the cello than Fauré. Have any of you learnt his sonatas yet? Or the piano quartets and trio?' Naomi put up her hand. 'Naomi!' Jean said. 'Lucky, lucky girl. At least one group will learn Fauré this week. Why is Fauré so great? He has purity of purpose. He is a scholar yet he delights in pure harmony. So. Have we time?' She glanced at her tiny, ladylike wristwatch. 'Yes. So. Back to the beginning. Do you all know what *Libera Me* means?'

'Save me?' Eustace boldly suggested.

'Yes. It is one of the prayers near the end of the Latin Requiem or mass for the dead. Spare me Lord from eternal death on that terrible day. Which day, dear Freya?'

Barely audibly, still wearing her woolly hat, Freya murmured something.

'Yes, the end of the world. And look what Fauré does! The pizzicato is relentless. It is the thing you cannot escape. It is your fate. Dum-dum. Da dum-dum. Da dum-dum. Or perhaps it's the beating of your frightened heart. But then the prayer!' She played the first phrase of the melody. 'The prayer is a melody that would unlock heaven. It's saying sorry, sorry for all my dreadful sins but it's also saying PLEASE! So, first the pizzicato. Let's try it again and now we know what it is, that it's Fate, it's terrifying, I want it *energized*. Can you do that? Of course you can! And—' She laughed. 'One, two, three, four.'

They played it again, only this time instead of joining in, she walked among them, now conducting, now simply crying out little phrases of encouragement, now singing in Latin in that high girlish voice. She was quite mad and utterly wonderful and Eustace would have followed her barefoot into a desert.

At home Eustace always had a bath before going to bed. It would have felt quite wrong putting his pyjamas on dirty. The other boys in the room just stood around brushing their teeth at the bedroom sink then pulled on pyjamas or, in the case of Fred, got into bed in their pants. He decided to seize the chance of a bath, guessing there would be competition for it in the morning. It ran slowly, with much coughing and gurgling from the pipes, which he hoped wasn't bothering people, and the chilly little room soon filled with comforting steam. The bath was extremely narrow, chosen to save hot water in the washing of children, or maids perhaps, so soon filled. He lay back, staring at cobwebs on the sloping ceiling nearby, feeling the chipped enamel hug his hips and, as usual, avoided looking at his body. The hot water stung where he had used the hair remover the night before.

On the wall to one side in a battered bamboo frame hung a large reproduction of Augustus John's Madame Suggia, demonstrating her formidable swan bowing technique. Like Jean's extended left foot, it was another family resemblance, evoking his earliest lessons with Carla, before she gave up her flat in Weston and moved to Clifton.

Quite possibly Carla had lain in this very bath at his age, though Naomi had implied that the rooms in the girls' wing were a little less spartan, as Jean's attitude to the differing needs of the sexes was quite conventional. He looked at Madame Suggia's magnificently haughty pose and thought of Carla's pretty handwriting spelling out the principles of good wrist and upper arm pronation. He remembered the curious thrill when she had first explained the term *panâche*.

The long evening had left him keyed up with its rush of unfamiliar people and new sensations. He was worried he still hadn't learnt everyone's names, and the boys his age were rather daunting, with their offhand familiarity with London and its great concert halls, the authority with which they recommended this or that brand of string or rosin and, most especially, with the casually shared assumption that they were all going to pursue music as a career. But he knew already that he wanted nothing more than to return there as one of Jean's full time students.

He was startled by a desire to cry and let out a little silent sob before stifling the urge with a hot, wet flannel across his face. He missed home he realized, as he never had on the nights he had spent in Clifton, missed his deeply carpeted bedroom and bathroom where the bath didn't pinch or scratch, missed his father's nervous good humour and his mother's casual glamour.

There was laughter in the corridor. Two of the older boys were talking quietly but their broken voices rumbled. He smelled tobacco and realized they must be smoking out of the little window off the end of the attic corridor beside the bathroom door. He tugged the flannel off his face, pinched his nose and plunged his head beneath the water. There was a large bottle of Vosene on the bath's edge. It smelled pleasantly of hot summer roads.

This unfamiliar pang he felt was homesickness, he knew. He recognized the symptoms from William Mayne novels about children sent away to boarding school but hadn't realized it could affect you in your teens. It made him want to live and study here all the more; like a thumb sliced open on an A string, it was part of the necessary pain of passion.

CHAPTER FOURTEEN

Eustace assumed Jean assembled a programme of compositions on the basis of the number of instruments represented
on the course, but it was tempting to think she *cast* the
pieces like roles in a drama after only one evening of hearing everyone play for her, sensing whatever natural affinities
emerged within the group. Ironically, given that most of
them had probably neglected sport and the development of
their bodies to allow more time in which to hone their technique, chamber music was just like sport. Having the wrong
player on the team pulled it down while being picked for a
team of a higher standard than yours could help raise your
game. And just as in the worst times of school sport there
was the abiding horror of not being selected or pointedly
being selected only when there was nobody better on offer.
At least they weren't lined up while two captains took turns
to choose their teams.

Eustace dressed and came downstairs ahead of the other
boys who, as he'd predicted, were queuing up to use the
one bathroom and making ribald jokes about bad smells
and people taking too long.

He met Naomi in the kitchen, where she was chatting in
impressively fluent-sounding German to one of the full
time students, who was solemnly layering some kind of
smoked fish on to toast for herself while Naomi stirred a

double boiler of porridge. The student was dark and pretty but grave, which Eustace instinctively trusted.

'*Guten morgen*,' she told him.

'*Guten morgen*,' he replied haltingly; Naomi giggled.

'*Ich heisse Brigitte*,' Brigitte said, tapping her chest where a little gold crucifix dangled. '*Und du?*'

'Er . . .' Eustace began.

Naomi prompted him, '*Und Ich* . . .'

'Ah, yes. *Und Ich, Ich heisse Eustace.*'

'Hey, Eustace,' she said with a brief flash of good humour.

'Brigitte has to speak German to us at all times, even if we don't understand it,' Naomi explained, 'because Jean thinks it's good for us and because it's the language of Bach, of course.'

She served them porridge and invited him to join her in having both demerara sugar and sliced banana on top. She explained her and Ralph's *famously unhinged* mother was German and had spoken nothing but her own language with them at least until they started school. He noticed how she kept touching her hacked-off hair and wondered if she was regretting having cut it so impulsively.

Suddenly there was a rush of people for breakfast. Naomi and Eustace bunched up in a corner of the long kitchen table with a pot of tea and Brigitte fled with her fishy toast and a murmured greeting. Eustace was dying to join everyone in examining the announcement Jean and Fraser had pinned up, which he had failed to notice when he first came in, but would have had to ask Naomi to get up to do so. She saw his eyes flick towards it repeatedly and smiled.

'Don't worry,' she said. 'You're not playing De Fesch

with those stuck-up girls from Cheltenham. Jean's put you with us to learn the Schubert quintet. Just the slow movement, I think. She must have been impressed by your pizz last night. And you've got your lesson with her straight after lunch, which is good as it gets it out of the way. Mine isn't until Thursday, so it'll loom.'

Freya was still wearing her hat, although the kitchen was probably the warmest room in the house on account of the Aga on which Ralph and Fred were now making industrial quantities of toast. She granted Eustace the nearest he had seen her produce to a full smile and stirred a half-teaspoon of honey into a mug where she had poured hot water over a slice of lemon. She pulled a face when Eustace gestured to the remains of his porridge.

'I can't keep anything down before lunch,' she said quietly.

'You're playing with us,' Naomi told her. 'Schubert quintet, slow movement.'

'Oh. And I'd been looking forward to a week of playing with those . . .

'Ssh,' Naomi warned, glancing over Freya's shoulder.

Eustace saw she meant a pair of tall, sharp-elbowed sisters from Cheltenham who had spent much of the previous evening telling anyone who would listen that their father had just finished recording a new Beethoven cycle with his quartet, which put all previous recordings in the shade.

'The Alice Bands,' he said. It was the nickname he had thought up in the bath the previous night. He was gratified when Naomi nearly sloshed her tea.

Because they didn't need a piano, they were assigned the

dining room to practise in. This lay across the way from the kitchen and similarly felt as though it was in a basement because you could only see out of the windows and across the garden if you stood up on tip-toes. It had been the servants' hall, Ralph explained.

'They didn't want servants looking out too easily. Here. Give me a hand.'

Eustace helped him rumble the table against one wall to give them enough space to set five old dining chairs in a circle.

'Jean says they're just the right height and encourage good posture,' Naomi said. 'Though that's only true if you get one whose seat isn't collapsing. Here. The hard ones are best for cellists,' she added, setting out two hard chairs side by side so that Eustace didn't need the cushioned one he had just picked up.

They had just set up their stands and begun to tune when their viola player arrived. He was an older boy, tall with striking black hair and blue eyes. Eustace hadn't noticed him the night before.

'I'm Turlough,' he said, with a shy smile around the circle and they all gave their names.

'You're Irish,' Ralph said. 'Sorry.'

'Stating the obvious,' Naomi said.

'Yes,' Turlough said. 'My flight from Dublin only got in first thing. Who's got a good A here?'

'Perfect pitch,' Freya muttered from under her hat and gave them all her A to tune to.

The music had been left in there for them. It was

interesting, Eustace thought, that Ralph and his sister took the first violin and cello parts as though by right and equally interesting that neither he nor Freya demurred. But perhaps chamber music, all music in fact, relied on such natural hierarchies. As the only viola, Turlough sat between the two paired instruments like a referee.

'So who's the second cello for this?' he asked, when they had tuned.

'Me,' Eustace said.

'Much the most important line in this movement,' Turlough said and winked at him.

Wishing he didn't blush so easily, Eustace glanced to Naomi's part and saw that it was a mass of long-held notes compared to his. And then suddenly Ralph was counting them in and they were playing.

As with the Fauré the night before, he sensed it was a piece he ought to know. The movement was slightly baffling. It began with one of those passages where time seemed almost to stand still. Ralph played a hesitant sort of interrupted monologue on the violin to which Eustace's cello responded with a sequence of pizzicato phrases while the other three players sustained harmonies that shifted so slowly the changes in tonality were barely detectable. It was like watching a square of moonlight slowly move across a floor. Then came a quite different, stormy middle section, in which Eustace finally got to snatch up his bow to play a repetitive figure that seemed to power the storm along until, in a magical transition, the stillness of the opening section returned, but somehow transformed by the knowledge of darkness at its heart. The square of moonlight was no longer just that but moonlight in a prison cell or stealing across the lino of a hospital ward.

He had never played with such strong, confident musicians, apart from in his lessons with Carla and Ebrahim. They were perfectly in tune; they made no mistakes, so far as he could see. You would never have guessed they were sight-reading. They somehow found space around their playing to watch one another, to smile, to communicate. In particular the tone Turlough produced from his viola was quite unlike the rather woolly one Eustace was accustomed to hearing from the viola player at St Chad's.

The experience was so intense that it left Eustace a little shaky and he was relieved that everyone else had so much to say the moment they finished that it gave him time to recover and quickly to pencil in some fingering that had come to him as they played.

They made a second attempt at the first section. Eustace had his back to the door, so only heard it softly open and close as they played. Then he saw Turlough and Freya glance up. They stopped as agreed just at the transition to the middle section and he heard Jean's voice behind him. He hadn't realized she had been standing so close.

'Thank you,' she said, briefly placing a hand on Naomi and Eustace's shoulders. 'Isn't it an extraordinary movement?'

They all nodded, shy suddenly.

'Have any of you played it before?'

Everyone said yes. Eustace must have looked surprised.

'And they didn't tell you? Oh, that was mean. You did

well, Eustace. One of the hardest things about pizzicato is
that it goes downhill. Very hard to control its tempo and
not rush. Ralph and Eustace, you're already getting the
hang of that exchange. Although it feels terribly exposed
for you both. In a way the hardest thing is sustaining those
long, long chords.'

'We were just talking about that, Mrs Curwen.'

'Turlough, isn't it?'

'Yes.'

'I pronounced it right?'

He nodded, with a grin.

'You all call me Jean, here. Mrs Curwen sounds as
though she breeds shelties and has no sense of humour.
And what did you decide?'

'I said I thought it was like staggered breathing in a
choir,' Naomi said. 'That perhaps we should aim to change
bows at different times.'

'Hmm. Yes. And did it work?'

Freya smiled.

'Not sure, eh? It is just hard. But Schubert was a string
player. He never asks the impossible the way Tchaikovsky
does. Let's just hear the three of you for a bit without Eustace and Ralph.'

She pronounced Ralph *Rafe*, at which Naomi gave Eustace a sort of secret smile with just her eyes. Jean counted
them in and walked slowly around them in a circle as they
played. Eustace took the opportunity to gaze full on at
Turlough. He had tugged off the jersey he had been wearing when he came in and his striped T-shirt revealed
very pale arms with well developed muscles, as though he

rowed boats when not playing the viola. As he bowed, his forearm actually rippled. It was in oddly manly contrast to the child's Timex he wore.

'That's it,' Jean said softly as she walked. 'Try to keep those chord changes so together and smooth that we hardly notice them happen. Smoother bow changes. That's more like it. Thank you.'

She clapped her hands and the three of them stopped playing. Turlough looked directly at Eustace in a way that made him sure he'd seen him watching. Freya scratched her scalp under her hat with the tip of her bow. As she talked, Jean rested a hand on Freya's shoulder very kindly, as if to show she knew it could not be spoken of but that she understood that she wore the hat because she was unhappy and felt self-conscious without it even though it drew attention to whatever lay underneath.

'Now let me hear those first thirty bars again with all of you. Ralph, what do you think this is about?'

Ralph paled. Eustace had already picked up from talking to him that his approach to music was deeply technical and that Jean's narrative interpretation made him uncomfortable.

'I'm not sure,' he said at last.

She laughed. 'I do like a man who says nothing when there's nothing to say. Well it's Deutsch 956 – opus 163 posthumously – so it's very, very late. He finished it just two months before his death. He almost certainly knew he was dying. He was desperately ill and being treated with mercury. We know that he wrote this, along with the great last three piano sonatas, just months from his death at only thirty-one – and that a few years earlier he had writ-ten these words. *On the road to martyrdom, nearing eternal ruin, my life is annihilated in the dust; a prey to unheard-of grief – kill it and kill me myself.* So imagine! His bones are in constant pain, all his body hair has fallen out or been shaved. Light hurts his eyes. He has pustules all over and he has lesions in his throat and on his tongue that mean he can no longer sing his songs or talk to friends. And yet he writes this! This wonder! Now Ralph, you're a sensible, scientific man just as dear Freya here is a sensible, scientific woman so let's not talk sad stories, let's talk the-ory. What key are we in?'

'E major?' Freya said it as a question but it was clear and they all knew it.

'Yes. Sunniest of keys for these strange, still outer sec-tions. But then where do we go? I bet Eustace knows.'

'F minor,' said Eustace.

'And is that odd?'

'Well it's completely unrelated to E major,' Naomi offered.

'Exactly! And it erupts into this tranquillity but the tranquillity isn't quite the same after. Traces of the tempest remain, see? There?' Jean leaned to point over Naomi's shoulder at her music. 'Right near the end he dips back into F minor then out again into E major. It's as though he's lifting a trapdoor in the floor in front of you to reveal the abyss. I always think it's rather terrifying. But the hard thing is not to over-egg it. It's Schubert, not Mahler. So, young Ralph,' she laughed, 'bearing all that grimness in mind, have another go. Remember it's a conversation, not a solo. Chamber music is always a conversation, even when only one of you is talking. But what's so strange and sad here is that the violin doesn't get proper answers. The second cello gives dusty answers, almost echoes. They're like poor Echo following Narcissus around, if you like, and Ralph says *I'm so sad* and all Eustace can answer is *So sad*. And now The Madwoman will shut up and let you play.'

But then she continued, 'Just two more things! You three, with your long, held notes, try thinking of them as lights. These two are walking sadly through the world's most beautiful wood at dusk and you three are like film lighting men holding them in this halo as their conversation, their circular conversation, winds on towards the eruption. And finally, finally, ask yourselves if the E major is as happy as it seems. Or is it like moonlight on the face of a dying man? So. Off you go.'

They lifted their bows and began the movement again. She had given them no technical advice whatsoever, just talked at them, ranted almost. And yet it seemed to Eustace their playing was changed for, as he concentrated on timing his pizzicato answers precisely, trying to make them sad echoes of Ralph's questions, he found he was picturing the Fort at home, in autumn, with piles of dead leaves and him walking a few paces behind Vernon, and finding nothing he said could catch his attention or make him turn around to face him again.

She left them alone soon after that, listening long enough to hear some of the middle section and telling Eustace they could look at that together in his afternoon session. They were playing when she left and continued until Freya complained that she had flunked an entry and wanted to try it again. Then Naomi said,

'You know this means she has singled us out?'

'What for?' Turlough asked warily.

'She usually leaves supervision of the morning sessions to Fraser and the others. But on most courses she picks one group and visits them every day and makes their piece the finale on the last night. Last time it was those sisters from Hungary, remember?'

'How could I forget?' Ralph sighed.

'Isn't that unfair on the others?' Eustace asked. 'I mean, everyone has paid to be here.'

'Music's never fair,' Freya told him. 'Like beauty.'

'It's good Jean wants to work with you on this,' Naomi added. 'How are you bowing that figure in the middle section?'

He demonstrated his idea, slurring the triplets. She frowned.

'I think that's too uneven, and bloody hard to keep up. Try just bowing it out; you'll end on an up bow, I know, which feels odd but actually that gives a nice propulsion and lets you swell into each repeat of the figure and start again with a wallop of a down bow.'

He tried it. She was right; that bowing had far better momentum. He sensed Naomi was right about most things.

At around eleven there were footsteps on the stairs and a rush of noise and chat in the kitchen as the others broke for coffee. By unspoken agreement, the five of them played on, working on the passionate middle section, and Eustace couldn't decide if they were showing off or simply single-mindedly dedicated, or both at once.

They broke when everyone else had gone upstairs again, stopping for instant coffee and banana bread, which Freya insisted they spread with butter and honey for energy. She wasn't sad, he was coming to realize, but furious. From little things she let slip, she revealed she had a great store of anger, like a banked-up boiler hotbox, against her school, her father, her teacher, her hair and most other people. She had extremely high standards about everything and he was honoured when she began to smile at his comments.

As they stood around the kitchen table munching their buttery honeyed banana bread, stretching out their backs after long sitting and dazed from intense focus on the Schubert in a badly lit room, Freya suddenly said, 'It's appalling you're not being allowed to take up that scholarship.'

'The important thing is my lessons with Carla. And those are nothing to do with school.'

'I can't believe you're taught by Carla Gold,' Naomi said.

He felt a glow of pride.

'I heard her play Beethoven in Cork,' Turlough said. 'She's pretty stellar.'

'Doesn't mean she's a good teacher,' Naomi said.

'She has *such* good hair,' Freya said and pushed angrily at her hat.

Lunch was a cauldron of vegetable soup and a mound of bread rolls heated in the Aga. The soup was thin and under-seasoned but there was a big block of cheddar to grate into it. The Klengel Variations for cello quartet were being worked on, a Haydn piano trio and the Fauré one.

Everyone enjoyed saying how amazing their piece was, but how challenging, how much fun they'd had with whichever tutor came in to work with them on it. Nobody mentioned Jean visiting their rehearsal and the quintet kept quiet about it. Pudding was tart apples and woolly pears.

Eustace's session with Jean was the first of the afternoon and she had written *BE PROMPT!* in capital letters at the top of the schedule so he decided to go straight to the library so as to practise there while he waited for her. But Jean was already in there when he arrived, eating the last of a plate of oatcakes, sliced apples and fingers of cheese.

'Oh sorry,' he said, making to back out. 'I'm early.'

'Come in, dear Eustace,' she said. 'It's quite all right. Punctuality is so important for musicians. You'll hardly ever be working alone and one late person holds everybody up. You set yourself up over there while I finish nibbling.'

The library was a beautiful room, panelled in oak. The shelves were packed with music and books about music and composers. A watercolour of the house hung over the mantelpiece and the silk curtains and cushions on the window seats were rotting, fabric hanging in strips here and there, but the effect on a fine day was pretty, their pinks and blues faded like old flowers.

There were two chairs and stands still in place from a piano trio rehearsal that morning. He set his Schubert part and pencil on one of the stands then perched on the piano stool and played himself a D minor triad to tune to.

'I can tell who taught you,' she said, with a smile.

'I don't have a piano at home,' he admitted. 'Just a tuning fork.'

'And what more does a boy need?' she said. 'What an interesting old instrument. I couldn't help noticing last night. Could I have another look?'

She came to sit in one of the chairs and he handed it to her along with his bow. She thanked him, sounded the strings to check his tuning and flattened the C string slightly. Then she played a few bars of the middle section of the Schubert.

She didn't play out, the way the rest of them tended to, parading their big tones to one another like so many peacock tails, she played inwardly, as though to herself. And yet the tone was rich. It was like someone playing at full volume but in a distant room.

'How do you do that?' he asked.

She grinned. 'Little finger,' she said. 'He just seems to rest there but on a piano up bow he does so much. What a nice cello. Did Carla find it for you?'

'Yes. In Bristol.'

'Ah. A famously good hunting ground. Well done her. I'm rather envious. There you go. Have it back before I grow too attached. Play me that very bit, from the key change, until I tell you to stop. I'll talk probably. I talk all the time while pupils play, but keep on playing.'

She sat back on the other chair. She sat as though about to play herself, very erect, as though at table but perching almost on the chair's front.

He began to play, trying not to rush, trying to remember how the other parts had sounded above him that morning. But she didn't talk. She listened intently until he

reached the end of the arco passage and began on the pizzicato of the last third.

'Thank you,' she said. 'Good simple bowing. Some
people fiddle around with it but that's a good solution for
that figure because it gives it the right propulsion.'

'That was Naomi's suggestion,' he confessed.

'Ah. Naomi is good at bowings. You know why? She
sings! Singers get it almost instinctively because there's a
natural grammar to stresses and uplifts when we sing, as
there is when we speak.'

'Carla always tells me to sing when working out bowing,' he told her.

'Good for Carla. Now listen. I'm appalled about Clifton.
She wrote to tell me when she signed you up for the course.'

'Ah.'

'You're at a crucial stage, you see. Two years in the
wrong environment could ruin your technique.'

'Oh but I'll still be learning with her,' he assured her.
'It's just school.'

'But it's not, do you see?' Her tone became suddenly
urgent, firm. He had heard the boys talking about Jean's
notoriously swift rages but this wasn't rage so much as
caring very deeply. He could not imagine daring to look
away when she spoke like this. 'It's about nurturing. If
you're a music scholar it's a clear, unambiguous statement
of priorities. If you're just another boy in just another
school, it wouldn't matter how marvellous your teacher
was, if the lessons happen elsewhere and outside school
hours, do you see?'

'I think so,' he said, although he didn't, not really, since he had always had his cello lessons away from school.

'You enjoyed this morning, I think. Playing with the others?'

He nodded.

'I could see it the moment I came into the room,' she said. 'You were glowing with it. We must see if Carla can help set you up with a quartet or a piano trio back at home or in Bristol.'

'I'm hoping to join the youth orchestra in Weston.'

'Well that's good,' she said, 'but the trouble with orchestral playing is you're so hidden within the group it might get you into bad habits, whereas in a chamber group you're effectively a soloist whenever you play. So. Play me that section again, but I'll fill in the first cello part. It's such a strong figure, such a strong rhythm that you need to lean into the other lines but sort of pull away from them at the same time.'

He had no idea what she meant but nodded and quickly retuned while she went to collect her own cello. She sat, played her A as a cue to him to play his so that she could tune to him, then she counted them in and he began to play. To his amazement she had the first cello line by heart and, because she had no music in front of her, she watched his playing closely as she played. Her look was hawkish and unsmiling, so he focused on reading his music instead.

She broke off abruptly. 'Would you like to study here, Eustace?' she asked. 'As a full time student, I mean. Once you're sixteen?'

'I'd like that more than anything,' he said.

216

She smiled. 'Dear boy. Such enthusiasm. Well I can't promise anything. You're still very young and we'd only take you after O levels. It was different when we were based in Ladbroke Grove but it is so remote here you'd have to board and we'd have to teach you everything. And we can't do that until you get most of the other subjects out of the way. But talk it over with your parents. There are grants and scholarships you can apply for if, well, if they can't manage fees. When you come back at Easter, we can see how you're progressing and then maybe lay plans. Yes?'

'Yes.'

'Good. Now. Back to the beginning and show me that pizzicato again. You're in dialogue with the violin, echoing him at least, sad little echoes, but we need a sense of direction in each phrase like the one you'd produce if you were bowing, not plucking . . .'

After the lesson he couldn't put his cello back in the ballroom because a group was rehearsing Klengel in there. A log fire had been lit in the intervening sitting room, as it had turned chilly since the morning, and Freya, Naomi, the Alice Bands and several other girls were flopped in there across the sofas and chairs, worn out from practising. He lingered a while to warm his back and pet Rowena, who was slumped on the rug before the fire, mumbling a toy made from an old sock stuffed with other socks and knotted. But they were talking about teachers and players he didn't know, then Naomi condemned someone's description of a concert programme as *so provincial* in a way that made him uncomfortable. Besides, his head was still buzzing from the things Jean had told him and he dreaded having them

217

made ordinary by thoughtless cross-examination so he gave the deerhound one last lingering rub behind the ears, which she seemed to like, then quietly slipped off upstairs.

He had thought to lie on his bed for a while so he would be at his best when they played again later. Turlough was practising Bach in the bathroom across the way. It took Eustace a few moments to place a piece he recognized as the sarabande from the second cello suite because it was up an octave. It hadn't occurred to him before that, of course, any cello piece could be borrowed for the viola, or vice versa, with only this simple transposition, as their string arrangement was the same.

Turlough didn't break off diffidently as Eustace would have done, but then Eustace would never have practised facing a wide-open door as though playing to an audience. He was standing with his back to the window and afternoon sunlight formed a halo around his curly hair and made his expression hard to read. Eustace had thought to walk heedlessly into their room, which he saw through its open door was mercifully empty, but Turlough shifted position in such a way as he played that the light fell full on his handsome face and their eyes met. After which it would have felt rudely dismissive to walk on, so he simply sat on the creaking floorboards and leaned against the wall to watch and listen until the movement came to an end.

Clapping would have felt silly and he was learning from the others to be cooler in his responses.

'That works well,' he said. 'I like the way you didn't draw out the last phrase the way some cellists do.'

'Thanks,' Turlough said, scratching an itch on his thigh

218

with his bow adjuster. 'Oh my God, you just had your Jean session. How was it?' His lazy smile did something to Eustace's stomach.

'She's incredible,' Eustace said. 'It's odd because, compared to my teacher at home, she doesn't give much technical instruction. It's more that she just inspires or talks in terms of phrasing or feeling.'

'It's flattery,' Turlough said. 'She takes your technique as read and talks to you as a fellow musician. Bet she'd have the same effect on a clarinetist or a trumpeter.'

'But she— Well, she cares so deeply about the music you feel you're sort of doomed to disappoint her just by being human.'

'Listen, you did well this morning. Weren't you intimidated?'

'By you lot? Of course. You're all so good. But you sort of swept me along with you.'

Then Turlough just looked at him without speaking so that Eustace rather wished he hadn't stupidly sat himself on the floor like a child and could just stroll on his way like an adult. 'You kept looking at me as though you wanted something from me,' Turlough said at last.

Eustace laughed and picked at some hard skin that was cracking painfully beside his left thumbnail. It would hurt if he had to play thumb position tonight but he knew better than to let it show or to risk bad tuning by wearing a plaster on it.

'Don't be daft,' he muttered, mortified at having his thoughts so easily read.

'It's a cruel truth,' Turlough told him, 'but you'll find the boys who get kissed the most tend to be the ones who want it least. Wanting is never sexy.'

He retuned and began to play the first minuet from the same suite, turning aside slightly as he did so as if to release an unwelcome supplicant from an audience.

Eustace scrabbled to his feet and continued to the bedroom. Luckily there was nobody else in there so he could flop on to his narrow bed and clutch the pillow for comfort. That morning the bed across from his had not been claimed but now, he saw, there was someone's holdall and coat dropped on it. The holdall handle had an airline tag attached so he guessed the things belonged to Turlough.

He rolled over, clutching the pillow again but facing the wall now. The sound of Turlough's viola was inescapable, warm, insistent. Why had he felt the need to say anything? It was simple cruelty. Somehow Eustace felt far more vulnerable to sharp words there, in a house full of glorious music and more sensitive, interesting company than he had ever had at St Chad's, but perhaps that was because he had always faced school on the defensive, expectations low and pre-armed against cruelty. He wished he had not come upstairs. He wished he had stayed safely by the fire with the deerhound and the girls. But then he fell sound asleep.

When he woke the viola had fallen silent and the light had changed. Quite unused to falling asleep in daylight, he was disorientated and took a moment or two to remember where he was and why. Then he sat up abruptly, worried it was late and he had missed supper.

Turlough was sitting on the neighbouring bed watching

him. He smiled perfectly kindly. 'I was about to wake you,' he said, 'but you looked so peaceful.'

'Is it suppertime?'

'Uh-huh. Time for another pear and cheese salad or whatever. I'm sure Jean puts us all on vegetarian diets because she thinks meat arouses passions. That woman has a deep mistrust of sex.'

It was the first time Eustace had heard anyone speaking disrespectfully of Jean and he was shocked. He sat up fully, swinging his feet on to the narrow stretch of old carpet between them.

'I quite like salad,' he said, which made Turlough smile.

'Do you want that kiss now?' he asked.

Eustace was trying to think of some suitably cool retort when Turlough abruptly took his head between his hands and kissed him full on the mouth. Once, twice, then a third time more lingeringly, pressing Eustace's lips apart with his tongue. He withdrew a little, gazing at him then rubbed his rather rough thumb across his lips, as though to wipe the kiss away, and said, 'Come on. Supper.' He jumped up and hurried out, leaving Eustace to compose himself and follow.

The week was at once so repetitive – in the unvarying routines of working on the Schubert in the mornings and playing *en masse* in the evenings and the equally unvarying menus at lunch and supper – and so rich in its content, that Eustace could not have looked back with any certainty and said what happened when every day something new was thrown into the mix. One day Jean made everyone lie on the floor of the darkened ballroom and *Listen. Really listen* to one of the new Philharmonia Hungarica recordings of the Haydn symphonies. Another afternoon he found himself roped into sight-reading a Dvořák string quartet just for fun. Although he was shy of them, behind his attempts to play the clown, he found he loved the novelty of spending time with the girls either flopped sleepily on sofas around the fire or talking intently at the kitchen table or, when the sun shone, on the flight of stone steps at the house's front.

It was odd, perhaps, to have travelled so far without seeing anything of the local countryside and its buildings but he felt he was exploring in his head, through the company of bright, gifted people and the great luxury of being somewhere where music was not a hobby or a mere accomplishment.

He experienced two instances of Jean's furies. One came the morning after his lesson with her. It wasn't late – perhaps five to eight – and they were all awake but enjoying just lolling in bed reading or chatting about nothing in particular when there was a sudden thunder of feet along the corridor, the door flew open and Jean marched among their beds with a face like thunder.

'Dairymen, nurses and miners have all been at work for hours,' she said. 'What on earth do you think you're all doing?'

The other instance involved Haydn, with whom she was currently obsessed. It was an afternoon and, on a whim, he and Pierre and one of the Alice Bands had stumbled on the so-called *Gypsy Rondo* and Pierre was driving them into playing it ever faster, which was fun: music as sport. The cello part was extremely simple, so it was easy enough for Eustace to keep up and join in the fun. And suddenly Jean burst through the library doorway and stood there glaring.

'How *dare* you?' she asked. 'How *dare* you play like that? Men and women were taken out of Viennese and Hungarian orchestras and sent to their deaths simply for being Romany or Jewish or communist, many of them great musicians. The Nazis made some of them play in the camps to cover the cries from the gas chambers, and still you have the ...' She was so furious her thick hair seemed to be crackling and she was having trouble finding the words. 'You have the *vulgarity* to play like that! No more Haydn for you this afternoon.'

She scrabbled the music off their stands and then, aware perhaps that she had made a spectacle of herself, strode out with it under her arm and slammed the door behind her.

In neither case did any trace of her anger show when they saw her next. It rose and spent itself like a summer storm and left only her usual smiles and intensity behind it. But in both cases it left Eustace only wanting the more abjectly to please her.

As for their morning sessions on the Schubert, he would not have thought it possible to work on one movement in such detail, day after day, and not become bored. But he was far too intent on perfection for boredom. He was particularly fascinated by their discussions about bowing, their experiments with trying a shared phrase now this way, now that, until they settled on unanimity. And as a fellow cellist, Naomi made him see how his fingering choices affected the sound of a phrase as much as his bowing ones, the same notes played in fourth position on one string could sound mellower but less confident than in first on the next string up, just as his first finger could lend an unwanted strength to a note better sounded with his weaker fourth. The course wasn't a competition; they were all friends on the same voyage of discovery.

'But it is a competition, of course,' Turlough said. 'It's inevitable. One group will play better on the last night and everyone wants it to be theirs.'

'We'll win,' Naomi said. 'We've got the best piece.'

It was impossible not to catch snatches of the other groups at work, especially as unofficial pressure mounted and some groups began to rehearse in the afternoons as well, casually demoralizing one another with a cascade of Vivaldi or a lush serving of Klengel's purple harmonies. But theirs was the only piece on the programme that could be described as intense. It had a compelling inwardness to it they felt sure would give them an advantage if they could only achieve perfection. Ralph practised on his own so hard that the girls began to speak of him in hushed tones as of some martyr and Eustace found himself fretting about things that had never especially bothered him until now, like how to maintain a smooth pressure at the very tip of the bow or how much vibrato to use on his pizzicato to be resonant without being, dread words, *vulgar* or *hysterical*.

As for his feelings for Turlough, these lurched between elation and humiliated despair because Turlough could go within a minute from smiling on him like the sun to blanking him out entirely. Just when he began to suspect Turlough gained some pleasure from treating him cruelly, Turlough would make a discreet gesture to follow him from a room and would lead him to a store cupboard or the cellar or a remote corridor to kiss him again.

Eustace was quite prepared, after his explorations with Vernon, to do more but all they ever seemed to do was kiss. And because Turlough, at nearly sixteen, was so much older, he didn't feel he could take the lead. And he began to sense Turlough liked him to be utterly passive, childlike, innocent even. Just once he let his hand touch the front of Turlough's jeans as they kissed in the chilly bathroom after the others had gone to bed. Turlough immediately pressed him against the wall so tightly he suspected he was taking his own private pleasure. He tried not to dwell on the fact that Turlough showed no curiosity about exploring Eustace's body in turn.

He was interested that none of the girls seemed to have the least idea about Turlough, although one or two of them knew him quite well from other courses and youth orchestras. Naomi clearly had a crush on him, as she reddened whenever she spoke to him or he to her, even in rehearsal, where she was normally so bossy. And Turlough flirted with the girls, or teased them at least. Certainly his regular absences with Eustace seemed to have aroused no suspicion among the other boys in their room but then, Eustace was coming to realize, he was more aware than most of them; taking their music so seriously seemed to have put the usual preoccupations of adolescence on hold. Looking around the room as they were brought together to sing madrigals or to play arrangements from Bach or Purcell of an evening, he couldn't imagine any of them doing anything so perverse as buying a porn mag and giftwrapping it in order to seduce a school friend.

Despite being married Jean retained this same purity and, one sensed, encouraged it in others. When they had discussed various musicians, not just cellists and conductors but composers as well, it was clear that she frowned on anyone associated with love affairs or scandal. Wagner one would expect to be disapproved of by her, and Carl Orff, as an enthusiastic Nazi, was not to be named, but her condemnation of Jacqueline du Pré came as a surprise. For her, it seemed, a preoccupation with sex or a prioritizing of it overlapped in her mind with that other crime against music: *hysteria*.

Prompted by Naomi and Ralph phoning home from the guesthouse after their penultimate supper there, when everyone else had gone down for the traditional minutes of noisy release afforded by the ping-pong table, he remembered guiltily that he had done neither of the things he had promised to do: send a postcard or call his parents to reassure them he had arrived safely. He waited a polite distance from the little telephone booth in the guesthouse lobby, pretending to read *Horse and Hound* but observing the constrained politeness with which the siblings spoke to their parents. Then he took their place and rang home.

He let it ring and ring but there was no answer. This was odd as they rarely went out, or not together. He thought about calling the number that went through to downstairs,

226

as this would be answered by whichever nurse was on evening duty, but decided it might give the impression that he was in trouble or homesick, so he decided against it and went to join in a last session of Round the Table. By sheer fluke, he did well and ended up facing Turlough, who made him lose concentration by smiling.

When they were sent to bed later he contrived to stay awake reading until the others had turned out their lights. Turlough, who ignored bedtimes, appeared silently in the bedroom doorway, framed in the wash of light from the corridor, and gestured with his head to summon him. Running a bath by way of cover, he kissed him up against the sink, sliding hands under Eustace's pyjamas this time while firmly pushing Eustace's hands back to his sides whenever he tried to touch him in return.

'Do you want me to lie you on the floor now and fuck you?' he muttered.

'Yes,' Eustace told him, though in truth he was not at all sure, being fairly certain that it would hurt and that Turlough would not be gentle and wouldn't care.

Turlough pulled back in a way he had, to look at him, examine him almost. 'No,' he said with a teasing smile. 'You want it too much. Now run back to bed so I can have a quiet wank in peace.'

CHAPTER FIFTEEN

Eustace tried to stay awake after returning to bed. He even had a mad thought of getting into Turlough's bed in the darkness to wait for him. The day had been as full and stimulating as all the days at Ancrum however, and sleep soon stole over him without his noticing. When he woke the next morning, Turlough had already dressed and gone downstairs to practise in the stables before breakfast.

The kitchen was busy and noisy by the time he came down. With grinning ceremony, Fraser pushed through to the notice-board where the various timetables hung and pinned up the running order for the evening's concert, mischievously aware of the fuss it would cause in his wake.

'We're last,' Naomi told Eustace. 'Oh my God, we're last!'

Freya tugged her hat down tighter for comfort. Ralph brought them over a plate of toast he'd just made. Naomi was buttering it for them all except Freya, who preferred it dry and even then only broke it into pieces, when Ralph said,

'Who's that?'

Eustace looked up to see his father getting out of his car in the courtyard and being met by Jean, who shook his hand and led him around to the front of the house.

Eustace's mind raced. 'That's my father,' he admitted.

'How cool. He's come to hear us! He's come all that way to hear us!' Freya had rarely been so animated as she was by this idea of parental devotion.

Eustace tried to pretend this was the likely, touching explanation but found he couldn't swallow his toast. He sat on for a few minutes, willing himself back into the moment of excitement and anticipation he had been in before glimpsing his father inexplicably alone, looking pinched and drawn, and in quite the wrong place, then gave up and, with an unconvincing shrug, said he'd better go upstairs to say hello.

When he reached the hall he found Jean there with his father and, bizarrely, Turlough coming down the stairs to join them with Eustace's suitcase. The smell of burning toast around them all felt as intimately domestic as the fug of a morning bedroom. Eustace's cello was standing at his father's side already.

'Thank you, Turlough, dear,' Jean said as he set the suitcase down beside her and slipped downstairs. Turlough caught Eustace's eye as he passed. He winked but his expression was tense and unsmiling.

Jean touched an arm to Eustace's shoulder and drew him briefly to her. She had on a Norwegian jersey, which smelled of nothing more feminine than fireplaces and Rowena.

'I'm so very sorry,' she said. 'You've done so well.' She held him back from her to meet his eye. 'I'll take your line in the Schubert tonight,' she told him. 'Keep in touch and I hope we'll see you at Easter.'

She let go of him and looked at his father.

'He's a strong player,' she said. 'With good instincts. Thank you for encouraging him.'

The noise of young voices from the kitchen was swelling, presumably as Turlough passed on whatever he knew.

Eustace's father finally spoke to him. 'Your mother's been in a car crash,' he said. 'She's in hospital and . . .'

'I think,' Jean put in quietly, 'it would be best just to slip away now. Goodbyes can get so very overwhelming and everyone's wound up pretty tightly because of tonight's concert.'

'I thought you'd come to hear us play,' Eustace said.

'Sorry,' said his father and picked up the suitcase as Jean walked to the front door to let them out on to the terrace. Eustace took up his cello to follow.

'Goodbye,' she said as they passed. Eustace looked at her to say goodbye and she touched his shoulder again. 'Come back.'

Maybe she didn't voice the last but simply mouthed it; he was in a state of shock where his normal senses seemed withheld.

Jean might have hoped to see everyone tidily shepherded off to the last morning of rehearsals but had not realized his father's hire car was visible from the kitchen. As Eustace opened the back door to slide in his cello and suitcase, Naomi, Ralph and Freya came out to say goodbyes in which the emotion was muffled by the inability to ask all the questions clearly in their heads, and by the inhibiting presence of his shattered-looking father. Ralph gave him a manly handshake. Naomi gave him a swift hug and said she'd find out his address from Jean and write to him.

Freya merely stood, adjusting her hat and silently weeping. And then, realizing his father had already climbed into the car and started the engine, Eustace took his stammering leave, climbed in too and suddenly they were speeding out through the park over the little bridge, past the church and away.

'That's the guesthouse where we have all our vegetarian suppers,' he pointed out as they drove past. 'Had.'

He became aware his father smelled – which he never did usually – and had a dark spangling of bristles across his jaw. A terrible thought occurred to him, as his father sped away from some traffic lights and followed a sign for Berwick and the A1.

As always, his father had the radio tuned to *Today*. Men – it always seemed to be men – were discussing concepts that were all but meaningless to Eustace. They spoke of the economy, strikes, the Common Market, trades unions and sport: the great drift of clotted, uninvolving subject matter Vernon referred to with withering dryness as *current affairs*. He usually suspected his father only played it to cover the awkwardness of otherwise having to make conversation, especially when driving, an activity that could invite dangerous confidences. Sometimes, however, he worried that he really listened to and understood it, and that current affairs, like shaving or gardening or carving a chicken or wiring a plug, were among those things he was going to have to embrace as part of the ghastly business of becoming a man.

'Have you been up all night?' he asked eventually.

Mercifully his father turned the radio down slightly.

'I slept a bit,' he said. 'In a motorway service station somewhere. When I started falling asleep at the wheel.' He let out one of his abrupt laughs that was all nerves and no delight. 'It's a six- or seven-hour drive from here to Bristol,' he added.

'Could we maybe have some breakfast somewhere?' Eustace asked.

'Didn't you get any?'

'No. I was just about to when you arrived.'

The battling scents of air freshener and unwashed father on a yawningly empty stomach were beginning to make him feel queasy.

'Good idea,' his father said eventually. 'There's a place I noticed between Berwick and Newcastle.'

Eustace wound down his window a tiny bit. It was hot in the car and he was starting to sweat. He concentrated on breathing slowly and training his gaze on the distance. It was a shock, after the rarefied atmosphere of Ancrum and the course to be suddenly passing wool shops and butchers, to be seeing men, women and children on the street doing everyday things, none of them giving a moment's thought to Schubert's last agonies or the finer points of how developing a stronger fourth finger on the left hand could improve one's tuning. He realized that the people he had begun to think of as new friends, and not just Turlough, would think less of them for that and promptly felt guilty by association. In a similar way he realized he was resenting his mother for having had the accident more than he was worrying about her chances of survival, and that made him feel nauseous as well as bad.

They stopped at last at a roadside café where the hire car was dwarfed by parked lorries. He hesitated about leaving the cello in the car. Touchingly his father seemed to read his mind.

'We can get a table by the window so you can keep an eye out,' he said.

It was a relief to be out of the car and the smell of baked beans and fried bacon made him ravenously hungry. Without consulting him, his father ordered two full Englishes and a pot of tea from the waitress. She seemed to guess from a glance at the state of his father that they represented a family in crisis and brought them their tea immediately with a basket of buttered toast on the house. When she brought their cooked breakfasts, the helpings were huge, with fried bread and sautéed potatoes as well as everything else. Eustace shocked himself by eating almost everything: even the mushrooms, which he'd spoiled with a squirt of fartily expelled ketchup from the plastic tomato between them. It was all good, the best cooked breakfast he had ever eaten, even the worryingly pink sausage. Coming up for air, gulping the rich, brown tea the waitress had poured for them both, actually saying, *Shall I be mother?*, he saw his father had barely touched his but was cutting things up on his plate and moving them indecisively around.

'Dad?' he asked. 'Aren't you hungry? I thought you were hungry.'

'Not very,' his father said. 'Sorry.'

'That's all right.'

He didn't know why he was politely accepting his

father's apology when he'd done nothing wrong and, in any case, was wasting his money not Eustace's.

'Where did it happen?' he asked, because he didn't like the way his father had fallen so quiet since they had sat down. He thought perhaps he was intimidated by the lorry drivers reading their newspapers and smoking at the tables all around them. He was never a very manly man but Eustace knew that talking about cars and roads was a manly thing to do so thought it might help.

'She was on the motorway the other side of Bristol. Heading towards London,' his father said quietly.

Eustace found he was picturing his childhood jigsaw of England, in which each county, even tiny Rutland and two-part Flint, was a separate piece illustrating principal activities and produce. He pictured his mother's car on it as a toy one. In the wrong place.

'But why?' he asked. 'Where was she going?'

He had been fiddling with a last piece of toast, although he was quite full and couldn't imagine wanting to eat again for hours, but now looked up and saw his father's normally quizzical, smiling face crumpling up in tears. He glanced around and saw a lorry driver notice and look hastily back at his tabloid. His father let out a sort of sob, almost a honk, and there was a big drip on the end of his nose that spooled out as Eustace watched, and landed in the egg he had cut open and left to congeal.

All at once the motherly waitress was at their side. She had come from behind Eustace, taking him by surprise. 'Is everything all right with the food, only you've not—'

'It's fine,' Eustace told her. 'Delicious. Thank you.'

She frowned minutely – little more than a twitch of disapproval – and placed the bill down between them on a custard coloured saucer. But then, talking to Eustace, she added, 'There's a nice, clean washroom out the back if your daddy wants to freshen up.' And she topped up Eustace's tea from the big brown pot.

His father took the hint, after she had moved on.

'Won't be a tick,' he said and left Eustace at the table while he went in search of the lavatories. He couldn't shave out there, obviously, but he must have washed his face in the sink because his eyes looked clearer again when he came back and the front of his hair was wet. 'Right,' he said brightly, then he sat down and ate his cold breakfast slightly too fast to look entirely normal. Then he settled their bill and led the way back to the car, belching.

Eustace spotted the air-freshening device that was smelling so vile as they climbed back in. His father saw it too and shocked him by tossing it out of the window as they drove off. It was only a cheap cardboard thing from some garage but it was litter and they were not a family who dropped litter, ever. In fact he had known his father pick other people's litter up and hand it back through their car windows saying, 'I think you dropped this . . .'

They drove for six hours. More. They listened to the radio all the way and ate the Jelly Babies his father bought when they stopped for petrol. But Eustace asked no more questions and his father said absolutely nothing. Guiltily, Eustace found himself glancing at his watch as the day passed, picturing what was happening at Ancrum, the practising, the stopping for coffee and banana bread, the serious, competitive talk over soupy lunch. He tried to picture Jean Curwen playing his part with the others, then wished he hadn't because she played so well, even the mere second cello line. It would make the Schubert remarkable and something that would be talked about on the train home the next day. It would certainly eclipse any talk of Eustace and his abrupt departure.

At the hospital Eustace insisted on bringing his cello inside. The hire car was newer than their old one and had locks that worked but he suddenly knew there could be nothing worse than to come back out and find the instrument gone, or damaged in some freak accident. His father respected his wishes and winced when a larky hospital porter in the lift looked at the cello case and said,

'You come to give us all a tune, then?'

His mother was in Intensive Care. Her hair had been cut so savagely short that it stood up in tufts. There were stitches near her hairline and little cuts all over her face and neck, from the glass presumably. And there was an ugly bruise peeping out from the top of her hospital gown. She wore no lipstick. Had a nurse not guided them to the bed, Eustace would not have recognized her. She was unconscious.

He found himself waiting for her breaths and realized they were coming more slowly than usual, perhaps more slowly even than in sleep. There were tubes attached to her he did not care to examine or speculate about.

His father went off to one side of the room to talk, very quietly, with a doctor.

CHAPTER SIXTEEN

Eustace couldn't sleep. There was no reason for this. He had carefully avoided coffee. Though, of course, the lack of wine with his hospital supper meant he had gone to bed without the usual glass or three to send him off. The street seemed noisy, which was a nonsense because, even allowing for the Cromwell Road's thunder of traffic just around the corner, the room was soundproofed and he could hear no more than the vibration of taxi engines as cabs slowed or idled in passing. Perhaps it was the *lack* of usual noise that made him wakeful. No chatter of departing guests, no passing pedestrians talking loudly on their mobile phones, no beeps and clicks of cars being locked or unlocked. The bed was perfectly comfortable and supportive but it was a hospital bed, not his own. And he missed Joyce who, though nominally curled beneath the outer layer of her whippet bed beneath the bedroom radiator, had acquired a sly habit of insinuating herself on to her master's bed once he was asleep and nestling in ever closer beneath his arm or behind the crook of his knees.

Perhaps he had spent too many hours in bed already when he should have made a point of spending at least the afternoon and evening sitting upright in the room's unappealing wipe-down armchair?

He got up, walked about, performed a few of the

stretches they'd been taught in Boot Camp, drank another glass of water, had a piss then tried going back to bed. This time he actively tried to stay awake, which had worked for him in the past.

He pictured Theo, heard his rumbling voice and the teasing, deadpan humour Eustace was slowly learning to read. Although they had spoken now for hours on Skype, during which Theo had occasionally stepped back from the screen to fetch something to show him, Eustace's impression of his body remained hazy. He knew he was fit and had a neatly furred chest and a long scar under one forearm from when he had been knocked off his racing bike by a car as a teenager. He knew, if the app hadn't lied, that Theo was five foot eleven, slightly shorter than him. But he had no mental sense of his scale, having really only seen him in close up through a small screen, had no sense whether he would be wiry or bulky, whether he had the legs of a runner or a rugby player.

It was odd, too, to have no idea of how Theo smelled. He had confessed to him on one of their last conversations before they left the frank environment of the app for the politer one of face-to-face conversation, that the nearest he came to a kink was liking the smell of a man's fresh musk, to which Theo had swiftly responded with a photograph of his sweat patches after a dawn run about the camp. He had offered to send Eustace a dirty T-shirt and Eustace had been regretting ever since his coyness in batting the offer aside with a silly joke.

He watched a breeze stir the lamp-lit leaves of the plane tree outside his window and worried that he wanted their meeting to be a success so badly that his need would doom it. He knew now that Naomi was right, in the way Naomi always was, and that he had been wrong not to tell Theo about the cancer in advance. This way their first date would be about sickness not happy anticipation. He thought about ringing him but it was the middle of the night and Theo would be in transit somewhere, inhibited among strangers. Quite possibly he wouldn't answer. Then Eustace remembered he had no mobile with him and had not memorized Theo's number, so couldn't have used the payphone, even had he thought to buy credit for it before his wallet was taken beyond the lead-lined walls.

He sat up, fluffed and turned his pillows, lay back and calmed himself with a mental slideshow of the modestly rare selfies Theo had sent him since their courtship began. He reminded himself that one of the first things they had established they had in common was that they were both quite shy and self-critical. He imagined them on the houseboat at Bembridge, imagined them kissing on deck in the moonlight, water lapping below them, halyards clinking against masts in the harbour around them.

Then he tried to imagine Theo meeting his mother and stopped when he realized they were meeting, and getting on infuriatingly well, at his funeral. He tried not to think of himself as having cancer or being radioactive, so of course did both. He tried not to think about his mother.

Like most cumbersome journeys, the one to visit her had shrunk, with repetition and familiarity, to a fairly painless commute. Circle Line to Paddington, train to Bristol

Temple Meads, Number 8 bus to Clifton then a ten-minute walk towards the downs. The weekly duty visit had reintroduced him to the pleasure of reading and, since her second widowing, he had been working his way through the novels that had once so enthralled Vernon.

She lived in one of the huge, Bath stone houses out towards the zoo that might have been built for ambassadors, had Bristol been a capital. Like so much architectural pretension in the district, they were a testament to just how much money the city once generated through slaves and sugar. He vividly recalled how, in his youth, many such houses had reached their nadir, as communes and squats and student digs, their gardens forbiddingly jungly, their decoration anarchic. But property values had escalated as steeply here as in London, and it was as though the entire district had been scrubbed to newly built freshness. With their electric gates, discreet, shoe-level lighting and glimpses of security systems, it was likely that many of the houses there had been restored to a degree of luxury far above their original architect's fantasies.

Any irony in his mother having ended up in a retirement home having nominally run one herself for years was annulled by Downs Court being as far removed from cabbage water, commodes and TV lounges as a five-star country retreat was from a two-star seaside guesthouse. Each resident had their own suite with the use, at a cost, of extra bedrooms should they have guests. Breakfast was brought to their bedsides on a tray. Three-choice lunches and dinners, cooked by a talented chef, were served in the dining room or available as room service. There were on-site nursing staff, a hairdresser and beautician, a brace of handsome masseurs, classes in yoga and more vigorous exercise, a tennis court (with handsome coach) and an indoor pool. In short it was a luxury hotel and, though Eustace had nothing to do with the man in life, he was grateful to Second Husband for posthumously settling monthly accounts that must have been eye-wateringly expensive. He had never seen his mother naked and never seen her bank statements.

It was all part of the double-damask service of the place that visitors to Downs Court could not simply march in off the street and knock on a relative's door. Several of the residents had dementia and all were rich so, by way of protection, visitors had to give their names at the reception desk and be escorted, much as though visiting the CEO of a multinational. The escort, usually pretty, female and English – though the masseurs and tennis coach were male Slavs, he gathered – would knock at the door and, despite having called ahead from the reception desk, would then slip in alone, for all the world as though fearful of interrupting the resident in a delicate merger deal, before coming back to say with a smile, 'She's expecting you.'

Eustace had observed that the world was divided between those who could not stop remembering, made wary or resentful by memories they could not shake or injuries they would not forgive, and those, like his mother, whose graceful progress was oiled by a selective memory. She had a breathtaking flair for ignoring the tasteless or painful and, seemingly, if she retained any conscience, having one that was efficiently smoothed by the progress of time. *Time heals all* had always struck him as a dictum favoured by the complacent. The version he and Naomi preferred was *Time picks every scab*.

'Darling!'

He was always *darling* to her now, and they always hugged and kissed like mother and son in a sitcom, which was odd as he didn't remember her doing either in his childhood.

She looked immaculate. He suspected she had her hair and nails seen to every week out of boredom and because it gave her someone to talk to. She turned off the vast television. She had never been a reader – she read the *Daily Telegraph* only nominally, having a way of folding it aside after a cursory flick with a sigh at the stupidity of *the World*. She had never been fond of television either, usually leaving the room when he had watched it with his father and implying that an interest in it was vaguely low, but she had now become an avid viewer. He was grateful for this as it lubricated his visits when they could pass a companionable hour watching people choose new houses in the country or sell unwanted antiques to pay for cruises.

'I like your hair,' he said.

'Thank you. They only took a little off. It's not too short? The horror of scraggy old necks!'

'It's fine. It looks *soigné*.'

'Oh good. Sit.'

He sat and let her fiddle with her espresso machine, although he would have to fetch the filled cups across to the table when she was done as her hands would shake and spill them. When alone, she drank her coffee standing up by the machine, he knew. He gazed out through her sliding doors at the terrace and the lawn beyond. It was all flawless and entirely without charm or character, like a face robbed of interest by plastic surgery.

She swore she had never been under the knife, though he clearly recalled her and Second Husband attending his father's funeral fresh from a 'holiday' with faintly oriental looks they had not possessed on departure. It did not bother him. It was her life, her face, her money. He suspected the beautician, as bored as all the residents, gave them all injections to amuse herself. The area beside his mother's mouth and eyes sometimes took on an unnatural, sausage skin smoothness. It all seemed a little pointless when her shuffling gait, withered shanks and rounded shoulders proclaimed her a woman fast approaching ninety.

He fetched the coffee and a saucer of chef-baked biscuits only he would eat, although she would be sure to say how good they were.

'So,' she asked, once they were settled. 'How are things? Did you sell that last flat to the Russian?'

'I did,' he said. 'Mrs Lee was furious as she wanted the whole building.'

'Better a Russian than a Chinese. They're everywhere. Not here, thank God.'

'You can't say that.'

'It's my house. I can say what I like.'

The racism, like the money, had come from Second Husband. Or perhaps he had merely helped give it voice.

'So. Great,' she said. 'What next?'

'Well . . . I thought I'd invest the profits for once and sit back for a while.'

'You're far too young to retire.'

'I've been living like a retired person for years.'

She flapped this remark aside. It troubled her when he spoke of his age and retirement as it gave her a glimpse of the end of her own conveyor belt.

'When my time comes,' she had told him on his previous visit, troubled by a neighbour who had made *a bad death*, 'I'd like you to shoot me, very quickly, in the temple, with one of those bolt guns they use on cattle.' Speed, violence and momentary pain didn't seem to bother her; loss of dignity was her great horror. And, just possibly, a not quite shaken fear of something beyond. Judgement. Punishment, even.

'The thing is,' he told her now, 'I'm not very well. I've got cancer.'

She set down her coffee cup with great care but it rattled against the saucer and redundant spoon.

'Really? You look fine,' she said. 'Where is it? The usual? Most men die with that, not of it, you know.'

'No, not prostate,' he said. 'Thyroid.'

She looked blank.

'In my throat. They already cut it out. Look,' he raised his head and pointed to the scar he was sure was clearly visible still.

'Can't see a thing,' she said, not really looking.

'She was a very good surgeon, I think. Anyway, with no thyroid it means I'm on a daily dose of thyroxine for life, and have to have regular blood tests, but I have those anyway. But tomorrow I go in for radiotherapy.'

'Will you lose your hair? I've always liked your hair.'

'Apparently not. It's just a pill. They deliver it in a lead casket and pass it to me with a long tube or something, it's so radioactive. Then we see. But. You know. It's still cancer. This one can come back in the lungs or bones, and neither one's a good prognosis.'

'But you're not coughing or anything?'

'No.'

'You'll be fine, then. It's amazing how good the treatments are these days. Now. You need to think about lunch as it's gone twelve. Shall we eat in here or go to the dining room?'

And that was an end of the subject.

He chose the dining room because walking there and back took time and provided subjects and people they could safely discuss, and because he had found the room-service food was never terribly hot.

He had hardly looked for expressions of emotion or compassion, that would have been out of character, but some concern, even along the selfish lines of *who will visit me once a week if you die* would have been reassuring.

As they made their way slowly along the jasmine-scented corridor pausing, as they always did, so she could comment on the enormous flower arrangements or blatantly assess her unsmiling reflection in one of the full-length looking-glasses, he consulted his own feelings to see if he felt anger or disappointment and found he felt relief, if anything, that his small, offstage drama left her placid self-regard untroubled.

They arrived in time to secure her preferred table, facing the rose garden and affording minimal eye contact with other residents.

'It's not that I'm not sociable,' she said, as she always did, as they took their seats there. 'I'm always very happy to chat over cocktails or if one of them joins me on a bench in the garden, but some of them are such messy eaters now that I feel embarrassed for them and it's depressing.'

After she had checked that he was not on a medicine that forbade it, they ordered large glasses of a delicious pinot noir with their boneless guinea fowl.

'I'm always meaning to ask you,' he said, 'if you ever run into Carla Gold these days.'

'Carla Gold.' She said the name slowly, placing it, tasting it almost. 'Oh. Her. Your . . . Well why ever should I?'

'She lived near here.'

'Yes, but surely she moved far away a long time ago. Even if I did, not that I ever go out really, I doubt I'd recognize her. It was all so long ago. What on earth made you bring her up suddenly?'

'Oh. I dunno. Clifton, I suppose. They had such a lovely house: she and the Boys.'

She dropped her head to stare hard at a piece of pancetta-wrapped bird before skewering it on her fork. She had wet macular degeneration but was in denial, unsurprisingly. She chewed thoughtfully. He considered a second glass of wine instead of pudding.

'Do you still go to church?' he asked her.

'What? Oh. Well they lay on a little shuttle service to

Christchurch, and the Catholic place, but it's always *Family Communion*.' She pronounced the words as though they tasted bad. 'So it never feels very special, with ghastly, uncontrolled children rushing everywhere and, well, it's such a palaver. There's a priest who comes here, though, once a week, C of E, offering takeaway, as it were. But really that's a bit embarrassing and she's a woman so it's really not the same.'

'Ah.'

He ordered them each a second glass.

'Naughty,' she said. 'You'll have me on my back,' and she produced a dry laugh. 'That woman. No. Not her. The one in the rather loud violet top. I hear her crying sometimes. At night.'

'But that's awful.'

'It gets so hot so I have my windows open and so does she, and I hear her crying. I actually went out on the terrace once, in the moonlight, and shuffled along in my dressing gown and slippers in the dew to check, and it was definitely her. Crying like a lost child. You'd never know to look at her. Nothing one can do, of course.' She sipped her wine, gazed out at the roses. 'I realized the other day that I don't believe in Hell any more,' she added. 'Not really.'

'How reassuring.'

She glanced sharply at him, well aware of his irony, but chose not to rise to it.

'Yes. Thank you. Delicious,' she said and let the waitress take away their dishes. 'It's just that, well, it takes away the rulebook somehow. Makes you wonder how differently things might have turned out. Coffee here? Or in the library, do you think?'

He had been given a relatively large dose, he gathered. For twenty-four hours or so after they gave him the pill, he was in total isolation in the lead-lined room. His meals were placed in a sort of airlock from which he could collect them only when a red light turned to green to show him the orderly delivering his tray had safely gone back out into the corridor and unlocked the inner door. He could see people down in the street, of course and, had he wanted to, could watch them on television, but he contented himself with music and thoughts.

He continued to think about Theo a lot, worried about him, worried that someone with so much yet to offer was so keen to attach himself to someone whose store might be about to empty. But then he remembered his younger self with Gilbert, who he had adored, and who had transformed his life, and made an effort not to worry.

He was enjoying Naomi's music. She seemed to have recorded hours and hours of it, though of course transferring sound files was now the work of seconds and hardly the labour of carefully curated love a mix tape had been around the time he met Gilbert. Half-way through her performance of one of the strange, stream of consciousness Britten cello suites, the telephone rang. He had not noticed there was one, so used had he become to telephones being something you carried in your pocket. It was the radiologist checking he was happy for her and a nurse to come in.

Rustling in their protective suits, they greeted him

politely. The nurse took his temperature and pulse and made a few notes. The radiologist then actually ran a Geiger counter over him.

'A little while to go yet,' she told him. 'Drink plenty of water, even when you're not thirsty,' and she poured and handed Eustace a glass of water, which Eustace obediently drank.

Once again the heavy door sealed him in, *kerthunk*. He replaced the ear buds and clicked to return to the beginning of the movement, because Britten's neurotic cello lines, thoughts-made-music, made no sense if you came to them half-way through.

CHAPTER SEVENTEEN

His mother didn't die. The nurses kept saying she was a fighter, though Eustace failed to see how they could know this when she simply lay there and breathed. He visited every day. It was the nearest he ever came to religious observance. Every afternoon he caught the train and a bus to the hospital to sit by her bed and watch her for a while. He managed to persuade his father to come as well and drive him just twice, but the one great dramatic act of driving overnight to Scotland to fetch him seemed to have sapped his father's reserves of energy and altruism. He was sliding deeper and deeper into a near-wordless passivity; cared for by Mrs Fowler and the staff in the home, he had effectively become a resident.

It emerged that Mrs Fowler was a formidable organizer. Sighing that his father could not be expected to continue under the circumstances with *all he usually did*, she discreetly assumed the reins of the house, receiving deliveries of all the goods he used to drive to fetch and occasionally asking Eustace to *play the man* by changing a lightbulb or putting out the rubbish, even though he suspected she only left such tasks undone to humour him.

So he got into the habit of visiting his mother alone, taking the train to Bristol then the bus to the hospital, and asking his father for the money to do so. The nurses began to greet him like an old friend and he soon knew his path through the hospital without needing to consult the coloured signs.

'Talk to her,' they said. 'Let her know you're there!'

And he did try, but he had never been an especially chatty boy and it felt artificial to become one now. He did touch the back of her hand however, and allowed himself to kiss her cheek and would simply say, 'Hello again. It's only me,' assuming that was enough and that she could recognize his voice.

The car was a write-off, apparently, so badly damaged the insurers said it was a miracle anyone had survived. If this could be called surviving. His father and Mrs Fowler took delivery of a brand-new version of the destroyed one. It sat gleaming and unused in the drive like a boldly stated lie asserting that nothing had changed.

As his father took to sitting in the day room with the guests, occasionally playing silent games of patience, Granny began to talk loudly to him about *that woman* and Eustace, listening patiently to her, realized she had never liked his mother, not even slightly.

'He should never have married that woman,' she told him. 'I knew she'd be trouble. A restless soul. Like trying to hold a cat when it doesn't want to be held.' And she mimed scratching his face.

He didn't pay this much attention as she was clearly beginning to go a bit peculiar, sometimes spending hours at a time flicking through her bible in search of a verse she could never find apparently, sometimes giving no sign of recognition for a few minutes after he entered her room.

'You've grown so,' she would say by way of apology, as though he was deliberately disguising himself.

He had not seen Vernon since their last meeting before he went to Scotland and Vernon's awkward departure had left behind it a worry about how the friendship would resume. Starting at Broadelm Comprehensive in September, their routines would be utterly disrupted and he feared Vernon would make new friends and leave him behind as a reminder of activities he would rather forget.

So he was touched when Vernon showed up at the front door with a bunch of flowers one morning and said, 'I'm sorry about your mother. Could I visit her with you?'

For a silly moment, glancing through the front door window, Eustace had thought the flowers were for him, but he was still touched. The train ride into Bristol and the short bus journey gave them a chance to recover lost ground. He answered all Vernon's questions, told him all about Ancrum and Jean Curwen. Or nearly all. He found he preferred not to tell him about Turlough.

'How did you hear about my mother?' he asked.

'Oh . . .' Vernon thought a moment, head slightly on one side in the attitude he sometimes adopted of a much older person. 'Let me think. Of course, it was Mrs Cobb. She cleans for us as well. Twice a week.'

Eustace was briefly bemused by this rare glimpse into Vernon's home life. He pictured Vernon and his father solemnly lifting their slippered feet as Mrs Cobb ran the Hoover beneath them, whistling tunelessly between her teeth. Mrs Cobb also cleaned at the hotel that catered exclusively to the blind. She said it had left her always meticulous about replacing things in exactly the same positions after she had dusted, though she knew her predecessor at the place had taken to moving furniture around out of malice.

Vernon surprised Eustace afresh when they reached the intensive care unit. He greeted Eustace's mother with something approaching tenderness, touching the back of her hands, as Eustace always did, and holding his flowers beneath her nose for a few seconds so that she might breathe in their scent. Scents, he assured Eustace, especially of herbs and flowers, were tremendously stimulating to the brain.

'Just think how readily you wake at the smell of toast,' he reminded him.

There was no change in his mother that day, but Eustace liked the thought that the scent of his friend's flowers might be stirring her steadily as she slept on.

Feeling their friendship had just reached another level, he dared to be bold as they walked back to Temple Meads from the bus stop.

'Tell me about your mother,' he said. 'You never mention her.'

'Because she died when I was very little,' Vernon said. 'People feel awkward when I mention her, so I tend not to.' In the thoughtful silence that followed this, Eustace felt Vernon draw his cloak of tweedy privacy back about himself.

On his way in one day, just after term had started, he met Carla Gold. It was unmistakably her, even from behind. She managed to look as though she had stepped briefly down from another, more stylish world but now was taking her gracious leave from this place where people waddled around in sports clothes or ugly uniforms. He even caught a faint whiff of her spicy scent as he walked over from the doors. She was standing with an overnight bag by her side, leaning on a crutch and, to his horror, with her right arm in a sling. She was waiting for someone.

She was equally startled to see him and he was moved that she evidently knew all about everything from the way she cried out his name and hugged him, rocking him slightly.

'I'm so sorry,' she said. 'So sorry. It was all so . . . And you had to cut short your course?'

'Only by a day. Your leg,' he said, 'and . . .' He gestured at her sling.

'Oh,' she glanced down. 'I managed to break both my hip and my arm. Actually the arm was just a simple fracture, thank heavens, and it's all fixed now and I can go home and lie on my own bed. It could have been so much worse . . . How is she?'

'No change,' he said. And her kindness and beautiful searching gaze made him melt inside in a way he simply couldn't deal with just then, so he coughed. 'Jean is everything you said she was.'

'She is, isn't she? You loved it?'

'I really want to go back. She said if I go back at Easter, she'll consider taking me full time.'

'No! Really? That's incredible!' She was overdoing her reactions somehow, which was odd. 'How's the new school?'

'Oh,' he said. 'It's not so bad. But I'd like to start lessons again. Maybe . . .' He glanced down at her crutch.

'Oh. Yes,' she said. 'Of course. And we must. Everything's a bit chaotic just now but, look, ring me at half-term. Maybe just after? And we can sort something out. If your father's, well . . . Oh. Here's Louis to fetch me. He had to leave the car miles away, I think.'

Eustace carried her case through the doors for her to where Louis was getting out of the car. Louis gave him a gratifying bear hug and ruffled his hair as though he were a child, but because it was him, Eustace didn't mind.

'Can we give you a lift to the station?' Louis asked.

'Oh. No. It's fine. I'm on my way in actually,' Eustace said and watched them drive off.

One day a priest was at his mother's bedside when he got to the hospital. Eustace stared at him from the far side of the room. He was strikingly handsome, with silver hair cut so short it was tempting to reach out and feel the buzz of it against his palm. He looked like a cross between Steve McQueen and Peter Graves, who played the silver-haired character in *Mission Impossible*. Or like some smooth hitman in a Hitchcock film. Vicars had no business being handsome, Granny said; it gave them an unfair advantage. They were supposed to look like Dick Emery or the owlish one in *Dad's Army*. Something made this priest turn on his chair, so he saw Eustace and jumped up.

'You must be the son,' he said and held out his hand. 'I'm the father. Haha.'

Eustace came forward, reached out his hand and was

disconcerted that the priest didn't simply shake it but clapped his other one on the back of it, making a sort of hand sandwich. His eyes were the blue of a hot sky, made all the more intense by his silver hair and early autumn tan. 'I'm Father Tony,' he said.

'I'm Eustace,' Eustace told him. 'Are you the hospital chaplain? Is she dying now?'

'I'm sure she isn't.'

He steered Eustace towards his mother's bed, where Eustace carefully placed a chair on the opposite side to Father Tony's. Quickly, with a touch of possessiveness, he touched the warm back of his mother's right hand and kissed her cheek, whispering,

'Hello. It's only me.'

'I don't work here,' Father Tony went on. 'I was just visiting a couple of friends who are in for operations. A friend who's a nurse here always tells me if there's someone who she thinks needs me or . . . who isn't being visited much.'

Eustace noted the waxy ridge on his mother's ring finger where the nurses had taken off her wedding ring for his father to keep safely at home along with Grandpa's special watch. It was a small reminder that hospitals were public places, almost the street, given the freedom with which complete strangers could come to one's bedside.

'I visit her every day,' Eustace told him quietly.

'It can't be easy for your father,' Father Tony said. 'I heard a little about—'

'He manages. We have help.'

'I should leave you in peace.'

'Thank you.'

'But shall we pray first?'

Eustace wanted to demur. He was not a Christian, not really, but neither was he bold or interested enough to be a professed atheist. He did feel, however, that prayer should be a silent, private activity. But Father Tony prayed anyway, loud enough for the nurses to hear, certainly loud enough for his mother to hear, and he used her first name, as though he knew her. It seemed to go on and on. It was deeply embarrassing, like spontaneously singing in a public place, and Eustace focused closely on his mother's hand and the nearby laundry label on a hospital sheet until Father Tony was done. He was quite proud of himself for resisting the impulse to say 'Amen' at the end.

Father Tony finally stood up to go, coming round to lay a hand on Eustace's shoulder as he did so.

'Good boy, Eustace,' he said. 'God sees you.'

Then he padded away. He wore Hush Puppies. Granny would have hated him on sight. Unlike her daughter-in-law, she was impervious to charm and impressed only by principles.

'It's all right,' he told his mother. 'He's gone now. That was awful!' Then he continued his visit in his usual companionable silence. When he reached home that evening, he reported to his father as always, if only to say that there was no change, but he said nothing of the priest. He didn't like to risk passing on Father Tony's implied criticism of his father's not visiting.

He had assumed it was a one-off thing, a chance meeting in a huge building where strangers came and went all the time. The next time he visited, however, Father Tony was there again, almost as though timing his arrival to coincide with Eustace's. Eustace stopped far short, before the priest could spot him, and went instead to fetch a cup of strong tea and a soothingly bland iced bun from the canteen. He dawdled, making himself read a chapter from a geometry schoolbook before he returned, to give Father Tony time to leave.

When he touched his mother's hand to greet her, he found the priest had tucked a simple wooden crucifix under it. He could see that this was meant in kindness but he was disturbed at how it emphasized her lack of choice in the matter. A doll, a book, a bar of chocolate, a bottle of beer, all could equally have been placed in such a way and each would equally have implied a choice she hadn't made. Eustace pocketed the crucifix and, when he left, slipped into the hospital chapel, which lay on his route back to the bus stop. He left the ugly thing on a seat in there, where someone might pick it up, out of choice.

He caught a slightly later train and bus the next day and there was no sign of the priest. There was, however, a bouquet of very beautiful white flowers with a card propped up against it, which said, *We're all thinking of you. X.*

'There are some lovely flowers,' he told his mother. 'From people who are thinking of you and send a kiss. The picture is of . . .' He turned the card over. 'Oh. That's nice. It's a view of the suspension bridge.'

Because Vernon's flowers were still looking good and the new bunch was still wrapped he decided to take it home in an effort to cheer his father. When he arrived he found a vase, filled it with water and arranged the flowers as best he could before setting them on a table in the sitting room window. They looked lovely and smelled even better than Vernon's had. The houses in the magazines always had flower arrangements. He had looked at the gorgeous bucketfuls outside florists and been astonished at how much people were prepared to pay for such a fleeting pleasure. He imagined a future in which he regularly bought himself flowers with no thought of the cost.

'Look,' he told his father when he came in. 'She already had Vernon's by the bed so I brought these home for you.'

His father didn't exclaim over their beauty or scent but merely asked whom they were from.

'I don't know,' Eustace told him. 'The card doesn't give much away.'

'Let me see.'

He took the little card from Eustace.

'I don't recognize the handwriting,' Eustace said. 'Do you?'

But his father only read the card with a frown, tossed it into the wastepaper basket and drifted from the room without further comment. It was unlike him to be so graceless. The next morning the beautiful flowers had vanished. Eustace spotted them later in the day room, where they were already wilting in the heat.

That night there was a letter waiting for him at home, from Naomi. Her handwriting was very young for her age and he remembered how she almost boasted of neglecting all her schooling for the cello. It was a funny letter, full of silly jokes and catchphrases from their short week together. *Did you do D minor?* it began. *Well, did you?*

She had discovered the Italians made nicknames by shortening from the front.

So you can be Ace or Azio and I can be Omi, which is easier to spell than Na, which would need a Y not to be pronounced Nah.

She gave a full account of the last night's concert and gratifyingly added that Jean had explained that she was taking the place of a *fine young player we hope to have back with us as a permanent student before too long. So get you, Maestro.*

After supper he felt he must write her a letter in reply. He had no paper and envelopes so went to his mother's little desk. There, sure enough, he found a pad of the Basildon Bond she liked – the smaller one because it meant short letters could be made to look longer. She was not one of Nature's letter-writers, tending to resort to paper only when she needed to say thank you to people for presents or hospitality, neither of which happened very often. And she had recently abandoned her proper fountain pen for a Parker biro his father had given her for a birthday present. It was very smart, made of shiny metal Eustace liked to think was silver but which was probably just stainless steel. It wrote far better than the leaky plastic ones he tended to use at school, which had a way of unpredictably releasing blotches of sticky ink, which his hand then smeared across the exercise books as he wrote. So he picked up her Parker biro now, thinking to use it for a more impressive effect in his letter to Naomi.

One old-fashioned concession his mother maintained was a heavy address embosser. It had belonged to

Granny – it belonged to the house really – and as a small boy he had been allowed to use it for his mother on the rare occasions when she had a letter to send. You tucked the paper carefully into a slot, pulled down a handle that was decorated a bit like her old manual sewing machine, and there, very chastely, was a colourless imprint of their address and telephone number. Only the machine was so old that the number was now too short and his mother had to spoil the elegant effect by writing in the extra digits when it was a letter to someone who needed to know them.

He tore off the top sheet in the pad, slid it in and pressed, admiring, as always, the neatness of the imprint produced and lamenting in advance that the messiness of his hand-writing could never match it. He picked up his mother's biro but had written no more than the date and *Dear* when he saw quite clearly the ghostly imprint of his own name where he was about to write Naomi's. There were more words. A whole letter in fact.

He turned on the desk light in an effort to read it better but his mother's incisive, rounded script looked like so many Os and Ys. He could make out the greedily scooping loops on her Gs, which Vernon had once told him were an indicator of *need for pleasure and depth of sexual desire.*

All the pencils in her pen pot were HBs, so much too hard, but he remembered she had sticks of charcoal some-where from a short-lived attendance at art classes. He opened a few little drawers, having broken off to intercept and redirect huge Mrs Knapton, who had lost her way yet again, and drifted up the wrong stairs into the private area. He held the charcoal stick flat against the writing pad and gently swept it from side to side until his mother's handwriting stood out white against the surrounding grey.

Eustace. (He took the Dear as read.) *By the time you come back from your course, I will have left to begin a new life where I doubt very much your father will want you to join me. It is nothing you or he have done wrong. I am simply in love, deeply in love, in a happy way I realized I had never been before. And once you love someone, it is hard to unlove them. I love you. I am proud of you. You will do very well without me. Mother X*

He read it twice to be absolutely certain of its sense then used her good paper scissors to cut the letter into the smallest pieces he could manage. Then he crumpled them into his pocket so that he could drop them safely in a public litter bin next time he went out. But where was the original? He went to search his room carefully, looking in all the places she might have left a letter she wanted only him to find but there was no trace of it. Perhaps she had posted it and it was somehow delayed, but that was hard to credit, even with strikes and so on. Perhaps she had changed her mind and destroyed the original, as he had just destroyed its ghost? More disturbing, of course, was that his father might have intercepted it and been worrying how to break the news to him less abruptly.

Mrs Fowler summoned them to eat their supper shortly afterwards. They ate together in strenuously polite near-silence. Eustace realized it was completely out of the question either to tell his father what he had just discovered or to ask him even indirect questions about where his mother had been going when she had the accident.

He wrote the letter to Naomi after supper. He kept his tone light, said only that his mother was still in hospital and that he hoped to begin cello lessons again soon but that Carla Gold was out of action for a bit. He signed himself Azio *because Ace looks like bragging.*

He thought back repeatedly through the rest of the evening, while companionably watching television with his father and lying awake until sleep claimed him, and over and over again through his classes the next day, thought of her increasing absences and naked cheerfulness in recent months. And he saw that she was right: even had he not been so distracted by his music or by Vernon or whatever, there was nothing that could have been done, short of his father imprisoning her. Love had infected her as inevitably as any virus. He could no more have stopped her falling in love than he could have prevented her accident. This did not diminish a creeping feeling of desolation; whatever the fragility of her bond with his father, her maternal love had not been strong enough to hold her to them. Neither did it stop him idly speculating on what the man was like who had so inflamed her or feeling a curious envy of the passion she had tasted, poisonous fruit so seductive it had made her prepared to abandon them all, assuming their disgusted rejection of her in turn.

And, of course, she had left them nonetheless, vanishing into her medically managed unconsciousness as completely as she had planned to do into her mysterious lover's house.

For two days he could not bear to visit her, although he loitered in the public library after school to let his father assume he had been to the hospital rather than risk raising the question of why he suddenly hadn't gone. When guilt, love and curiosity overcame him on the third day and he returned, two things struck him as he entered the intensive care unit. Father Tony was there again, at her bedside, holding her hand, and her eyes were open, looking directly at Eustace as he approached.

The uncomplicated joy that burst up in him on seeing her restored to life made him break down in tears for the first time since early childhood. As he approached the bed, his knees buckled, and he found himself gasping and sobbing into her blanketed lap like a five-year-old. He felt her hand spasmodically grasping the back of his head and heard her voice, croaky from dehydration and underuse, saying *hush*, and *there, there* and *Eustace*.

And the priest, alarmed perhaps at this unexpected upwelling of raw emotion, was saying, 'It's perfectly natural. It's to be expected.' And also, 'Thank you, Lord Jesus!'

At last embarrassment overcame relief and Eustace composed himself sufficiently to sit up and look at her. 'Sorry,' he said. 'I . . . I thought you were dying.'

'Blow your nose,' she said wearily and slowly nudged the tissue box towards him.

She looked at once herself and much older, and slightly mad with her tufty hair. And her face had lost its symmetry; one side hung back from expression now, like the other half's shyly reluctant twin. Perhaps it was just the trauma or residual sleepiness at work, but her voice appeared to have lost entirely the edge of irony that since childhood had made him brace himself slightly for each encounter with her, just as adults and painful experience taught one always to handle knives with care.

'I did die,' she told him slowly and there were tears in her eyes suddenly. 'I left my body. I was up there in the corner of the room and it felt so good to be free! No more aches and pains. No more body. And I looked down and saw you at the bedside.'

'Who? Me?' Eustace asked. Had he stopped her dying?

'No,' she said flatly. 'Him.' And she gave Father Tony a mad, lopsided smile as though she had known and loved him all her life. 'I saw light. A long, long tunnel with light at the end, where I longed to be, but there was a voice saying: *Not yet. Go back.* And then I was back and I heard him praying. Who are you again?'

'I'm Father Tony.' The priest seemed to grow an inch. 'Shall we all pray?'

'Yes,' she said. 'Oh yes.'

'I'll phone home,' Eustace said and hurried out to the payphone in the hall, passing two nurses and a doctor who were running towards the intensive care unit, alerted to the drama playing out in there.

Mrs Fowler answered and cried when he told her, which made him nearly cry again and realize she had been cooking in the house for his entire life.

The pips went before she could fetch his father.

CHAPTER EIGHTEEN

His mother had to stay in hospital for another month. She was moved twice in the next four weeks, once to a post-operative ward, where everyone had undergone head injuries or brain surgery and then to a rehabilitation unit. She had suffered a brain-stem injury through whiplash and, with it, a debilitating stroke. Her speech was slow and often slurred. Her right side was not quite paralysed but severely impaired, so that she had difficulty walking and grasping, though the nurses assured them all that most of these effects would pass with daily exercise and regular visits to a rehabilitation or physiotherapy centre. More disturbing was that her powers of reasoning were damaged. She regularly came out with the wrong words for things, just like Granny, and when she picked up a biro and tried to write a postcard, her writing was that of an infant, broad and uncontrolled.

She knew who they all were, though she sometimes stumbled saying Eustace and took to calling him angel, which might have been heartwarming were it not so entirely unlike her old self. She had become tactile in a way she never used to be, either. The old her had been controlled, even niggardly in her expressions of affection, but the returned her, as Eustace found he was thinking of her, was a toucher of cheeks and holder of hands. He might have welcomed this had it been more discriminating, had he felt occasionally singled out, but he soon saw that she called doctors angel as well, and touched the nurses' cheeks with the same childlike wonder with which she touched his.

He tried in vain now to make his father visit. He lied. 'She's asking for you,' he said. 'She keeps asking where you are.'

But his father closed down at any mention of her or shrugged or left the room on some mumbled pretext. Thinking of the letter he had uncovered, Eustace could only imagine that his father had received something similar and was upset and angry and needed to punish her by withholding himself. Certainly Mrs Fowler made no attempt to urge him to go and just shook her head and wiped bleachy cloths over surfaces. Eustace could understand his father's anger and withdrawal. His pleasure at his mother's stumbling return to a kind of normality was tempered with the knowledge that she had reached the point of leaving them both for ever and with gladness.

He mentioned his father to her whenever he could, continued to lie to her as well about how often he spoke of her and how much he wanted her home.

'He doesn't visit because he hates hospitals,' he told her. 'And because he's so sad. He's very sad all the time.'

But she just said things like, 'Poor man. Poor, poor man.' And sometimes she cried a little, as though his father were a wounded pet or dying bird whose suffering she was powerless to assuage. Just once, when she was on the rehabilitation ward and he was keeping her company on one of the shuffling walks she was now encouraged to make the length of a long corridor supported on two sticks, he ambushed her. He had the change ready in his pocket and as they slowly approached an unoccupied telephone booth, he darted from her side, rang home and stuffed in coins when Mrs Fowler answered.

'I've got Mother here,' he told her. 'Dad said I should get her to ring him.'

And while she duly hurried to bring his father to speak, he held out the receiver to his mother. 'Dad's coming to the phone for you.' She took the receiver carefully with both hands, still not trusting her right one to work on its own, and held it to her ear, long fingers splayed out along it in a way that would have looked elegant had it not been strange.

'Hello?' she said uncertainly. 'Hello?' Then she looked confused and terribly sad and held the receiver out to him again. 'No one there,' she said and he could hear the deep purr of the dialling tone that meant his father had hung up.

The longer his father held himself apart, the more Jesus and his handsome friend Father Tony were filling the vacancy he left. The priest visited every day. He quickly intuited that his presence made her son uncomfortable and would take his leave of her soon after Eustace's arrival at her bedside, touching his shoulder with a big, muscular hand the way he always did and saying,

'I'll let you have Mum to yourself.'

But still Eustace was aware of the territory Tony and Jesus were stealthily annexing in her heart. He often watched from the far end of the ward and saw their heads bowed together in oddly intimate prayer or in confidential conversation. He saw how Father Tony's manner began subtly to alter around her, the way an interloping friend's did when increased confidences and shared private knowledge let them assume new assurance in a circle of old intimates.

The old her had never been what one would call religious, merely ticking Church of England on forms and knowing how to behave when attending Midnight Mass on Christmas Eve or Communion on Easter Sunday. She expected Eustace to be confirmed at twelve with his classmates, simply as the preparation for becoming an adult and passing for normal, as she often used to put it, but she always approached religion as she approached politics, wearing her irony like a pair of irreproachable Sunday gloves. But now she routinely had a bible on her bedside and took to devouring other books people mysteriously brought her, books with rainbows or clouds on the covers and with heart-on-sleeve titles like *Summoned By Grace* or *Christ the True Friend*. And she began to be visited not only by Father Tony but by two or three women who had not been her friends before. They were her age or older and had in common a fondness for folksy, homespun clothes, a lack of make-up and a very slightly reserved, even assessing manner towards Eustace, as though waiting for him to leave so they could return to less guarded conversation with his mother. She had never had much in the way of friends before, which was why her friendship with Carla had been so transformative. He quite liked Barbara, the tall, bony-faced one closest to her in age, because she laughed at things and didn't refer to Jesus as though he were a friend who happened not to be present.

The increasing presence of these new confidantes at her bedside, with their little posies of wild flowers, plastic bags of home-baked flapjacks or mottled windfall apples, made it all the stranger that he never saw Carla there, especially given how kindly Carla had asked after her when he ran into her downstairs that time. He made a point of ringing her, although they had agreed not to arrange a resumption of cello lessons until after half-term. He reached her answering machine, a device that few people had and which made him shy so he hung up and wrote a little message down on the telephone pad as he always did, then rang her back to leave it in as lifelike a manner as he could muster.

'Mother's much better,' he told her. 'She's had a sort of stroke but she's walking and talking and I know she'd love to see you, if you were passing.'

He was inexperienced at the dynamics of friendship but he was observant and had seen the way people at school protected their pride after an argument by drawing stand-in, second-best friends to them while the principal friendship recovered or died. He felt sure that, once Carla swept up to his mother's bedside with her bouncing hair and long limbs and beautiful clothes, the proper order would be restored and these new women and Father Tony and Jesus, especially Jesus in fact, would slip back to their proper places on the margins of her life.

He imagined Carla encouraging his mother to make a

virtue of her new short hair with a good salon cut and some hoop earrings to show off her exposed neck and ears.

Carla didn't call him back – he hadn't suggested she should and had been quite clear that his mother was still in the hospital, on Carla's doorstep, in fact – but he left it a few days until, sitting with his mother and Father Tony in the rehabilitation ward's day room, he said, as cheerfully and as naturally as he could, 'So has Carla been to see you yet? I ran into her and Louis the other day and she asked how you were doing and I told her she could find you here.'

Father Tony cleared his throat, as though to cover a rogue fart, and his mother looked Eustace in the eye and said, 'I can appreciate how much she has done for you, darling, but Carla Gold is no longer my friend.'

'But—' he started.

Only Father Tony touched him on the shoulder and said, 'Eustace? I think we have to accept that your mother knows her own mind.'

They were distracted just then by the arrival of the tea trolley and the conversation was swiftly swung around to focus on Eustace and how he was doing at his new school, but he realized afterwards that it was the first time the priest had been there when he arrived and still there when he left.

The head of rehabilitation had made it clear that his mother would be ready to leave hospital at the end of that week, on the understanding that arrangements would be made for her to attend regular physiotherapy sessions to improve her motor control and continue to see a therapist to restore her speech. They had warned her that some of her brain damage would be permanent and that she could not expect to recover all her lost faculties. When she was tired, her symptoms were likely to become worse.

Eustace and Mrs Fowler had been preparing for her return. A second, sturdier hand rail had been fixed on the stairs up to their private part of the house and grab rails fixed beside the bath and lavatory so that, short of the installation of panic bells and a commode, there was not much left to distinguish the elderly guests' territory from his mother's.

But on the Friday when he returned from school expecting to find that a hospital car or ambulance had dropped his mother off, Mrs Fowler told him a very nice, tall woman he guessed was Barbara, had called round instead to help pack a suitcase of clothes for his mother to wear during a recuperative stay at a Christian community some way inland. Mrs Fowler seemed to think this perfectly understandable and possibly was slightly relieved at not suddenly having to take on the care of her employer's wife as well as the management of the home.

They did not even have an address or a name for where she had gone until the first of her postcards arrived for him after that weekend. It was a beautiful old manor house with orchards and a vegetable garden. Whatever its old name, the Christian community who owned and ran it called it Grace Manor.

The food is all vegetarian and very healthy, she wrote in her new childish handwriting. *Lots of pulses! And we all help cook and clean. I'm a bit clumsy at dusting. But it's so very special. Father Tony calls by most days.*

Eustace was cross with her at first for going there without warning so he didn't write back until her second postcard – a view of the gatehouse – and then did so carefully without a hint of surprise or disapproval at her defection. He showed her postcards to his father, who read them without comment and passed them back.

CHAPTER NINETEEN

Eustace had begun his first term at Broadelm in a daze, his head still full of what he had learnt and experienced at Ancrum, his heart full of unexpressed fears about his mother, who was then still comatose and possibly dying in hospital. Most boys and girls began there aged eleven, moving directly from primary schools. He and Vernon were an anomaly, arriving from a fee-paying prep school – so marked out as posh – and two years older, so expected to slot into a year group who had already spent two years establishing their pecking order and networks of friendship and antipathy.

The day before term started they and a handful of other boys and girls who were also, as Vernon put it, private-school refugees, had the humiliating experience of being herded through a brief induction day with that year's intake of eleven-year-olds who were, of course, far more numerous and felt much smaller and younger. Eustace was shocked by how big and impersonal the school felt compared to St Chad's. Its classrooms were twice the size, its desks Formica, not wood, its corridors as wide and long as streets, its lavatories unimaginably large and frightening.

Mulling over the challenges in their shelter afterwards, Vernon said that the way to fit in was to begin silently and discreetly, to avoid speaking out in class unless it was unavoidable and to smile if teased or mocked rather than mounting a challenge.

'And there are words to avoid saying,' Vernon told him. 'Like *actually* and *however*. I've been studying their speech patterns. We have to avoid complex sentence structures. Try to speak in single clauses and you're less likely to be beaten up.'

It was at once better and worse than expected. As at St Chad's, they had to wear uniform, though at Broadelm it was almost office wear: grey trousers, black jacket, white shirt and a school tie of indestructibly stiff nylon. Like St Chad's, Broadelm was sports mad, although the only sports it recognized, which were compulsory for the entire school, were football and, in season, rugby not cricket or tennis, and the girls played netball and hockey. Like any school, St Chad's had its share of bullies and teasers but, off the sports field, violence had been confined to the occasional threatening shove or Chinese burn. Nothing had prepared Eustace for the fights at Broadelm. These were proper knock down, punch, kick and hair-tug fights, which broke out at least once or twice a week and would swiftly gather a circle of baying, whooping spectators. Girls, he soon discovered, could be equally the fighters – which got the boys hideously excited – or, more chillingly, they could be instigator-spectators. Fights broke out over simple arguments and rivalries but were also often tribal. They were studying *Romeo and Juliet* in English, reading it with antidramatic slowness around the class, but the savagery of Montague and Capulet paled beside the sworn enmity between pupils from the rival estates of Bourneville, Coronation and Oldmixon.

It made him realize how little he understood his own town, how he had spent the last decade ignoring whole tracts of it, unaware of the social niceties of living in one street or another or being related to this or that notorious family.

Fights, he found, were easily avoided by giving no offence, drawing no attention to oneself and generally keeping out of the paths of the more obviously dangerous people as a well-trained housemaid would strive for invisibility from the gaze of her employers. If ever he heard or saw a fight breaking out, he walked swiftly in the opposite direction and so was never at risk of being drawn in as witness or, worse, second. Happily, Royal Crescent and its district were too under-represented to constitute a tribe worthy of battling.

Girls, however, were unavoidable and insistent. The week spent with the nicely brought up, if single-minded ones at Ancrum had been scant preparation for encountering most of the teenage girls of Weston *en masse*. With their uniforms daringly modified, their hair as big as ingenuity and a brush could make it, their breath alive with artificial fruit flavours and cigarettes, their tongues as sharp as their glances were withering, they were every bit as frightening to him as the boys. As new blood, thirteen and possibly rich – the bush telegraph having swiftly informed everyone in days that he had been at St Chad's – Eustace found himself the object of curiosity rather than disdain. Girls in his own year group were entirely fixated on boys in the year or years above or with a handful of particularly well developed boys their own age who could pass for older, but both he and Vernon were soon being tailed around the place and even along the streets after school by girls of twelve or eleven whose boldness was like nothing he had ever encountered. Who was he going out with, they demanded. Who did he like? Did he fancy this girl or did he prefer that one?

'No one you know,' he would tell them. 'Never you mind,' and he would remember to smile, trying to convey worldly experience beyond their years even as he broke out in a sweat at how unconvincing he felt he must sound.

What he could not have predicted was how interesting the lessons were. Compared to the teachers at St Chad's, many of whom were either dry as dust or bored to cynicism, many of his teachers at Broadelm showed an abiding enthusiasm for their subjects, even if forced to teach them to classes so large that keeping order throughout the room was an impossibility. The trick, he found, was to sit sufficiently near the front to be able to hear above the constant chatter from behind, yet not so far forward as to seem too keen or attention-seeking.

The library was well stocked, calm, often largely empty and safe.

Somehow two of the most daunting girls in his year, a complementary peroxide blonde and Gothically black pair called Sasha Hedges and Suzanne Cassidy, quickly discovered that his mother was unconscious in hospital and quite possibly dying and took it upon themselves to keep a protective eye on him. In his first week, when, despite Vernon's frantic warning signals, he couldn't resist putting up his hand to solve an algebra question that was baffling everyone, one of the bigger boys, a known rugby thug, started to mock his accent but Suzanne Cassidy silenced him with a tongue-lashing so impressive that even their maths teacher waited for her to say her piece before continuing without rebuke.

If asked to predict their fates there, Eustace would have said Vernon was the more likely to be picked on, because he was more obviously what Sasha called *lahdidah* and, where Eustace was merely what St Chad's boys called wet, he was overtly eccentric. Having urged Eustace that they could best survive by speaking the simpler language of their neighbours, Vernon perversely began to reveal his true nature in class by degrees. Speaking in long sentences, using his driest, most middle-aged wit, even slightly emphasizing his Trollopian cadences rather than, like Eustace, making an effort to ape the long vowels and dropped consonants of Bourneville and Coronation. And though there was the odd attempt to imitate him, there was laughter on his side.

'You're funny,' Suzanne Cassidy declared prominently when he had said something withering about Marie Osmond in the lunch queue. 'You I like.'

And so it was that Vernon unpredictably went from being a class oddball to being almost popular, or as popular as a boy could be with no sporting ability and a taste for nineteenth-century fiction. His eccentricities, his way of speaking, his habit of wearing his nasty nylon tie like a dandy's cravat were inimitable, which lent him a kind of rock-star cool.

And like a small fish benefiting from swimming in the wake of one much larger and more noticeable, Eustace was granted a measure of protection by association. Thanks to some quick thinking from Vernon, it was soon established that his name was Stash, whatever it said on notices or forms; even the friendlier teachers began to call him that.

Even though the youngest children there were only eleven, which Eustace remembered as feeling very young indeed, there was a strong sense that pupils at the comprehensive were largely independent of their parents. No parents were ever at the school gates at the end of the last period or at the start of the first. Pupils who lived out in the countryside made their journeys to and from the school on a fleet of battle-scarred buses. He and Vernon had long fallen into the practice of walking themselves to and from St Chad's but most of their contemporaries there had been scooped up at the longer school day's end by parents, as though preserving a myth that fee-paying children were somehow more delicate and in need of protection.

Eustace began to understand why the children from the three estates behaved so tribally. As they left their houses and flats in the morning they joined with one another in the streets, forming battalions that grew as they neared the school. He and Vernon were not the only ones who headed towards the older streets and promenade on leaving the last class of the day. There was a handful of Greeks, children of hotel proprietors, who also walked their way and he was fascinated to hear them talk Greek together, though in class they sounded as Somerset as anyone else.

Suzanne and Sasha each had a male cousin in the same year group, Jez and Tyler, big, sullen boys who smelled of Brut and fabric conditioner but already had the thickened ears and noses of rugby-playing brawlers. They padded around together but always within yards of the girls, quite as though they were their bodyguards. Privately thinking of them as Paris and Tybalt, Eustace began to like the sense that, if he was walking near either girl he, too, could probably count on her cousin's protection.

Before long it felt only natural for Sasha and Suzanne to mooch over to Vernon amid the chaotic stampede that always followed the day's last bell and say, taking in Eustace with a sweep of mascaraed eye, 'So where you going now?'

In Broadelm-speak this passed for a polite invitation and soon the four of them, guarded at a studiedly relaxed distance by Jez and Tyler, were strolling towards Suzanne's home on the Bourneville estate. Sasha's was closer, she explained, but currently mayhem as her mother was splitting up, or possibly not, with her latest man which apparently meant that everything was broken. Her mother's rages were legendary, he gathered, as were her sprees for new curtains and furniture when she was ready for a change of paramour.

'It happens in spring, usually,' Sasha said. 'When her sap rises.'

'Yeah, right,' Suzanne said. 'Or her child support comes in.'

So they went to Suzanne's, in the estate's heart.

On the face of it all the houses were identical but of course they weren't, because each family had expressed itself in a more or less maintained patch of front garden, in the cars and vans parked outside, in the different ways windows were decorated. Sasha reserved especial scorn for a couple of houses with no net curtains downstairs and Indian bedspreads upstairs where curtains should be.

'Junkies,' she said. 'And that lot are Gyppos.'

Suzanne seemed to know something about the tenants in almost every house they passed, which made Eustace feel inadequate for knowing almost nothing about his neighbours in the small crescent where he had spent his entire life. Her parents were both out at work still – her mother in a hairdresser's, her father, as a plumber – but she was able to give them all out-of-date Mivvis from a full freezer because her father also drove an ice cream van in the summer and got to keep the old stock.

The house was spotless and everything looked brand-new. She had an unexpected clutch of younger siblings who raced downstairs at the sound of her key in the lock and were suddenly all over the kitchen like so many hungry kittens. Eustace was impressed to see the calm authority with which she set about conjuring them supper, which she called tea. While the children were eating, she led the rest of them up to her bedroom where they all smoked mentholated Consulate – Eustace only pretended and still coughed – and flopped around on her pink candlewick bedspread listening to her records before having to leave in a hurry when her father came home. He was currently convinced Jez was a bad influence. It was hard to see how Jez could influence anybody for the bad, except perhaps by hitting them, though his shirt had ridden up on the bed earlier, revealing a thatch of black hair around and below his belly button, which perhaps suggested animal propensities.

A few days later, Eustace suggested they go to his and Vernon's shelter in the park, where they drank cider and pretended to get drunk, although it was only Strongbow.

Then perhaps he was a little bit drunk because some madness made him suggest they all come back to his place for tea. Lest there be any misunderstanding, he added, 'Some cake and a cup of tea,' which made Jez laugh.

'Go on. Say that again.'

'Some cake and a cup of tea,' Eustace told him and Jez laughed louder, giving him a playful backslap on the chest.

'What are you like?' he said, but kindly.

Suzanne, who was their unofficial leader because she had the biggest hair, most spectacular breasts and most dangerous father, stopped in the street to gaze up at the house.

'What? You live here, Stash?' she said.

'Well, yes,' Eustace admitted. 'But only in the rooms at the top. Most of it's my parents' old people's home.'

'That is so . . . Gothic,' said Tyler, who spoke so rarely and had such a deep voice that everyone listened when he did.

'I love old people,' Sasha said. 'If they're not smelly.'

Perhaps they were all a bit drunk after all. Anyway, Eustace confidently led them in at the front door. Mrs Fowler greeted them warmly, as it was well known that young things visiting brightened an elderly day. They were soon having a surreal tea party in the conservatory with Mrs Bagnold and huge Mrs Knapton and ancient Mr Fryer, who remained fast asleep even when Sasha squirted him with some of her Charlie. The unexpected appearance of two young women cheered up his father no end, to the point where Suzanne outraged the others the next day during physics by declaring that he'd been so sweet and funny that she quite fancied him.

There was no question of Jez or Tyler ever entertaining.

'I mean,' Suzanne said, 'their houses are quite nice and everything but there's never anything in the fridge but cold takeaway.' And so it was that, a few days after that, on a Saturday afternoon when they all met up as if by accident as Suzanne and Sasha came off their Saturday jobs, that Vernon surprised Eustace by inviting everyone around to his place.

'No mad old ladies here, then?' Sasha said.

'Only you,' said Suzanne.

The house was utterly silent. Downstairs was peculiarly orderly, every book on its shelf, everything in a drawer or cupboard. Mrs Cobb must have loved cleaning there, as there was no clutter to be tidied away before she could start dusting, and every surface sparkled. Tyler looked with longing at a painting of a naked woman looking over her shoulder. Suzanne scanned the crammed bookshelves.

'Have you read all these?' she asked.

Vernon shook his head a little sadly. 'But I've never bought a book in my life.'

'So how many of you live here?' Sasha demanded. 'It's so peaceful.'

'Oh. Just the two of us. Dad can't manage stairs any more, so he lives in the front room on the first floor.'

'What's wrong with him?' Suzanne asked.

Eustace marvelled at how her effrontery didn't seem rude, merely honest.

'It's a kind of Parkinson's. It's been getting steadily worse. He can still think and feel and everything but he can't talk any more and his body doesn't work very well. He's a prisoner in his body, basically.'

'Christ,' she said. 'Will he die?'

'Suzanne!'

'Yes,' Vernon said gently. 'I hope so. He's ready, I reckon.'

Eustace was appalled that he had not thought to ask after Vernon's father amid his preoccupation with his mother's accident and time in hospital.

'You didn't say,' he muttered.

'I know. Sorry. I preferred not to.'

'That's OK.'

'Can we see him?' Suzanne asked boldly.

'Suzanne!'

'Yes of course. He likes visitors, especially sexy girls. And the carers are all men now because of the heavy lifting.'

He led the way up the stairs the sunset was gaudily painting, past portraits of women, still-lifes of fruit, flowers and then more women, most of them calmly displaying breasts and hair and everything, and took them to a big, dazzlingly bright room where his father sat in a wheelchair facing the view through the park to the promenade and water.

'Dad?' he said. 'I've brought some friends home.'

'Hello handsome,' Suzanne said and walked directly over and kissed Vernon's father twice, once on each cheek, and then, after looking at him a moment, on the lips as well. Bending over his wheelchair displayed her breasts to full advantage. 'Your paintings are beautiful. Oh look at your view . . . Amazing!'

One by one they stepped over to introduce themselves. Eustace said, 'Hello again,' and gave a kind of truncated wave as he remembered they couldn't shake hands.

'We should take him out in the wheelchair,' Tyler said. 'It's nice on the prom.'

'He doesn't like it.'

'Er. How do you know?' Sasha asked.

'Before his speech went finally, he told me. He made me promise. He said it made him feel like a big baby when he still felt like a man inside.'

'Fair enough,' Jez said.

'There's cider downstairs,' said Vernon. 'We get everything delivered. Bye, Dad.'

They all said goodbye then trooped back downstairs to where Vernon produced icy cold bottles of cider, not Strongbow but proper country stuff from some farm.

'This is really strong,' Sasha said. 'I'll be anyone's. Not you, though, Jez.'

Vernon showed them the rest of the house. His father's studio at the back with its broad antique daybed and paint-spattered armchairs and the large purple-painted room at the front with all the floor-to-ceiling bookshelves containing what looked like every English or American novel worth reading. Now he had finally decided to talk, Vernon told them everything. The purple room had been his mother's. She was an English lecturer at Bristol. She had died very young of breast cancer.

'The worst,' Suzanne said, cradling her pride and joy.

Everything was taken care of by a lawyer, who would become Vernon's guardian if his father died before he was sixteen. There was Mrs Cobb to clean, and a gardener once a week and the two alternating carers who washed, dressed and fed his father. He was fed by tubes, now that he couldn't swallow any more. Vernon cooked for himself. He was quite good. He even made pastry and cakes. And casseroles. Casseroles were good as they lasted a week and he could have them with baked potatoes, pasta or even on toast.

They returned, via the fridge and more cider, to the studio, which Sasha preferred as she said the books were judging her. There was a big, paint-dotted sound system in there, as his dad had liked to paint to music as it helped the models relax. First Vernon played one of his father's old Doors albums. Eustace thought it a terrible caterwauling racket, though of course didn't say so, and he watched as the girls drunkenly danced together, hands above their heads and in their hair, then drew Vernon and Tyler in to join them. Despite his lifelong insistence that music was just noise to him, Vernon was an unexpectedly good dancer, actually flexing his thighs and hips rather than just shifting from foot to clompily-booted foot like Tyler. Jez just sprawled on the daybed beside Eustace, intently picking the label off his bottle. The scent of sweat and Brut coming off him was making Eustace's nose tickle. Then Vernon put on *Dark Side of the Moon* and he and Suzanne and Tyler and Sasha started kissing where they stood, lazily but persistently. Soon Eustace could clearly see both boys' hard-ons pressing through their jeans. Suzanne slid an exploratory hand over Vernon's, her weekend bangles clattering down around her wrist as she did so.

It was awful. Clearly Eustace couldn't pair off with Jez, although symmetry and desire required it, and walking out would have looked prissy. But simply to sit and watch felt all wrong. But then Sasha broke off and glanced at him – Tyler remained eyes shut, comically open mouthed – and she smiled at Eustace before continuing, so it seemed that having an audience was part of the couples' pleasure.

After a while first one pair then the other stopped and yet more cider was fetched and there was more drunken chatting and lolling around.

It became a pattern, getting together like this after school or at weekends, up at the Fort if it was fine or in the shelter but most often at Vernon's house because they could do as they liked there. But Eustace did not always join them. He used cello practice and his mother as excuses he knew would go unchallenged.

He felt he was losing Vernon, just as Vernon had so surprisingly revealed himself.

CHAPTER TWENTY

His mother returned to them from Grace Manor and everything changed. She had greatly improved in her speech and mobility but it was noticeable that her symptoms flared up again if she was crossed or checked in anything. She repeatedly cut short disagreements now by alarming and ugly choking fits, explaining afresh between whooping gulps of air that part of her throat was now permanently paralysed and thus dangerous if a crumb landed on it. The air was full of her harsh little yelps of pain and frustration as she strained for things she couldn't reach rather than *be a bother to anyone*. She banished his father to sleep in Grandpa's old room, claiming that her sleep patterns were haywire since her brain damage and that it better suited a man.

She always called it that now – *my brain damage* – as though it was peculiarly hers and extra special, an exclusive torment nobody else could understand. Her medication haunted every mealtime in a little Tupperware box, supplemented by various herbal nostrums her new friends had recommended.

This challenging new version of her was only for private. If any of her Christians visited, she displayed yet another persona, more like how she had been after she woke up at the hospital, softly spoken and much given to touching people and to staring with tears in her eyes. In this guise, she spoke frequently of how she had died but come back, been *asked* to come back.

And in returning she brought Jesus with her. Suddenly Jesus was everywhere in the house, in books, in inspirational cards she stuck in places like the fridge door and the car, in holy music she now played in preference to *Spanish Flea*, and in her conversation. She said things like, 'He loves me. I can see and accept that now.'

And Jesus's friends were there as well. Every day. Calling round to drive her to the doctor or physiotherapy or to Father Tony's church, which quite clearly was no longer for Sundays only. In fact, 'It's more special on weekdays,' she declared. 'When there are no noisy children and fewer of us there.'

Far from celebrating that she had, in most senses, returned to him, his father withdrew yet further. Since her accident he had been spending a lot of time watching the loud television with the residents or sitting with them in the conservatory, silent, as though prematurely aged. Mrs Fowler said it was shock and would pass. Granny said it was *That Woman*. But now he spent hours every day in the bedroom to which he had been banished. At least, he was there when Eustace left for school and often there when he came back. And frequently now he just cried. He didn't wail or sob, nothing making much noise; the tears simply welled in his eyes and ran down his face and he sighed or just closed his eyes, and let them run.

'We all pray for your father,' his mother told him. 'He's in a dark valley.'

'Are you sure he doesn't need medical help?' Eustace asked.

'We will pray and it will pass. He's not as strong as you or I.'

Eustace tried sitting with his father. He would take school books into his room to work there and keep him company in their joint retreat from Jesus, but that often only made his father leave the room and take his unreachable sorrow elsewhere, which made Eustace feel guilty.

Granny died finally. She left her life as she had lived it, with the utmost discretion and lack of fuss. The doctor said her heart had given out but Eustace thought it quite likely she herself had stopped her heart with a final surge of willpower. Remaining in her room, she was spared the proofs of her daughter-in-law's new friendship with Jesus, but she knew all about it as Eustace had continued to bring her regular bulletins with her breakfast tray as he left for school.

He found he could not cry for her. Her dislike of displayed emotion was too strong and her death had been too clearly a release. The contrast with Grandpa's death could not have been greater. For all her late fumbling with her bible, her last gesture was a quite shocking rejection of the Church. A brutally coherent letter, filed with her will at her solicitors when she was still of sound mind, made it plain she wanted to be cremated without ceremony, religion or family witnesses and her ashes were to be scattered at the Fort, since that was *where my late husband proposed to me and wooed me, even though the views are criminally overgrown now, I gather.* So the only ceremony was the ash-scattering, which Eustace did alone with his father and Mrs Fowler because his mother couldn't manage the steps and thought the rejection of God's grace at the end too sad. Mrs Fowler baked an extra special and enormous cherry cake to be shared between them all and the residents afterwards.

She handed in her notice the next day. She had been cooking and increasingly managing the home from when it was Granny's private house and thought it time, she said, although Eustace suspected she was driven out by the increasing incursions of Jesus into her territory.

His mother began to host Bible Study and Julian Meetings in both day room and conservatory, co-opting baffled or compliant residents sitting nearby. She found a new cook through her church, a young, comfortless woman, rescued by Father Tony after a bad marriage turned violent. And she, in turn, introduced pairs of bright-eyed Christian 'cadets', who astonishingly volunteered their strength and skills around the home in return for being able to sit in confidential huddles with already confused residents assuring them that, yes, they might not remember meeting Jesus but he met them on the road to Emmaus and remembered them every day. They were local youths for the most part, with accents that made it sound as though Emmaus was one stop before Filton Abbey Wood. The new cook said she only baked cakes at weekends, and that white sugar was a poison and Eustace needed to lose weight. He did not warm to her.

It was assumed that Granny had nothing to leave beyond the contents of her jewellery case, which were scant and characteristically unspectacular and her room, which were battered and shabby apart from a very pretty watercolour of a pleasure steamer docking at the old pier. They knew she owned the house, of course, which she left to Eustace's father. Had she left it to a cats' charity, Eustace considered, the shock might have done everybody good. But then, the will read and probate completed, he and his father received identical letters (because Eustace was still a minor) from her solicitor informing them that she had left Eustace what seemed a huge sum of £5000 *to further his musical studies.*

This was a complete surprise since she had never seemed to take much interest in his cello-playing even when he was small. It was enough to pay for lessons for the rest of the year as well as for two more courses at Ancrum.

As she had suggested at the hospital, he rang Carla just after half-term. It was so good to hear her voice. Their voices, in fact, because Louis answered. He hadn't realized until then just how much he'd missed them both, missed not just the lessons but the calm, unregulated Friday nights with them in Clifton. It was as though he had to pretend everywhere else – at home, at school, especially at school – increasingly even with Vernon, and hearing Louis kindly saying in that gravelly tone of his, 'Hey, Man-Cub, how are the hormones? We've missed you,' let him breathe out and be himself even if all he said was the usual awkward nothing much.

Carla sounded breathless, as though taking the call had diverted her from something in a rush and flustered her.

But she, too, said it was good to hear his voice. She asked how his mother was and he said she was home and out of the woods but . . .

'But what?' she asked.

'Nothing. It's easier if I leave it till I'm not here.'

He heard a telltale creak on the landing below and glanced round to see his mother was coming up the stairs. He was convinced that her breathing and movement were not at all laboured until she saw him looking at her. He turned back to the phone.

'School days aren't as long as they were at St Chad's, but I was wondering if you still had a space on Saturday mornings.'

'First thing?'

'Yes.'

'So you could still stay over on Fridays?'

'Yes.' He saw now that he wanted this more than anything.

'I hope you've been keeping up your practice.'

'Of course,' he said, although he had become a little lax that term, first distracted by all the hospital visits then by not having cello lessons to keep him focused, then by the fun of hanging around after school with Vernon, the girls and the cousins.

'Well let's see.' He heard her flick her diary's pages, heard his mother arrive on the landing behind him, breathing heavily. 'We could do that,' Carla said. 'I think it's time you learnt the next Beethoven, get you working on nice clean runs and clear, fast string crossing.'

'Great.'

'And how about the Easter course? Are you able to go back?'

'I just had a little legacy,' he told her, loving how that sounded. 'I'm paying for it myself.'

'Brilliant. So. Be here for supper on Friday?'

'Yes please.'

She laughed. 'Eustace?' she added.

'Yes?'

'This is all OK with your parents, I take it?'

'Oh yes. My dad said to call you.'

As he hung up, his mother put on the most appalling display, at once crying and enraged.

'You are *not* to go back there!' she insisted.

'But I need to carry on with my lessons or my technique will slip.'

Standing so close reminded them both he had been growing in the last six months and was now taller than her by an inch or more. Since taking up with Jesus, she had stopped wearing scent along with lipstick. She smelled of effort – women's sweat had a different tang to it than men's – and of some mentholated embrocation one of her new friends liked to rub into her neck because they were both convinced she still had whiplash damage there.

'There are other teachers,' she said, taking a step back.

'This is Weston,' he reminded her, 'not Budapest. If there are, they won't be as good as Carla. I need a pupil of Jean's. Anyone else will teach me all wrong.'

'Don't be precious.' She had raised her voice.

'Music *is* precious. That's the whole point. You have to

be fussy. You don't know anything.' He realized he was raising his voice back at her, shouting nearly. They had never done this but he found he couldn't stop.

'Don't talk to me like that.' She started to work up to one of her choking attacks. 'I'm not well.'

'We gathered. Anyway, it won't be for long. I'm going back to Jean at Easter and I want her to take me on full time.'

'What about school?'

'Only till I'm sixteen. Then she can teach me everything I need.'

'Stop this! Stop this at once!' his father shouted at them. They were both so startled they stopped and looked over at where he stood, leaning woozily in a doorway. He never shouted, especially these days.

'Oh darling.' Her tone was so false it made Eustace queasy, like Dream Topping. 'Have you taken too many again? Valium aren't sweets.'

'I'm aware of that. He goes back to her for lessons and that's that. We agreed.'

'But—'

'We agreed. Or have you forgotten?'

She never gave in to him, especially since Jesus and brain damage had fortified her against all criticism, but on this occasion something in his expression made her crumble.

He returned to Grandpa's room, she lumbered back downstairs to whichever ladies were visiting and Eustace shut himself away, tuned up and took out his Beethoven sonatas to look at Opus 5 Number 2.

CHAPTER TWENTY-ONE

The following Friday Eustace caught the train to Bristol after school, guilty that he had enjoyed airily telling Suzanne and Sasha that he couldn't go to see *Jaws* again with them and Vernon as he was staying the night with friends in Clifton. His father had roused himself sufficiently to help him open a bank account in which to sink Granny's legacy and had gently shown him how to write a cheque to Carla for his lesson and how to go into a branch and write one to Cash when he needed spending money.

He had spending money in his pocket now as well as the chequebook in his duffel bag. It felt very grown-up to stop in the little corner shop in Clifton when he climbed down off the bus to buy chocolates to take with him.

'Never arrive empty-handed,' his mother always said. 'People will always say *Oh, you shouldn't have* but they never mean it.'

That there had been some major changes in the household was apparent the moment he walked in. The basement door was never locked when Carla was teaching, so that she wasn't bothered by having to interrupt a lesson to open it. This had always struck him as foolhardy in a city where there were likely to be robbers around but Carla said the noise and frequent comings and goings would confuse any onlooker as to how many people lived there. This time, as he pushed open the door, glimpsing a lesson still in progress, he immediately saw new things, or things in new places. Furniture, pictures, everything had shifted and the usual smell of oranges and cinnamon had gone. Though still dramatic and full of interesting objects and Louis' big canvases propped here and there like so many pieces of theatre scenery, the house seemed to have lost the quality that so seduced him when he first set foot in it. Or maybe he was just older and more experienced. He had seen other houses. Ancrum. Vernon's house. Maybe this one needed a good clean.

In Carla's last lesson of the day, her student was playing a piece he had learnt with her early on – *La Cinquantaine* by Gabriel-Marie – and not very well in tune. This had never happened to him before. Cello lessons had always seemed to exist for him in a self-indulgent bubble setting him apart from the rest of life, in particular from school. But of course they were lessons and, as with any lessons, a teacher, however good, was bound to repeat themselves with each pupil, bound, at least, to cover some of the same ground. It was no different from Latin teachers always using Caesar's *Gallic Wars* or maths ones, trigonometry tables or slide rules. But still, he felt a small convulsion at what felt like betrayal.

And there was none of the usual smell of Friday-night cooking. It was something of a ritual with Ebrahim to cook supper or at least to bake something, to unwind after a day's rehearsing. And Fridays when he didn't have a concert were always cause for making an extra effort.

Eustace rounded the first-floor corner into the kitchen. Nothing was cooking. There was no Ebrahim. Louis had a

newspaper spread out on the table and was cradling a bottle of beer as he read. Offering chocolates in a house where
supper seemed unlikely to happen felt odd, but Eustace
held them out anyway.

'I brought these,' he said.

Louis looked up, smiled his big bear smile.

'Hey! Man-Cub,' he said and surprised Eustace with a
big hug. He smelled of man and turps and the funny cigarettes he smoked, which Eustace suspected were cannabis
but didn't like to ask. 'You're growing at long last,' he said.
'Soon going to have to stop doing this,' and he ruffled Eustace's hair, which made him feel about eight but in a good
way. 'How tall's your daddy?'

'Six-two, I think.'

'Huh. Soon lose your puppy fat. How's your mum?'

'OK. Weird. She nearly died, and made friends with
Jesus when she didn't.' It felt so good to talk lightly at last
of something so ghastly.

'Never a good idea. How is your dad coping?'

'Um . . . Could I sit?'

'Oh. Sure. Here.'

As Eustace took a seat at the table, Louis fetched him a
beer.

'Wait. Shit. How old are you?'

'Fourteen.'

'Drink it very slowly. Do you want lemonade in it?'

'What's that like?'

'Less nice.'

'Then no thanks.'

Louis sat again. His bulk was comforting in the same

way Rowena the deerhound's had been. The cello down-stairs stopped for a bit then started again, now with Carla unmistakably playing as well. A simple Bartók duet, another piece he used to play with her.

'So how's the new school? Is it rough?'

'Actually I quite like it. It's just a bit big and noisy but . . . I've got a new name. Stash.'

'Stash?' Louis wrinkled his nose. 'Can I keep calling you Eustace?'

'Of course. Where's Ebrahim?'

Louis took a swig of his beer. He sighed, turned a page of his paper, although he wasn't reading it now.

'Ebrahim left me,' he said.

'Oh. I'm . . . I'm sorry. I thought you two were . . .'

Louis smiled wryly. 'So did I. He met someone else and he's joined them in New York. All his things went off in a huge crate today. He even sold his piano.'

'No!'

'He gave Carla a second-hand upright to replace it. She's here full-time now, of course, which is lovely. But, I dunno.' He shrugged and said, '*Het is heftig*. We'd been together since, well, for fifteen years. The house is full of gaps. You try not to think things matter. They're things. They can be replaced. All of them. But then things have a way of stand-ing in for people. He would go on long concert tours but I coped because all his things told me he was coming back. But . . . your bed is still where it was, Man-Cub. And all my dirty books you like to read.'

'I don't.'

'Eustace, it's fine. Curiosity is good. You must take

down and read whatever books interest you.' Louis smiled sadly, reached out to ruffle Eustace's hair again. 'Sorry. Bit pissed. I said I'd make pasta.'

'I can help.'

'*Uitstekend!*'

They both stood, Louis a little unsteadily, and Eustace put a large pan of water on to boil.

'Let me teach you something,' Louis said, his big hands reaching into a basket for an onion and into a cupboard for a tin of tomatoes. 'Fetch me butter from the fridge, would you?'

'Sure.'

'So . . . Every student's mother tells them to start tomato sauce by frying onion and garlic. But the best tomato sauce, the *only* tomato sauce you will ever make after tasting this, involves no frying at all and no garlic. Open that can and tip it into a pan.'

Eustace obeyed.

'Now peel the onion. That's it. Top and tail and peel and slice in half just once across the waist. Now put the whole thing into the tomatoes. Yes. I know. Weird. But that's what you do. Now a really big slice of butter. About three or four ounces. Bigger. That's it. In it goes.'

'Really?'

'Trust me. Now, on to simmer, really low. That's it. And a lid on it. Now we measure out our pasta then we can sit down again. You do nothing for about forty minutes then boil your pasta, fish out the onion chunks and throw those away and . . . perfect, creamy tomato sauce. You will never forget, especially once you've tasted it.'

They heard the last pupil of the day leaving with her mother and soon afterwards Carla joined them. She greeted Eustace warmly and cannily bound him to her afresh with a dismissive comment on how the pupil would not be coming much longer as she did not seem to be able to hear when a note was sharp or flat and how she was beginning to think it was not a defect that could be remedied by instruction.

'It's like teaching driving to someone with no understanding of speed or the difference between forwards and back. I mean tuning is so *fundamental*. God, I need a drink. Thanks, Louis.'

Over supper, which was indeed revelatory in its simple deliciousness, she quizzed him in detail about the course, in particular the other cellists and whether they, too, wanted to be taken on by Jean at sixteen.

'The hard truth is that, though she's an idealist, and wants everyone to have their lives transformed by Haydn, she is also brutally realistic about excellence. And she will only ever have space and energy to teach a handful of full time students. Between now and the Easter course we have to improve you as much as we possibly can. You've no school exams, have you?'

He shook his head.

'Good. So what are your two weakest points as a cellist?'

'Carla . . .' Louis began but she raised a hand to emphasize that the question was important.

Eustace thought carefully. 'Agility,' he said. 'My left hand is OK in fast passages but my right lets me down and my string crossing gets inaccurate and can't always keep up.'

She nodded and he gained the impression she already knew this but, Jean-fashion, needed to hear that he knew it as well.

'And the other weak point?'

Here she smiled slightly to show that she knew she was being a bit intense but also that they both understood why.

'Finding high notes first time,' he said.

'You know we all cheat,' she said. 'The greatest cellists probably still have little pencil marks or even scratches on their fingerboards to help them find some of those notes without hesitating. But yes. We can work on that. It's a confidence thing and a muscle-memory thing, and both can be built. Talking of which, did you make this sauce?'

'Louis showed me.'

'Memorize this recipe,' she said, 'and you will never lack friends.'

And so saying, she brought fruit and cheese to the table and diverted the conversation into easier areas, asking him about friends at school while she and Louis contributed their own tales of secondary-school friendships. Each in turn spoke of a great love from their teens. Louis' had been another boy at his school who had brutally dropped him and taken up with a girl the moment his father found out and threatened to move him to a different school. Carla hesitated a moment, glancing at Eustace before her confession.

'Are you old enough for this?'

'He's fourteen,' Louis said. 'Plenty old enough.'

And so she confessed how she had been crazily in love with her best girlfriend at Ancrum but far too innocent and young for her age to realize their feelings could find a physical expression.

Her words petered out.

'What?' Eustace asked.

'Fourteen is far too young,' she said, 'and it's past my bedtime and probably past yours. Night both,' and she kissed them both a little drunkenly and went up to bed.

Eustace could not believe he had been so naïve. 'So . . . So does Carla prefer women?' he asked.

Louis smiled. 'Prefer implies that it's a choice. It is very rarely a choice with any of us.'

'Is she OK? She seemed a bit sad.'

'Well . . . We both miss Ebrahim. Three in the household worked well for us. Carla and I are both naturally rather intense and his mischief kept us on our toes. And with him gone, it's depressing how often we feel like a straight couple with a dead sex life. It is SO past your bedtime, Man-Cub!'

'Yes, yes, but . . .'

Louis sighed, measuring his words like precious pigments as he cut them both a thin slice of cheese. His eyes, which so often looked almost black because they were so deep set, caught the light from the table lamp and flashed green. He rubbed a hand through his short hair.

'She would kill me for telling you even this much because, well, she's your teacher but . . . She has recently lost someone too. Like I lost Ebrahim.'

'Another woman?'

He nodded. 'She was more in love than I've ever seen her. They both were. It seemed so absolutely the real thing. They were going to set up home together, keep cats, grow vegetables, the full menu and all four courses. Then something happened and the . . .' Eustace sensed he was about to say a very rude word but pulled back from it at the last moment. 'The other woman changed her mind and cut her off, just like my friend Lars did at school. No explanation. No contact. There is nothing more brutal because it gives you no closure. At least Ebrahim looked me in the eye and explained, so I could see it was beyond persuasion or argument. If ever, Eustace or Stash or whatever we call you now, I prefer Eustace, God I'm drunk. If EVER you love someone and they decide they love someone else, NEVER try to argue them back in love with you. It will only make them love you less. Now come on. Bedtime.'

He led Eustace back down to his usual little bedroom in the basement, found him a bath towel, put a new bulb in the bedside lamp so that the room, which also had Ebrahim-gaps, looked cosier. He started looking at the books on the shelves before he left.

'Don't read Genet yet,' he said. 'It'll only worry and depress you and adolescence is bad enough. Frankly you'll learn more from the trashy stuff. And the comics. Borrow whatever you like, OK? Just bear in mind it's trash, it's fantasy and being gay doesn't mean you have to drop everything and move to New York or San Francisco. And you can prefer string quartets to Donna Summer. Just, you know, be yourself. I'm going out for a bit but you know where everything is. Night, Man-Cub.'

He closed the door behind him but Eustace stepped over to open it again as the lack of a window in there disturbed him. He saw Louis heading up the steps from the area to the pavement, light from a streetlamp glinting off the studs on the leather biker jacket he was now wearing.

He was so busy wondering where Louis could be going at an hour when everyone else was in bed and then so rapidly drawn into poring over a book of cartoon strips from some gay magazine in America, that it was only at three in the morning, when someone bumping into a dustbin woke him and he found he had fallen asleep with the light on and his cheek pressed into some outrageously exciting pictures by someone called Tom of Finland, that he realized Louis had recognized and greeted his secret self without Eustace having made any declaration.

CHAPTER TWENTY-TWO

Through that winter and into the early spring, Eustace's life settled into a fragile stability. He found various ways to make school and home bearable. At school he did well at maths once again and slipped steadily and without panic to the middle of the class in other subjects. He learnt that nobody much minded in such a competitively sporty school if he skipped football and rugby sessions, beyond awarding him a D in his report; as a hopeless player he could only prove a liability and as a cellist he could not afford wrist or finger injuries such as Tyler or Jez so often displayed.

As for home, his parents now seemed barely to interact. It was tacitly accepted that his father was afflicted with depression, if not actively suffering a nervous breakdown, for which the family GP continued to prescribe Valium. As a result of this, his father now spent most of his days in bed or, if dressed, then asleep in a chair. Pursuing her now ceaseless round of early morning Communion, Christian socializing, prayer groups, bible study and evensong – for which friends would drive her to Bristol Cathedral – his mother left him to the care of the humourless cook and whichever shiny-eyed volunteers might visit his room. Eustace found it easy enough to avoid them both in the name of homework, of which there was actually very little compared to what had been set at St Chad's, and cello practice, which they both understood was a duty without end. The schoolwork and cello practice were genuine; he felt entirely justified in pursuing them. They very rarely ate a meal together. In fact the nearest he now came to family mealtimes were his Friday evenings at Carla and Louis' kitchen table, where he felt he could be himself, uncensored and genuinely interested in whatever the two adults had to tell him.

And alongside these two strands of his education, he was pursuing a third, thanks to the contents of Louis' shelves of paperbacks in the basement. He did indeed read the Penguin translations of Genet and of Cocteau, of Mann's *Death in Venice* and *Tonio Kröger* and Forster's recently published *Maurice*, which were all, more or less, very depressing. But alongside them, at Louis' urging, he read the more recent Americans, not just the hypnotically strange *Myra Breckinridge* and *Myron* and the inspiring *Giovanni's Room* but *The Lord Won't Mind*, *One for the Gods*, and *Forth Into Light*. It amused him that the titles of these last might have adorned the Christian books his mother now read. There was also *Forgetting Elena*, a waspish satire set somewhere called Fire Island, which he felt compelled to read several times, convinced he had yet to wring all the meaning from its strange overlapping of gay beach house with oriental court ritual. The men in all these seemed to be uniformly handsome, virile, rich and expensively educated but they came to believe in their right to happiness and the stories ended with them neither punished, unhappily married nor dead. The novels had about them a strain of self-mythologizing breathlessness, full of precious feminine references which confused him.

'Fret not, Man-Cub,' Louis told him. 'It's called camp. Time enough for that when you finally get the hell out of Weston-super-Mare.'

So Eustace read on, devouring *The Persian Boy*, *The Front Runner* and a memoir called *The Best Little Boy in the World*. And the books taught him things by inference, such as that, though Louis apparently remained single, his late-night trips out in his leather jacket were not for fresh air and that gay, lesbian and bisexual people were all around, frequently disguised as high-achieving straight ones.

He continued to exchange occasional letters with Naomi, though she was not an assiduous correspondent and, once they had established that they had both booked to return to Ancrum in the Easter holidays, the need to stay in touch felt less urgent. He did not like to let slip too much detail of what he was learning and practising, alerted by Carla to the not so covert competition for Jean's attention and long-term favour.

He also watched Carla fall in love. She did so slowly and very discreetly. At first she just mentioned *a friend* who taught German at the university. Then they all began to meet. Margit arrived a couple of times as he was leaving on a Saturday morning – a short, owlish woman with a radiant smile – then she was there at supper on Friday evenings; not always, but often enough for it to become unremarkable. And when she was there, there was delicious black rye bread at breakfast, which she baked herself.

Sensing his mother's new disapproval of Carla must be linked to her having finally understood Carla's true nature, he was careful never to go into any detail about what happened at Clifton, whom he met or whatever. The one thing he did let slip was that Ebrahim had moved to America, so that it was now just Louis and Carla living there. He knew this was cowardly and wilfully misleading. He said nothing of Margit and her homemade bread and radical politics, knowing his mother had yet to forgive the Germans for the war and not wishing to goad her. Interestingly he found he told Vernon equally little. His trips to Clifton were precious territory he did not wish to pollute with the curiosity of friends.

He was always extremely careful with the books he borrowed each week. He transported them into the house in his cello case – which nobody but he ever opened – only read the books in his bedroom and, when not reading them, hid them deep under his mattress, not just pushed under near the edge, in the way he used to hide Vernon's magazine, but lifting the mattress right up so as to hide the books at its very middle, where even somebody changing the sheets would be unlikely to stumble on them.

He had read his way through most of the 'good' books. Responsible Louis always asked to see what he was borrowing or what he had borrowed and they would have a short discussion, like a little tutorial, when a book came back. In his head Eustace liked to think he went to Carla for cello lessons and to Louis for gay ones. But Louis had recently gone on a visit to Gouda to see his mother, who was unwell, and Eustace had taken advantage of his absence to borrow two publications he had often looked at in bed of a Friday night but was fairly sure Louis would not willingly have let him take back with him to Weston.

The first was a novel, though one glance told you it was not a book one read for the quality of its prose. It was called *Chains* and its tawdry yellow cover featured a naked man wearing only leather riding boots, with his clenched buttocks to the viewer, ankles clasped by a second naked man over whose back and buttocks he trailed a thin chain from his fist, promising pain. This was by someone described as *the Author of the Leatherman's Handbook.*

His other unauthorized loan was a copy of a lurid, if monochrome little magazine from America called *Physique Pictorial.* It was a few years old, so Louis was obviously keeping it because he had enjoyed it. It had photographs of naked men just standing around and doing nothing, as crudely invitational as the women in Vernon's magazine. The cover, graphically betraying the nature of the publication, displayed the first of several Tom of Finland drawings. In this an extremely well-endowed man leaned proudly back against a fence outside a barn, wearing an odd combination of baseball cap and, yet again, black leather riding boots. On a bench set at a convenient height, sprawled an even bigger, equally thick-lipped man, bare-chested above his bulging jeans, his muscular top covered in an unbuttoned leather jacket, just like Louis', and with a jaunty leather cap to match. And he was making a gasping, close examination of the standing man's thickening cock. It was preposterous, the set-up and clothes as ludicrously impractical as anything spotted in *Mayfair,* but Eustace's response to it was instantaneous, as though the pictures had pressed a button in his head. They were insistent. They said *Look. This is who you are. This is what you want. This. Look!*

He had yet to read *Chains* because he kept turning back to the magazine. His desires, he supposed, were in their infancy and, like an infant, they were still responding primarily to pictures.

He planned to keep both publications well concealed and to slip them back into Louis' bookshelves the following Friday. In the meanwhile he found himself thinking about his room in his absence and counting off the hours until he could be back there, as though he had a secret lover hidden there, not an old black and white magazine. He looked around in classes and wondered how many of the other boys poring over their textbooks were feeling the same about the busty pouters under their mattresses and at the backs of their big brother's underwear drawers.

He had bunked off games as usual – a cross-country run that day as the playing fields were still waterlogged from an overnight downpour. It had turned into one of those crisp spring days when it felt miraculous that the town was not yet overrun with visitors. Unusually his mother was not in the day room with one of her friends when he came home but sitting on the garden bench in the sun. For the first time since her accident she looked like her old self. She had put on lipstick and a dress that showed off her figure. She had a cardigan draped over her shoulders in an old way of hers he liked to think made her look French.

'Hello,' she called out. 'You're early.'

'It was only games,' he said. He sat beside her and dropped his rucksack on the gravel.

'Let's both bunk off,' she said. 'Drive somewhere nice as it's sunny.'

'Really? Are you up to it?'

'I'm driving myself quite a lot now. Come on. Just us.'

He laughed. 'Come on, then.'

She already had the car keys to hand so he threw his bag on to the back seat and they sped off. She wound down the front windows and drove them swiftly inland to Wells and a tea shop, one that was comically unchanged though they had not visited in years. She made him order a slice of gâteau though she only wanted a toasted teacake.

'Your new hair looks good,' he said. 'Have you had it trimmed again?'

'Yes,' she said. 'I decided not to grow it back. It was only that length out of habit and like this it's so easy to look after. Like an old French woman's, only I shan't be dyeing it those lurid colours they like there. Is this dress too young?'

'No,' he said. 'I like it.'

All her scars had gone. Despite her new piety she must have been obsessive in her use of creams. The dress revealed a bit of cleavage, just enough, and he saw she was wearing the old amber beads that were her sole wearable inheritance from Granny and had taken off the crucifix she had been wearing night and day since she had been given it in hospital.

'So,' she said. 'Tell me everything. How's school?'

'OK,' he said, picking at stray crumbs. 'I quite like it, actually. Though you wouldn't like the girls Vernon and I go around with now.'

'Are they a bit rough around the edges?'

'They're a bit . . . local,' he said and she laughed, as he knew she would.

'And you've paid for the Easter course yourself?'

He nodded. 'Yup.'

'That's so grown-up. You know . . . if Jean Curlew.'

'Curwen.'

'Yes. If she does offer you a place, I'm sure we can find money to pay for it.'

'There are scholarships, Carla says. If parents can't pay.'

'Yes. Well. One way or another.' She waved at the waitress and made an elegant, ladylike *we'd-like-our-bill-please* gesture. 'And otherwise . . . how are things?'

'Oh,' he said. 'OK.'

'You're not to worry about your father.'

'Of course I worry. He cries all the time.'

'Not all the time.'

'Most of the time. When he's not asleep or so full of Valium he can't speak.'

'Thank you.' She handed the waitress back the bill saucer with money on it and stood. 'We're all praying for him. He still hasn't got over nearly losing me.'

Really? He thought. *Really?* But he merely shrugged because he was enjoying the sensation of having her full attention for a change. And perhaps that letter of hers had been only a mad impulse, no sooner penned than burnt.

She drove back by a slightly different route that took them into a secluded valley through freshly ploughed fields where last night's rain still lay in the furrows. There was a cluster of fine old buildings up ahead with a high wall around the garden to their rear, and an orchard.

'Oh look,' she said sharply.

'What?' he asked. 'Lovely old house.'

313

'It's Grace Manor,' she said. 'Let me show you.'

'But isn't it a retreat? I'm sure they don't want—' he started but she had turned up the drive and swung in under a gatehouse and into a gravelled quadrangle marked out by tightly clipped bay trees in pots. 'We shouldn't just show up here,' he said.

'It's fine,' she said, patting his forearm. 'They're friends. We can say we were just passing. I wanted to show you the garden. Even at this time of year it'll be—'

'Do we have to?'

'Come on,' she said. 'Just quickly.'

And she was out of the car so that he felt he had to follow her because since giving up her second walking stick she could be wobbly.

'Shouldn't you lock it?' he asked, glancing back. A woman in a pink fisherman's smock with a wooden crucifix pinned to it was standing near the car. She said nothing but smiled and raised a hand. He flapped a hand in response and hurried after his mother.

It was all very beautiful and astonishingly quiet: one of those rare country spots where there seemed to be no twentieth-century noise. Not even a tractor could be heard, simply the bleating of sheep. The stone was the local limestone, the sort that looked as though it had warm sun on it even on a dull day.

'It's Tudor,' she said. 'Well, the oldest parts are. It was rather fancifully extended by a history-minded vicar, I think. Oh look. Agnes, hello.'

Agnes was a smiling, rustling sort of woman, quite a bit

older than his mother. She reached out a hand to shake his and he saw she had strong, tennis player's arms.

'Hello,' she said. 'You must be Eustace. We heard all about you when your mother was with us.'

'Agnes is a nurse,' his mother said, with a glance at Agnes' little navy leather shoulder bag. 'In case anyone has a turn or something.'

'Well,' Agnes said. 'It's quite a drive along those back lanes to the nearest hospital. Have you been inside the walled garden yet, Eustace? The spring bulbs are just getting going and it's so pretty.'

'We were just going there,' his mother said.

'You're sure we're not disturbing anything?' Eustace asked Agnes.

'Heavens no,' she told him. 'I'll just pop inside and tell Father Tony you're both here.'

'Father Tony?' Eustace asked, but she was gone.

'He works here sometimes,' his mother said. 'I'm sure I told you. Now just look at this,' and she led the way through a little wrought iron gate that opened with a well-oiled silence on to a garden in another, smaller quadrangle where a chapel formed one side and a modern limestone crucifix loomed in a corner. The crucifix spoiled it all rather, making him think of how some people's gardens ended up with little pet cemeteries in one corner.

His mother's chatter was sounding nervous now. 'Of course it was late summer when I was here, autumn really, but there were still lots of roses. You'll just have to imagine those. But just look at all those narcissi out already. I always prefer the white ones. Those yellow and orange trumpets your father insists on planting are so very, well . . .'

'What a lovely surprise, young man.'

Father Tony was as handsome as Eustace remembered and had somehow maintained a tan through the winter. Perhaps he went skiing. Agnes was rustling in his wake as he shook Eustace's hand warmly and kissed his mother's cheek.

'Hello,' Eustace said, disturbed at how the priest was still holding his hand.

'You've not seen the chapel yet, I think.'

'Well we should probably be getting home,' Eustace told him.

'Oh, but you must see in here first. It's pretty special.'

And he dropped Eustace's hand only to envelop his shoulders in an arm.

He had no smell at all. Eustace found himself thinking of the peel-off faces in *Mission Impossible*.

'I swear you've grown since last year,' Father Tony told him. 'This way.' And he steered Eustace through the door-way to the chapel.

'I shouldn't have drunk so much tea,' his mother called out. 'I'll just nip to the . . .' and she slipped from their side.

'It's through the gate and first on the left,' Agnes called after her. 'But you'll remember the way.'

The chapel was fine. It had a roof like an upturned boat and stained glass that looked older than anything in Wes-ton. It was very plainly furnished, with pale oak benches and an oak table for an altar. A glass crucifix glowed in the fading light thanks to some ingeniously concealed lighting. Father Tony kept his arm over Eustace's shoulder and Eustace had a ghastly feeling he might be about to suggest that they pray together.

'See,' he said. 'I told you it was special.'

And for a second Eustace registered the faintly comical fact that he had a mouth not unlike a Tom of Finland policeman. He wondered just how thoroughly Father Tony would lose his cool if he kissed him on the mouth, tongues and all. Then the sound of a car's ignition firing made him flinch out of the priest's grip.

'Mum?' he called, and ran out to the garden in time to see her car swing around the outer quadrangle and drive out beneath the arch. She had left behind the tartan suitcase and a plastic carrier bag. He sprinted across to the little iron gate but it was locked now.

'Don't leave me!' he shouted, 'Mum!' reflecting as he did so that he never called her that, never really called her anything, so had no name to call out in such a crisis. He shook the gate but it held fast, then a wasp stung one of his shoulders. He slapped a hand to kill it but Father Tony caught his wrist in a fierce grip midstrike and he saw it wasn't a wasp but Agnes delivering a swift injection through his shirtsleeve.

She looked flustered and pink in the face from hurrying and opening her little medical bag at the same time, but she still managed a kind smile.

'Just to relax you,' she said. 'It's quite safe. Mum signed a consent form. I am qualified to do this.'

His knees began to weaken and he slumped on to a bench against the wall, feeling as though all his strings had been cut. The sun had dipped behind the buildings and the shadows seemed to spread across the paths and bushes. He saw Father Tony cast a worried look at his colleague, saw her mouthing *It's fine* back at him. Somebody unlocked the iron gate. The woman in the pink smock. She was carrying the suitcase and handed Father Tony the plastic bag through which he glimpsed the cover of *Physique Pictorial*.

'We helped your mother,' Father Tony was telling him. 'And now she wants us to help you.'

CHAPTER TWENTY-THREE

Two days later. Three. Four. He did what he should have done the first night had he not been so groggy. He slipped down to the chapel, to which, being in one of the inner rooms, he could enjoy access day or night, and used a teaspoon he had slipped up his sleeve at supper to jemmy open the little offerings box. Notes in there were no use to him and he left them, but he scrabbled up the one tenpence piece and thrust it safely to the bottom of his jeans pocket. Perhaps there was a God after all. Then he padded swiftly back to his room, knotted together his sheets and the ugly orange curtains as tightly as he could, tied one end to the bracket that supported the sink in the landing loo, dropped the rest through the window, squeezed through the gap, scraping and cutting his belly in the process and lowered himself as far down as he could before taking a deep breath and letting himself drop to the field below.

There was only a sliver of moon still up but the cold night was cloudless. There were sheep down there and he dreaded they'd start bleating at his sudden arrival among them but happily they were huddling at the far end beneath some old apple trees. He ran as fast as he could across one field, across another then on to the lane and back up the side of the valley down which he remembered his mother driving. He ran until a stitch and breathlessness stopped him then walked, breath whistling out of him, terrified he was making far too much noise, ready to leap into the hedge and hide if there were shouts or torches behind him, or headlamps. He had no coat – that had been taken from him with his shoes – but he could not have said if he was shivering from cold or adrenalin. It was more sport than he felt he had performed in his life to date. By the time he finally saw the yellowed light in a distant call box his slippers and socks were wet through from dew.

He raised the receiver and rang the only possible person. It was the dead of night, of course, and a forty-minute drive, so it was a good hour or so before they could be with him. Before the pips went, Vernon was marvellously calm and controlled.

'I seem to remember there's a little sign in there for emergency calls,' he said. 'It gives your Ordnance Survey grid reference or something. Just read it all out to me, then we can use our brains and find you.'

There was a big old barn across the way. Nervous of being far too visible if he stayed in the light of the phone box, Eustace walked in there and groped around in the dark until he found what smelled like clean enough straw, lay down and bedded himself in, curling himself up for warmth. Somehow – an effect of shock perhaps – he fell asleep. He woke with a start, and was instantly afraid as he heard an engine running. Then he heard Suzanne's distinctive voice, not remotely sotto voce, asking,

'So where the fuck is he? It's two a.m. and I'm getting nipples like fucking Spangles here.'

They were all far too young to drive, of course, but he

knew from tales of their wild nights out in Bristol that at least one of her tribe of older brothers would be up for a spontaneous mercy dash. When he stumbled out of the barn, Suzanne gave a little scream and ran to envelop him in herself and a very smelly blanket from her big brother's minibus. It was the middle of the night but both girls had come along as well as Vernon and the cousins. They were all a bit drunk, including the driver who, Eustace remembered, made money since doing time by ferrying holidaymakers to and fro from various campsites and beaches. He also remembered the brother had a record for GBH so was probably proof against a few charismatic Christians wielding a syringe. Vernon was up front with Suzanne, because he had been map-reading with his big black torch. Tyler and Sasha were canoodling on the back seat, so Eustace sat in the middle with Jez.

'All right?' said Jez and he welcomed him on board with a lazy grin, as though midnight rescue missions were nothing out of the ordinary.

The brother dropped them at Vernon's then melted away. It was too late for anyone to go home and risk waking their families so they all piled in. Vernon and Suzanne went to his room – Eustace suddenly realizing they'd been sleeping in there for a while – Tyler and Sasha began a whispered argument about something and took it off with them to the spare room, so Eustace drifted into the kitchen where Jez took a long, expressive piss in the sink with a tap running while Eustace carried on through to the studio at the back. Being nearly all window and as it was long past the hour when the central heating switched off, it was cold but there was a pile of blankets and pillows and an old patchwork quilt on the daybed. He made himself a sort of nest there, tugged off his soaking slippers, socks and jeans, switched off the light and bedded down. He could tell it was going to be a very short night, with no curtains or blinds to stop the light searing through once the sun was up. Even now the sodium wash from a nearby streetlamp lay across everything.

He had assumed Jez would fall asleep on a sofa in the purple room but he came into the studio as well. Eustace had been facing the wall in an effort to shade his eyes for sleep but heard his heavy tread and half-turned to see him standing there beside the bed, noisily kicking off his boots.

'Hi,' he whispered.

'Your teeth are chattering,' Jez said, incapable of whispering. 'You're still frozen. Budge up.'

He slid under the quilt behind Eustace and, without a moment's hesitation, flung a meaty arm around him and pressed tightly into him, belly to back, thigh to thigh, foot tucked under foot.

'Commandos do this,' he mumbled sleepily, 'when one of them's got exposure. You smell of straw.'

'Sorry,' Eustace whispered.

'No. It's nice,' Jez said and fell heavily asleep against him.

Just then, Brut, beer and sweat were the best and safest smells in the world.

CHAPTER TWENTY-FOUR

In the morning he slept late, after stirring briefly so Jez could extricate himself to dress and leave at some point. When he finally woke in earnest, everyone had gone and he remembered it was a school day. He showered, borrowed some clean clothes of Vernon's then sat upstairs with Vernon's father, whom the morning carer had washed, fed, dressed and wheeled to his usual position.

'Hello,' he told him. 'Vernon rescued me last night. He was a bit of a hero. He doesn't need any sorting out, you know, like you once said . . . I hope we didn't make too much noise when we came in. I'll not be here long, don't worry.'

But of course there was no way of knowing what Vernon's father thought of his being there. Perhaps he liked the company. Perhaps not. It felt good to sit there for a while in the brilliant sunshine, basking like a heedless cat, but he knew the lunchtime carer would arrive before long and also that there was a risk one or other of his friends might let something slip at school and bring the authorities after him, social workers, policewomen, whoever.

He imagined his mother had told the school he was in hospital or some plausible lie to explain his absence but now that he had broken out, for all he knew the police had been alerted. She had signed a consent form, Father Tony had showed him her signature, so, however it felt, it was voluntary treatment, not kidnapping and assault.

He wrote a note to Vernon, explaining he'd borrowed the clothes and thanking him for everything and saying he'd be in touch. Then, after a few minutes' deep breathing and telling himself he was fine and couldn't be hurt in broad daylight in crowds of people, he let himself out and headed down to the waterfront and along the prom for home.

He had planned to hide in the shrubbery opposite and wait if the car were there but it wasn't so he took the risk that it was she who had taken it and not his father and let adrenalin carry him in at the front door, which he unlocked with the key they kept hidden, and hurried up to his room meeting nobody but mad old ladies who either smiled or just stared. No reliable witnesses there.

His rucksack was on the foot of the bed. Presumably when she came home from abandoning him at Grace Manor, his mother had left it there. Moving as fast as he could, he changed into his own clothes, swept others and a toothbrush into his rucksack along with whatever textbooks lay to hand and his chequebook. Then he snatched up his music case, slung his cello case over his shoulder and fled out of the house, across the town and on to the waiting Bristol train.

In his panic and confusion, he realized as he let himself in that he had no idea what day of the week it was. He became aware it was Friday only when he walked into the kitchen, where Carla was finishing lunch, and she said, 'You're several hours early.'

But then she saw his expression and his bulging rucksack.

Once he'd finished talking and crying and pulled himself together as best he could, she was forceful in a way he would not have predicted. First she made him eat something while she swiftly rang Louis' studio to summon him and called her three afternoon pupils to cancel them with profuse apologies and a smoothly fabricated account of a family emergency. Then she crouched by his chair and held his hands and looked deep into his eyes.

'Eustace, forget about your mother for a moment,' she said. 'And if you can, forget about the priest and that nurse. Do you trust your father?'

'Yes. He's . . . Well he's depressed and taking Valium for it but yes, I trust him. He wants what's best and he's not like her.'

'Does he answer the phone?'

'Hardly ever. But you could ask for him. They'd fetch him if you asked for him. You could say you were calling from Dr Linwood. That's the psychiatrist he's been seeing. They might call to change an appointment, I suppose.'

She went to the phone and dialled then suddenly hung up. 'Your mother might answer, mightn't she?'

'So?'

'She'd recognize my voice.'

At that moment Louis arrived, looked down at Eustace with concern, none of his usual smiles, and cast a questioning glance at Carla. He was immediately drawn into her plan as she passed the receiver to him.

'When they answer,' she said, 'even if it's a man, say you're Dr Linwood calling for his father. Then hand it to me when he comes on.' Swiftly she dialled the number again.

Someone answered. Louis put on a perfect English accent.

'Oh hello,' he said. 'I'm so sorry to bother you.' And he asked to speak to Eustace's father on a confidential matter. When the woman on the other end queried this, he said, 'Tell him it's Dr Linwood's office calling for him.'

There was a long pause during which Eustace pictured his mother, for he was sure it was her, walking to rap on his father's bedroom door because she always enjoyed waking him during the day. Finally Louis raised his eyebrows and handed Carla back the receiver.

'Hello,' Carla said. 'This is Carla Gold. Yes. Whatever you've been told by your wife, Eustace is now completely safe but if you don't want to involve the police and social workers and a High Court Judge having him taken into council care, you and I need to have an urgent talk. I suggest you come here. Say you're going to Dr Linwood's then drive here. Shall I remind you of the address?'

When she finally hung up and Louis turned to him and said, 'Hello Man-Cub,' he burst out with it.

'I'm sorry, Louis. I'm so sorry,' he said, and it came out so loudly he could see he was startling them both. 'I took your Tom of Finland magazine and the *Chains* book and they made me throw them on a bonfire. I'm sorry.'

Louis took a while to understand and then said that of course it didn't matter. He proceeded to get angry in a way Carla said really didn't help, although Eustace found he didn't mind at all because Louis was angry on his behalf. 'Bloody Christians,' he kept saying.

Carla suggested Eustace take his bag to the room

downstairs. *Your room*, she called it, which touched him.
'We just need to talk things through before your father
gets here.'

'Of course,' Eustace told her and left them. He didn't
like to unpack straightaway in case they decided they
couldn't have him to stay after all, but he lay on the bed
and was aware that his heart was racing.

He must have fallen asleep. The next thing he was aware
of was the mattress squeaking and tilting as someone sat
heavily by his feet. He opened his eyes and saw Louis. He
rubbed his eyelids and sat up.

'You're shattered, Man-Cub! What did those bastards
do to you? No. Tell me later.'

'Is Dad here?'

'Yup. He's having a nice cup of tea. Poor man. He was
in a bit of a state when he arrived but he's better now. He
loves you very much, you know.'

'You think?'

'Come and say hello.'

'Sure.'

Eustace followed him back upstairs.

His father and he didn't hug or anything like that, because
they were not hugging people, but his father jumped up
from the kitchen table as Eustace came in, which was more
animation than he had demonstrated in months.

'I had no idea,' he said. 'Truly.'

'I know,' Eustace told him. 'I can't come back, Dad.
Don't make me. I mean . . . Unless . . .'

'It's fine,' Carla said. 'We've talked it all through. You
can stay here and commute to school on the train, at least

until you go back to Ancrum at Easter. By which time things may have—' She glanced apprehensively at his father. 'But we need to talk to your mother.'

'No!'

'I need to,' his father said. 'We owe her that much. She needs to know you're safe. She's been worried.'

Louis let out a *huh* so explosive he sloshed his tea. He mopped it up with his handkerchief then poured tea for Eustace and slid it towards him along with a mute offer of a rock bun.

'May I?' his father said, indicating the bright red telephone on one end of the dresser.

'Of course,' Carla said. 'Or there's one on the next landing up if you'd like privacy.'

'Actually,' his father told them all with a ghost of a smile, 'I'd rather appreciate the moral support. She can be a bit . . .'

'Yes,' Carla said. 'I—'

'Oh. Yes. Of course you— Well.'

Leaving the table for the telephone, his father met Eustace's eye briefly and raised his eyebrows as if to say, *Here we go.*

He dialled. They all waited. Eustace took a bite of rock bun then wished he hadn't because he found he was much too tense to swallow it. He took a mouthful of hot, rather stewed tea to wash it down and nearly choked. He became aware his father was talking and must already have been passed over to his mother.

'He's here,' his father said. 'He's fine. We're at Carla and . . .' He turned to Louis. 'I'm sorry,' he told him.

'Louis,' said Louis.

'Carla and Louis' house.'

He was briefly interrupted as Eustace's mother began to say something so forcefully they could all hear her voice. Then, astonishingly, his father cut her short.

'No,' he said and Eustace's heart swelled so that he thought he might cry. 'He's staying here. What you did was . . . repellent. No. Let me speak. I—'

Again she started shouting. His father slowly moved the receiver away from his ear so they could all hear her rage turned to tinny impotence and he turned on Eustace a look full of apologetic affection.

'I can't,' he began, then seemed overwhelmed by emotion. He took a breath and started afresh. 'I can't begin to tell you how sorry I am,' he said. Then he turned his back on them all and raised the receiver again. 'Have you finished?' he asked. 'Good. If you'd like me to involve the police and social workers and his headmaster, I can, but I'm fairly sure what you all did was illegal and it was certainly enough to have him put into the care of strangers. And just now I'd rather he was with people he trusts and loves.' He let her talk some more. She wasn't shouting now, apparently. 'My feelings on the matter are neither here nor there. These are the people he instinctively chose and I reckon, despite having you for a mother, his instincts are pretty good. I'll give them something for his board and lodging and he can stay here until you do what you have to do . . . It means exactly what it sounds like, woman. Dear God.'

For a second his usually mild voice turned savage. He checked himself, took an audible breath and let her talk.

Carla reached out a hand and briefly laid it on Eustace's where he was fiddling with cake crumbs. Eustace looked up and she smiled kindly at him. As did Louis.

His father was holding out the receiver, one hand covering the mouthpiece for privacy. 'I'm sorry, old chap,' he said. 'It's going to be fine but she needs to talk to you. Do you mind?'

Eustace made himself stand and went around the table to take the receiver from him. He held it to his ear. He could hear her laboured breathing, a sudden fruity sniff as she wiped her nose. She was crying, or had been.

'Hello?' he said gingerly.

'Oh, Eustace. Oh thank God. I was so worried.'

'You left me.'

'I know, I know and I hated doing it but they helped me and I thought they'd help you in the same . . .'

Her voice was distorted by tears in a way that set his teeth on edge. He wondered where she was. Had she answered in the hall and found her ugly emotions on display or was she somewhere private? He pictured her on the edge of her bed; a crucifix now hung above the headboard where a pretty watercolour of apple orchards used to be. She would be doing the things she did during difficult conversations, kicking off her shoes so as to grind her toes together, twisting and untwisting the telephone cord around her wrist.

'I'm hanging up now,' he told her.

'But what about clothes? Do you have enough?'

'I can always drop by after school.'

'I wanted you to be happy.'

This took him aback. It was such a preposterous thing to say that he could think of no adequate response.

'Eustace?' she said. 'Hello?'

His hand shook as he hung up, so the receiver bounced heavily on its tangled flex and smacked against the wall.

CHAPTER TWENTY-FIVE

He had thought the return to Ancrum, so longed for and dreamed of in the intervening months, would feel like a simple resumption. It couldn't do, of course, because most of the participants were of an age where their moods and bodies were in a state of flux. Freya had sprouted breasts and left off her woollen hat to reveal a great shock of Titian hair that stood out from her head like a fiery dandelion clock and now seemed in a state of constant surprise at the arbitrary gift of beauty. Naomi, by contrast, had retreated from the mother-bought Laura Ashley look of the previous summer and was now scowling about the place in army surplus fatigues and a big jersey that flopped off her shoulders and reached half-way down her thighs. Ralph looked much the same only taller and with several shaving cuts. Pierre had piled on weight unexpectedly and peroxided his hair himself in a gesture towards Punk that simply made him look ill. Amidst them all Turlough looked quite unchanged apart from five o'clock shadow, as self-possessed as ever, as though he knew where the money was hidden and wasn't about to tell.

They all hugged on Berwick platform just as he remembered the old hands hugging the previous summer.

Turlough looked him up and down and said, 'Just look at you,' in that way he had that could have been nice or nasty and set off fluttering in Eustace's stomach. And there were several faces missing – where could they possibly have preferred to go? – and a handful of new participants who looked impossibly young and vulnerable but were probably at least thirteen, but with that inward-looking immaturity Eustace was coming to see was peculiar to musicians-in-training. Placed among even the oldest of this group, Vernon and Suzanne would have seemed mature enough to start a family.

But those who had returned wanted nothing to have changed so pretended nothing had and clung to rituals. They all called out *Ancrum!* as the house came into view beyond the little church and bridge, and *Jean!* as Jean appeared on the top of the steps, waving to them as Young Dougie's van and Peg's minibus crossed the park. They would drink unspiced tomato juice as a starter and eat cheese and apple salad and play Round the Table and sing madrigals and gorge on banana bread and play Fauré. Eustace joined in and was nice to the newcomers just as people had been to him, but a part of him kept sitting back, mentally, and seeing they were clinging to the comforts of repetition and tradition as some people, poor Pierre evidently, clung to the comfort of food.

Jean hugged him, saying, 'Dear Eustace of the Stag,' which was mad and meaningless but sweet and she still smelled of Imperial Leather and wet walks. 'How's your mum?' she asked and he said,

'Better, thank you. Getting better every day,' and realized that protecting her innocence so that she could continue to be herself and change young people's lives was part of what made Ancrum what it was; in all probability she knew nothing of Carla's life with Louis and, increasingly, with naughty, owlish Margit. She would pass her life without ever seeing a Tom of Finland drawing or knowing there were priests who believed they could cast out homosexuality devils from fourteen-year-olds, and that was somehow all to the good.

He was in the same boys' dorm, up in the attics; though Pierre was now somewhere else, perhaps because Jean had divined he was unhappy. Pierre's place had been given to a cherubic young cellist from the Menuhin School called Solly. Solly had bee-stung lips and a quick, knowing manner. He was tiresomely, relentlessly cheeky but an extremely good player. He was good not simply with the technical flashiness of a child prodigy but seemingly with an ability to intuit the emotions behind a phrase. Even if he was simply parroting the phrasing of older players, and one suspected he must have at least begun by doing that, because he was far too young at barely twelve to understand the emotions he was conveying, you would not have known, had he been playing behind a screen to conceal his youth. There was absolutely no evidence that he had any warmth in his heart; he had the shrewd, hunter's ear of a born mimic and tease. Within minutes of arrival he was blatantly assessing who had influence, who did not, and where the shames and pains were in anyone he encountered. Eustace disliked him intensely on sight and soon decided that his antipathy was so strong that if Solly took up an offer to study at Ancrum full time, that would make it impossible for him to do so as well. However, Solly soon loudly made it plain that he was only there for his older sister, an unexceptional violinist, as the course was *good for her.* Though they had barely met yet, he spoke of Jean with a patronizing familiarity as of a harmless eccentric.

Eustace was fairly sure he was not the only one at the guesthouse table longing to see Jean take him down several pegs, though he suspected she would do this, and devastatingly, in private. There was a school report phrase he'd heard her use ironically regarding the unsuitability of fitting very self-regarding performers into chamber groups – *does not play well with others* – and, for Jean, it was chamber music, the creation of music with others, not pyrotechnic solo playing, that was the benchmark of true musicianship.

When Jean gathered them all in the ballroom that night to play the *Bachianas Brasilieras* number five, with the higher instruments on the soprano line along with anyone who felt like singing instead of playing, Eustace managed to catch Turlough's eye a couple of times. They were sitting almost opposite one another, with Jean playing between them in front of the big marble fireplace, and he'd thought Turlough was looking at him. Then, when Jean shifted him to one side to move an extra cello on to his line, he realized it wasn't he who was drawing Turlough's attention but Solly, who was showing off to cover for the humiliation of having been placed on an accompaniment line rather than the trickier first cello part.

He watched them move off into a corner to chat when cocoa was served and slip from the room when Jean had them all sing *Non Nobis Domine* before heading up to bed. They didn't slink into the dormitory until all lights had been out for a while. And their bedtime absence became a pattern in the days that followed, as did their way of sharing little jokes and smiles.

Solly was very young, a child in fact, but Eustace didn't feel he could approach him to check he was happy with whatever the situation was because Turlough was sure to be so unpleasant about it, and didn't feel he could report them to anyone for fear Turlough would come out and say it was a jealous fantasy.

Turlough ignored him, actively ignored him, had said not a word to him since his initial teasing greeting on the station platform, and this hurt as it was surely intended to, but he surprised himself at being able to regard it with the same equanimity he did when finding himself not in the group learning the variations from the first Brahms sextet – evidently that course's lead ensemble. Instead he had a lovely time learning the top line of the fairly challenging Klengel Serenade and Humoreske for cello quartet with three lovely Scottish girls who had not been before and who seemed to think he was outrageously outspoken and funny. They were set to rehearsing in a first-floor bedroom which seemed to double as Jean's dressing room and they had great fun daring to play while wearing various hats of hers. He chose a smart brown felt with a pheasant feather trim.

He listened with genuine sympathy to Naomi's tales of how Solly had insisted on pushing her onto the second cello line in the Brahms, although she knew the first already and was much older, and how he was rushing her in the tricky variation with all the scales, but he felt absolutely no envy, no wish to be worrying at her side in Solly's place, catching Turlough's eye and wondering if his gaze meant anything.

His session with Jean wasn't until the Thursday, the penultimate day. As Carla had suggested, he played her some of the second Beethoven sonata. She was impressed, said she could see how much work he had managed to put in since the summer *despite everything*. She asked about school and whether there were other musical outlets for him. He said Carla was putting out feelers to other teachers to see if he could form a string quartet and that he planned to audition for Weston's Youth Orchestra which gave a couple of concerts a year.

'That's so good,' she said. 'What's the standard like?'

'Er . . .' he said. 'Actually they're fine. Fine for Weston.'

And she smiled. 'The wonderful thing about your music,' she said, 'is that it's hardwired into you now. It'll never leave you. Even if you have to neglect it for a year or two for your maths or university or a job or whatever. It will be a faithful friend throughout your life, helping you meet new people, lifting your spirits like a bottomless larder. There's far too much emphasis on music as a career but one of the glories of music, especially in this country, is its army of amateurs, many of them with professional standards of excellence like Carla has instilled in you. Do you see?'

'Yes,' he told her.

And that was that. He was not one of her chosen few. He would not be returning as a full time student to receive a magnificent but undoubtedly lopsided even wayward alternative education to Weston's sixth-form college. And he would not become a professional cellist. Not even a teacher, like Carla. With one intense, compassionate pronouncement, Jean had set him free from yearning and striving. He would join the youth orchestra and enjoy it, love it even. But he would focus on other things, like his maths. He would go to university. He would have the career his poor father had never quite managed.

Stealthily the Klengel Quartet was the hit of the last night concert, perhaps because the Humoreske was one of those pieces that made everybody smile. The Brahms, which was last in the programme, of course, where expectations were always highest, was a bit of a mess because Turlough had a newly replaced A string that kept going flat despite him tweaking at its adjuster whenever the music allowed, which was rarely, and Solly rushed the scales. He didn't play well with others.

There had been no suggestion Eustace's father meet the train at Bristol. Eustace was quite old enough now to cross unassisted to the little train on the branch line platform and travel to Weston and walk home on his own. But his father surprised him on Weston Station. He surprised him yet further with a quick, clumsy hug. Perhaps he was on new pills.

'How was it?' he asked.

'Good. It was really good.'

They started walking over the footbridge towards town and the car park.

'Do you still want to go there full time instead of the sixth form?'

'Do you know? I don't think I do. Not any more.'

'That's a pity. Isn't it?'

'It is. And it isn't.'

As they emerged from the station, Eustace glanced across the parked cars to the nearby art deco houses. Mr Buck's was still unsold, empty and beginning to be vandalized.

His father hadn't walked, as they usually did, but had brought the car. Eustace slung his bag in the boot and carefully slid his cello across the back seat. His father didn't start the engine immediately. The train from Bristol had been full of people paying a weekend visit to the big shops, all laden carrier bags and flagging good tempers. The crowd dispersed slowly past them, some towards the seafront and hotels, some towards the estates and bus stops for the villages.

'I told your mother to move out,' his father said.

'You *told* her?' Eustace almost smiled but found himself oddly torn. 'Where has she gone?'

'Back to Grace Manor for now. I don't think she'll be there for long. People like that prefer their guests weak and, underneath it all, she's very strong, as you know.'

'Yes.' Eustace thought of amber beads, the burnt cinnamon smell of toasted teacake, a locked iron gate. He knew his father was offering all this up as a tidy happy ending, or a new beginning, in a spirit of kind hopefulness. He decided to play along with him, although he knew there would be anger, tears, jagged edges still to come.

'You're safe now, old chap.'

'Thanks, Dad. Will you . . . divorce?'

His father shrugged. 'It would make sense, although it means she can sue for half of the little I'm worth.' A seagull dropped down to pick at something on the wet tarmac before them. A burger bun. 'She was leaving us when she had the accident.'

'I know.'

'How?'

'I found out. Doesn't matter. Who was she in love with?'

His father paused then distracted himself by fastening his seatbelt and starting the ignition.

'You need never know,' he said. 'It doesn't matter now.'

He drove home by a circuitous route. He had already received a generous offer from a property developer for the house and had a mind, once he could rehome the remaining guests to their satisfaction, to buy a shop with a two-floor maisonette above and a sunny courtyard garden.

'It even has a studio over the garage at the back. I thought you'd like that as you'd have your own back door and you could play your cello as loud as you liked.'

It was a pleasant enough pair of buildings in an attractive part of town, away from the chip fat and hurly burly.

'But Dad. A shop?'

'I thought I could sell books,' his father said. 'Second-hand and new. Less bother than residential care and, I mean, how hard can it be?'

CHAPTER TWENTY-SIX

One further Geiger test and Eustace was released back into an oblivious world having duly left his brand-new bamboo outfit behind him in a special bin and dressed in the clothes that had been stored for him outside the lead-lined room.

'What about the sheets?' he asked. 'Aren't those radio-active as well?'

'Yes,' the nurse admitted, 'though not as much as your T-shirt and boxers will be. It's the sweat, you see. We wash them in dedicated machines just through that wall, where the contaminated waste water can be isolated from the rest of the system until it's safe to release. Now remember, you're still not entirely safe to be around. No holding children or babies for a week and, ideally, no hugging or close bodily contact with anyone else for twenty-four hours.'

He thought of Theo, who even now must be travelling across the desert to some central army base, Eustace really had no idea, prior to flying home. He thought of kissing Theo. He thought of not being allowed to kiss Theo and having to explain why.

'Really, though,' the nurse added, 'you're fine so long as you keep clear of kids. Oh, and anyone pregnant.'

He had stepped out of the lead-lined room before he remembered the little MP3 player, so discreet they had both forgotten he'd been wearing it all this while.

'Oops,' said the nurse as he dropped it and the ear buds into the bin with the clothes. 'Seems a waste.'

'It served its purpose,' he said.

Hospitals woke earlier than the rest of the world and it was still fairly early. He stopped at a patisserie he liked to pick up a bag of treats for a second breakfast for Naomi.

As usual, Joyce ran into the hall to greet him, carrying her favourite hot pink toy which Naomi had long since christened the Double Ender and hid on a high shelf during teaching hours to stop Joyce presenting it to the startled parents of her young pupils. Joyce growled, her invitation to be chased, and he followed her, laughing, into the kitchen where the first thing he saw was an army kitbag. Naomi was at the table with Theo.

In the flesh he looked reassuringly older and more solid, not willowy and certainly not innocent.

'Look who got here a day early,' she said, as Theo pushed back his chair and stood up, beaming.

'She told me everything, you daft bugger,' he said.

'I did,' she admitted.

'You were right,' Eustace told her. 'You need to learn from the off,' he told Theo, 'that my best friend, Naomi, is always right.'

He glanced her way and saw tears in her eyes, although she was smiling.

'Are you OK?' Theo asked. 'You could have told me. How was it?'

He stepped towards him but Eustace held up both hands to keep him away.

'Sorry,' he said, wincing. 'Not allowed to touch anyone

until tonight. Well, strictly tomorrow morning, but let's say tonight. Around the cocktail hour. It was fine,' he added. 'Just boring. Non-event. And lots of lovely cello music. Hello.'

'I thought it was just pregnant people,' Naomi said.

'I'm not pregnant,' Theo said, deadpan. 'Cross my heart,' with a look that told Eustace exactly how it would feel pulling his T-shirt over his head later.

'You'll just have to take Joyce out for the whole day,' Naomi said. 'It's a beautiful morning. You can be tourists. Cross all the parks. Catch a boat to Greenwich. Cruise along Regent's Canal. Just be absent. My first pupil arrives in fifteen minutes and she wears Alice bands and is extremely judgemental.'

'I thought they came tomorrow.'

'They do. But I moved or cancelled them, remember, because it was tomorrow we were expecting Pornstar Bambi.'

'Who?' Theo looked confused.

'Oh, that's you,' Eustace admitted. 'Doesn't begin to do you justice.'

'Get a room,' Naomi said. 'Oh. I forgot. You can't!' And she laughed wickedly as she walked through to the sitting room and started tuning up.

'She was playing when I arrived,' Theo said. 'She's amazing.'

Eustace nodded. 'She is rather,' he sighed. 'Christ you smell good.'

'I've been flying for hours. Are you really not allowed near me yet?'

'Really.' They stood on either side of the hall just looking, the sound of Naomi's scales all about them. Joyce had sensed a walk was about to begin and scratched peremptorily at the front door, where the same gesture, repeated twice a day, had removed a layer of paint slightly larger than the width of her paw. Theo grinned, revealing the fetchingly chipped tooth.

'Go on,' Eustace told him.

Theo reached down to fasten her lead on her. He looked back.

'After you,' Eustace told him.

AUTHOR'S NOTE

This novel would never have happened without the input of my cello teachers, Fiona Smith and David Waterman. Thanks also to Andrew Brown, who lent me a cello to set me playing again at forty.

I'm indebted to the memory-jogging recollections of two of the lucky full time students at the real life Ancrum, Steven Isserlis and Justin Anderson and to the cellistic proofreading of Joely Koos.

I'd also like to thank Clayton Littlewood and my old friend Nick Hay for their detailed memories of Weston-super-Mare in the 1970s, and Dan and Jon, for letting me borrow their impossibly romantic long distance courtship.

Thanks to Richard Lingham, for his expertise on 1970s child protection procedures,

to Ian Pitkin, Principal Physicist in the Nuclear Medicine department of Bupa Cromwell Hospital for the fascinating tour of the radio iodine suite,

to the Corineus Quartet for inviting me to play the Schubert Quintet with them, and giving me the part with Jacqueline du Pré's fingering in it,

to Bertjan ter Braak for *heftig*,

to Caroline Dunn and her Bristol book group for the inspiring excuse to remind myself of the loveliness of Clifton,

and to the librarians of Weston-super-Mare, whose hospitality a few years ago unwittingly set me wondering what it would have been like to grow up in such a place.

TAKE NOTHING WITH YOU

Bonus Material

My Childhood Bully

Q & A with Patrick Gale

MY CHILDHOOD BULLY

One day my agent forwarded a letter to me. Nothing unusual there; some of my readers are of an age where they regard email and direct messaging as an unmannerly introduction. But this letter proved to be a thoughtful, clearly heartfelt, two-page apology from a man who had done his best to make my life a misery at school.

'I wanted to say sorry,' he wrote. 'I am sure there are many reasons why I behaved the way I did. Sadly, I think people who experience abuse and bullying are vulnerable to passing it on and I know at the time I felt quite helpless and demeaned by my behaviour. However, no explanation amounts to a justification. It was bullying. I was vindictive when you were entirely innocent, and it was wrong.'

When the bullying started, I was a plump and bookish child at preposterously elitist Winchester College, as deeply uncomfortable in my skin as any nerdy thirteen-year-old can be. But the growing sense that my sexuality was increasingly marking me out for unwelcome notice made puberty 10 times worse. My most recent novel, *Take Nothing With You* is not autobiographical, but its portrayal of a gay child in the 1970s draws heavily on my own memories. My young hero Eustace is as inured to daily insult and mockery as any LGBT child will tend to be, but I spared him the direct torment of a school bully – something I could all too easily have drawn from memory.

As was the norm in boarding schools in the 1970s, Winchester's disciplinary system relied on a network of prefects; sixth-formers who effectively ruled each boarding house while the housemasters, though resident, ruled remotely. Outside classroom hours and lunches, it was quite possible to have no contact with anyone over the age of 18 from six at night until the first lesson the following day, apart from a brief interlude for evening prayers. To a very young, very gay thirteen-year-old, these prefects with their muscles and lordly arrogance seemed like men in a world of boys. They were often cruel, but in the lofty manner of feudal lords, they dealt out punishment and mercy with a casualness that declared how far beneath notice their juniors were.

But they weren't bullies. They were simply the beneficiaries of a system in which ageing and endurance ensured that most boys would eventually rise to such heights. Bullies tended to be younger and relatively powerless: fourth and fifth-formers were especially dangerous, as was anyone who was insecure. Torments varied from ugly practical jokes, in which only the foolhardy would refuse to play along as a good sport – such as tipping a carton of rotten milk down a boy's back – to terrible moments of mob cruelty where a victim watched as their possessions were scattered across a muddy ground, or found themselves held head first over an invariably filthy lavatory.

The luckier victims had nothing much wrong with them – an embarrassingly foreign name, perhaps, or simply ginger hair – and possessed enough self-control to grit their teeth and endure, or even laugh along; thus subtly becoming part of the pack and not much fun. The unlucky were the thin-skinned, the hot-tempered and the unforgivably odd. I can think of two such boys: one deliciously upper crust and furious, the other desperately unappealing and unhygienic. They were picked on again and again, to the point where it became as much a part of daily routine as mealtimes. Even new boys, boys younger than them, would swiftly learn to have a go at them too, so as to prove their mettle. I'm pleased to see that one of them has gone on to become unassailably distinguished in his field; the total vanishing of the other, in this age of social media, leads me to fear the worst.

My bully was like none of these. As Margaret Atwood so memorably illustrated in her novel *Cat's Eye*, the worst tormentors begin as friends.

It was an inappropriate friendship. He was fifteen. At this stage I had yet to move on from the adjoining school that shared Winchester's music facilities, so we met in the chapel choir. He played the flute and I was a precocious pianist. Against all unwritten rules, but intoxicated by regular contact with an older boy, I learned the Hindemith flute sonata's piano part so as to rehearse with him. Nothing bad happened; there was no sexual contact and, for all that I was gay and flirtatious, I believe he was no more gay or paedophilic than most teenage boys in a single-sex boarding school. But he wrote me fairly saucy letters and short stories, which my mother found when I was home for the holidays.

She said nothing to me, but raised a genteel stink by passing them to my choir school's headmaster. A stern announcement was made, ordering that all fraternisation between the choirboys and the teenage musicians cease. But that autumn I started at Winchester – and was placed in the same house as him.

It rapidly became clear that not only did students assume we were lovers, but that he was curiously friendless. As in any boarding school of the time, there were several such pairings – sexless but intense friendships. If both older and younger boy were outstanding sportsmen or committed members of the army corps, they were accorded a discretion worthy of ancient Greece. With me – an obviously gay, musical, unsporty showoff – and the friend – an unpopular dissenter in our little feudal world – we had no such protection. I was quickly warned that any continued association would be disastrous. Some fifth-formers made their feelings clear by destroying my bicycle, then setting fire to my cubicle curtain with lighter fuel while I sat in it.

So I told him: no more Hindemith, nothing more to feed the fuel of suspicion. That was when he turned on me. Apart from a single, poisonous letter thrust into my locker, it was a single-minded campaign waged against me without a grain of evidence. From then until he finally left the school three years later, he couldn't pass me without saying something vile, spitting or pointedly pretending I wasn't there. His muttered comments became openly homophobic – a word that, of course, was not used in the late 1970s. Despite our age difference, our penchant for music and shared boarding house ensured that our paths crossed several times a day. Mercifully, I was one of the school's day boys, so escaped back home at night and on Sundays. I breathed not a word to my parents. Only my body cried out, breaking out in such bad eczema that I regularly woke with my sheets glued to the backs of my knees with dried blood; I blamed a reaction to bleach, soap or hard water, and was prescribed a sequence of ineffective creams. And I have never got over a lingering aversion to Hindemith.

I suffered in silence, but didn't think of myself as a victim. I wasn't the smelly boy goaded into losing his temper, or the posh one shrieking, yet again, as some nouveau-riche underachiever emptied his books across the floor. I had friends. Amazingly, by my second year, I even had a sort of gay gang, and our achievements made us fairly untouchable. And I understood enough to see that my tormentor had almost certainly been tormented himself.

When I mentioned receiving the letter on social media, the response startled me. Numerous friends turned out to have been hounded at school or felt ashamed at having once been bullies. Some said they wished their tormentors only ill, others admitted to having tracked them down on Facebook, with a view to confronting them with their crimes. The one thing common to all our stories is that nobody told their parents. There was a code of honour among victims.

But my tormentor, it seems, had turned victim with no other agency than time to work on him. One of his children had been bullied at school. It was the crisis of ineffectuality brought on by that, the crisis so many of us spared our parents with our silence, that caused him to contact me.

Of course, I accepted his apology. I gave him and his suffering child my best wishes. But I could not forgive him. The scars run too deep for that.

This article was first published on www.theguardian.com

Q & A WITH PATRICK GALE

The title of this novel, TAKE NOTHING WITH YOU, is a phrase used when adult Eustace is having treatment for cancer. What persuaded you to choose it for the novel as a whole?

Like several of my novels, this is a deeply psychotherapeutic story in which the central character needs to revisit his past in order to reassess or even edit his personal narrative in order to move on. At first we think the title refers only to the instructions Eustace receives for his radioactive iodine but by the end, once we have relived his boyhood traumas and obsessions with him, we realise these are memories to be left behind in the hospital along with his disposable clothes and Naomi's MP3 player, so that he can have a chance of new happiness with Theo.

Many of your books are set in Cornwall, but this is the first set in Weston-super-Mare. Was there a special reason for choosing that town? Does location anchor a book for you?

Weston-super-Mare was a happy accident in my life. I'd been invited to talk at the library there and, never having visited before, spent some time walking the streets and examining the houses and soon realised I was going to set a novel there; it simply struck me as the perfect setting for a story of a provincial gay boyhood in the 1970s and the very antithesis of 'smart' London.

Eustace lives with elderly grandparents, and is an only child. Do you think this makes him a good observer of others?

I think his rather odd home makes him at once more innocent than other boys – siblings being a great source of information – and more formal. The old are very useful to a novelist, just as the very young can be, for their habit of directness. I was far from an only child, being the youngest of four, but I soon developed an only child's habit of watchfulness. My brothers thought me sly because I'd fall very quiet and just listen and watch . . .

You've used music as a background to some of your other books, and you are an accomplished cellist. Did you find music a comfort in your own childhood?

Music was everywhere in my childhood. My mother played the piano and sang to us and encouraged us to sing with her and there was always music playing but then, when I was seven, it was found I could sing and I was sent to a cathedral choir school where music became a sort of career, with hours of rehearsal or private practice every day and two instruments to learn as well as all the singing we did. So it was a discipline, something more active than a comfort, but it was always my source of safety and happiness. I never felt more secure than when making music with friends.

Eustace doesn't feel uncomfortable about his sexuality; it's the actions of others that hurt him. Do you think we've become more open about talking about our differences now?

What I was keen to show was that, for the LGBT child, their overwhelming sense at first is nothing to do with sex but everything to do with feeling that they don't belong and won't, somehow, 'pass'. I was incredibly lucky in having gay friends of my own age when I was not much more than fourteen or so, and although I was still the butt of jokes and cruelty from the majority, I never felt alone and I knew it was simply a matter of marking time until I was older. The laws have changed for the better now, and manners and practices are slowly altering to match them, not least in school, but children will always be horrible to those among them who are different. Difference in sexuality is especially hard for children to bear because it's invisible so the temptation to hide it is overwhelming, and that concealment brings with it a whole raft of stress and self-hatred. The wonderful difference now is that parents and teachers can feel empowered to be supportive rather than feeling obliged to express disgust. That said, there continue to be horrible exceptions. Readers might be tempted to comfort themselves that the 'ex-gay' treatment to which Eustace (and his mother) are subjected is something from the bad old 1970s, but they need to realise it is still carrying on, at the time of writing, in faith-based schools (of various religions) throughout the western world.

You've said that the music school experience in this book is close to a holiday course you followed yourself. How conscious are you of blending fact into your fiction, and does it ever become a problem for you?

Yes, Jean Curwen is closely based on Jane Cowan and her inspirational teaching methods just as elements of Eustace's mother's experience of religious commitment following a severe car accident that nearly kills her echoes closely my mother's own. I have always blended streaks of fact into my fiction; it's what gives me confidence to proceed, I think. I like to have some element in each story that I know really well and that I know to be true. And yet often what really then fires up my imagination are the points in my material where the facts run out, where there is something – like my great-grandfather, Harry Cane's private life – that isn't known and cannot be discovered.

The mother in TAKE NOTHING WITH YOU puts her own needs and feelings first. How much do you think this affects Eustace's understanding of her, and shapes his life?

I feel really sorry for Eustace's mother. She is of that generation that were blighted by shortages and deprivations and, indeed, traumas in the Second World War who then thought themselves too old and set in their ways to benefit from the sexual liberation of the 1960s and the new wave of feminism that came hard on its heels. She and her husband were ill matched and utterly inexperienced when they married and a deeply concealed tragedy has blighted their intimacy further. I think each, in their way, is suffering from depression, born of unspoken grief. She is not one of nature's mothers. Or, it must be said, one of its wee wifeys. Having neglected Eustace rather, to pursue her own chance of happiness, she then sees in him (typical narcissist!) a reflection of her own 'wrong-doing' with Carla and hands him over to be normalised. But we have to understand – as I believe Eustace does – that she does this not to be nasty, but because she wants him to be happy and doesn't see how being different can bring any-body joy or fulfilment.

You've talked about the fact that you loved LP Hartley's THE GO-BETWEEN. Did TAKE NOTHING WITH YOU come out of that affection? What other novels have influenced your writing?

I describe *Take Nothing With You* as having two literary godmothers: *The Go-Between* by Hartley, and Noel Streat-feild's *Ballet Shoes*. Eustace's odd name is a homage to Hartley's hero in *The Shrimp and the Anemone*, another sad little chap first encountered at the seaside. I was keen to revisit the dynamic of *The Go-Between* with key differ-ences. Unlike poor Leo, Eustace keeps his innocence to the end and, through his music, learns resilience to withstand the forces that ruin Leo's life. As for *Ballet Shoes*, it stands in a tradition of novels about children striving to escape poverty (of experience, of opportunity, as well as financial) through the discipline of sport or art. I was keen to show how learning the cello requires a similar, profoundly phys-ical commitment to ballet or gymnastics which in turn gives the deeply awkward Eustace a new confidence in his phys-ical self as well as new attentiveness in the schoolroom.

You are invited to join us behind the scenes at Tinder Press

TINDER PRESS

To meet our authors, browse our books
and discover exclusive content on our
blog visit us at

www.tinderpress.co.uk

For the latest news and views from the team
Follow us on Twitter

@TinderPress